PRAISE FOR MICHAEL JOHN SULLIVAN'S
EVERYBODY'S DAUGHTER:

"I applaud Michael John Sullivan for bringing his beautiful story to life."
– Eric Wilson, *New York Times* bestselling author of *Fireproof*

"A suspenseful page turner.... The novel is rich in its plot, sub-plots, characters who readers will long remember with a craving to read the next one."
– Examiner.com

"The last time I remember talking about a book this much was after I read *The Help*."
– Rainy Day Reviews

"This is a unique blend of Science Fiction and Biblical Historical Romantic Suspense Fiction, so there is bound to be something for just about every book lover's genre!"
– Reviews from the Heart

"Part mystery, part suspense and filled with exciting time travel, this book kept me interested from beginning to end."
– Just One More Paragraph

"I could not lay it down. I loved it!"
– My Favorite Things

The Greatest Gift

Michael John Sullivan

THE
STORY PLANT

To you, the reader, for allowing me inside your mind.
It has been a privilege to share my words with you during
this trilogy.
I hope we meet again.

The Story Plant
Studio Digital CT, LLC
P.O. Box 4331
Stamford, CT 06907

Copyright © 2014 by Michael John Sullivan
Jacket design by Jeff Fielder

Print ISBN-13: 978-1-61188-157-8
E-book ISBN: 978-1-61188-158-5

Visit our website at www.TheStoryPlant.com

First Story Plant paperback printing: October 2014
Printed in the United States of America
0 9 8 7 6 5 4 3 2 1

A NOTE FROM THE AUTHOR

Dear Reader,

Welcome to the third book of my trilogy, *The Greatest Gift*. Originally, I planned to write this novel under the title *The Greatest Christmas*. However, I realized halfway through writing the story, it was necessary to change it. *The Greatest Gift* properly allows each of the characters to find their destiny or not. The important conclusion is we each have our own choice in what path we take.

When I last left you, there was the wonderful ending to *Everybody's Daughter*. Yes, miracles do take place in everyday life, no matter what century we are born in. We just have to recognize them. Before you there might stand a child ready to give you unconditional love in return for yours. Look above you – today there could be a beautiful, clear, blue sky. Take a moment to let the warm sun fill your body and soul with enough strength to persevere through a dreary day of challenges.

Where there is life, there is beauty. It is how I wanted *Everybody's Daughter* to be remembered as I began to write the next book. I wanted each character to benefit from the ending of *Everybody's Daughter*. There had to be a reason why this incredible moment was allowed to happen.

It also took the element of time travel to help us truly understand how alike we are with our ancestors from past centuries – whether we are spiritual or religious or young or old or believers or not. What we truly have in common is the desire to be loved and share our precious gift of time.

The Greatest Gift starts off shortly after the ending of *Everybody's Daughter*. Michael and Elizabeth Stewart were given a great gift. It's a chance for them to cleanse their pasts, to be grateful for the prized time of today, and to realize the future is only valuable if we have achieved the previous two goals.

I spent a lot of time changing significant plot points so I would be able to present a book that allows you, the reader, satisfaction that the characters are better off today than they were when we started with the series five years ago.

It was important to understand that each of us must confront the daily struggles of life and in the most inopportune moments, tragedy. How we move forward after we each encounter some of life's cruelties truly paints our next portrait.

I thank you for being a part of this series. I'm already at work on my next novel, *The Second World*.

Always remember, all works of art are connected to each other. Thanks always for connecting with me.

Michael John Sullivan

CHAPTER 1

ELIZABETH WAS GONE. *She could have gone outside to the bathroom. Yeah, that makes sense. I've got to relax. She freaked out last night when I told her we had to leave first thing in the morning. She's different since she came back. How can she not be happy to be here with me now? Why is she confused? Upset? She seems angry at me. I need to settle down. I can't have a meltdown every time she's not right beside me.*

Michael yelled, trying to stifle his panic. "Come on, girl, we have to get a move on and find the tunnel so we can head on home and get out of this century." He forced a chuckle. "Bet not too many dads can say that to their kids, huh?"

He waited a few more minutes before letting the next burst of panic flood his heart.

"Elizabeth," he shouted louder this time, making his way to the edge of the cave and peering around the corner to check the make-shift facility. "Hey, are you going to hog the bathroom just like you do at home?" he asked, injecting a teasing tone while trying to stifle the nausea building in his gut. "Hurry it up. It's my turn."

When he heard no response, he barged inside the bathroom. It was empty.

Dear God. Where is she? Is she that angry with me? There's something wrong with my daughter. The trauma she endured to her head, the loss of blood, dying and then coming back to life. I could see she wasn't in her right mind, the way she acted and talked.

I pray I'm overreacting and that she just went out for a short walk. Michael grimaced. *Why did I fall asleep? I should have stayed awake all night and made sure she didn't leave my sight. Enough. This isn't helping her. I have to stop berating myself and get a grip.*

Michael shook his head. *I thought I had given her enough time to adapt.*

He went outside and scurried up a hill, ignoring the morning's heat and humidity. He cupped his hands together and screamed with all his might, "Elizabeth. Are you out here? Answer me." Nothing.

He ran down the hill as fast as his legs could take him, his heart racing as he hurried to the other side of the cave.

He spotted his friend tending to sheep in the field. "Abel!" Michael yelled, trying to catch his breath. "Please," he shouted, waving his hands. "I need your help."

Abel wiped his hands on his garment. His brow furrowed as he looked at him in confusion. Michael reached him, gasping for air. Abel spoke in Aramaic and Michael had no idea what he was saying.

His fingers shook as he reached into his pocket and pulled out a cross, which was attached to a string. This allowed him to communicate in Aramaic. "Have you seen a girl, about this high?" Michael asked, pointing to his shoulders. "She has brown hair and green eyes."

Abel nodded. "The words you spoke before, I have never heard them. Where did you learn them? What do they mean?"

Michael shook his head. "What?"

"Your words. They were strange."

Michael hesitated. "Forgive me. I was running, out of breath. I could not speak clearly."

Abel rubbed the side of his head. "Who are you looking for?"

"My daughter. Elizabeth."

"Your daughter? Your daughter is dead. Is she not?"

Michael paused, realizing he had told Abel about Elizabeth's fate a while ago. *He knows she died. I told him I only had one daughter. How do I explain this to him?*

"She is like a daughter to me," he fibbed. "She is the daughter of my sister. She was visiting and I did not talk much about her for fear the Romans would come after her as well. Do you know how far she has gone?"

"She was running toward the aqueduct," Abel said. "I tried to talk to her. She gave me an unpleasant look. She looked to be grieving, crying. Has a family member died?"

Michael shook his head and ran back toward the cave to seek the supplies and weapons he needed to safely get her back home. He knew she had been through a lot. He could see she was confused and distraught the night before but chose to ignore it. Perhaps he should have been more cautious and watched her more closely. Even so, Michael was also angered by her behavior. She knew he was worried about her. How could she just up and leave and not wake him up? This was a dangerous time and place for them to be.

Michael picked up a rock and scraped it against the wall, sharpening its edge. *Protect her Lord. I need you to do this for me. If you won't, I will.* He looked at the rock and placed it in his pocket. He kicked at a big branch and sent it tumbling down a small hill. He reached the edge of the cave and let out an angry growl. Grabbing a makeshift weapon, he placed it in a small pouch. He picked up his bedroll, threw it away and picked up some silver.

What else do I need? Think. Get a hold of yourself. I can't panic now.

He noticed one of his garments was missing.

She must have taken it.

He saw some scribbling on the wall. The doodle usually made him smile. It was definitely Elizabeth's. Yet there was no heart placed above the "i," her signature artwork that usually brought a smile to his face.

Right now, everything enraged him. He threw his pouch down and kicked at the smoldering fire, sending some of the wood still simmering against the concrete wall. It splintered into several pieces as Michael stormed the kitchen area looking for more weapons.

He punched at the wall and roared. He looked briefly at his bleeding knuckles. "I am going to shake some sense into you when I get my hands on you."

Michael grabbed the leftover bread from last night's meal and stuffed it inside the pouch. He took a few steps toward the opening of the cave and stopped. Feeling faint, he held onto the wall while his heart continued to race. He ran to a wooden box, opened it and saw the second cross was missing. "She took it. Thank God. At least she'll be able to communicate in Aramaic." He tossed the box away. "My God, why are we still in this forsaken time?"

CHAPTER 2

CONNIE THANKED SEVERAL PEOPLE as she stood outside her brother Michael's house. "I'm not sure when we will get together again," she said, exhausted. "We've done this a while now and I'm sure everyone needs a day or two to rest." She gave them a tired wave. "I appreciate so many of you joining me on the searches."

Connie turned and went inside, never losing stride as she stopped at her niece's bedroom. The quiet and stillness flooded her mind with horrific scenarios at what might have happened to her brother and his daughter.

She poked the door with her index finger and peeked inside. The creaking sound echoed through the empty house. Connie walked past a dresser, touching a picture of herself holding Elizabeth when she was a toddler. *Where are you, my sweet niece?*

The little stuffed Pikachu she gave Elizabeth nearly fifteen years ago sat on top of her pillow. She patted it on the head as if expecting a response. Picking it up, she sat on the bed and held it against her face. She breathed deeply and could smell Elizabeth's scent.

"Are you safe?" she said, lifting her head. "Did your dad find you? Is he safe, Elizabeth?" The silence of the house shouted back at her. "Why haven't either of you called?"

She placed Pikachu back down on the pillow, keeping her hand on top of the stuffed animal's head, and sat motionless, gazing around the room. The walls were filled with movie stars, music icons and pictures of Jerusalem. Connie stood and walked around the room a couple of times, mentally absorbing each one. She rubbed the top of Elizabeth's desk each time she passed it.

Connie went back to the dresser and stared at the picture, wondering what year it was. *Was that the time I took her to the circus? Or was it for Disney on Ice?* She stepped back and sighed. She knew she just had to try to do something to help. "Well, I wouldn't be much of an aunt if I didn't look again to see if there are any notes or clues." *Maybe Michael doesn't need me but would he even ask me for help if he did? No. He wouldn't. He's stubborn. Just like me. Well, too bad.*

She pulled open the top drawer and began dumping out papers. Maybe something was overlooked the last time they did this. Elizabeth could have left a note behind that hadn't been found yet. Connie couldn't help but wonder if the FBI guys had come across anything while they were here. *Maybe they missed something. It's possible. They're human. They're not God's gift to investigating.*

Connie kept tossing papers to the bed after examining them. She shook her head as she came upon a poem entitled, "Why Are We Here?" *Wow. Very deep for a teenager. I wonder if Michael knows about this poem. I thought he was the goofball with the religious stuff.* She folded the sheet and tucked it into her pocket.

After she finished searching the top drawer, she opened the next one, removed several t-shirts and stuck her hand deep into the dark corners. Nothing. She did the same for the third and fourth drawers, throwing the items on top of the bed.

When she was done, Connie backpedaled and sat on top of the clothes. She rubbed her eyes and stretched her arms and legs. She had no idea what to do or where to go looking for them. Connie considered whether she needed to buy a gun. Perhaps they'd been kidnapped. Michael surely had some enemies. It occurred to her that he might be broke – might have gambled his money away. Maybe he owed some mobsters a lot of money. She thought of every possible doomsday scenario – the absurd and not so crazy possibilities.

She had to get a grip. Michael might be a lot of things, but one thing he wasn't was a gambler. *He is always watching sports though.* She took a deep breath and consciously tried to relax. She had to stop jumping to conclusions. The FBI was involved and looking. *But I still can't just sit around here.*

Connie left the room and went down the hallway and into Michael's bedroom. *Sorry, bro. I've got to do this. I just can't do nothing and hope you're going to give me a call whether you're safe or not. You would do the same for me.* She opened every drawer and looked in every corner but found nothing. *Those FBI guys are good.*

She stepped back and sat on the edge of the bed, hands covering her face. *I don't know how to help you, Michael. I hope we have enough of a relationship that you would call me if you were safe. Or you wouldn't have so much pride that you wouldn't call me for help.*

"I can't sit here all day and worry," she said out loud, standing and giving a defiant look to the mirror. She began to put away some papers and saw a letter tucked inside a small envelope. *What is this?* She unfolded it. "A love letter? I wonder if it's to that Leah woman."

She dug deeper into the drawer, pulling out a small black Bible. It read "1969."

"Is this my Bible?" she whispered. She fingered through several pages and then looked at the inscription on the inside of the back cover. "The day me and Con became friends. April, 1969."

"I can't believe he's had it all these years." She looked at the mirror above the dresser. "Where are you, bro?"

She sat in silence for a few more moments until her cell phone rang. She dropped the letter on top of the dresser and ran downstairs to the kitchen. She grabbed it off the counter. "It's me," the voice on the other end said.

"Who's me?"

"Who do you think? Susan."

"Tell me you have news. Did they find Michael? Elizabeth?"

"No. But we have to do something. Any thoughts?"

"Well, what can we do? The FBI is looking for them. If anyone can find them, they can."

"Can't sit around. I have to do something. Pastor Dennis called me and asked if we can meet him in his office."

Connie hesitated. "Church makes me uncomfortable."

"Are you coming or not? He said to come as soon as possible."

Connie paced the hallway.

"Hello?" Susan said. "Are you still there?"

"I'm here. I'm here. See you over there soon."

CHAPTER 3

SPECIAL AGENT HEWITT PAUL SHOWED HIS ID and was waved to the stairwell by the policeman sitting behind the front desk. "Second floor. Room two thirteen. She's a wreck today," he said to Hewitt. "Not sure which planet she's orbiting around now."

Hewitt gave him a military salute. The hallway was short and with only two rooms opening off the corridor. *Stupid hicks. All about appearances, I guess.*

Allison twitched several times as she sat on a bench in her four-by-six cell. Hewitt put his hand under her chin and pulled out a sheet of paper from his front pocket. "Are you being treated all right here?"

She nodded and brushed some hair out of her eyes.

"I understand you fired your attorney."

She nodded and stretched out on the bench. "When do I get my meal?"

"I'll ask when I go back downstairs."

"I hope it's something more than bread and water."

"I'm sure it'll be something more nutritious."

She sat up again and folded her hands. "I don't want meat. I'm becoming a vegetarian. I don't believe in eating animals."

"But you do believe in shooting innocent human beings?"

"Michael Stewart is innocent?"

Hewitt sat down next to her. "Everyone is innocent until proven guilty."

"Even me?"

"Yes."

"How do I get out of this pigeon hole?"

"By cooperating with me."

Allison frowned and turned sideways, away from him. "Is Pastor Dennis feeling better?"

"He's fine. The wound is healing."

"I'm glad."

"Why were you trying to kill Michael Stewart?"

"Why do you keep asking this?"

"I'll keep asking until I get an honest answer."

"Or the answer you want?"

"Well?"

"I wasn't trying to kill him. I was just trying to hurt him."

Hewitt glared. "Look at me."

Allison turned and faced him.

"I need the honest truth. This is important. The pastor has decided not to press charges. The Suffolk DA is willing to give you time in a comfy mental hospital. You do enough time and show you're stable, you can have your freedom eventually."

She nodded. "I'll do whatever I can to help you."

"Good. I only have one interest right now – finding Michael and Elizabeth Stewart."

"You still don't know where he is?"

"He disappeared within seconds of you shooting him. You were one of the last people to talk to him about the case."

"I did speak to him about his daughter but I don't know where he might have gone." She shook her head. "But I'd bet Susan and Connie know. Those two tramps are up to something. Susan came running down from Massachusetts to be with Michael when his daughter went missing and has been hanging around since. Connie, well, she's just a nosy, miserable person. She's been around a lot lately. Strange. The relationship between her and Michael has been cold for a long time." She looked up at Hewitt. "Go ask Susan and Connie; those two hags would know where he's gone."

"The report says you gave a statement that you decided to take a shot at Michael Stewart because he humiliated and embarrassed you. How?"

Allison hesitated and looked away. "You have the report."

"I want to hear it from you."

"He lied to me in our interview."

"You shoot at every person who doesn't tell you the truth in an interview? And how do you know he was lying?"

Allison stood and walked to the metal cell door. She tried to stick her finger through the tiny keyhole. "Of course not, but his story was so bizarre. He said he traveled to Jerusalem."

"So?"

She turned around. "At the time of Christ? Come on."

"Go on." *This woman has lost her mind. How am I going to get any kind of useful information out of her? What will the boss think if I utilize her as a source? They'll run me straight to Bellevue along with this nut job.*

"Michael said he found a tunnel in the church."

Oh, yeah, she's crazy. Wonderful. This is hitting a dead end.

"He said he witnessed Jesus' death after falling in love with a woman. He said he knows Elizabeth is back there, trapped."

"You printed the interview?"

"Why wouldn't I? I quoted him. I did my job as a reporter."

"So what's the problem?"

"The problem is another newspaper, our competitor, asked for a response from Michael and he said his quotes were taken out of context. He said he was a believer and nothing more than that."

This lady needs to take a long rest inside a small room. "Why would you print that story? Michael is obviously a wacko. Didn't you realize the ramifications of publishing a story from a religious nut?" Hewitt asked.

"I do now."

"Didn't you realize what the response would be? Did you have any other motivation?"

She leaned back against the wall. "Sure, I wanted to embarrass him. Hurt him as much as I could." She sighed. "Instead, I was humiliated. People laughed at me. Do you know how much I was mocked online? Readers called for my job. I was trending on Twitter." She paused and let out a big sigh. "They called my editor. The publisher called me into his office and berated me. He asked if I was crazy and wanted me to take a drug test."

"Did you?"

"No. I couldn't. Not then. I wasn't having one of my best weeks."

Hewitt shrugged his shoulders. "Perhaps Michael was playing a joke? You did say in your statement you've known him for a while. Were you friends? What sort of relationship did you have?"

"We're not friends. I was a friend of his wife, Vicki. He treated her horribly, always stressing her out with his dream of being a bestselling author. The guy can't write. I know what good writing is. And the poor woman never got a break financially. She worked her butt off. While she was paying the bills, he was home sitting around with a career that was going nowhere. I can't tell you how many nights I spent on the phone with Vicki, consoling her. I heard her anxiety every night. I felt her stress." She clenched her hands. "He made me so mad."

"Why did you think it was any of your business to get so bent out of shape over their marriage problems?"

Allison sneered. "It's what friends do. Don't you have any friends you would lay your life on the line for?"

"I'm asking the questions here. You haven't told me anything that can help me find Michael and his daughter. I'll ask you again – besides this hate you have for the man, do you have any solid leads I can follow? Are there any people I can contact besides the two you mentioned before?"

"I told you I have no idea where they went." Allison paused. "Does that mean I'm stuck here for a while?"

"I hope you find a good attorney. You'll likely land in a psych ward for a bit. But I don't see you there for a long time. Go make a new life for yourself when you're released."

She grabbed onto his jacket. "So I should pretend I'm crazy so later on I can get out?"

"Do what you want. You can rot in here for all I care. I need to find the Stewarts one way or another. And you're not the way for me. I have my boss up my rear and the media making jokes about how a middle-aged man eluded the country's top law enforcement agency. I'm not in a sweet mood today. Good luck to you. You'll need it."

"Can you get me into a place where I won't have to watch my back? I'd rather spend my time with a bed and TV, away from this place. This town is full of crazies. Wackos. You've seen it, haven't you?"

She tugged harder on his dark blue suit, pulling a button loose.

Hewitt yanked her arms away. "You need to get yourself some help."

"You haven't lived here like I have," Allison said. "The pastor and Michael. They know something. I saw them locking the door to his office many times. When I tried to listen, they would stop talking."

"Step away from me and keep your hands to yourself," he said. "Maybe your information can make more sense. Whose office are we talking about?"

"The pastor's."

"What were they doing in there?"

"They were reading this black book."

He took a few steps toward the door. "The Bible? No surprise ... "

"No. Not the Bible. The book of miracles."

He waved his arms in the air and walked out. *Book of miracles. What a waste of time. This woman is not only insane, she's delusional.*

CHAPTER 4

FIRST-CENTURY JERUSALEM

THE SMELL OF DEATH INTOXICATED TITUS. He raged around the top of the impressive structure, strutting in his shiny armor like he was Caesar in his chariot. He bellowed out orders to the soldiers below who were dragging a lifeless body inside the Antonia Fortress. "Hang him upside down," he said, slamming his spear to the ground.

Nearby, another man was welcomed with Roman force. The sound of his head striking the ground echoed across the courtyard. A group of soldiers roared in delight as Titus broke up the group. "Why is he up here?" He raised his spear toward the fallen man's head.

"We thought he was important enough to bring him to you, sir," said one of the soldiers.

"Who is he?"

"Another follower of that preacher."

"What preacher?"

"The man who was once said to have come back from the dead," the soldier said.

"Those are lies spread by religious zealouts. No man can survive being nailed to wood," Titus mocked. "Do not deceive me. Send him where we are keeping the others. Make sure the one who writes sees his bloody head." He kicked the man in his ribs, eliciting a faint groan from the victim.

The thirst for beating and maiming another prisoner only invigorated Titus more while the heavy heat suppressed his Roman comrades. Many were taking an early morning break from the strenuous activity.

Titus clamored for more action as he gained the steps leading back inside. He scraped the walls with his spear, echoing its chilly tone through the downstairs chambers of the fortress.

"Myah, who is next?" he asked, slapping the soldier in the side of his helmet with a sword.

"Sir, we have our friend back."

Titus sneered. "Barabbas?"

Myah grinned. "He awaits your presence."

"Where?"

"In the deepest dungeon."

"Good." Titus grabbed a nearby spear, scraping its edge against the bloodstained, concrete wall, sending hot flickers showering around them. He made his way down several flights of charred stairs, each step slower so as to relish the mental images he could conjure up in his devious mind.

"I know it is you, Titus," shouted a faint voice. "You do not scare me."

The sound of Barabbas' voice, courageous indeed, enraged Titus. "I will torture you and let your filthy, beastly blood spill one drop at a time until your pain avenges every Roman you have killed."

Barabbas stood tall, taking a few steps toward Titus and then backing away just as quickly. He dodged side to side near the bars, daring a response.

Titus tantalized his prisoner with the tip of his weapon, pricking him just below his eyelid. "An eye for an eye," Titus said. "Is that not what you believe?"

Barabbas pushed away the spear, giving a disgusted look. "You can never avenge the cowards I slaughtered."

Titus adjusted his shield.

"I have killed far more of your filthy pigs than you have of my brothers." Titus jabbed at Barabbas' neck, creating a gash as a short spell of blood sprinkled the grimy floor. Another droplet of blood slithered down the side of his neck to his bare shoulder.

Barabbas picked it off before it could fall, looked at it and sucked it dry. "I am stronger than a thousand Romans."

Titus poked several times through the metal opening of the door as Barabbas continued to evade the weapon, using the far ends of the prison room to his advantage. "Stay still, coward."

Barabbas growled as if mocking Titus. "Coward? It is you who fears me, Roman. You hide behind your armor and weapons and a metal door." He moved side to side, never allowing Titus a clear shot. "Come and get me, Roman. You are strong with your spear and weak with just your hands."

Titus pinned Barabbas in the corner, poking his spear into his rib cage. Barabbas winced. Titus pressed harder, trying to penetrate bone. "How do you feel now, murderer?"

"Ready as always for you, Roman, weapon or not. My brothers stand ready to fight you." He let out a loud gasp, as if struggling to breathe. "We are ready to kill more of you, until the last soldier leaves."

"You will die before we leave."

"Kill me." Barabbas extended his arms. "You martyred the preacher. Martyr me. Kill me like you killed the preacher."

"You filthy pig." Titus spat. "The preacher was a peaceful man while slime like you lives."

"You gave him Roman justice."

"He gave his life so yours was spared. Now that was an injustice."

Barabbas leaned over, gasping, holding his side. "You should know about injustice, Roman. The smell of your blood pollutes this prison."

Titus clipped him again in his side, drawing another round of blood. A few droplets raced down the side of Barabbas' leg, too quick for him to stop them from reaching the floor. Barabbas growled and grabbed the end of the spear in a furious rage.

"Titus," said Clavius, another Roman soldier, as he bounded down the final steps of the dungeon. "We have some terrible news. Come."

"Help me," Titus said.

"As you wish, sir." Clavius jerked the spear away from Barabbas and smacked him in the side of the head. He watched the prisoner fall to the floor as he handed the spear back to Titus.

"It takes two Romans with weapons to stop me," Barabbas said.

Titus thrust his spear one more time, shearing the outside of Barabbas' ear. "Silence, you fool. The next spear that comes your way will take your tongue."

Barabbas groaned.

"Not so courageous now, are you?" Titus asked.

"Sir, we need to go," said Clavius.

"I am going." He walked toward the stairs. "Do not kill Barabbas. He is mine to avenge."

They climbed a few steps when Titus turned around. "What could be more important than butchering the murderer?"

Clavius stepped forward. "I have dreadful news, sir."

"What is it?"

"Marcus has been found."

"My brother?"

Clavius nodded.

Titus grabbed his arm. "Where? How is he?"

"He was found washed ashore."

"Alive?"

Clavius' head dropped and he let his spear hit the ground, its noise charring the darkness of Titus' heart.

"I will take vengeance on those who have done this to my blood."

"I think we should take this up with the governor, sir," Clavius said.

"I do not need a politician to tell me what to do."

"Sir, do you think it is wise not to consult with the governor? This is an extreme matter for the empire."

Titus grabbed his throat, bending his neck back and pushing him to his knees. "Listen and do not misunderstand my words. No one kills my brother without vengeance. An eye for an eye, a heart for a heart. Do you understand?"

He gagged as Titus released his grip. Clavius nodded.

Titus leaned down to him still gathering his breath. "No one needs to know about this. Understand?"

Clavius nodded again. Titus grabbed his spear. "I will need this. Call upon Aegidius."

"What do you want with him? I will need permission from the commander to speak to him."

Titus placed his spear under his neck, lifting Clavius up with it. He trembled and backed into the wall.

"There is no need to carry this word to the commander. Go. You have your instructions. Tell Aegidius to meet me outside the gate."

Titus pulled out several pieces of money. "Make sure he knows there is a lot of silver for him waiting outside. The trip will be short."

"Sir ... sir ... where should I say you have gone?"

"Tell whoever needs to know I am visiting a Jewish widow and need to give her a proper Roman greeting."

CHAPTER 5

LEAH PUSHED AND SWUNG HER ARMS, falling off the bedroll and away from her husband. "Stop," she screamed. "No more."

Startled, he shot up and grabbed a nearby spear. "Who is there? Show yourself!" he demanded, ready to strike any intruder.

Leah rose, putting her hands in front of her face. "No, it is me, Aharon," she said.

Aharon grabbed a nearby flickering candle and shone it on her face. "Leah. My darling. Again?"

She stood and touched his hand. "Yes, I was having a bad dream."

"How many times must we suffer like this?"

She shook her head and hugged him.

"Did that man in the cave frighten you again?"

Leah didn't answer.

"What did he say to you?"

"I am troubled."

"It is the man. Am I right?" he asked.

"My love, it is more. More than I can tell you."

"Speak to me, Leah. I am here to listen."

How will I explain this to him? She took a deep breath and inhaled Aharon's smell as if a loving, protective shield encompassed her heart.

"Tell me, my darling," Aharon said. He held her tighter.

Leah looked away. "I saw him."

"Saw who?"

She flinched but did not speak.

"The Roman?"

She nodded and rested her head against Aharon's chest.

"What did the Roman do?"

"There was a fight."

"Who was the Roman fighting? That man?"

Leah shook her head.

"Yochanan?"

"No. Elizabeth."

"The girl? Why her? Tell me, Leah. I am here for you."

"We are not safe here."

"It is just a dream. You have had many. We have been safe for many sunsets."

Leah released her hold on Aharon.

"Why are you pulling away?" he asked.

"Sit," she said, her eyes gazing into a lit candle. She placed it in front of him on a table. Leah touched his arm. "Let me heat some water. I have made some warm water. It makes my stomach feel better. Do you need some?"

"What I need is the truth. I cannot sleep this way anymore," he said. "You need to tell me how you feel." He pressed his hand on her heart. "What is in here?"

She went to the fire and warmed the water. It was several minutes later she was satisfied and placed a small cup of water on the table. Then she joined him.

They each took a sip, delaying the discussion. "I am in love with you, Aharon. Never doubt this. The man whom you have seen me speak with in the cave ... " She sighed.

Aharon raised her chin with his hand. "Speak honestly."

"I was in love with him before I met you."

Aharon stood. His anguished face tore at her heart. "Is there any more you need to tell me?" he asked.

"My feelings for him are in the past."

"Why were you talking to him at the gravesite?"

She bent her head. "I was going to pray for his daughter. It is his daughter who rests inside the cave. It had been some sunsets since we had seen each other. I did not know he had returned."

Aharon sat down and thumped the table with his hands. "Where does he come from? Why did he leave his daughter here and not bury her near his home?"

"I do not have those answers. Perhaps he was lost. He does not come from here. He has strange customs and beliefs. He is not like us."

"If he is not like us, how did you fall in love with him?"

She threw her hands in the air. "Love chooses us. We do not choose love. Do we?"

Aharon pushed his cup away. "Chooses us? How can you say that? I risked everything to give myself and my life to you."

"Do not be angry. I never sought out your love. It chose us, much like the stars that watch us when we sit on the rooftop."

"Were you ever with him?"

Leah shook her head.

"How would you know you were in love with him?"

"It is not important now."

"How can you say that?"

"It is gone, my love. You are my love."

"I can tell you still have feelings for him." He thumped the table again with his hands. "Is he the one you have been dreaming about?"

She looked up at the ceiling. "I do not know," she said. "Sometimes I think it is Yochanan, sometimes Michael, sometimes ... "

"Yes?"

She picked her head up. "Sometimes you."

"What happens?"

She waved her hands in the air. "No. No. I cannot talk any more about this."

He pulled her chair close. He placed his hand on hers and wiped away a single tear at the top of her cheekbone. "Leah, tell me. You are my life. My love. I live my life for you. You have to know this."

"I do. My dreams tell me it is not safe for us to be here."

"Do not believe your dreams. What is in your mind when it is dark is not here with us in the light. We are safe. The Roman soldier was dropped in the sea. He is dead. You saw he was dead."

She nodded, got up and looked out the lone kitchen window. "I know he is dead. Yet my dreams tell me there is a soldier coming to get me."

He followed her to the window and she felt his big arms envelope her. "You have had these dreams many times and yet we are safe. Do not fear the soldier who is dead. He cannot hurt you. The fish ate him."

"We do not know that. Did you see the fish eat him?"

Aharon didn't respond.

"Tell me," she said in a low tone.

"He is gone. He will never be found."

She heard him yet her thoughts drifted. "I miss my tree," she said. "I found God near my tree when I was so lonely."

"I am sorry. You know why we had to take it down?"

She did not answer.

"For us to be safe," he said.

"Why do I not feel safe?"

"You must have faith in me to protect you." He touched her stomach. "And to protect our baby."

CHAPTER 6

MODERN-DAY LONG ISLAND

DENNIS IGNORED THE FOOTSTEPS ECHOING IN THE CHURCH as he greeted Susan and Connie in his office. "I wanted to speak to both of you for several reasons. I know Michael is important to each of you in your own way."

He paused a few moments until Susan and Connie sat down. He went behind his desk and held up a black book. "I do know that it is possible."

"What's possible?" Connie asked.

"To travel to and from places and times."

"Where and when?" she asked.

"To Jerusalem, the time of Christ."

Connie shook her head. "Come on, Pastor. We've been over this a few times now. No one is going to convince me that my baby brother has the power to take trips to Jerusalem in this broken down old church. Are you telling me he has done something no one else has done? You want me to believe he has used time travel to go to another place and time in history? I love an entertaining story, but I'm not a fool."

"It's here," Dennis said, pushing the book over to her. "There are stories told by the previous pastors of this broken down old church as you call it talking about such occurrences. I didn't believe it could be true either, until a man named George Farmer convinced me. Michael isn't the only one who has done this."

Connie smirked. "Despite some unusual things I've seen, I still find this hard to believe," she said. "I need a lot more proof. My brother has always had an imagination for the paranormal. He's always watching that idiotic *Ghost Hunters* show on the Syfy channel. He was obsessed with that basement of yours too. He actually had me convinced at one time. I bet he was behind that snake trick. He was always planting fake bugs and snakes in my bed when we were kids. The worst part is he's got my niece brainwashed with this religious crap."

Connie paused, pulled back on her tone and glanced at the pastor. "No offense. But then he was up there with you by the manger and just disappeared into thin air," she said, waving her hands. "What are you all trying to pull? What about the doorway where he disappeared? Did he go down there? Where does it lead? Did he leave the country?" She regained her composure for a short moment. "Tell me, Pastor, are you protecting him? Sure looks like he's running away from this."

Susan looked away and shook her head. "How could you say that about your brother?"

Connie glared. "Excuse me, miss perfect. I'm trying to look at this objectively. I'm worried about my niece."

"We're all worried about Elizabeth," Susan said. "I'm also worried about Michael."

Connie softened her look for a brief moment. "I wonder what your role is in this nonsense. All of a sudden, you show up and things get worse. Since when have you been part of his life? He hasn't mentioned your name until recently. You leave the state and come back at a very odd time. I know what you've been after – a husband. Did you think he was vulnerable with Elizabeth missing?"

"Why you little … " Susan said, slapping Connie in the face.

Connie shrieked in pain and surprise. "Little miss perfect has a temper!" she said as she shoved Susan back.

"You'd better get yourself another shrink, you nut job. The one you have now isn't working," Susan yelled as she stumbled against the side of the pastor's desk.

"Stop it! Now!" Dennis shouted. He stood up and hurried over to the two women, putting himself between them. "Do you realize you're in church?" He pointed to chairs on the opposite sides of the room and gestured to both of them to sit down.

Susan pointed to Connie, glaring. "That woman has had it in for her brother since the day I met her. She rips him and tears him down every chance she gets."

They sat in silence for a few minutes. "Now this is nice," Dennis said. "Isn't it?" The women looked away from each other while Dennis paged through the book.

"I'm sorry," Connie finally said in a pointed tone. She lowered her head. "I'm just upset about my brother and niece."

Dennis sat on the desk between them. "Look, I'll admit I don't know much about women. I wasn't very good reading my ex-wife's moods or finding time to listen to my kids with their problems. I usually tempered her frustration with chocolate. Hmmm." He reached over and rummaged through his top drawer. "Do either of you want some? Would that help?" He held up a couple of Kit Kat bars. "Left over from Halloween." He waggled them in front of Susan and Connie with a smile.

Connie and Susan looked at each other. "Oh, pul-ease," they said simultaneously.

"Okay," he said. "I see I struck out with that suggestion. Forget the chocolate. I need your help, both of you." He winced, pressing the bandage so it stayed intact.

Connie crossed her arms. "Only a religious nut would believe my brother's story about traveling back in time and meeting Jesus of all people. Jesus." She rolled her eyes. "Could the doorway lead to another part of town?"

"Sure," he said. "But I doubt that's where he ended up."

"How can you be sure?"

"George Farmer told me some amazing stories. When George first told me about his travels, I didn't believe him. But when I saw Michael leave with my own eyes, all my doubts vanished." He held up the black book again. "I've read the stories about the miracles in here. It all adds up now. Didn't you see what I saw?"

The women looked at each other.

"I wasn't inside the church when he disappeared," Susan said. "But, I was outside and I was in the back of the church. I would have seen anyone leaving." She hesitated and opened her mouth, yet no words were formed.

"Tell me," Dennis said.

"I saw what the cloth did when we were in the car accident."

"What cloth?" asked Connie.

"Michael was carrying around this cloth. It had these red-stained markings on it. He kept pulling it out of his pocket, looking at it. We were driving to the church when some car comes out of nowhere and hits us. I had this big gash from the glass cutting me. Michael placed the cloth on my neck, and it stopped bleeding. It not only stopped the bleeding, the wound disappeared. It was a miracle."

"Are you kidding me?" asked Connie. "Okay. You get hurt. You're bleeding. My brother puts a cloth on your wound. It stops the bleeding. Wow, what a miracle."

"I thought I was going to die," Susan said. "I felt my body float. I could see myself sitting in the car from above."

"Oh, you are the drama queen of Northport. I wouldn't expect you to react any differently."

Susan glared. "Pastor, you know about the cloth. Right?"

He nodded. "I didn't see it do anything like what you said, Susan. So I can't be sure."

"I know what I saw, and I know what I felt," Susan said.

Connie stood and waved. "I'm out of here. There are way too many crazy theories being discussed in this room. I'm going to do what any normal sister would do when her niece and brother go missing. I'm going to organize another search party. I do care about Elizabeth and Michael."

"I guess that makes sense," Dennis said. "I'm not sure searching here though will lead to finding them. I do know what I saw."

"I know he was up near the manger with you and you handed him the doll. Then, poof, he's gone. Magicians do this all the time. There's nothing supernatural about this, Pastor. So he could have disappeared behind it and gone out another door. I know the church has hidden doorways. Right?"

"It does," he said.

"The FBI agent told me he went down that stairway by the manger," Connie said. "I believe what he said. I don't believe in fantasy. Perhaps it's a good way to draw people to your church, collect some more money after a sermon. Get everyone excited about miracles." Connie's voice spun a cynical tone. "Then pass around the big collection basket. A great way to sucker in the suckers."

Dennis shook his head. "I'm not like that."

Connie leaned forward. "What are you like, Pastor? Why don't you tell us? Are you being truthful about everything you know? Or are you hiding secrets just like my brother? Why don't you come clean and tell us about your relationship with Michael? Why have you been so friendly with him?"

He looked away, not sure where Connie was moving the discussion. He was relieved when Susan spoke.

"We're getting off track here," she said. "Our concerns are Michael and Elizabeth. If he went down the stairway, we need to follow the tracks and see where they might have taken him. It's the only logical conclusion we can come to right now."

"Don't you think the FBI has done that?" Connie asked.

"But do they really know where all the tunnels are in this church?" Susan asked.

"Well, wouldn't it be logical to first talk to this George Farmer person?" Connie asked in a triumphant tone.

"George has passed on," Dennis said.

"Oh, great," Connie replied.

Dennis dropped the book on the desk. "I don't know why it happened for Michael or for George Farmer. Or anyone else who's mentioned in this book."

Connie grabbed it and started flipping through the pages. "This is nothing but scribbling by religious freaks. It doesn't make any sense. Anyone can write this nonsense. I could have made up a story like this. My brother's a writer. He's always talking about far-fetched stories."

A hard rap on the door halted the conversation. "Yes, who is there?" asked Dennis.

"Special Agent Hewitt Paul."

"Um, okay. One minute, sir."

"Please go home. Pray," Dennis said, rushing Susan and Connie to the door. "Pray that the Lord helps Michael and Elizabeth to find their way home again. If you want to go out the back door and avoid the media, it's open."

Connie shook her head. "I'll drink instead. Do you want to join me, Susan?"

"With you?" Susan grimaced and looked away.

"You can help me draw up another list of people we can call who might know Michael or Elizabeth. As much as I hate to admit it, he cares about you. You might know someone I haven't thought of who could help us."

Susan hesitated.

"I'll buy," Connie said, turning around. "I'm sorry about doubting you, Pastor. I'm just angry." She looked down. "Sometimes I show it in the wrong way. But I would do anything for them. If he needed help, I'd give it to him. If he needed a place to hide, I'd help him."

"Check his home. Maybe he left some notes or a journal in how he was able to travel," Dennis whispered.

"What?" Connie asked as she opened the door and brushed past the special agent. Hewitt Paul gave her a look.

Connie sneered. "So arrest me. I love my brother. I hope you never find him. If he comes to me, I'll give him whatever help he needs. I hope you rot in hell for this. I hope you never find him." She slammed the door before Hewitt Paul could make his way into the office.

"Sweet girl," he said.

"She's upset about her brother and niece," Dennis said.

"I know. I'm upset too. I don't need you to sermonize me about her love for him. I heard the drivel." Special Agent Paul sat down, stretched his long arms and legs and yawned.

"How can I help you, Mr. Paul?"

"Call me Hewitt. We have a fugitive situation and possible kidnapping or murder. Not a wonderful circumstance for a special agent to be in while the media has a field day highlighting our supposed incompetence. They're laughing at us. Have you seen what they're saying on TV and the Internet about the FBI? This makes me angrier."

He frowned. "Pastor, I will tear this place apart, brick by brick, pew by pew, curtain by curtain. No one disappears in front of me. We had this entire church surrounded. The only way he could have escaped is through a passageway we haven't found yet. You know this church better than anybody. I believe you helped him escape."

Dennis pushed the black book across the desk. "Read it. I didn't believe it at first until I heard another member of our church tell me about his experience."

"Who is this person?"

"George Farmer."

Hewitt opened the book and read the first page. "How do I get in contact with Mr. Farmer?"

Dennis sighed and rubbed his chin. "You can't."

Hewitt frowned. "Why?"

"He passed away recently."

"Does he have any living relatives?"

"Yes. His wife."

"Terrific. I'll get his address and number through my office."

"Please leave his widow alone. She's been through so much. She's old and frail."

"I'm here to solve this case. If she can somehow help me find that poor girl, I'm going to sure as hell knock on her door and get some answers."

Dennis stood, placing his foot in the small garbage can. He pressed down on a newspaper article, mashing it into little pieces. He grabbed an empty Styrofoam cup, dropped it onto the crushed article and wiped his face with a tissue. He tossed it in and turned around.

"I have to bring a special unit in here to lift fingerprints and gather more evidence," Hewitt said.

Dennis glanced past Hewitt. When he didn't respond, Hewitt reached over the desk and grabbed his arm. "Did you hear me?"

"I heard you."

Hewitt's phone rang, and he answered it. "Hello. Yes." He turned his back on him. Dennis leaned back and grabbed the garbage can. "I need to take this out before the men come for the pickup."

The special agent grabbed the black book and put it in his pocket.

Dennis looked back and saw Hewitt was following him out of the church. He stared at him as he placed the garbage into the big, green metal bin at the rear of the parking lot.

"You do everything around here, don't you?" Hewitt asked.

Dennis shot him a nervous grin. "We're not exactly a profitable church, Mr. Paul."

"You can call me, Hewitt," he said again.

"I don't feel comfortable doing that."

"Why is that?"

"I'd rather keep my distance from you. Number one, you don't trust me. Number two, you don't believe me. Number three, you don't have much faith."

Hewitt shrugged and grabbed his arm. "I don't care about faith. I deal in reality. I have a job to do. And I'm going to do it until I find Mr. Stewart and his daughter. I'm going to feel like a mosquito on the back of your neck during a hot August night, buzzing around your head even when you're sleeping. I'm going to find that girl, dead or alive, if it kills me. No one is above the law. Not even you. A collar doesn't give you immunity."

"I want to find them, too," said Dennis, shaking his arm loose. "But you won't find them pushing those around who can help you."

"Prove to me you can help," Hewitt shouted, kicking at the bin. "Show me that you are willing to help me, or I will make your life miserable here."

Dennis smiled like he had done so often when consoling angry churchgoers. "And what good would that do, Hewitt?"

Hewitt took a few steps away. "I won't sleep until I find Elizabeth Stewart. I don't care about the religious babble you spout with your microphone every Sunday. You're just like any Joe out there. With or without you, I will solve this case."

Dennis sighed. "I know, but you're going about it the wrong way. Do you realize where Michael has gone is someplace many have read about in history books but can never visit?"

"Don't con me, Pastor," Hewitt warned as he went back inside the church.

CHAPTER 7

FIRST-CENTURY JERUSALEM

IT WAS A BUSY EVENING AT THE ANTONIA FORTRESS. There was an order given to capture a rebel who had been spreading the news that the rabbi killed on the cross had risen from the dead. The reward was sizeable. There was a measure of disbelief among the soldiers preparing to spread out across the countryside to quell the blasphemous rumors. Despite this important edict handed down by his superiors, Titus ignored his orders.

Instead, he hid in the lower bowels of the prison and closed his eyes. He couldn't avoid being noticed.

"Titus, you are to join the first army," said Plavius, his superior officer. He kicked at his head. "Awake, you lazy fool. A Roman soldier should be prepared."

"I am not well," Titus said.

"Do not disobey my order or I will have you hung from the top walls of this prison." Titus didn't answer and instead gathered up his spear and put his helmet on as he joined the group. He walked behind them as they left the barracks and waited for an opportunity to escape. It came when he hid behind some brush.

Titus delayed several moments before peering out and then seized his opportunity. He raced the remaining steps back to the fortress and bribed the guards at the gate. He returned inside to find the soldiers were still sleeping.

He crept up the stairs until he came to the top floor where they agreed to meet and plan their attack. "Wake up, it is time for our hunt," he said.

The four soldiers looked up and held out their hands.

"You will receive your silver when we kill the widow and drag her body back here for a showing," said Titus.

He sharpened his spear for good measure against a wall, taking a moment to relish the sparks that flickered from the friction. "Wear your most defensive armor," he demanded.

"Sir," one of the soldiers said, "you talk about killing. I thought this was not a military mission."

"Is the silver not enough for you?"

"I have no silver in my hands, sir," the soldier said.

"You will get it when our mission is done," Titus promised.

The tallest Roman stood up. "With respect, sir, I say this. This is not common among our orders. If this is not a military mission, I do not understand why we are bringing so many weapons to arrest the Jewish woman. We are taking her prisoner. Are we not?"

Titus glared, slamming his spear against the side of the prison wall. "I will decide whether it is my right to kill or keep her alive. A great Roman soldier is always prepared for the worst."

The soldier gave him a puzzled look. "She is just a widow. Why is she so dangerous? Does she have weapons like us?"

Titus grabbed the soldier's arm, twisting it backward. "What makes you think she is not dangerous?"

"She is just a Jew, a woman, a widow, a peasant."

Titus released his grip and shouted, "Come with me. I will show you what they did to my brother, a Roman soldier."

The soldier cowered in the corner.

"Let him be," said Titus. "We do not need sheep in our flock." He laughed and led the other three past several tall marble stanchions. "Over here," he yelled. He gestured to the corner of the grounds. "My brother, your brother, a Roman who risked his life for us in many battles," Titus said, kneeling. His brother lay in a decorated, well-cut casket. Marcus was clothed in the best attire and wore a helmet.

"Come closer," said Titus, standing.

As the three surrounded the casket, Titus lifted up the center of Marcus' vest and the soldiers gasped. "Tell me, my fellow Romans, do you now doubt my claim that my brother was murdered?"

"Vengeance will be ours," he said as he covered Marcus back up. He turned and led the soldiers away. "Do not be deceived," he added. "This could be a dangerous mission. The widow might have friends and neighbors to defend her. When we approach her home, look for any weapons and take them. Do not kill her. It will be my honor to do so."

He guided them down the stairs into the basement. "Prepare," Titus said. "Sharpen your weapons, drink plenty of water and get some sleep. We stay quiet about our mission. The only task another Roman needs to know about is our quest to aid a Jewish widow in the name of Marcus. There is no other reason to offer."

CHAPTER 8

JAX'S BAR WAS TRIMMED AND DECKED OUT WITH HOLIDAY DÉCOR. Red and green ribbons hung on the high wooden beams protruding from the ceiling. Christmas lights dazzled and blinking patterns of fluorescent colors danced in rhythmic motions. A large tree, its lower branches bent from the weight of heavy ornaments, stood majestically in a nearby corner, inviting even the shyest patron to utilize the beauty for a photo op or selfie.

Susan sipped red wine while Connie preferred white. They drank as the speakers belted out "Twelve Days of Christmas."

They watched a young couple slow dance to the next tune, Bing Crosby's "White Christmas." Connie watched the woman's happy face for a brief moment and then looked away.

Susan smiled and recalled the evening she and Michael danced to Frank Sinatra's version of "Silent Night" several Christmases ago. She took another sip of her wine and relished how it slid slowly down her throat, hugging her chest, warming her arms. She let her mind drift.

She remembered how Michael's hand felt on hers, how they moved in unison, step by step, cheek to cheek, chest to chest. It was perfect. They were one. She took a deep breath to collect herself as she drank some more. It didn't matter she and Connie weren't talking. In fact, she was happy for the silence. *I'll always have that night. No one can take it away from us. No one. Not my mom. Not Connie.*

She finished the rest of her glass while Connie played with her cell phone, frantically pulling and pushing at the touch screen with her thumbs. She dropped it to the table and looked up at Susan.

"Now what?" Connie asked.

Susan shrugged, still smitten over the memory. "I guess we wait to hear from Pastor Dennis."

"Come on, do you really believe what that kook said? It sounds like he's off his rocker. Do you think the pastor and my brother planned this disappearance? I'm fine with that, but don't talk to me like I'm an idiot. I'd like to be in on it if this is what's going on."

"Pastor Dennis isn't that way," Susan said. "He's an honest man. I've known him for a long time."

Connie looked away. "Believe me, he's not honest."

"Believe whatever you want," Susan said. "I've seen some strange things happen. What do you want? Evidence?"

"Yeah," said Connie, with a sarcastic edge.

Susan leaned forward and pointed to her neck. "Look here."

"So what?"

"Do you see any marks?"

"No."

Susan leaned back in her chair. "Right. No marks. The car accident."

"Oh, jeez. Here we go again with the dramatics." Connie smiled. "Wow. You really have it bad for my brother. He's got issues like the rest of us. Like you. Like – "

"You?"

"Like the pastor, your honest man. If you only knew what he's been hiding."

Susan ordered another glass of wine, trying not to show she was intrigued by Connie's remark. *Don't sink to her level. She's trying to pull you into her dirty pool of gossip.* The waitress returned with another glass of red wine. Susan took a long swig. "What's he hiding?" *Ugh. I can't believe I took the bait.*

Connie drained the remainder of her wine and signaled for the waitress to return. "This stays between me and you," she said. "Got it?"

Susan pushed her glass around in a small circle. "Sure."

"The pastor was married several years ago."

"I know."

Connie looked around. "Let me finish."

"So finish."

"He had a drinking problem, so his wife took the two kids and left him. Demanded a divorce. He was such a mess he had no choice. They decided to settle this out of court to save money. The pastor and his ex agreed that she got the house and he kept his insurance policy. A big one too."

"So? Isn't that normal when people split up? They split the assets."

"That wasn't the strange part."

Susan pushed her glass to the side. "Go on."

"So instead of naming his kids on the insurance policy he named my niece as his beneficiary."

"Elizabeth?"

"Yes."

"How do you know this?"

Connie gave her empty glass to the waitress. "Can I get another?" Then she put a couple of fingers over her lips. "My friend was the lawyer for his ex and gave me the info after he heard Elizabeth went missing."

Susan shook her head, lifted the glass to her mouth and put it back down. She stared at Connie. "What does this mean?"

"It could mean a lot of things. It could mean maybe one of the pastor's kids or the ex had something to do with Elizabeth's disappearance."

"Why don't you go to the cops?"

"I can't. Not yet. I have to think this over."

"Why?" Susan asked.

"If word leaked out, my friend would lose his job and perhaps his partnership. I haven't seen the document, either. I only know because he had a few in him one night and he told me."

"This sounds crazy."

"Oh, and my brother time traveling and talking to Jesus isn't crazy?"

Susan winced. "I don't know what's crazy and what's not."

"Well, I know I'm not crazy. I might be the only one in this hick town who's thinking rationally."

"You have to go to the police with this."

"Not until I'm sure. I need to find out a few things. I don't want to come across as some crazy person. You saw what happened to that woman Allison."

She looked from side to side to make sure no one was listening in on their conversation. "The pastor could be the only one who knows where my brother is. I don't want to upset or anger him. If I find out he's lying, I'll go to the cops. I love my brother despite what you think."

"I love him too," Susan said.

The waitress returned with another glass of wine, and Connie took a big gulp. "Yeah, I know all about your love. What do you know about real love? If you loved him so much, why did you leave Northport? Women like you are a dime a dozen in this town. Maybe he wasn't making enough money for your snooty lifestyle? Was that it?"

Susan smiled. "You are one pent up, frustrated woman, aren't you? You don't know anything about me. You don't know what's in my heart, what Michael and I share, how much I care about him. You have your own issues, and the biggest one is you. You're so bitter and lonely after your husband left you that you can't be happy for anyone unless they're miserable with you. I'm sorry you're unhappy with your pathetic, lonely life."

Susan took three quick sips of the wine, her eyes never leaving Connie's. She released the top part of the glass before she could break it.

Connie drained her glass and stood. "I'm leaving."

"Go ahead, go back to your big, fancy home with the high ceilings and chandeliers and the twenty big bedrooms. It must be so cold and lonely in that mansion of yours. How does it feel walking around all those empty rooms?"

Connie stopped and turned around. "I don't live there anymore."

"What happened? Did you relocate to the Taj Mahal?"

"Not that it's any of your business, but our house was a short sale. The only stinking rich person at this table is you. I've lost everything."

Before Susan could think of a response, Connie continued. "Are you thrilled now that my wonderful life is as miserable as you say?"

Susan felt a surge of guilt. She drank the rest of her wine in three gulps. She stood. "I'm sorry. Don't leave. We're both worried about Michael. We both love him. Can we agree on that?"

Connie hesitated and took a few steps toward the front door. She stopped and walked back to the table and sat down.

"Another glass? It's on me," Susan said. "Let's work on that list."

"We'll have to walk home if we do."

"So we'll walk off the calories."

The waitress came by with two glasses. "Compliments of the gentleman over there." The waitress pointed to a table beside the Christmas tree. The man in the familiar dark suit sat alone and raised a glass to them.

"Oh my," Connie said.

"Oh no," added Susan. "Now what?"

Hewitt Paul walked over, carrying his glass. "Hello, ladies. Mind if I join you?"

Connie and Susan didn't answer.

"I'll take that as a yes. I think we have a lot to talk about."

CHAPTER 9

HEWITT PAUL SAT STRAIGHT UP, his broad shoulders towering above Connie and Susan. His arms were folded. He smiled as Connie and Susan played with their cell phones and drank their wine. "Sally, another one for my friends," he said, gesturing to the waitress passing by. "She's such a fine waitress, isn't she?" he asked.

Connie and Susan shrugged.

"Sally. You know her, don't you?"

"Sorry, don't know her," Susan said. "Do you, Connie?"

"Nope."

Sally placed a glass of wine in front of each woman.

"Put that on my tab," Hewitt said with a wink.

"Will do, cowboy," said Sally.

Hewitt tapped the table, startling the women. "So ladies, what brings you out here tonight?"

"We're secret lovers and decided to come out in public to show our affection for each other," said Connie before she took a sip.

Susan laughed. "You wish, sister."

Hewitt grabbed a few pretzels from the untouched basket sitting on the table. He offered the snack to them.

"I'm on a diet, *cowboy*," Connie said, rolling her eyes.

"I hope you're not driving tonight," Hewitt said.

"No. We aren't. We're walking," said Susan.

"Is that against the law, *cowboy*?" Connie asked.

"I'm glad to hear you aren't on the road tonight. I'd hate to write you up with a DUI."

"Isn't that a cop's job?" Connie asked.

"It is. But I like to help out. Don't you like to help out in your community?"

"Depends on what it is," Connie said as Susan continued to sip her wine.

The lights dimmed inside the bar as the hour passed midnight. The room was still buzzing from chatter as late-night shoppers stopped by for the evening revelry. Susan's vision was fuzzy. *I hope Connie keeps her mouth shut about the pastor. We have to get out of here.*

They made small chitchat about the weather. As both finished their drinks, Connie motioned to Susan to join her in the bathroom. "Excuse me, Hewitt," said Susan. "Need to powder my nose."

"Take your time," he said. "I just have a few questions about your relationship with Michael."

She waved her hands in the air. "There was no relationship."

"Not what I heard."

"Susan," Connie called from the far side of the room. "Are you coming?"

Hewitt stood as Susan stumbled into a chair. "Oops."

"Do you need help?" Hewitt asked.

Susan put up her hand and waved him off.

Once inside the restroom, Connie shut the door. "All right, what's his angle?"

"Angle?"

"You think he's looking to take one of us home?"

"What?"

Connie pushed hard against the door to prevent anyone from entering. "It's how these guys do their work. Ply the woman with liquor, take her to bed and extract info from them. Don't you go to the movies?"

Susan moved past her and went into a stall. "Um, no. I think you've seen too many movies."

Connie paced back and forth for several minutes. "Are you done, yet?" she asked.

"Cool your jets. I drank a lot."

They both heard a thump as something struck the door. Then there was a rapping sound. "Hey, are you ladies in there?" Hewitt asked.

"Yes. Go away. Give us some privacy. We need two more minutes." Connie locked the door. "Hurry, Susan. Cowboy is waiting."

"I'm hurrying. Jeez." She emerged from the stall. Her blouse hung over her jeans and her hair was ruffled. She looked into the mirror. "Hey Connie, do you think I'm fetching?" Susan laughed.

"Knock it off."

"How is … is it … you … don't seem … like me?"

"You mean, like drunk?"

"Yuppers."

"I took one of those anti-alcohol pills before we started drinking."

"Really?"

"Yeah. We've got to get out of here. You've had way too much to drink. Who knows what you will say to this guy."

"Okie dokey," said Susan as she unlocked the door.

"No," shouted Connie, slamming it shut, then locking it.

"What's wrong, ladies?" Hewitt asked.

"We have to leave," Susan said.

"Yes, but not that way." Connie went to the lone window and pulled it up. A cold breeze brushed through the room.

"Whoa," Connie said.

"Are you expecting me to climb down a couple of floors?"

"It's only two," Connie said. "I'll go first and catch you if needed."

"Catch me?" asked Susan. "Are you expecting me to fall? Oh no, I'm not going through that window."

"As much as I hate to admit it, you're as light as a feather compared to me. I'll have no problem catching you. Take my coat and purse. Throw them down when I tell you."

Connie slid through the window, her feet dangling until she landed on the fire escape platform. "See, no problem," she said, holding a thumb up. As she turned, her blouse caught on the metal railing. "Oh, great." She twisted back toward the window and pulled at the knot. "Terrific. I just bought this blouse on sale at Macy's. One day and I can't even get it off when I need to."

A ripping sound caused Susan to giggle.

"Oh, joy," Connie said, looking down at her torn blouse.

"Well, looks like the *cowboy* will want you."

"Shut up," Connie said. "Wait until I'm on the ground before you start down."

She staggered down the fire escape to the last step, some ten feet off the ground. "Here goes." She let go and her heels crumbled. Her backside met the cold ground. "Ouch."

"Are you all right?" Susan asked, peering out the window.

"Yeah, I'm fine. Throw me the coats and purses."

"Wheeee. Here they come."

Connie set them aside against the wall. "Hurry."

"Cool your jets. I'm coming." Her legs came first, and a shoe fell, tumbling to the sidewalk. "Did you get it?"

"Forget the shoe," Connie yelled.

"I love that shoe."

"Stop yakking."

Susan made it to the last step and looked down. "Oh, I think I'm going to get sick. That's a big jump."

"Stop being a baby. Let go."

"Can you catch me?"

"I'll catch you."

"Are you sure?"

Connie grimaced. "I'm sure."

"Count to three."

"Oh, Lord. One, two."

Susan let go and fell on top of Connie.

"Three."

"Well, that wasn't so hard," Susan said.

"For you."

Susan laughed. "Are you hurt?"

"Only my pride."

They both lay there for a few seconds and laughed. "I guess we're friends now?" Susan asked.

"Frenemies is more like it. Can you get off of me?"

"I'll help you with that." A strong arm lifted them both off the ground.

"Oh hi, Hewitt," Susan said.

"Where are you ladies going?"

CHAPTER 10

LEAH PICKED UP MICHAEL'S TORN SHIRT with a picture of Bruce Springsteen on it. *I never did ask Michael who this is. Maybe I can ask if I see him at the burial place.*

She held it up to her face, smelling the fabric. She wiped some tears away, ashamed and confused. *What do I do about my feelings? Michael, you are here, without your daughter. You are alone and sad. I am not. I am happy with Aharon. This is not fair. My God, I plead to you for answers.*

She placed the shirt inside a small drawer. As she did so, she noticed a tiny robe, bringing back sorrowful memories. She picked it up and held it against her heart. *Why, my God, must there be so much pain in our world? Will it ever end? Why did my daughter have to be taken from me?*

Leah rocked back and forth with the robe, humming a song. She felt a wiggle in her stomach and stopped singing. She listened and rubbed her belly, caressing it from side to side. "What are you trying to tell me?" she asked in a whisper. "I am listening. Mommy is here for you. Tell me what you need."

She took a deep sigh and closed her eyes, rocking again back and forth, holding the robe in one hand and stroking her belly with the other. She cuddled the robe tightly to her face and breathed in until Aharon's voice startled her.

She tucked it back inside the drawer quickly as Aharon walked into the bedroom. Leah turned to see he was wiping his hair with a cloth.

"What are you doing?" he asked.

Leah took a deep breath and swallowed. "Cleaning the room," she said in a faint voice.

"I do not believe you."

She turned her back. "Why do you say that?"

He stuck his head around her shoulder and kissed her cheek. "Your face is wet. Why were you crying?" He noticed the open drawer and the tiny robe. "Oh, my love."

"I am fine." She laid her head against his shoulder.

"You must think of what we have now and not what has been."

"What will we do if our child becomes ill?"

"Children become sick. We will be sure our child stays healthy. I cannot change what happened to you and Yochanan many sunsets ago. I will protect our child from any illness." He gripped her shoulders. "I will."

Leah looked away.

"Are there more troubles?" asked Aharon.

"Yochanan spoke those words when our daughter was born." Leah dropped her head. Aharon put his arms around her. He kissed her forehead. "We will make sure our child lives."

He kissed her again. "I must go. My brother called upon me while I was cleaning. He told me to join him now. Do not be sad, my love. I will be back before the sun sets."

I am sad. I cannot tell him of my dreams of losing another child. When will I sleep again? When can my body rest? My mind will not allow me to rest without fear. I am a prisoner. Nowhere to go but inside these walls.

CHAPTER 11

HEWITT HELPED SUSAN AND CONNIE TO THE CAR. Susan leaned on the front passenger door as Connie ducked into the back. "Are you coming, Sue?"

"Yupsters." She pushed Connie over, the tip of her head hitting the ceiling. "Ouch."

"Are you ladies okay back there?" asked Hewitt.

"Tip top here," said Susan.

"More like tipsy," Connie said.

The heat whooshed from the dashboard, soothing the chill of the spacious Cadillac. Connie and Susan leaned against the windows, hands folded like good Christian girls waiting for a Sunday service to begin. Susan's eyes shut a few minutes later.

"Aren't you lucky I stumbled upon you ladies? It could have been costly and dangerous for both of you to be out there in this condition."

Annoyed that the window was cold against her face, Susan edged over and leaned against Connie, who frowned. Susan backed away as Connie jostled her shoulder.

"Where are we?" Susan asked.

"You're in the car with Special Agent Hewitt Paul, Susan. Do you not remember getting in the car with us?"

Susan didn't answer.

"I'll be taking you home."

Connie laughed out loud.

Susan's brows knit together.

Connie giggled, slurring her words as she spoke to Hewitt. "Hey, *cowboy,* where are we going riding tonight?"

"What was that?" he asked.

"You and me?"

Susan mouthed, "What are you doing?"

Connie laughed and hugged Susan as Hewitt's gaze followed them in the rearview mirror. She watched his eyes focus on her.

"I'll drop Susan off first. Where can I take you?" he asked.

"Make a right here. I'm up the road somewhere," Susan answered while giggling some more.

"You're in a good mood," said Hewitt to Connie as he made a turn onto Susan's block.

"Right here," said Susan. "The house with the big blue lamp."

The car pulled up in front of her home. The lamp lit the front steps. Hewitt turned the car off and helped Susan to the door. He said something to her and gave her a card.

Thank God he took her home first. I wouldn't have been able to help her. Miss college girl can't handle her liquor. Who knows what she would blurt out now, Connie thought.

Hewitt returned to the car and turned around. "Why don't you sit up here?"

"Another time."

"All right. Where can I drop you off?"

"My brother's house."

"Why there?"

"I water his plants."

Hewitt stared.

"Have I broken any law?"

"If you're harboring a fugitive, yes." He turned around and started the car.

Connie sat silent for a minute or two and then burst out laughing.

The car stopped on top of the hill, several yards away from the front door. She climbed out before Hewitt could help her. She stumbled and fell on top of the hood.

"Are you going to throw up?" Hewitt said as he raced to close his windows.

"I'm fine. Relax."

"Let me help you into the house."

"Mister big shot agent, I'm not that kind of girl."

"Well, good, because I'm not that kind of guy."

"Are you married?"

"I was."

She giggled.

"That's funny?"

"You must have been a peach to live with."

"I hear you weren't."

Connie stopped. "What?"

"Keep walking."

Connie reached the front door and fumbled with her keys, dropping them. Hewitt picked them up. "Let me handle this."

"You're so strong."

"How much did you have to drink tonight?"

"Oh, four or five or um, I don't remember."

"Where's the light?" he asked as he led her inside.

She watched him move his hand up and down the wall, searching for a switch. He finally found one and turned on the hallway light. "There."

"Do you want a cup of tea?" Connie asked as she kicked her heels off into the living room and tossed her coat on the floor.

"I'd prefer coffee."

"I'm not a chef. You're getting tea." Connie staggered to the kitchen, pouring water into a teapot and lighting the stove.

She sat down at the table as Hewitt took off his coat and jacket, impressing her with his well-built shoulders. He sat across from her and stared.

"How are you doing with everything?" he asked with a slight hint of empathy.

"Aw, you really do have a heart."

"Of course I do. I had a child. I hurt like anyone else. I know what it is to lose a loved one."

Connie looked down. "I know. I'm sorry."

"I can help you and your family if you let me. I can make sure Michael gets a good lawyer, a fair trial. I'll ask for leniency and make sure he's given a chance to avoid the worst prison time."

Connie picked her head up. *Wow.* She shook her head.

"Is everything all right?" he asked in a soft tone. "Do you need help?"

Connie put her hand in the air. "I'm fine." She looked at him loosening his tie. She gathered her composure. "I don't know where he is."

"Are you sure? Look, I know you love your brother. I can sense you're as frustrated as I am. I only have your best interests at heart. *Like you.*" He reached to touch her hand.

Oh, no you don't. No way, cowboy. She straightened up. "If I did have any information where he was, I wouldn't tell you. Is that hard to understand?"

Hewitt pulled his hand away from hers and glared. "I think it's time I make *you* understand."

The teapot whistled, and Connie poured the steaming water into a ceramic cup. She placed it in front of him and dropped a teabag on the table as her phone rang.

"Oh, Lord, what does he need at this hour," she said, answering it. "Hi Dad. What's up?"

"I'm worried about you, Connie."

Connie rolled her eyes at Hewitt. "Why Dad?"

"Because you're alone. Do you know how embarrassing it was to tell your aunt that Craig walked out on you?"

"I don't care what anyone thinks."

"Well, you should. You aren't getting any younger. Don't you want to have children?"

Connie placed the phone down at her side and sighed.

"Are you all right?" Hewitt asked.

She put the phone back to her ear. "There's nothing I can do to change it now. I've got to go. I have a guest."

"A man?"

"Yes, Jim, a man. Is that okay? Would you like to interview him?"

Click. Connie looked at Hewitt. "Can you believe he hung up on me?"

"I think you gave him a reason to hang up on you," Hewitt said.

"Oh, great. You men all stick together."

"Give the guy a break. He's checking in with you. Probably worried a single girl like you is out late."

"I'm a grown woman."

Hewitt poked the water with the bag several times, as Connie handed him a napkin. He looked at her. "Yes you are. I'm glad you realize that. We can make this easy for everyone involved. I can be your best friend or your worst enemy. It's up to you. If you're involved in any way, I won't be Mr. Nice Guy anymore. I am going to pay your father a visit too."

"Leave him alone. He's an old sick man."

"That's life. I have a job to do." He took a few sips and winced.

Connie smirked, taking some joy in his discomfort.

"I do my job well," he said. "I'll find your brother. He has a lot to answer for."

"What does he have to answer for?"

"Have you forgotten that your niece is missing and her blood was found in your brother's car? We have witnesses who say he was abusive to her in church. Now they're both missing. I know you have information that could help me find your niece and brother, so now's the time to tell me what you know."

Connie looked away. *He sounds convincing. No. He's trying to coerce me. I need to stop staring at his shoulders. I need to focus and concentrate. He doesn't want to help Michael or Elizabeth. He's looking to put my brother in jail. Michael is a religious nut, but he's not a murderer.* "You're asking the wrong person."

"Okay then, is your ex-husband the right guy to ask?"

Connie clenched her hands.

"You don't think I know about your ex? Why he left? How embarrassing it would be if it got leaked to the local papers here? How embarrassing it would be for your father to find out? I'm sure it would send him to his grave quicker if he knew. How humiliating it would be if your friends discovered the real reason? I'd bet your boss would just love that publicity."

She stood and pointed to the door, screaming, "Get out."

Hewitt stood, dropped his card on the table and walked to the door. "Perhaps I should have a chat with your ex."

Connie grabbed a wine glass and ran to the door. "You ... " She threw the glass, and it flew past Hewitt, shattering into several little pieces as it crashed against the door. She stood on her toes, pulled on the top of his shirt and swung with all her might at the tip of his chin. Hewitt grabbed her hand before it connected.

"You want to add assaulting a federal agent to harboring a fugitive?"

Connie ripped her hand away from his. "Screw you."

Hewitt turned his back to her.

"You have it all wrong," Connie said, sobbing. "I didn't mean to lose the baby. I didn't. I did everything I could."

Hewitt stopped, closed the door and then turned to face her. "I'm sorry. I know. I know." He watched Connie continue to cry. "I shouldn't have gone there." He escorted her back to the kitchen table. "I'm not really a jerk. I just do my job well."

Chapter 12

ELIZABETH CRINGED AND GRABBED HER HEAD. "Oh, this hurts," she said, staggering to a nearby well to rest. She took a deep breath, drew some water up in a bucket and splashed it on her face. "Mom, I know. I know all about the danger. Yes, I know about Dad. He wouldn't listen to me. I tried to explain it to him. He thought I was losing my mind. Just let me do what I have to do. I just want to get out of this awful place."

She looked into the distance and noticed a series of concrete homes that looked similar. *It could be any one of these houses.* The excitement of seeing Leah again was both joyful and mournful. She relished the thought of giving her a hug but was equally full of anxiety. *She'll think I'm some sort of freak. Will she run away? Attack me from fear? Will she think I'm a ghost?*

She bent down and patted the air. "Hey, boy, what are you doing here? I've got to run. Behave."

Elizabeth hoisted up another bucket of water. She cupped her hands, savored the moisture and repeated the process several more times. Leaning her head in, she lowered the bucket down.

A hand touched her shoulder, and she jumped. She turned and saw Leah. Elizabeth smiled and reached for her, but Leah pushed her away.

"It's me, Elizabeth," she said. "Do not be frightened."

Leah shook her head, turned pale and fainted.

"Oh no," Elizabeth screamed. She reached into the well and pulled the bucket back up. "Wake up, Leah. Here, I do not have time for this," she said, splashing water on her face. "Snap out of it."

She tapped her cheeks a few times and cupped some water. Elizabeth dropped it on Leah and hit her face with short, swift slaps. "Wake up, please."

Leah blinked several times. Elizabeth continued to splash her with water. "Are you okay?"

Leah mumbled a couple of words that Elizabeth couldn't comprehend.

"What did you say?" Elizabeth offered her water. "Drink this."

Leah held the bucket, staring. "You are alive."

"Yes. For now. We need to get going."

Leah stepped back, putting her hands in front of her face. "Are you a spirit?"

"In a way," Elizabeth said. "But I am as real as you are."

"You cannot be real," Leah whispered, backing away. "I saw you take your last breath. We buried you. I visited you at your grave. You cannot be alive."

Elizabeth walked toward Leah. "I am. Feel my hands." She extended them. Leah first moved away and then touched them, backing quickly away again.

"You do not feel warm. You are cold. You are a spirit." She backed up several steps.

"No, Leah. I am not." She picked up a sharp rock and cut the tip of her finger. Blood dripped out. "Look. I bleed. Just like you."

Leah touched Elizabeth's hair. "We buried you. You cannot be my Elizabeth."

Elizabeth opened the locket around her neck. "Matthew. You remember him. We spoke about him."

Leah blinked several times, shook her head and ran back inside her house. Elizabeth stood frozen as her stomach lurched. "I know, Mom. I don't need a lecture right now. Yes, yes, I'm going back to Dad as soon as I help her. At least I know where her house is now."

Elizabeth grabbed her head. "Ugh. Not again." She straightened up and rubbed her eyes. "I will do my best, Yochanan. I know how much you love her."

A noise nearby startled her, and she jumped behind the well. The line to the bucket shook and bounced back and forth. Roman soldiers with metal shields across their chests and shiny helmets on their heads pushed their way into nearby homes. They shouted and grabbed men and women, lining them up only a few yards away from Leah's courtyard.

Two soldiers pointed their spears at a man's neck. The man held his arms in front of his face, screaming. *Oh, God. Leah. She's in danger. We have to get out of here.* Her eyes scanned the outer area of the small community, looking for something to use as a weapon. She raced to the back of Leah's house and grabbed onto the top of the shower stall, hoisting herself up onto the lower portion of the roof. She crawled down the ladder and stumbled to the second floor.

She heard pots and cups crashing and breaking downstairs. Elizabeth crept down a few steps. She leaned and saw Leah struggling with a soldier, her face etched in horror. The soldier swung his spear, missing her head as she fell to the ground.

Haven't we done this before?

Leah screamed.

"Let her go," Elizabeth yelled, racing down the remaining steps. She picked up a water jug and rolled it toward the soldier.

He pushed Leah to the ground and leaped over it.

The jug hit Leah in the back as the soldier chased Elizabeth back up the stairs. She climbed to the top and crawled toward the steep portion of the rooftop. The soldier took three big steps and lunged toward her. Elizabeth rolled out of the way and the Roman tumbled several feet, falling off the roof.

She lay on her stomach and held onto the edges with her hands. She looked down and saw the soldier groaning, his helmet bent into his cheek, blood pouring from a big gash. Elizabeth took a deep breath and saw the ladder shaking. Eyeing the proximity of the roof to the ground, she prepared to make her escape with a leap.

As two soldiers climbed up, one ordered, "Stop, woman!"

Elizabeth held her arms up in a gesture of surrender. "Stick it." She turned, held her breath and sprinted off the roof.

Her legs stung as she fell to the ground. She protected her head as she tumbled several feet. "That wasn't so bad," she said, wiping off her legs as she looked around. "Leah," she cried out.

Elizabeth took several steps back inside the courtyard. "Come with me, hurry!"

She turned to look toward the well as a sharp ping opened a gash on her back. She grimaced. A soldier grabbed her arm and spun her around. Another Roman pulled her hair and pushed Elizabeth to her knees.

"Halt," one soldier yelled, pointing his spear at her throat. Leah was behind them, her hands tied. She lowered her head as the soldiers picked Elizabeth up.

Another Roman took his helmet off and sneered. He pulled back his arm, spear in hand. Leah struggled to get loose. A soldier struck her in the side of the head. She fell to her knees. A Roman on a horse galloped into the courtyard and put his arm up. He dismounted and grabbed the spear pointed at Elizabeth, pushing the threatening soldier away.

"I am trying, Yochanan," Elizabeth said. She struggled to get loose from the Roman holding her arms. "Where is the weapon, Yochanan? Tell me."

CHAPTER 13

CONNIE STOPPED ALONG MAIN STREET and walked into a medical office. She watched a woman sitting on a bench, dabbing her eyes with pink tissues. The woman fidgeted and kept reaching into her purse, fishing her cell phone out of the bag, looking at it and placing it back inside. She repeated this process three times before Connie looked elsewhere.

She then stared at an old lady wearing a black overcoat holding a young girl's hand. The lady had one arm wrapped around the girl's shoulder whose face was mashed into her chest. *Must be her granddaughter.*

In the far corner of the room, a man paced back and forth. He was talking quietly on his phone, wearing a big smile while holding a small teddy bear.

Connie smiled. *At least someone is happy here.*

She looked back at the woman with the cell phone issues. She was weeping. *I wonder what's wrong. I've seen that look before. I should probably get up and go talk to her. No, it's none of my business. Would I want some stranger bothering me while my world was falling apart? Who knows what types of issues she has.*

The woman pulled two more tissues out of her purse and wiped her nose a few times. Connie sensed the woman staring back, so she lowered her head to avoid eye contact. She brushed a lone fuzzy off of her coat and looked up. *She's still crying. Poor soul. I wonder if it's a guy problem.*

"Denise Ranakowski," the woman behind a glass partition called out. The old lady and young girl went up to the front desk. A nurse greeted and guided them away.

Connie moved over to the row of seats where the woman was crying. She sat two seats away and pretended to look at her phone. When the woman behind the partition left, she moved to the seat next to her. "What's wrong?" Connie asked.

The woman sniffled a few times and shook her head. "Everyone has a sob story, right?"

"I guess. What's yours?"

"I shouldn't say."

Connie leaned over and whispered, "I've seen that look before. I had it many days and nights after my husband left me. I wish I'd had someone to talk to during that time. Look, if you don't want to talk, I respect that. But I'm here."

She nodded and wiped her face. "I look like crap."

"Don't we all?"

The woman laughed. "I guess you're not a counselor."

"Why would you say that?"

"A counselor wouldn't say that."

"What would they say?"

The woman placed the tissues back into her purse and took a deep breath. "They would say, 'Oh, you look fabulous. Life has so much to offer you. Focus on the wonderful things in your life.'"

Connie grimaced. "I guess there are no wonderful things in your life?"

"I'm sitting here, but my stomach is out the door. No job. Not a penny to my name. My boyfriend took off once I told him about the baby. My mother thinks I'm a slut, and my father isn't around to help." She shrugged. "I've got no one."

Connie was silent, waiting for her to continue.

"So, I guess I've left you speechless?"

"Not speechless. I was absorbing what you said."

"I guess you can become my new stranger."

"What does that mean?"

"Not a friend. Just someone who waves to you and asks how you are doing when they don't really mean it. You see, since my friends and family heard I'm pregnant and not married, they treat me like the weather – fair."

"I'll admit I used to judge people." Connie shook her head. "But I've learned the hard way I have no right to judge anyone."

The woman pulled a big Hershey's dark chocolate bar out of her purse. She unwrapped it and broke off a piece. "Would you like some?" she offered. "It's healthy."

"I never turn down chocolate." Connie took the piece and put it in her mouth.

"This is my medicine, my new stranger." She started munching on the remainder of the chocolate bar. "By the way, I'm Virginia," she said, extending her hand.

"I'm Connie," she said, shaking it. "I'd need more than that small chocolate bar if I had your troubles."

"Well, Connie, since we've taken the next step of being best strangers forever, why are you here today? Or is that too personal?"

"I had three miscarriages a long time ago. I'm seeing if it's possible to have a child at my age."

"Really?"

Connie looked at her. "I'm old. But I'm not that old."

"How old are you?"

Connie laughed. "You don't have any filter on, do you?"

Virginia grinned. "No."

"You're my kind of stranger," Connie said.

"Why would you want to burden yourself?"

Connie looked down. "My ex and I went through a very difficult period in our relationship. It's the reason why everything went south. Maybe I'm trying to alleviate the guilt I have."

"I'm sorry, but you shouldn't feel guilty."

"I know. I know you're right. I guess I'm trying to learn how to treat myself better. I guess we're all still learning."

"You're taking a brave approach to this."

Connie went to the vending machine and bought some M&Ms. She ripped the bag open and let a pile of them drop into her hand. "My turn," she said, offering Virginia a few.

"Why, thank you," she replied.

They chewed on the candy in silence for the next few minutes.

"I'm not so brave," Connie finally said. "You are. To deal with people abandoning you and raising the baby with all your challenges is admirable."

Virginia lowered her head and wiped her hands with some stray tissues. "I haven't made up my mind whether I'm going to go through that hell."

"Can't you get in touch with your boyfriend's family?"

"He's an ex-boyfriend now. They want no part of me."

"What about other family? Other friends? A cousin? There has to be an aunt or an uncle or grandparent who can help."

"You would think there would be. But you're the only one who's listened to me about it without yelling and judging me."

Connie sighed. "Do you want to have the baby?"

"Yes. But I want the baby to have a better life than me. I don't want to worry about where the next meal comes from or whether I can afford to go to the doctor's when my baby has a high fever. And we're not even talking about paying for childcare or a babysitter if I'm able to find full-time work."

Connie stood up. "I need some more chocolate."

"Bring it on," said Virginia.

CHAPTER 14

HEWITT SAT ON THE EDGE OF HIS BED and stared at the pictures lining the dresser. As his eyes scanned them one by one, his daughter's voice rose inside his head and soaked his body with sadness. He reached for the picture, pushing his wedding ring away. He watched it spin and fall to the floor.

He closed his eyes, remembering a summer day.

I'll push you, Hailey. Let's see how high you can go. Up you go. Wow, how high you are. Look at you, my little girl. You are reaching for the stars, baby. Then it'll be the moon. Then another galaxy. He could hear Hailey laugh. It softened the edge in his heart.

"Look at me, Daddy. Look at me. I'm flying like a bird in the sky."

"I can see that. You're an eagle gliding across the Grand Canyon."

Hailey smiled from ear to ear.

He took a deep breath and stood. He picked up another picture of Hailey, her face covered in chocolate. Hewitt pressed the picture against his chest. "I am doing this for you. I will not fail."

He reached down and removed his socks. Straightening up, he lifted his arms pretending to shoot a foul shot. "Bingo," he whispered as he tossed it into a laundry basket at the far end of the room. "I've still got it," he said.

Hewitt walked past a picture of them in Disney World. "I will break that pastor, no matter how long it takes, until he tells me the truth. I don't care if God sends me to hell."

He turned to the walls behind him. There were four detailed pictures of the Lady by the Bay Church interior with doors, windows and offices marked. Profile pictures of Michael and Elizabeth Stewart were hung beside it. Below Michael's face, Hewitt had written several pointed thoughts about his personality. Under Elizabeth's photo several friend's names and phone numbers were listed.

He struggled to think clearly, shaking his head several times as if that might remove the sorrow and anger and release him from his emotional stranglehold. *I've donated my marriage to this job ,but I don't care.*

Hewitt stayed silent, staring at his wedding day photo. *No. I've dedicated my life to helping families find their sons and daughters. You were wrong, Veronica. Dead wrong.*

He shook his head. *I know I can't replace her, but every time I see a young girl, I see Hailey's face. Every teenager I see, I see what she would have been. She should have had birthday parties with her friends. She should have been able to graduate from high school and go to college. I should have been able to walk her down the aisle at her wedding. We were robbed. She was robbed.*

Hewitt stared at himself in the mirror above the dresser. *What good am I if I couldn't protect my own child?*

CHAPTER 15

Go NOW, MICHAEL IMPLORED HIMSELF. He raced out of the cave, his pouch dangling on his side as he bounced uphill and down. He passed a field filled with sheep and scattered the last group while heading toward a cluster of similar-looking homes. He tightened the pouch around his waist and fingered a sharpened wooden weapon inside his pocket.

He pulled the top part of his robe over his head like a hoodie to conceal his identity. *I hope Elizabeth doesn't give Leah a stroke or heart attack. Leah has no idea Elizabeth has risen from the dead. That will either scare her or kill her. There's no good ending to this.*

His thoughts pushed his legs to move with more urgency. He couldn't decipher how long he ran in sheer panic so he stopped. *Calm down. I won't get there any faster by falling apart. Maybe Elizabeth had a reason why she wanted to visit Leah.* Michael shook his head. *No. The reasons she gave didn't make sense. There's something terribly wrong with her.* He bent down to catch his breath for a brief moment. When he straightened up, he noticed Leah's town in the distance.

Initially he wanted to complete the journey by finding the apostle, hiding the relic and getting Elizabeth back to Northport. That all changed when she left. Selfish as it seemed, he wanted no part of the journey asked of him.

Lord, please help us get home. My daughter's been through so much. I want to see her graduate from high school. I want to take pictures of her on Prom Day. See her off to college. Hold my grandchildren. I've had enough of this running around in the First Century.

He sprinted, pushing himself so hard he staggered to the front of the courtyard. He took a quick, desperate sip of water from the well. He threw the bucket back down and ran inside Leah's house.

Shattered pieces of clay littered the kitchen floor, and a wooden table lay broken against the wall. A smoldering fire clung to its last spark in the stove.

He raced from room to room, his weapon drawn at shoulder level. He climbed to the second floor, stepping on the dinner mats and crushing a plate.

Furious, he yelled out as if his daughter were standing in front of him. "You make me so crazy, Elizabeth. This time you've really done it. This time we both may not get out alive. Are you happy about that? How many times must I battle these Romans? How many?"

He scurried to the room at the far end of the second floor, shouting out the window. "Lord," he screamed. "Where are you? I'm trying to help you. Why aren't you helping me?"

He slid down the wall, his head pressed against the lower part of the window. "I want to go home, Lord. I want to take my daughter home too. Now. Right now. No more delays. No more instructions. No more chasing people. Is that too much to ask? I've done everything you've asked. Is this how my faith is rewarded?"

He took a deep breath, waiting for an answer. He heard absolute silence. He stood, leaned out the window and saw the vacant courtyard. He looked out to the horizon and turned his head to the right and left. He saw nothing.

Where are they, Lord? Tell me. Point me in the right direction. I'm a desperate man. I need your help right now. He climbed the last step to the roof, hand clenched on his weapon and looked around.

Empty.

He circled around the steep and short elevated parts. *What's this?* He leaned down and picked up a shoe he had made not long ago. *Elizabeth. This was the one I gave her.* There was blood on it.

He bent over and squeezed his head with both hands. "No!" He raged around the roof and looked skyward, shouting, "Elizabeth!"

Michael fell to his knees but then got up immediately. He grabbed his chest and threw up. He gagged and staggered around the roof a few more times before tucking the shoe inside his pocket.

He raced down the stairs, leaped and fell, never touching the last three rungs. He cursed under his breath and got up, swatting a piece of broken wood from the table. He looked around for other weapons and found a spear buried under a bedroll. He searched in a small box and grabbed several pieces of silver.

Michael heard two men approaching the house, sounding like they were engaged in an argument. He remained quiet and listened, taking a quick peek out the window.

Michael recognized Leah's husband from when he observed them at Elizabeth's gravesite. *He looks upset. Oh, I hope it's not bad. He has to know where Leah and Elizabeth went. We can find them together.*

He heaved a deep sigh, got control of his emotions and ran outside, yelling to the two men. "Please help me." He put his hand out in a gesture of friendship. "My daughter is in trouble."

Leah's husband glared at him. "Who are you? What are you doing in my home?"

"I have come looking for my daughter," Michael said.

"Are you the man from the burial site Leah has spoken about?"

"I am."

"Go on your way."

Michael shook his head. "I cannot leave until I find out what happened to my daughter. Her name is Elizabeth. She has hair like mine," he said, pointing to his head. "The same color eyes."

"Elizabeth? The woman Leah and I visited at the burial site?"

Michael thought fast on how to spin this without having this man think he was insane. "No. A different daughter. I renamed her Elizabeth after my first daughter died."

"I cannot help you." Leah's husband walked past him.

"Something terrible has happened," said Michael, following him.

"It was the Romans," Leah's husband said, turning around. His face was pale. "The soldiers have come for us."

"What soldiers?"

"The ones looking to avenge us for killing another one some sunsets ago."

"My God, Aharon," his friend yelled. "Is this so?"

Aharon jolted the man with a thrust to his shoulder. "Stay silent. Do you know how many hands around here would love to fetch a reward? Go home. Protect yourself."

The man ran out of the house as Michael took a few steps toward Aharon. "It was Marcus. Right?" he asked.

Aharon nodded.

"Where would they take Leah and Elizabeth?"

Aharon went to the bedroom and came back with a spear. "The fortress."

"The one by the wall?"

"Near the big temple," Aharon said.

Michael smothered a loud sigh of intense fear. "There have to be hundreds of soldiers there."

"Many," said Aharon with a frown as he walked away.

"Where are you going?"

"To the fortress to get my Leah back. She was not responsible for killing that soldier. I am. I will give myself up to save her life."

Michael ran after him and grabbed his arm. "No. There has to be a better way. We can think of a plan, find a way that can save everyone."

Aharon turned toward Michael and knocked him to the ground. "Get your hand off me or my sword will take it."

Michael backed away on his knees.

"There are many Romans with better weapons than we have," said Aharon. "How are two people going to take on the most powerful army?"

Michael stood and thought about what Aharon had said for a few moments. "I do not have the answer for that question. I do know two of us are better than one."

Aharon walked several paces out of the courtyard. "Well, I know I have to go there and defend my Leah. I am prepared to give up my life. You should do the same for your daughter."

"I cannot disagree with you, my friend."

Aharon took several steps back to him, facing Michael nose-to-nose, and glared. "You are no friend of mine. We can help each other. Whatever happens, I will go my way with Leah or not. You will go your way with your daughter or not. Do you understand?"

"I do. But you understand as well. I will save and protect my daughter at all costs. We can either help each other or not. That is your choice. Are we clear?"

Aharon didn't respond and kept walking, picking up the pace with each step. Michael stayed behind a good distance for fear of antagonizing him more. *I am going to need him to help me get Elizabeth out safely.* His thoughts percolated, ideas swarmed in his mind. Yet, none seemed reasonable and rational against the odds he faced.

I'll make this journey alone if I have to.

Michael looked skyward, fighting off his peaceful instincts. "I don't give a damn about any commandment. I'll kill any man who lays a hand on my daughter."

CHAPTER 16

HEWITT STARED AT THE CEILING, looking at more white paper boards with case information on them. He read and stared, never blinking.

Michael Stewart – middle-aged man. Devoted to his wife. Changes and becomes a recluse with his daughter after his wife dies. Closest friend is the pastor. Pastor is friends with him for suspicious reasons. Pastor has motivation to silence Michael. What is Michael's motivation? Churchgoers saw him upset about daughter's boyfriend. Motivation there. Michael is a Type-A control freak.

Hewitt sat up and pulled out the side drawer. He grabbed the black book he had taken from the pastor's office, flipped it open and began to read. *Let me find the reference to the old man the pastor spoke about. Farmer. Where are you, Mr. Farmer?*

He flipped through the pages and found it near the back of the book. Hewitt put his finger on the lines and read them over and over again. The passage described how George Farmer appeared from the basement one afternoon, bloodied. "My God, this can't be real."

Hewitt turned the pages in disbelief. "No. This can't be true." He put the book down at his side, his index finger holding his place, and took a deep breath. *It's time I suspend reality and think like these fanatics do. I wonder if this Pastor Vincent is still alive.* He read another page.

I heard the terror in the mothers' screams. I felt powerless, as I had no weapons. I finally got up enough courage to find a rock and throw it at a soldier. It hit him in the head. I raced and picked up the baby. A woman chased me.

I kept running. I stopped until I came upon this small town, unlike any I had seen before. They lived like the Amish. No cars. No electricity. Just candles. The woman who was chasing me caught up and started talking in a language I had never heard before. She yanked the baby out of my arms and left.

I ran back to the field and tried to help as many mothers as I could. One soldier speared me. That's why I have this wound. I know you're thinking otherwise, but I would never hurt myself. I swear this is what happened.

Hewitt closed the book and put it back in the side drawer, went downstairs and grabbed his coat and keys. His phone buzzed, but he didn't glance at it. Instead, he walked into the dark living room where his wife had spent her last days with him, sleeping alone. He touched the pillow before going outside to his car.

As he walked toward the car, he read the text and then replied with, *thanks*. Hewitt tucked his gun inside his holster and then flipped a switch on a small tape recorder and slid it in his front shirt pocket. After pulling on his coat, he buttoned it up to the top.

He heard the beep as the car door unlocked when he pressed the button on his key fob. He climbed in, buckled his seatbelt, turned the key in the ignition and backed out of his driveway. He arrived at the psych ward in no time.

"Good evening, miss," he said, flashing his FBI identification. "I'm here to see a Pastor Vincent Hornichek."

"This is outside our visiting hours, sir," the nurse behind the desk said.

"It's official business." He walked past her.

"Don't you need the room number?"

"I already have it."

Hewitt strode by several doors. He came upon an open door at the end of the hallway and tapped on it. "Pastor Vincent? Pastor Vincent?"

The old man was talking.

"I'm sorry to bother you, Pastor. I didn't realize you have company, but this should only take a few min ... " Hewitt stopped as he walked in. The pastor was talking to an empty chair. He looked at him.

"Are you Pastor Vincent?"

"That's what they tell me."

Hewitt pulled a chair beside the pastor's bed and sat. "Vincent, I'm Special Agent Hewitt Paul from the FBI."

"Hello, Hewitt Paul from the FBI. I'm Pastor Vincent from the CBI."

"CBI?"

"Yes. Haven't you heard of us?"

Hewitt shook his head. "I'm afraid not."

"Neither have I."

Hewitt grinned. "Pastor, I need your help. Do you remember George Farmer? He attended your church."

"Who is George Farmer?"

"That's what I'm asking you."

"Why would you be asking me about someone I don't know?"

"Then you don't know?"

"Know what?"

Great. He leaned closer to the pastor. "Let me see if I can help you with your memory."

"Fine with me," he said.

"George Farmer attended the Lady by the Bay Church. You were the pastor when something strange happened to George. You wrote it in a black book. George told you this story. Do you remember this?"

"Lady by the Bay. Hmmm. It's familiar. I believe I officiated at George and his wife's wedding."

"Good. Now could you tell me more about him?"

"Sure. He married the actress Sandra Bullock. Lovely ceremony. Too many cameras. I hate those flash cameras. She was a lovely person. Drop dead gorgeous but too much makeup. Lucky man that George. Lucky man."

Hewitt rubbed his eyes. "I need a new life."

"Do you think what I have here is a great life?"

Hewitt smiled. "No."

"Did I help you?" he asked, smiling.

Hewitt stood. "You did. Is there anything I can do before I go?"

"Yes. I could use a glass of water."

"You got it."

Hewitt walked back to the front desk. "Pastor Vincent needs a cold glass of water. Where can I find one?"

The woman shook her head. "No. If he starts drinking water before he goes to sleep, we'll be taking him to the bathroom all night."

"Excuse me?"

"No water. It's the rules."

"Whose rules?" Hewitt asked.

"This is a psychiatric hospital, sir. He can have his water tomorrow morning."

"Screw this," said Hewitt, walking away. He went to a vending machine and put a couple of dollars in. Pressing a button, he scooped up a bottle of water and showed it to the woman. "He's getting his water."

"You can get him up then when he needs to go to the bathroom."

Hewitt sped back to the desk. "You can get off your ass and help the man if he needs to go. Or one call to the *New York Times* and I can give them the inside scoop of what's going on in here. Capiche?"

He didn't give the nurse a chance to respond as he hurried back to the pastor's room, uncapped the bottle and handed it to him. Pastor Vincent drank it like a man who had found a fresh spring in a dry desert.

Hewitt gave the pastor his business card. "If anyone gives you a hard time here, call me." Hewitt pointed to Pastor Vincent's phone at the side of the bed. "You know how to use it, right?"

"I sure can. But when I do, they tell me to stop and take it away from me. They tell me I'm bothering people with my calls late at night. But I get lonely."

"Don't worry about that. I know all about loneliness. You call me."

"Thank you."

"Is there anything else you need?"

"I'm fine."

"Pastor, I'll put your bottle here if you need it. If you need help with it, call a nurse. Okay?" He looked for space on top of the dresser. He pushed aside a little box, and a coin fell to the floor. He reached down and picked it up. "This is one odd coin you have here, Pastor."

"Oh yeah. I've had that for a while. It was a gift."

Hewitt held it up to the light. "Whoa. This is some coin. Who gave it to you?"

"Ah, a woman. Cecilia. Always attended church when I was there. She didn't have much, but she was always a giving woman."

"Cecilia?"

The pastor didn't answer as he had fallen asleep. Hewitt pulled the sheet and blanket over him and left the room. *Cecilia Farmer. Wife of George.* His mind formulated questions he intended on asking. *Where did you get that coin? Did George talk about the importance of the coin? Did he talk about his travels and what he was doing? Did he drink a lot? No. I know I want to believe that, but I need to suspend reality at least for a moment.*

As he approached the front desk, he noticed a man with a long ponytail, wearing a black leather jacket, heading out the front door. He immediately recognized him.

"What's Pastor Dennis doing here?" he asked the nurse.

"He was here to see a friend."

"Who was he seeing?"

"I can't disclose that information. You should know that. Do you have a warrant?"

Hewitt laughed. "I don't need a warrant." He grabbed the sign-in sheet and walked away.

CHAPTER 17

CHAINED TO A WALL, Elizabeth struggled to breathe. The stench from the bowels of the Antonia Fortress snaked through her stomach. She recoiled in horror as she saw Leah. Her face was swollen while blood dripped from her nose, and her right eye was barely open from a harsh bruise.

My God. What do I do now? Get us the hell out of here! This is crazy. Someone help me. Now! Dad? Where are you? Why did you have to go back to this terrible place? I was happy with Mom. I was happy. At peace. I want to scream.

"Dad, did you read my note?" Elizabeth thrashed about, pulling and yanking on the chains. "Let me out of here," she screamed. Her voice echoed down the dark corridor and elicited no response. She took several deep breaths and relaxed her arms. *Get a grip. I'm so mad at Dad. Why won't he answer me?*

"Leah, can you hear me?"

She mumbled a couple of words.

Elizabeth placed her hands on the ground and inched over to Leah on her backside. Leah held up her hands. Elizabeth swatted them away. "Knock it off. Do you think I want to be here? Yochanan told me how you needed help."

Leah shook her head. "Yochanan is dead. You are dead."

"Do I look dead?" Elizabeth slapped her on the cheek. "Did you feel that?"

Leah pulled away. Elizabeth slapped her on the other cheek. "Did you feel that?" Leah nodded. "Can a dead person do that?" Leah didn't answer.

"Let us just say I took a momentary rest from this hellhole."

They stayed silent for a few moments. "You spoke of Yochanan," Leah said.

"Yes. I spoke to him. He told me that you were in danger and I needed to help you."

"How did you speak to him?"

Elizabeth leaned back against the wall and turned sideways to face Leah. "I spoke to him when I was not here anymore. Or I think I did. I do not know. I am not sure of anything right now. Since I have been back, I think I am seeing and hearing people. People from the past. People who are not with us anymore. I can feel their worries and experience their loves."

"You see him?" Leah asked.

Elizabeth nodded.

"Can you see him now?"

"Not right now. But I saw him after the Romans took us."

"What did he say?"

Elizabeth hesitated and pulled on the chains again. "These clamps just will not budge. We have to get these off of us."

Leah edged closer to her. "Tell me. What did Yochanan say?"

She took a deep breath and looked away. "He said he loved you."

"Look at me," Leah said.

Elizabeth turned to face her.

"I know he loved me. Did he say anything about what will happen before the next sunset?"

"Only God knows."

"Then how did he know I was in trouble?"

"God shared it with him. He shared it with me. Every thought, every feeling, every emotion goes through God."

"What does God look like?"

Elizabeth paused and looked away for a brief moment. She turned back to face Leah. "There's no face on God. It's a feeling. A feeling of joy and peace. A feeling when someone is kind to you. A feeling when someone tells you they love you. It sweeps over you like an ocean wave and fills you in a way I do not know how to describe."

Leah touched her hand and took a deep breath. "What about Michael? Does your father know you left to see me?"

"He knows or I hope he knows."

"What do you mean?"

"I did not tell him when I left."

Leah tried to stand. "Why?"

"He did not want me going back to you."

"You should have obeyed him."

Elizabeth gave her a look. "Did you think I could stay in that grungy cave with him while your life was in danger? I could not walk away knowing you were in trouble."

"Your father will be worried."

"He is used to it. He should have been here by now. I am tired of this awful place. I was happy, you know. I was happy. I saw my mom."

She stopped talking and glared as a guard walked by. "Hey, moron," she said.

The guard turned toward her and gave a puzzled look. "What?"

"Moron. Do you know what it means?"

"No."

"Let me tell you then. It means someone like you is given this job because you do not have the ability to think like your commanders. So they give men like you this job because all you can do is beat up defenseless women and children. That's you – a moron. I bet you are the biggest moron in this prison."

The guard opened the door and smacked Elizabeth. Her head bounced into the wall. She laughed and spit at the guard. Some of her blood splattered his face. "Wow, moron, you are so tough. Picking on a woman whose hands are chained to a wall."

"Elizabeth, stop," Leah pleaded.

"Go ahead, moron. Hit me again." She spit again at him.

The guard raised his spear.

"Stop," shouted a man behind him. "Titus, what are you doing?"

"This woman was being disrespectful, sir."

"Now is not the time to administer punishment. She will have her time to answer for the crimes committed against the Roman Empire."

Titus turned and walked away.

"Moron," Elizabeth shouted.

A commotion distracted Titus and the other soldier. A group of soldiers bellowed and raised their weapons. They ran in different directions. "I wonder what is going on." Elizabeth said, getting to her feet.

Leah pulled on her arm and shook her head. "Sit, we cannot do anything now."

Elizabeth could see a group of Romans surrounding a man. His brown hair was streaked with gray, and through his torn clothing, she could see bruises covering his legs and arms. The soldiers opened the cell next to them and placed him in there. One soldier stood guard as the man got to his knees and closed his eyes. He started whispering.

After a few moments, the man groaned, obviously in pain, and sat back against the wall, keeping his eyes closed. Elizabeth struggled and settled down on the other side, near the man's cell. "Sir, are you all right?"

The man shook his head and reached through the bars to touch her hand. He gestured to the ceiling and put his hands together. "My time is short here. Please pray for me."

CHAPTER 18

MICHAEL GAZED AT THE ANTONIA FORTRESS, its tall and magnificent structure casting shadows of doom all around it. He rubbed his eyes and let them circle the vicinity. *How am I going to get her out of this forsaken place? I can't walk in just to see if she's even there. I need to formulate a plan, but how? There have to be several hundred guards, all with armor and weapons.* He cringed, as the adrenaline faded from his body and the reality of the situation became all too clear – it made him feel ill. *I can't do this alone. I need help. I'm not going to have much time to do this. I wish I had more money. I guess what I have had better be good enough. If not, I'll have to find a weapon and take my chances.*

Michael took out some silver and showed it to the two men standing several yards within the shadows of the Antonia Fortress. "I need help to get inside. Do you know a way past the guards?"

The men took several steps away from him and had a quick conference. They returned a few moments later.

"Why do you need to do this?"

"My daughter. She may be in there."

The tall man shook his head. "Your daughter will not live for long."

Michael glared. "My daughter is not going to die in there." He clenched his fists and moved closer.

"Do not lose your temper," the tall man said. "They will give you the sword."

"Please help me. I can get more silver."

The tall man turned to his friend. "Shalim, what to do?"

"Heber, it is too dangerous."

"His daughter, Shalim. It is not a place for a woman. No woman should be held here."

They again took a few steps away from Michael and whispered to each other.

"I do not have much time," Michael said, glancing back at the prison. "I need help now."

"We can help but we cannot join you. It is dangerous for us to even help you at all being who we are."

"Fine," Michael said, holding out the silver.

"We do not require silver to help a father find his daughter," Shalim said. "Come with us, brother."

Michael suddenly stopped. "Aharon is gone," he mumbled, taking several paces in each direction looking for him. He squinted. *Where did he go? I have a plan now. A good one, and I think it might actually work, but I need him.*

"Why are you waiting?" asked Heber. "Come with us."

Michael followed as they led him past several stands of food and approached the big temple. They washed themselves and went through a back entrance. The men led the way down a flight of stairs and into a long corridor.

"You will now need the silver," said Heber, pointing to a lone guard standing by a gold-plated door.

Michael showed them five coins. "Is this enough?"

The men nodded.

"Wish me luck."

"What is that?" Heber asked.

"Wish me good fortune."

"We shall. We will wait here to be sure you are safe," Shalim said. "Show the guard your silver. Hold it out in your hand and let him see it."

Michael walked toward the guard, making sure the soldier could see the silver from a distance.

"Halt," the guard shouted. He raised his spear chest high. "Do not take another step." The guard jabbed his spear forward three times as he approached. "What is your business here?"

"My business is this," Michael said, extending his hand full of silver.

"This interests me. Why do you need to take this path?"

"To see if my daughter is in the prison."

"Why is she being held?"

Michael shook his head. "She was mistaken for another woman. We were just passing through town and got lost. She was arrested by the Romans but was with me at the time the incident took place. I need to get her home. She hit her head and is sick."

The guard took the silver. "Do you know your way around the prison?"

"I do not."

The guard opened a small door and pointed inside. "Put the armor and helmet on and act like a Roman soldier."

"I shall," said Michael, as he reached down and put the armor over his chest and helmet on his head.

"Be careful," the guard said. "Do what the commanders say you must do, or you risk your life and the life of your daughter."

The guard opened the gold-plated door and Michael stepped inside. As the door closed behind him, he saw a tall stairwell. *Act like a soldier. Don't flinch or hesitate. Be decisive. Kill if necessary.* He took his helmet off for a brief moment to wipe some perspiration as he reached the top step. He composed himself to stop his heart from racing. *Now where?*

Several voices echoed down the chamber as he saw a line of cells. He walked past the first. A bearded, dirty man reached through the bars and grabbed his neck. "You dirty, filthy Roman," he hissed. "Where did you take my wife? Tell me or I will kill you."

Michael jabbed the man with the back of his spear. "I do not know. Let me try to find out."

The man fell to the back of the wall and spit at him. "I will track you down."

A young man lay in the second cell. He had bruises on his back and a gash on the side of his face. "Are you okay?" Michael asked.

The young man didn't move or answer. He was leaning sideways against the wall. Michael reached in and poked him with the back of his spear. "Sir, sir, are you hurt?" He pushed the man again with his weapon, surprised when he tipped over. His arms and legs were motionless. *Oh, Lord, he's dead. Take a deep breath. Stay focused. Find Elizabeth and Leah.*

He turned a corner and a group of Romans were chatting. "Well, what do we have here, someone from Pilate's renegade?"

Michael tried to walk past them, but two soldiers blocked his path. "Are you a spy from Pilate? Checking up on us? The last one to be loyal to Pilate never made it back. Speak."

"I am not Pilate's soldier. I am here to make sure these rebels face their deaths for their crimes against the Roman Empire."

"Let him go," called out a man decked in brightly colored garbs.

"Yes sir," the soldiers shouted.

"I need a few of you to help me move the prisoner. You," he pointed to Michael. "And you."

"Yes sir," Michael said.

"Come with me, both of you. We have an important mission for you."

The commander led them down a darkened hallway. Candles were melted down to their holdings. The resistance from the prisoners in the cells was silent. They lay beaten, listless. "This is an important prisoner for us. He must be protected until his trial. Many in the city are calling for his death. We had to hide him down here. His name is Paul. He is one of the followers of the rabbi."

"The rabbi? Which one?" Michael asked.

"The one hung on the cross."

Michael stood before the cell. Paul sat against the wall, his eyes closed and hands folded. The commander unlocked the gate and picked him up. "Here, take him," the Roman said. "Bring him to the top of the fortress for his trial."

Michael grabbed an arm, looked sideways and saw Elizabeth and Leah. *There they are!*

CHAPTER 19

THE MOONLIGHT MADE AN UNINVITED ENTRANCE into Hewitt's bedroom. He shielded his eyes with two pillows. He sat and let the reality of the situation hit him first in the stomach and then in his head. He tried Veronica's cell number three more times, but the calls went to her answering machine. Finding her old goodbye note, he crumbled it up without reading it and tossed it into the wastepaper basket.

He staggered to his feet and let his shirt hang out as he went into the bathroom. Looking in the mirror, he grabbed his toothbrush, held it up and dropped it into the sink. He smashed the neatly pushed up toothpaste tube with his hand, squirting its contents all over the sink and then tossed a bottle of hand soap against the wall.

The level of anger rose inch by inch in his body. He shook his head as he continued to build his case mentally against Pastor Dennis. With each thought, his anger was redirected. *Enough of this nonsense about people taking trips to Jerusalem. They're all a bunch of wackos. No time for a shower.*

He made a quick call to his office. "Is that his name? Robert Cantone. Yes. Thanks. I'll be waiting."

Hewitt tied his shoes and went downstairs. Sitting in front of his computer, he battered the keyboard in a furious fashion. "Whoa," he said, sitting back. *Which one to choose?* He clicked on the first few links but came up with nothing. *How about this one?* "Well, there's Robert Cantone's picture. No wonder he's in the hospital." Hewitt read the local newspaper article entitled "Woman Dies After Giving Birth."

"What?" he said as he stood up and stared at the screen. He printed a copy of the article and paced around the kitchen, confused thoughts swirling in his mind. *Why is the pastor visiting someone who killed his best friend's wife? This is an odd way of showing loyalty to a friend. Yeah, he's a pastor. I know. I know. But, this goes beyond being a pastor. Especially if they were close friends. Something is not adding up here.*

Hewitt made another call to the office. "I have the info on Mr. Cantone. Let's do some more background work on the pastor. You have his four-one-one. I have some visits I need to make in Northport. Some questions need to be asked. Call me on my cell. Thanks."

Finally getting somewhere. Looks like it's going through the pastor after all. Hewitt looked at his cell phone and frowned. "Come on honey, at least return my calls."

CHAPTER 20

Elizabeth grabbed her head and groaned. She shook the chains back and forth. "Oh God, not again," she said between short breaths.

"What is wrong?" asked Leah.

"My head. It feels like it is exploding again." She wiped away the sweat running down her face.

"You look ill," Leah said. "Your face. I can see through it. Oh my. Am I going crazy? My eyes are deceiving me. My mind is failing me."

Elizabeth gazed at her. She got to her feet, waved her hands sideways and tried to walk. "Who are you?"

Leah shook her head. "Sit down. You are not well."

"I do not understand. Who are you?" asked Elizabeth.

"Can you not see?" asked Leah.

Elizabeth shook her head. "No. Who are you? Who do you know?"

Leah stood and reached for Elizabeth. "Sit. Rest. I will call a guard. Do you need water?"

"Beth?" Elizabeth asked.

"What?" Leah moved closer to her.

"Bethia?"

Leah stepped back and fell to the ground.

"Bethia. What do you want?"

"Who are you talking to, Elizabeth?"

She didn't answer. "I understand, Bethia."

Leah watched Elizabeth gather her breath. "You said, Bethia," she said.

"Yes," Elizabeth said. She coughed several times, gasping for air.

"Bethia was my daughter."

Elizabeth calmed down, taking short breaths and nodded.

"My Bethia was just a baby when she died. How could she talk to you?"

"Her soul spoke," Elizabeth said.

"What did she say? What did she look like? Does she look like me? Like Yochanan?"

Elizabeth shook her head. "It is not like that." She touched Leah's hand. "I can feel the emotions."

"What did you feel?" Leah asked, leaning over her.

"Joy. Bethia said joy will come to you."

CHAPTER 21

A ROCK STRUCK MICHAEL IN THE HEAD, ricocheting off his metal helmet. Stunned, he fell to his knees.

"Fight the Romans," yelled a man in the crowd. "Free the man of peace."

The commander pointed to the rebel. "You will pay the price for striking a Roman soldier. Take him away."

Michael watched several Romans surround and beat the man. His blood left a trail as they dragged him down the stairs.

"Bring the preacher here," said the commander to Michael.

He got up and helped guide Paul out to the courtyard at the top of the Antonia Fortress. The crowd screamed and shouted opposing messages at him. "Death to the preacher," some in the crowd yelled.

"Save him," shouted others.

More rocks came hurtling toward them. Michael stood and faced Paul, taking a couple of rocks in his back. His armor shook from each strike. The mob became unruly, and more Roman soldiers pushed them farther away from the podium.

One dignitary stepped forward to the lip of the crowd and put his hand up. "This man should be given the right to speak."

The crowd hushed and Paul spoke. "I am a humble man, like all of you," he said, straining to speak over the buzz of the crowd. "I am only expressing what my heart tells me to say. What I say is, find a place in your heart for our Father's kingdom."

Several men in the audience stepped forward, throwing fruit and rocks. Michael moved in front of Paul again and was struck by pieces of watermelon.

"Nail him to a cross like his king," yelled a man, wielding a sword.

"Where's your king now?" another man shouted.

Paul's words were lost in the chaos and noise. Michael drew his spear as a man took a few steps forward and threw a rock. It struck his chest armor, making him flinch. *Now, that hurt.*

The commander gestured to him and the other guard. "Take him back to the cell. This crowd will kill him."

Michael took Paul's arm and followed the guard down the stairs. "I will handle this," Michael said. "Go find some water. Refresh yourself."

"Thank you," the other guard said.

Michael lowered Paul down but didn't clamp the chains around his arms. "Are you all right?"

"I am."

He lowered Paul down and watched him sit. *My God. I'm here with one of the apostles. He doesn't look like I thought he would. I wonder how old he is. I wonder if he realizes he's going to die a violent death. Maybe he doesn't have to die that way. Maybe this is the reason I'm here. Am I supposed to help him too? To help him live longer? Write more? Preach the word more?*

He shook himself out of his thoughts. *No. Keep it simple. Rescue Elizabeth and Leah, find a safe way to travel and get back.* "Rest, Paul," he said. "Watch for my signal. I am here to take you out of this forsaken place."

"Who are you?"

"Well, I am certainly not a Roman soldier, but your rabbi sent me to help you."

"My rabbi?"

"Yes. I saw him by a small cave in a mountain. He gave me instructions to get you out of here safely."

Paul got to his feet with some energy and looked to his left. "Can you see over there?"

"Where?"

Paul pointed.

"What's wrong?" Michael asked, looking with him.

"The women." He gestured to the cell.

Michael froze, dropped his spear and released his grip.

"My daughter! And Leah."

Paul strained to turn his head. "Your daughter? You must go now. I believe the Romans took them to where I was."

Michael raced a few steps, stopped and turned around. "Keep your hands behind you. I will tell them I have locked you up."

Paul fell down and groaned, holding his head.

Michael watched for a brief moment. *I'm sorry, Lord. I'm doing the best I can. What you ask may not be possible. I want to help. Paul will have to wait.*

CHAPTER 22

MANY OF THE DIGNITARIES HAD LEFT when Michael returned to the top of the Antonia Fortress. The crowd had also thinned as only a few hours of sunlight remained. Some scattered calls for the return of Paul went unanswered. Elizabeth and Leah stood shackled together.

Michael hoisted his weapon to give the impression he was there to help secure the hearing. He watched Elizabeth pull and tug at her chains and was shocked to see how frail she looked. His mind started to churn, wondering if they had touched her. Michael dismissed the thought immediately, shaking his head and hitting his helmet with the tip of his spear. He had to stop thinking like that – it would drive him mad. He knew he would kill anyone on the spot if he found out they had touched her. Michael couldn't deal with that and wouldn't hesitate to lay down his life for his daughter.

The shouting inside his head drove him crazy. He tried to settle down, taking deep breaths, telling himself to relax. *I need to be calm if I am to get them out safely. I have to act like every other soldier here. I don't want to stand out.* He took another deep breath, and his thoughts turned to Elizabeth again. *They better not have touched her. Stop. Stop it, Michael. Enough.*

He looked over at Elizabeth. She appeared defiant while Leah kept her head down. *Good girl. Stay strong. Don't take anything from these bastards.*

A man with a fancy robe and a bright red, long ribbon draped over his shoulder paced in front of Elizabeth and Leah. They remained quiet. He was addressing the crowd. "The women held before you are to be judged for the murder of one of our own, a Roman soldier."

Michael moved closer and found a big concrete column to shield his location. He edged near the guard behind Elizabeth and tapped his shoulder. "Soldier," he said, "you look weary. Let me help you. Go and get some rest. I will make sure the prisoners are secure."

The soldier pulled off his helmet. He bowed and lowered his weapon to the ground in a gesture of gratitude. He handed Michael the key. "This handles both."

Michael nodded. "Rest well."

"I shall." The guard walked back to the stairwell and disappeared.

Michael stood and held his weapon like the guard did before him. He was listening to the dignitary try to shout over the chatting crowd when a jolt to his back startled him.

"Where is Flavius?" asked a Roman soldier.

"Who?"

"Flavius. He was standing here before."

"He needed rest."

"Rest? This is not usual protocol. I will inform our commander."

When the guard turned to walk away, Michael called out to him. "Come back; I asked him to leave."

"Why? A guard never leaves his post during a trial."

"I asked him to leave because I want to avenge my friend's death."

"Whose death?" asked the guard as he took off his helmet.

"The man in the box," Michael said, pointing to the casket.

"Marcus?"

"Yes, Marcus. Marcus was a friend. These women are his murderers."

The soldier laughed. "I did not know Marcus had any friends. Or even one friend."

"He did."

"So be it. Far be it from me to stop a friend of a Roman soldier for avenging his death. I will give you the means to do so later."

Michael bowed and lowered his weapon. The Roman did the same.

He turned back to the proceedings as the dignitary faced Leah. "Were you not married to the Roman soldier?"

Her voice barely audible, Leah answered, "I was not."

"She is lying," said a soldier, stepping forward from the crowd.

"Titus, we will hear from you later," said one of the authorities. "Let the woman speak in her defense."

The dignitary turned sideways and spoke to Leah and the crowd. "There is a wound mark on Marcus, near his heart. Did you plunge a weapon into him as witnesses have described?"

Leah did not answer. Michael could see her hands clench.

"You will answer the Roman Empire for the crimes you have committed." The dignitary slapped Leah in the side of the head.

The crowd, now strengthening in numbers, hissed.

A man at the front of the crowd shouted at the dignitary. "Why does a weak woman give you fear?"

"I will ask you once more – did you kill Marcus?" He approached Leah and raised his hand.

"Leave her be," said the man, emerging from the crowd.

"No," yelled Leah. "Stay back."

Elizabeth moved to defend her, but a guard pushed her back.

Michael took several steps closer and squinted to get a better look at the man. It was Aharon. Michael slipped through the crowd on the side and waved at him. He took his helmet off for a brief moment and signaled toward him again.

Aharon's eyes widened and his mouth dropped. "What are you doing?" he mouthed.

Michael gestured to Leah and Elizabeth and raised his spear. Then he nodded toward the sun and pointed down. He held his spear up higher and tipped it in the direction of the front gate. He watched as Aharon disappeared into the crowd.

Michael returned to his post behind Elizabeth. Another guard approached him. "What are you doing?" he asked.

Michael felt his stomach lurch, unsure how to answer at first. "I was not sure whether my cousin was in the crowd. It is hard for me to see that far on this day."

The guard laughed. "You have been drinking."

"Yes. Yes."

"Only keep your eyes on the prisoners." The guard walked away.

The dignitary continued questioning Leah. "How long did the two of you share a home?"

"I do not remember. Some sunsets he was there. Many sunsets he was not."

"He was there enough to be married to you."

"I was not married to him."

"Did you obey the rules of the Roman Empire in the laws of marriage and act accordingly as his wife?"

"He was not my husband. He was a pig."

The crowd cheered.

The dignitary frowned. "You have spoken ill of the Roman Empire. It is a crime to do so."

"Pigs deserve to be slaughtered," Leah said.

Michael watched as the dignitary had a conference with Titus. He came back to the front a few moments later and faced Leah and Elizabeth. "I rule Titus can avenge his brother's death."

"I shall," shouted Titus, raising his spear.

"So be it. At sunrise, you shall be turned over in custody to Titus. Your daughter shall receive the same sentence."

The dignitary waved his hand to Michael and the guard standing on the side. "Take the murderers back to their cell. May their last sunset be a peaceful one."

He grabbed Elizabeth's arm while the other guard secured Leah. They walked them back downstairs to their cell.

Michael locked the latch. "I will take the first watch," he said, disguising his voice.

"Sir, we are not responsible for this."

"For their last sunset, it will be my reward to guard these women who have murdered Romans. I will not be given my right to avenge my friend's death. Let me have this."

The guard bowed and lowered his spear, the bottom of the rod striking the concrete ground. He left and Michael paced back and forth down the hallway several times before stopping in front of

Leah and Elizabeth's cell. He put his hand through the bars. "Take this."

"What?" Elizabeth asked.

He pulled off his helmet for a brief moment. "It's me, your dad. Take this."

"Dad? What … ?"

"Shhh. Take the key."

Elizabeth reached and took it from his hand.

"It will unlock your chains and the latch on this door. Do not unlock it until I give you a signal."

"What kind of signal?"

"I am not sure yet. It will come after the sun has set. Do not fall asleep."

He backed away and looked down the hallway.

"Michael, Michael," Leah said, moving forward, her chains jingling.

"Quiet," he said.

"My Aharon. I saw him in the crowd and – "

Michael nodded. "I will try to contact him." He reached through the cell door to touch her hand. "When you are free, you and Aharon must leave. Never come back. Seek a place far away from here."

Leah put her head on his hand.

Michael heard another soldier walking down the corridor toward them. "Remember," he whispered, "do not fall asleep. Wait for a signal. Close your eyes – now!"

They both nodded and feigned sleep as the guard rattled the cell with his spear. Elizabeth tightened her hold on Leah.

"Look at this scene," the guard sneered. "Like mother. Like daughter."

"Yes," whispered Leah. "Like mother, like daughter. To the last sunset." She squeezed Elizabeth's hand.

CHAPTER 23

Dennis bent over and groaned, holding his side. "Lord, forgive me for my self-pity, but this is quite painful." He opened the bottom drawer and let his fingers perform a dance inside it.

"Where is that book?" He pushed the chair away and fell to his knees. "I'm praying, Lord. Help me find my treasure." He put his face closer to the inside of the drawer. "Where did it go? Where's my secretary? Katie Adams, where did my book go?"

"Pastor," she said as the door closed behind her. "What are you doing?"

"Praying."

"From there?"

"I'm looking for a book. Small. Black."

"The Bible?"

"No. A small, black book I had scribbled some notes in. I thought I left it in the drawer."

"Get up, Pastor, please. I'll look. You shouldn't be bending over like that with your pain."

"I'll take you up on your offer, Katie," he said. He held onto the desk, pulled himself up and plopped into his chair. "Try the middle one," he said with some encouragement.

"Sure," Katie said. She rummaged through it several times. "I don't see any book in here."

Dennis opened the top drawer. He pulled out several small notebooks filled with sermon notes. "Nothing."

"Let me check the bookcase," she suggested.

"You do that," he said, shaking his head while rubbing his eyes again. He blinked several times and yawned. He stopped midway to answer the phone.

"Hello?"

"Pastor, it's Connie."

"I haven't heard anything today. Sorry. Did I give you the black book?"

"No. Did you lose it?"

He groaned. "Nah. Just misplaced it. Call me later. We really should talk. Don't you think?"

"Yes, Pastor, we should talk."

Dennis hung up and grabbed his side again. He pulled up his shirt and saw the gash was bleeding. "Why isn't this healing?"

"My God, Pastor," Katie said. "Let me get you some help."

"I'll be fine. Keep looking for that black book. I need it ASAP."

He tucked his papers away, slipped on his coat and opened the door.

Hewitt faced him. "Hello Pastor. Where are we running to now?"

"The doctor. I'm in a lot of pain."

"Not as much pain as I'm in right now trying to solve this case."

"Special Agent, I must go. I'm hurting."

"The wound?"

"Yes," he said, wincing.

"This won't take long."

"I don't have the time. We can talk later."

Hewitt blocked him. "We can talk now. How bad is the wound?"

"It's awful."

"Forget the doctor. I'll drive you to the ER."

"That will be better, Hewitt. We can get there quicker on my Harley."

"Sorry, Pastor. This is official business. We'll use my transportation."

He helped him through the church and into his car. Hewitt pushed his head down and buckled him up in the front passenger seat. "You okay there?"

Dennis nodded. He leaned his head against the window, taking slow breaths. The ride was bumpy as Hewitt navigated up and down the hills of Northport. He peppered Dennis with questions every few seconds.

"Did you know Robert Cantone was driving that car that killed Michael Stewart's wife?"

"Yes."

"Is it not odd that you're friends with someone who wrecked a close friend's life?"

"I'm a pastor. We forgive. We comfort."

"Does Michael know this?"

"He does."

"Has he forgiven Robert?"

"You'll have to ask him."

"I can't find him. Where is he hiding?"

"We've gone through this several times. I told you."

"You told me nothing. You made up some wacky story about him traveling to Jerusalem."

"Look. Whether you believe it's wacky or not, I know he's not here."

Hewitt slammed his fist against the dashboard. "Where is he then?" He drove past the emergency entrance to the hospital. "Just a few more minutes."

"What are you doing?" asked Dennis.

"You're hiding something, and I want to know what it is. When you tell me, I'll get you the help you need. You help me, I help you. This is how it works."

Dennis' eyes started to blur. "I'm dizzy."

"Why are you involved with Robert Cantone?"

He shook his head. "Help me."

"Answer me," Hewitt shouted.

"I was the tru ... " Dennis struggled to finish the sentence but couldn't.

Hewitt stopped the car and slapped him a couple of times in the face. "Wake up. What did you say?"

"I was asking for ... for ... giveness."

"Forgiveness for what?" Hewitt asked.

Dennis looked at him. His arms flailed, and he gripped the passenger side doorknob. He grunted and groaned. "I'm having a hard time breathing," he said, gasping. "Everything is fuzzy and dark. I can't see."

"What? My God. Wake up."

Dennis slumped forward.

"Wake up!"

Chapter 24

Michael sat against a wall among several Roman soldiers in an upstairs barracks, pretending to sleep. He opened his right eye every so often to watch five men on their knees in a circle rolling a die. Several pieces of silver were piled in the middle and were removed after a burst of cheering. More Romans, helmets in hand, stood behind the game, sipping liquid from their cups. The smell of heavy wine intoxicated the area. Michael shook his head several times to escape the aroma.

The scene reminded Michael of a college frat house. These hardened men looked like idiots in their drunken state and they were behaving like children. Michael knew they all believed they were part of the world's greatest army, but he had seen that all they truly did was conquer and oppress weaker people. *They're all disgusting, gutless pukes. I wish God's hand would wipe them out now.* He shook his head. He had to stop thinking that way.

Michael figured he was smarter than any of them. He was from the Twenty-First Century and had knowledge these men couldn't even fathom. More than likely, none of them even knew how to read. He might be outnumbered, but he knew he could outthink them all.

He watched one man stumble over another and fall down. They were all drunk. *Wait until they drink themselves into oblivion. Then, kill them. Kill them all.*

Michael sighed and let his body relax. He knew he needed to ignore them for now. Maybe he could deal with them after he figured out a way to get Elizabeth and Leah out of there.

He was exhausted and started to doze off. As his body relaxed, he slumped to his right and then jerked awake. He shook the sleepiness off and stood. He was drenched in sweat from keeping his helmet on all day and night. He needed a break and was frustrated that the soldiers didn't appear any closer to going to sleep. There was no way he could move Elizabeth and Leah until they did. He stretched and joined the others at the dice game. *I need to make it look like I'm interested.*

The revelry was high after sunset as the wine kept flowing. "Join us, brother," a voice said behind him as the soldier slapped Michael's shoulder and handed him a cup of wine. "Drink up."

"I am fine."

"Why do you not join us?"

Whoa. It's Titus. Be careful. "I do not feel well enough to drink." Michael made a gesture of gratitude.

Titus sneered. "You are odd. Why are you still wearing your helmet and armor?"

"I am prepared in case I am needed."

"Why are you needed after sunset?"

"Did you not hear?" said a soldier with a die in his hand. He shook it several times and threw it into the middle. He groaned while the others cheered.

Titus gripped his arm. "What do you need to tell me?"

"Your hand is hurting my arm, Titus. Ease."

"Forget your arm. Speak."

"There is a prisoner to be moved."

"Which one? Not the daughter and mother."

"No. The prophet."

"What prophet?"

"Paul. The man who preaches."

Hearing that, Titus relaxed his grip and Michael took a couple of steps away. Hearing a cheer from the rowdy soldiers, Titus turned back to the game. Michael took the opportunity to walk toward the stairway, soon coming upon Paul's cell.

Elizabeth and Leah stood. "Now?" Elizabeth asked.

He shook his head. "Where did Paul go?"

"A bunch of soldiers came a while ago and took him. They brought him back for a little bit. It was not more than a few minutes before they took him away again."

"Did Paul say anything?"

"He said you would find what you need in Caesarea."

Michael leaned on his spear. He took off his helmet and wiped the sweat from his forehead. "This complicates the plan now."

"What is the plan?" Elizabeth asked.

"I don't have time to explain. Rest but do not sleep. I will be back once the soldiers have fallen to the wine. It should not be long."

"Is Aharon safe?" Leah asked.

"He will be outside waiting. You and Aharon should follow us out of Jerusalem. It will be the best path to safety."

"We will," she said and sat down.

Michael adjusted his helmet and threw down the face clamp. He wiped some perspiration off his hands on his garment. Turning to Elizabeth, he asked, "Do you have the key?" When she nodded, he turned and walked away.

He returned back upstairs and saw the dice game was slowing down. Three of the five Romans were slumped over each other. Cups of wine lay beside them. The chatter had died down, and the silence of the fortress was a welcome relief until he heard Titus' bellows.

Michael wondered what to do with Titus. He decided it was time to join him for a cup of wine. It might be his only chance to get rid of the man.

He leaned down and grabbed a cup, dumping most of the wine on the floor, and began stumbling around.

"My brother, Titus, you were right. The wine is delightful this evening. I am feeling much better already." He waved the cup around as the Roman approached him.

"You talk unlike any I have heard in the Roman Empire," Titus said.

"I have had too much of the wine."

Titus glared. "I am glad you have joined us, brother." He poured some wine in his cup and took a big gulp. He raised his cup high and said, "To the Roman Empire."

Clang. Their cups met and some of the wine sloshed to the floor. "My apologies, my friend," said Michael. He poured the wine to the top of Titus' cup and poured some in his own cup as well.

I wonder what's wrong. He looks even angrier now. Michael sipped his wine slowly. He dumped most of it on a soldier who was passed out behind him when Titus looked away. He sat down to catch his breath. "Sit with me, soldier. You must be exhausted from the day's worries."

Titus sat across from him, away from the wall. "You are right. It has been a day of sweat. My brother is here no more, murdered by those peasants. The commander has now taken away my right for vengeance." Titus paused briefly and then bellowed, "It is my right to avenge my brother's death!"

Michael straightened up. "Why did the commander do that?"

"They are taking them back to the empire."

"The empire? Where?"

Titus gave him an odd look. "You do not know?"

"Yes, yes, of course. Rome."

"They are to be tried there like the prophet. They murdered Marcus. I will take revenge in my brother's name before they are able to get on the boat."

"You cannot. The commander – "

Titus growled and stood. "The commander had his say, and now I will have my say."

"You will be punished," said Michael as he stood, gripping his spear.

"I do not care about being punished. I will go past the commander and to the Roman Empire with my plea."

"Titus, think it over. This is against protocol. You will risk your high standing in the Roman army."

"The blood of my brother was spilled by that whore and her daughter. I do not care about my standing. The honor of my brother is at stake."

Titus put his helmet on and grabbed his spear. "I will need you to be on guard while I do this."

"You are doing this now?"

"I am."

"I cannot help you."

"Take off your helmet," said Titus, moving closer.

Michael backed up against the wall. "All right, I will help you. I am ready. Whatever you need me to do, I shall." He looked away. "I do not want the women to see my face."

"So be it. I want them to see my joy when I kill them."

CHAPTER 25

HEWITT OPENED HIS DOOR AS HIS CAR CAME TO A FLYING STOP. "FBI, get out of the way," he shouted to a woman dressed in white packing equipment into an EMS truck. He pulled Dennis out of the Cadillac and carried him to a stretcher stationed outside the emergency vehicle.

"Step aside sir, we'll handle this," said the woman.

"Move," Hewitt demanded as he brushed past her.

"Sir, stop, now," she said, racing to catch up to him.

"Lady, you can either help or go back to your lunch break," Hewitt said.

He laid Dennis on the stretcher and pushed him toward the door. "Open it," he yelled.

He barreled past several people and into the emergency room. "I need a doctor," Hewitt yelled.

"I'll take it from here," the woman said, grabbing the stretcher.

"It's his side," Hewitt said, opening the door to a hallway. "It's his side, the right side. He's bleeding badly."

The paramedic raced him through another doorway and into a room at the far end. Hewitt pushed past two doctors.

"Sir, we'll let you know how he is as soon as the doctor allows it," the paramedic said. "There's a waiting room. You need to go sit there."

Hewitt retreated a few steps and looked down the hallway. He went back to the door's window and watched as the doctor ripped open Dennis' shirt, pressing paddles against his chest. He jerked up and down several times. "I hope he makes it," Hewitt whispered.

The doctor shouted out instructions, and one nurse inserted a needle in Dennis' arm, starting an IV, and placed an oxygen mask on his face. Two other nurses and a doctor grabbed the stretcher and quickly pushed Dennis through the door past Hewitt and on down the hall.

Running behind them, Hewitt said, "Is he going to make it? Is he?"

They wheeled him into an operating room where several masked nurses and technicians were waiting and then moved into action once he was positioned on the table.

Hewitt watched the medical team until the door clicked shut, obscuring his view. The thought crossed his mind that they almost looked like ants retrieving a big kill.

"Sir," a nurse said as she approached him from behind, "this will likely take a while."

Hewitt looked away, back down the hall.

"We'll let you know his condition as soon as possible."

Hewitt nodded, returned to the waiting room and left his business card with the nurse.

As he was leaving, he spotted the EMS workers finishing up packing the truck. "Could you tell how bad he was?" he asked, catching up to them as they were closing the back door.

"Don't know," said the man.

"What do you mean you don't know?"

"He's lost a lot of blood."

"What are his chances? Tell me. Tell me now. Do you want me to run you in?" Hewitt said, showing more edge while pulling out his badge.

The woman stepped between them. "Settle down, sir. Pushing people around won't get you anywhere. It's understandable you're concerned about your friend, but you have two choices – sit in the waiting room or go home. It's going to be a while before anyone knows anything. He's in good hands. These doctors are among the best around. If he's able to survive the blood loss, this is the best place for him."

"If he survives?" Hewitt turned away, holding his head. "I need him alive."

"Go take a break and get something to eat. Go relax with some friends."

"I don't need to eat. I need him to live."

CHAPTER 26

SOLDIERS SNORED, slumped against the walls across from the prison cells. "Look at these sorry men," said Titus. "They hold their wine like women. They are not Romans."

"Sir, are you sure this is the best time to take vengeance?" Michael asked. "I would like to continue celebrating with wine."

Titus turned around on the stairway and pulled up the top iron of his helmet. "We have celebrated enough. You can walk away and show no courage if you wish."

Michael shook his head. "I am with you, brother."

Titus flashed his yellow teeth. His bottom lip and chin were stained from wine. "Let us do this for one of the greatest Roman soldiers." He walked down the remaining steps, holding onto the walls to keep his balance.

Michael was tempted to kill Titus right then and there, but he knew it wasn't a good strategy. He had no idea what he would do with the body or how he could explain what had happened if he were questioned. It might even prevent him from rescuing Leah and Elizabeth.

Michael let his spear scrape the ground a couple of times. He needed to come up with a better plan. He knew he wouldn't hesitate to kill Titus if it was truly necessary. It might be the only way to save them all. Michael still wondered if it might not be better to do it now. The Romans were all drunk, making it easier to fight them. He might not be in the greatest shape, but he was certainly younger than any of them. All that was needed was a quick jab at Titus' neck and there would be one fewer problem to worry about.

Michael raised his spear. If he was going to do it, he had to do it now. *Stop hesitating. Kill him. He's a Roman. They deserve to die.*

Titus turned around, and Michael withdrew his spear quickly. "May I ask you something, Titus?"

"What is it you wish to say?"

"When are they taking the man to Rome?"

"The one the crowd wanted to kill?"

"Yes, that one."

"Why are you so interested in this man?" asked Titus.

Think. "He is said to know where a treasure lies."

"Treasure? What kind?"

Not a good response, Michael. "Where there is silver and gold. I could have heard wrong. He talks strange."

Titus shook his head. "No, soldier. You talk strange. I think we both should seek out this man who knows about this treasure you speak of."

"Where are we going?" Michael asked.

Titus turned around and continued to walk without answering. They passed several cells and came upon Elizabeth and Leah. They stood as Titus opened the latch. "Come out," he said.

Elizabeth quivered and shook her chains. "No. We aren't going anywhere with you!" She bent over and held her head. "No. No more pain."

"Are you all right?" Michael asked, running to her.

"Leave the crazy woman alone," Titus said.

"Can't you see she's hurt?"

"My head. It's pounding. I cannot take this anymore. Let me go home."

Michael rubbed her back. "Elizabeth, what's wrong? Tell me."

"You know this woman?" Titus asked.

"He does not," said Leah, standing in front of them. "He is concerned. He has a daughter like her."

"How would you know?"

"He told me so."

"I do not believe you." He pushed Leah aside and glared at Michael.

"Is this woman your daughter?"

Michael pushed Elizabeth back behind him. *Now what? What do I say now?*

"Answer me, soldier."

Michael took a deep breath.

"You will die like Marcus, Roman," Elizabeth said.

Titus took a step toward Elizabeth, and Michael put his spear to his neck. "Move away," he said.

"Are you threatening me?"

"Yes."

Titus moved to attack and Michael defended. "I would gladly go to hell to make sure you could never hurt my daughter."

"We can both go to hell and continue our battle there," Titus said.

Elizabeth stepped forward. "Marcus said you killed innocent women and children while on duty during the high holy days. You took their lives and their money. He said you deserve to die like him."

Titus lifted his spear higher and sneered. "How do you know that?"

"He told me."

"He would not say such words to someone like you. Your tongue breathes fire, and I will kill you here." He backed up and straightened out his spear.

Michael raised his own spear higher and felt a hand on his shoulder, holding him back. "Get your hands off of me. Stay behind me, Elizabeth. Leah, move over to the right."

"I am behind you," she said.

"You cannot protect both," Titus said. He swung and struck Leah in the leg. She fell to the ground.

"Dad, she's pregnant."

"My God."

Titus snickered. "Two times the pleasure now." He swung as Michael defended her with his spear. The weapons clanged together.

"I do not want to kill you," Michael said as he grimaced. "I do not believe in killing."

"I do," Titus said, and he pushed him back with a short thrust.

Titus retreated a step and then quickly struck Michael. He winced and saw blood dripping from the side of his leg.

Titus lunged at Leah. "No," she screamed, holding her stomach.

Michael flung his spear, piercing Titus in the side.

Titus grunted. His spear fell to the ground, and he grabbed his abdomen. He gagged, uttering some inaudible words.

Michael dropped to his knees. "No one and I mean *no one* touches my daughter."

CHAPTER 27

MICHAEL TRIED TO LIFT TITUS UP. "He is too heavy for me," he said, dropping the body to the ground. "Grab his legs," he said to Elizabeth.

"Where are we going to put him?" she asked.

"Just follow me." He looked at Leah. "Are you able to walk?"

She nodded.

They walked slowly down the corridor, past the drunken, sleeping soldiers, carrying Titus about a foot off the ground. When they reached the top, Michael rested and Elizabeth dropped his legs.

"Okay, we need to move him over there," he said, pointing to the far end of the courtyard. A lone casket stood upon a stanchion. Michael opened it and glanced only a brief moment at Marcus dressed in his Roman red colors and steel-plated armor. His hands held a red-tipped stained spear.

"It doesn't even look like him," said Elizabeth, looking in. "Are we sure it's him?"

"Yes. They can tell by the scars on his body," Michael said. He turned to Leah. "I believe there's the one you gave him." He pointed to the wide mark near his heart.

"It does not look like the man I killed."

"Believe me, it is him," Michael replied.

The sea had ravaged his face and arms.

"Help me with him," he said. Titus moaned as they dragged him over to the casket. Michael rested for a brief moment. "He's going to be heavy to lift."

"We should make sure he dies," Elizabeth said.

"No. Why?"

"Marcus said he should die like he did."

"You were dreaming," Michael said. "No one can talk to the dead."

"I was not dreaming. I know the difference between dreaming and reality." Elizabeth glared.

"Look, I don't have time to deal with your moods right now," he said, glancing around the courtyard to see if any other Romans were near. He leaned over the wall to see how many guards were near the front gate. He noticed Aharon several feet away, bending down by a bush, holding a torch.

He went back to the casket. "On the count of three we lift and drop him in the box. Got it?"

Elizabeth stared. "I understand."

"Good." He took a deep breath. "One, two, three." Thump. Titus groaned.

Michael heard a commotion below and returned to the wall. There were several Romans leaving their post near the front gate. He could see Aharon waving his torch.

"Help Leah get to her husband. He is near the front gate, behind the brush to the right as you come out."

"Where should I meet you?"

"Ask Aharon to take you to the fruit stand with the watermelons on the sides."

"We are going home?"

He nodded. "Go now. I will be there shortly." Michael watched Elizabeth help Leah down the stairs. He looked over the wall and gestured to Aharon to look for them. Michael was relieved when he saw Aharon, Leah and Elizabeth meet up a few minutes later.

He grabbed the coffin lid and placed it over Titus and Marcus. Michael could still see Titus breathing, his eyes glassy.

"I will chase you down."

"It will not be today," Michael said as he nailed it shut by pounding four small spikes with the bottom of his spear. He took the tip of the weapon and carved three holes into the wooden frame where Titus' head was. He pressed his right eye to the opening and was satisfied with his work.

It was good enough. *Now what*, he wondered. Was he really going to leave him here? Michael knew if he escaped, Titus would surely come after him. Perhaps he should have killed him before. Of course, he could still kill him now.

Michael peeked through the small hole again and looked at Titus, staring in his menacing eyes. He knew Titus deserved to die, just like Marcus. From what he had seen, every single one of the Romans was the same. All they seemed to care about was oppressing, raping and killing. He had never observed any of them give a thought to the suffering they caused.

He pulled up a spike and started to lift the lid off with his spear. He stopped suddenly, wondering what in the world he was doing. Was he about to take a life? It would be first-degree murder in any century. He was shocked he was even considering it. What was going on in his head? He would never have thought like this in the past. Was he going to let this Roman darken his heart? What kind of effect was this world having on him?

Michael muttered, "I hate this world!" He shoved the last spike back into the corner and dragged the box under a small covering, out of view. Racing over to the wall, he stood on his toes and looked down. He saw Aharon, Elizabeth and Leah moving toward the city wall. They turned and looked up at him. He waved frantically and motioned for them to go farther. Elizabeth hesitated, turning several times to look at Michael. He gestured each time to keep moving.

When he saw they were safe, he returned to the stairway and mapped out a plan of action. He'd stay calm and continue to act like one of the Roman soldiers. He must find a way out of the fortress, meet the others by the fruit stand, and leave.

Two soldiers were rising, stumbling around. Four more had stripped down and were heading out the front gate. *Perfect.* He followed the group of six and took off his helmet like the rest. He groaned and rubbed his head. "What a night of celebration."

"Has any man seen Titus?" a soldier asked.

They all shook their heads.

"Odd," the soldier said. "He is supposed to give us our silver for grabbing the Jew widow." He took a couple of steps back toward the front gate. "I am not getting cheated out of my silver."

"I will join you," another soldier said, putting his helmet back on.

One soldier glanced at him, fell to his knees and vomited. The remaining men moved toward the baths. Michael walked past the soldier and pushed his face into the dirt. "Best you stay down there for a while," he said.

"Ugh," the soldier said, coughing up some mud.

"Consider it breakfast in bed." He pushed the Roman back into the wet mess again. "There's your dessert."

He watched the men remove their clothes and walk down into the baths. *I'd better move as soon as possible.* Michael walked to the last one at the far end of the facility. He waited until every other Roman had submerged in the water. Since no one was paying attention to him, he removed his armor. He squinted and looked up at the top of the Antonia Fortress. There was still some darkness on the horizon. He squinted again and didn't see anyone. He caressed his chain and cross and tucked it inside his shirt. *Now is the time to go.*

He made his way inside the city wall. He came upon a lone man organizing some fruit on a stand. "Sir," Michael said, "I am to meet my family here. Have you seen two women and a man?"

The man put the melons down and came out from behind the stand. "They were taken away by some soldiers."

"Where?"

"The soldiers spoke amongst themselves."

"What did they say?"

The man didn't respond.

Michael pulled out some silver and showed him. "Tell me, or I will throw every melon on the ground."

"You risk much in threatening me."

Michael picked up two melons.

"Stop," the man said. "They are taking them to Rome."

Panic seized Michael. He swatted a lone melon sitting atop a wooden counter, and it broke into several pieces. The man grabbed at his hand.

"Take your silver," Michael said, placing it on the counter. "Where do they ship from?"

"Caesarea. You must move and do not waste any steps," the man said.

It's not like I have a GPS available, Michael thought. "How do I get to Caesarea?" he asked the man.

"Follow the smell of the sea. The city is not far from there. You will know when you get there. It is not like here. It is big and beautiful."

Michael became dizzy and grabbed onto the ledge of the stand.

"Are you ill, sir?" the man asked.

"Do you know the fastest way to Caesarea? My daughter was taken. I need to get my daughter home now."

The man returned his money. "You will need this to get your family back," he said. "Silver is your greatest weapon with the Romans."

"Thank you."

As he began walking, he noticed the sun was almost up. Michael was hopeful he would be able to spot them easier with the help of the additional light. He passed the aqueduct and saw eight Romans scouring the neighborhood. Michael hid behind a well, the same one where he aided Leah when she was sick. He scooped some water out of a bucket and splashed it on his face. Peering around the well, he saw two Romans were pilfering Leah's house.

He waited until he saw the Romans go upstairs and then made his way to Abel's home. "I need your help. The Romans took my daughter, Leah and Aharon. They are to be taken to Caesarea."

"I will take you halfway there." Abel gathered up a couple of weapons, put some bread in a pouch and then tied it around his waist. "Are you ready?"

"As ready as one can be."

Abel stepped outside his home but held up his hand when he noticed a Roman soldier shouting at a man herding sheep in his front yard. Abel turned to Michael and quietly said, "Come this way."

Michael quickly followed him behind his home.

"This is the only safe path," Abel said. "It is rough in some areas. There are not many travelers going this way."

"Mountains?"

Abel shook his head. "The wind off the sea." He handed Michael a piece of ripped cloth. "You will need this to cover your face."

CHAPTER 28

CONNIE INDULGED IN A PIECE OF CHOCOLATE CAKE. She soaked up the taste by rolling it slowly in her mouth, allowing it to sit as long as possible on her tongue. She scraped the last bit of icing off the plate with her finger much like she did as a child dipping into fresh cake batter. She swallowed the remaining water and checked her phone.

"How are you, honey?" asked the waitress. "Can I get you another piece?"

"On the house?"

The waitress smiled. "If you want."

Connie laughed. "Nah. I'm starting my diet now. Thank you. The chocolate cake came at the right time."

"I'm glad. I wasn't sure if those were happy tears or breakup tears."

"Was I crying?"

"Oh, yeah," the waitress said, sitting down.

"I guess things can always be better. So I'm hoping."

"Good."

Connie picked up her purse and took out her wallet. As the waitress left, she placed a ten-dollar bill on the table.

She stood and saw Hewitt sitting alone in the corner. She slung her purse over her shoulder and stormed toward him. "Well, well, look at what dregs have crawled into one of Northport's finest drinking establishments. Who are you bullying today, King Hewitt? What peasants are you blackmailing?"

Hewitt lowered his head and fingered his drink.

"Are you FBI guys supposed to be tying one on in the middle of an investigation? My niece and brother are missing and you're sitting in here partying."

Hewitt looked up and took a sip.

"Cat got your tongue?"

He finished the drink with his next swallow.

"Whoa. Take it easy there, big fellow. It's a little too early to start drinking. Hold on. Keep drinking." Connie put her purse down on the table, dug around inside, and pulled out her cell phone. "Smile, jerk." She sat down and snapped a few pictures. "Let me get the glass in the picture too." She took a few more shots. "I bet you never thought you would be modeling for me today, did you?"

"Gina," Hewitt called out to the waitress. He put his hand up in the air, holding the empty glass. "Another vodka." He looked back at Connie. "Make sure you take a few as I drink."

"Aren't we brave?"

"Will that satisfy you?"

Gina brought another glass of vodka.

"Are you staying?" Gina asked Connie.

She leaned back and exhaled. "Yeah. This looks interesting. I'll have some of the bubbly stuff."

"Champagne?"

"Seltzer."

"It's on me," said Hewitt, dropping a twenty on her tray.

"Why thanks, sir. I didn't realize you were a gentleman. Sorry about the tirade," Connie said with sarcastic bite.

"No, you're not."

Connie frowned. "Wow, you can read my mind. Yeah, you're right. You're a jerk. I think my hate level for you is as high as it goes. Speaking of high, what's with the drinking party?"

Gina placed a seltzer on top of a small napkin and pushed it over to Connie.

Hewitt took a couple of gulps of the vodka.

"Yikes," Connie said as she sipped her seltzer. "Take it from an expert. Drinking will never solve your problems. And I've had a lot of problems as you know."

Hewitt took off his jacket and threw it on a chair behind him. He unbuttoned his shirt and removed his bright blue tie, stuffing it into his top pocket.

"What happened?" Connie asked. "Oh no," she said as her mind wandered into terrible scenarios. "Did something happen to Michael and Elizabeth? Were they found? Are they dead?"

Hewitt shook his head.

"Oh, thank God."

He motioned to Gina for another drink as Connie continued to sip her seltzer. "Don't you think you should finish that one first before drinking another?"

He frowned and held the glass up to his face. "Does it really matter?"

"Yes. It matters that you have your wits about yourself so you can find my brother and niece."

Gina brought another glass of vodka. As she turned away, Connie grabbed it. "Look, I'm not your mother or your friend, but don't force me to call a cop. I know we haven't gotten off to a great start but I need you too. I love my brother. I adore my niece. You drinking yourself into oblivion won't help find them."

Hewitt reached across the table, snatched the glass from Connie's hand and took a big gulp.

Connie grabbed her cell phone. Hewitt grasped her hand, pressing it down. "Wait," he said. He held the glass up to his mouth. "Okay, take it. I'll give you my boss' email so you can send it to him."

She pulled her hand away and texted Susan. *I'm at Jax. Come ASAP. FBI dude drinking up a storm. Need your help.*

Hewitt wrote on a business card. He slid it over to Connie. "The email is on the back."

She pushed it back to him. "No. You're going to do me no good if you're fired and slobbering over more drinks. I need the arrogant SOB back because it's the only way you will find Michael and Elizabeth. And I'm going to help you."

"How are you going to help me?"

"I have some info on the pastor."

Hewitt buttoned up his shirt. "I'm listening."

"Promise you never heard it from me. My brother would kill me if he knew I was telling you this."

Hewitt nodded.

"I was told when the pastor got his divorce, he decided to leave his insurance to Elizabeth and not his kids."

Hewitt sat back.

"Isn't that crazy?"

He shrugged his shoulders. "He's best friends with your brother. Maybe his relationship was terrible with his wife and kids. I've heard of worst things involved with divorces, things that would really twist your mind. This I know."

"Really?"

Hewitt nodded. "Write the name of the wife down."

"Give me your card back."

He pushed it toward her and rolled a pen in the same direction. She wrote "Cathy Evans" and returned the card.

"Where does she live?"

"Not far from here. Greenlawn."

"Have you ever met her? What does she look like?"

"No. Never met or spoke to her."

"What about Michael? Did he ever talk about this?"

"No. But my brother would never talk about stuff like this to me."

Hewitt got up. "I'll check it out." He stepped outside.

Connie watched him talk on the phone near the front door.

Her cell phone beeped. "About time, Susan. What took you so long?" she said out loud, looking at her screen. *Delayed. Is the GQ hunk hitting on u? He he. Go for it ;) Meet later?* She battered the iPhone with her thumbs. *He's wasted. No go. Ha ha. TTYL. Fake hugs.* Hewitt returned as Susan's response rang. Connie took a quick peek. *Later, Gator.*

He sat down and stretched his legs. "The boys in the computer room are working on it."

"Could be something, right?" she asked.

"Could be nothing."

Connie leaned forward. "You can tell me. Did this case drive you to drink?"

He hesitated. "Yes. In a way." His phone rang, and he looked at the screen. He answered it and ran to the front door. *Just like a man. Always running out on a business call. Enough of this. I'm leaving.* Connie grabbed her purse and dropped her phone inside. She left another ten-dollar bill. "See you soon, Gina," she said while waving.

"See ya, sister."

Connie approached the door, hoisted the big bag over her shoulder and went outside. She noticed Hewitt bent over at the side of the building, his hands covering his face. "Are you all right?" she asked.

He didn't answer. She watched his shoulders tremble up and down.

"Are you sick? There's a bathroom inside. Here, let me help you." She reached under his arm and tried to budge him. "Hey, FBI guy, help me out a bit. I'm a tiny tot. You're a grown man."

Hewitt shook off her grip and covered his face.

CHAPTER 29

FIRST-CENTURY JERUSALEM

AS DARKNESS DESCENDED, Michael kept his head skyward, walking a few steps behind Abel. It was so peaceful he could hear the crackling of wood burning in the distance from homes. He stopped for a brief moment to watch a star race across the horizon. He recalled the moments back home at Crab Meadow Beach in the winter. Through tearing eyes, numb fingers and toes, he would sit on the boardwalk bench for about ten minutes and appreciate the beauty of God's landscape.

"I can smell the sea," said Abel, stopping. He turned and tied a piece of cloth over his face.

Michael dug his cloth out of his pocket and did the same.

"The sand can hit you hard," Abel said as he started walking again.

"You are a good friend. I am going to miss you."

"Will you not return?"

"I do not know. I must find my friends and take my daughter home."

"I thought you were home."

"I have another one. Far, far away." He paused. "I will never forget what you did for me," he said.

"You would have done the same for me."

"I am not sure I would have been so brave."

Michael looked down, realizing the conversation was leading to saying goodbye. "If I do return, we shall share a meal."

Abel took his cloth off and smiled. "My friend. There is a meal waiting for you if you return."

"I wish I could show my gratitude more."

"You have. You saved my son with that white food. You saved me by saving my son."

"We saved each other."

Abel moved closer. "How did I save you?"

"I was alone. Sad. Grieving. I had no one to talk to. I had no means of making any silver. You helped me." Michael grasped his hand. "This is how good friends wish each other the best where I live."

Abel smiled. "May the wind be at your back. Follow the sea, my friend. Be careful of the Romans. They will use their force upon anyone who is weak. Be strong. Do not be timid in using your sword. They will have no fear in using theirs." He turned around and began his trip back home.

Michael watched him disappear into the night. He could still hear his voice shouting out instructions. *It's time to go home.* He felt some uneasiness knowing he was leaving Abel behind to fend for himself in this world. *I wish he could come back with me. He would be safe in our time. Could make a decent living and not worry about the Romans taking his food and profit.* He looked up at the sky and let the crispness of the air fill his body.

Goodbye, Abel. By the time I get back, you will have lived your lifetime. I hope it is a wonderful life. I hope you have your dream fulfilled, working with your grandchildren. I know how much family means to you. While we come from centuries many years apart, we are much alike. Goodbye, my friend.

Chapter 30

"Hey, FBI guy, I need you to get a hold of yourself." She looked behind her and saw a crowd was forming. Some were even taking pictures. "Hey, knock it off. Can't you see my friend needs help? Get away from here." She waved her hands in front of a teenage boy. "Don't you have school today?"

She looked down Main Street and watched as the crowd continued to grow. She noticed a couple of boys holding up cell phones. "Hey," she said in a stern tone, "you'd better get up now before it's too late."

Hewitt staggered to his feet.

"There you go. Want me to call you a cab?"

He shooed her away with his hands. "Leave me alone."

She took a few steps back and sent a text to Susan. *Help! GQ agent folding like a house of cards.*

She placed her hand on his shoulder. "Do you want to talk about it? I'm here to listen."

He shook his head and took a deep breath.

"I can be a good listener. I know you don't believe that but I am."

Hewitt turned and put his phone in his front pocket. He took out his sunglasses and covered his eyes. He tucked in his shirt and adjusted his jacket.

"There you go. We're back to being the big, strong, arrogant FBI agent I so love to hate." She grinned.

He didn't. "I shouldn't drive. I've broken every conduct rule in the book."

"Welcome to the club. I've broken a few myself. We're not perfect. I don't see anybody here flapping their wings like an angel."

"I don't need your sympathy. I do need a ride."

"No problem. Wait here." Moments later, Connie pulled up to the curb, and Hewitt hopped in the front passenger seat. His head slumped forward against the glove compartment.

"Hey, you're going to hurt your neck that way. Sit back," she said.

He put his hands on top of his head.

"Where am I dropping you off? Your office?"

Hewitt turned his head to face her and took his glasses off, giving her a look of disbelief.

"Oh. Right. Can't go there. Where?"

"I've got nowhere to go." He put his sunglasses back on and leaned his head against the window.

Connie slowed down along Main Street and parked near the theater. "I don't know anything about you, but what about family? You've got a ring on. Can I take you home to your wife?"

Hewitt mumbled a few words.

"Come on, big guy. Help me out here. Speak up."

"My divorce is final. I don't have anyone."

Connie hesitated, began a sentence and stopped. There were a few more moments of silence before she spoke. "Sorry."

He sighed. "Do you want me to get out? I will if you want."

"What happens now?"

He shook his head and didn't answer.

"Let's get something to eat. We both could use some real food."

Hewitt shrugged his shoulders.

"I'll take that as a yes."

"Take me to your place. I can't be seen in public."

Connie pulled away from the curb. "Hate to break it to you but you've already been seen in public. I'm not sure what to say in this situation."

Hewitt grabbed her hand. "Stop."

"The car?"

"No. Talking."

"Oh. Okay."

"Thank you."

"You're welcome."

"You need to get in the last word, don't you?"

Connie stared at him as they waited for the light to turn green. As it did, she spoke. "Yupsters."

Hewitt sighed.

"Sorry. Trying to cheer you up."

"No more."

"All right."

"What part of no more didn't you understand?"

"I understand it all." She turned to him and pretended to zip her lips closed with her fingers.

"Good."

"Almost home."

Hewitt banged his head on the window a couple of times. "I blew it. I ruined it."

"Does that help? I get migraines sometimes, and I always wondered if you hit your head a few times, would it help you forget the pain on the other side?"

"There is no pain relief for what I am going through now."

"Are you insulting me?"

"You're starting to make me wish you'd drive the car over my head and put me out of my misery."

Connie turned onto Waterside Avenue. "Oh, I'm that bad? Sorry. I'm trying to listen."

Hewitt scrunched up the tie in his hand. "I just could never let go of the possibility she was alive."

"Your daughter?"

"Yes."

"I'm sorry. So sorry."

"The marriage fell apart because of me."

Connie pulled into Michael's driveway. She noticed her father's car parked a few yards down the block. "Oh, great. Now what?" she said, unbuckling her seat belt.

"Problem?" asked Hewitt as he climbed out of the car.

"I hope not," she said, retrieving her purse from the back seat.

She walked ahead of him and saw the front door was open. She called out once inside the hallway. "Dad? You here?"

They walked a few steps toward the kitchen and were shocked to see Special Agent Holligan. "Why, Special Agent Paul, what a surprise to see you here," he said.

"Why are you here?" Connie asked.

"Your dad needed a ride to the hospital. I'll pick him up later. He was due for a checkup."

"Holligan," Hewitt said, shaking his hand. "Good to see you. Have you any news for me?"

"I was hoping you would have some for me. After all, you're the lead agent on this case."

"I'm working on it."

"It's a little dark in here for sunglasses," Holligan said.

"The sunlight has really bothered me the last couple of days. Been having migraines too. I haven't been getting much sleep because of the case."

"Relax. Take your glasses off."

"Kev, I'm going to put some burgers on. Want one?" Connie asked, standing in front of him.

Kevin kept staring at Hewitt.

"Hello, anyone in there?" Connie asked, snapping her fingers in his face.

"Medium rare, Con," he said.

"Where's the bathroom?" asked Hewitt. "This water diet is taking its toll on my kidneys." He gave a high-pitched laugh.

"Upstairs. First door you see staring you in the face when you reach the top floor," Connie said. She grabbed some frozen patties from the freezer while Hewitt ran up the stairs. After unwrapping them, she placed three burgers on a frying pan and lit the stove. She watched Kevin peeking upstairs from the corner of her eye.

Kevin returned as the pan started to sizzle. She flipped the burgers over.

"What's he doing here with you?"

"I'm trying to help him with the case."

"Don't you lie to me. I'm not your average guy you can con. I know the games you play and the nonsense you spread."

Connie flipped the burgers again, the grease spitting up off the pan and into her face. "Ugh." She wiped it off with a dishtowel from the nearby rack. "I'm not lying. I'm trying to do whatever I can to help them. Or don't you care?"

He swiped the towel and waved it at her. "Don't play that guilt game with me. If you're protecting that loser brother of yours, I'll make sure you personally rot in a maximum-security prison for aiding a fugitive. You can spend the rest of your days in a small room with just a bed and toilet."

Kevin pushed the towel into her face as Hewitt returned to the kitchen.

"What's your problem?" Hewitt asked, striking him in the back. "Is that any way to treat a woman?"

"Keep your hands off of me, agent," Kevin said, slapping at Hewitt's face.

His sunglasses fell to the floor. He quickly retrieved them, putting them back on just as quickly. "You messed with the wrong guy on the worst possible day."

"Okay, fellas, there's too much testosterone flowing here. Let's drop the macho FBI act," Connie said, stepping in between them, showing her weapon – a spatula.

"Move out of the way, Connie," Kevin said as he grabbed the spatula and threw it against the wall.

She stayed between them. "Please. This isn't the best way to settle scores."

He pushed her aside.

"I told you to keep your hands off her," Hewitt said, throwing a punch to his face.

Kevin swung back, knocking Hewitt's glasses sideways. "Let's see those eyes." He reached for them, and Hewitt snatched his hand. They grunted and fell to the floor.

"Stop it," Connie yelled.

"Shut up," Kevin said with a grimace. He pulled the sunglasses off and laughed. "You've been drinking. Strike one. On top of that, striking another agent can get you suspended. You'll also be taken off this case."

They scrambled to their feet, each with a hand on the other's throat. They tumbled into the hallway pictures hanging near the front door. Connie ran back to the kitchen.

"Stop it now or I'll call your office," she threatened.

They released their grips on one another. "You wouldn't," said Kevin.

"Try me," Connie said. She wiggled her cell phone showing a picture of them fighting.

"She would," said Hewitt. "I know she would."

Chapter 31

THE SMELL OF THE SEA SWEPT OVER MICHAEL, as his feet grew tired from the long walk. The urge to reclaim his favorite bench at Crab Meadow Beach inspired his desire to continue the trip. He walked and walked, keeping his head high. He took a deep breath and gathered in as much of the aroma as he could. He finally stood at the tip of the shore, watching the waves tumble forward, as he cleaned some sand out of his ears. Removing his sandals, he took several strides into the sea and let the salty water soak his aching feet. He sat down and allowed the next couple of waves to massage his legs.

Are you up there, Vicki? He looked skyward. *Can you hear me? If I haven't said it lately, I want you to know I miss you. I miss the times we walked on the beach. I miss holding your hand. Remember the time when we were at Crab Meadow and we saw the small plane coming our way? We both thought it was having problems and was coming toward us. I shouted to you, and you calmly picked up Elizabeth and got her to safety. Remember that?*

He paused. *Okay, the plane was fine and we were too. I just wanted to say how grateful I was to have you in my life. I know the time was short for us. Dreadfully short. I miss kissing you. I miss your hugs.*

Michael rubbed his toes, trying to gather himself. *I miss talking to you, especially at night. Our room is so empty now. I'm alone. I can't stand it. There's no one to rub my back anymore. I have no one to touch, to love. I didn't realize how important you were to me until you died. Now I understand how much I needed you. I'm sorry it's taken me so long to appreciate it.* He sighed and looked up to the sky again, letting some tears leak down his cheeks. *I'd really appreciate it if you ask the man in charge for some help. I understand I ...* Michael stood and saw two men rowing. They were casting nets and shouting to each other. He dropped his pouch and took several more steps into the sea. Before he realized how far he'd gone, Michael found himself about one hundred yards from the beach.

They'll know how far Caesarea is from here.

He removed the cloth from his face, cupped some water in his hands and splashed himself. He looked down the shoreline but couldn't locate any city markers. *I'm so tired I can barely feel my legs. I need help. I'll take any kind of help.*

Michael waved at the two men. "Hello, my friends," he shouted.

They didn't answer and continued to remove fish from the net. The water rose to the top of his chest and waves touched the bottom of his neck. "Can you help me?" he yelled.

The men were almost done as he approached the boat. One fish slipped away. Michael caught it and held it up. "Here."

"Thank you, my friend," a man said, smiling. He was elderly, certainly a veteran of the sea as evidenced by his gruff, wrinkled face. "Are you lost?"

"I am."

"Where do you need to go?" the man asked.

"Caesarea."

The man turned to the other and said, "This is him. Right?"

"Yes," his partner said while looking up at the sky and pulling down his hood. He pulled the net up into the boat and picked up an oar. "Are you ready to catch more, George?"

"Same way?"

"Yes."

The man went back and forward with the oar as the boat now had gone some distance. "Can you tell me where to find Caesarea?" Michael asked.

"Stay along the shore and follow us."

"I am coming," Michael said.

He waded back to the beach, picked up his pouch and walked parallel to the boat, the wet sand clinging to the inside of his toes. He stepped hard against rocks as he walked the shoreline to dislodge it.

The men rowed at a faster pace so Michael jogged a few yards. "Hey, what is the hurry?" he called out.

Michael stopped and bent over, catching his breath. He took off his sandals and banged them against a rock, removing the last bit of wet sand. He looked up, and the boat was upon him. "Oh no," he said, stepping back.

George got out of the boat and handed him a bag.

"What is this?"

"Food."

He looked inside and counted four fish.

"You will need it," George said.

"Am I near the city?"

"You are. By the time the sun is at its peak, you will be in Caesarea."

The other man pulled the boat back into the sea, keeping his back to them. "We have more people to feed."

"I am coming," George said.

"I will row."

"How can I ever repay you?" Michael asked.

"You can. On the twenty-fifth of December, you can bring the same number of fish to Cecilia."

"Cecilia?"

"Yes, Cecilia Farmer." George smiled and got back into the boat.

"Wait! Cecilia Farmer? Did you say Cecilia? Stop, George," he shouted. "I know your wife. She loves ... "

Michael watched them row away. "You."

George nodded, waved and smiled as they continued to row. They didn't take a path along the shore. Instead, they rowed straight ahead, disappearing into the fog.

CHAPTER 32

HEWITT WENT BACK UPSTAIRS to recover from the brief fight. Connie followed and watched him attend to his eye. "Oh, that looks bad," she said.

"I'm fine," he said. "Go back downstairs with Holligan." Hewitt kept staring at his phone.

"Look, divorce happens," Connie said. "Happened to me. There'll be some rough days. If you need someone to talk to, hey, I'm here."

"That's nice to hear, but it's the least of my problems."

"Is there something more?" Connie asked.

Hewitt hesitated.

"I'm not leaving until you tell me." She watched his eyes stare at her from the bathroom mirror.

"It's the pastor."

"What about him?"

"He was hurt bad before. I took him to the hospital."

"What?"

"I took him to the emergency room. I can't believe what I just heard."

"Tell me. Is he okay?"

He faced her. "He died."

Connie covered her mouth. Hewitt brushed past her and went downstairs. Kevin pressed a washcloth with ice in it against his right eye. "I have to go. I have a job to do," Hewitt said.

"Are you sure you're doing the best job you can?" Kevin asked, removing the washcloth. "The way I see it, you're a miserable failure. You're a drunk, your wife left you and you've screwed up this case."

Connie walked over to Kevin, now standing in the hallway. "Please don't tell anyone in your office about this. I need you. I need him. We all need each other to help find Michael and Elizabeth."

Kevin walked a few steps toward the front door and turned around. He pointed at Hewitt. "He doesn't belong on this case anymore. I love my niece as much as you do. I can't ignore the behavior."

"You were always after my job," Hewitt said, approaching.

"Okay, fellas," said Connie, stepping between them. "We're not going to have round two here." She faced Kevin. "Give him a couple of days. Maybe we can all figure out something. Let me dig through his dresser drawer."

"We've already done that and I have his computer," said Kevin.

"He wouldn't leave everything on it," Connie said.

"How would you know? You're not even close to him." Kevin gestured at Hewitt. "The only thing I can promise is that I'll make sure this investigation isn't compromised or conducted poorly." He slammed the door behind him.

Hewitt rubbed his eyes. "I'm going to get myself straightened out, and I'm going to pay some visits to Cathy Evans, Mrs. Farmer and your friend's mom."

"What about the pastor?"

"There's nothing I can do about him now."

He grabbed a cup out of the sink, rinsed it, filled it with water and drank it all. "I'd better hurry before I'm taken off the case."

As he opened the front door, Susan stormed into the hallway. "Did you hear?"

Hewitt walked away and out the door.

"Stop. Please. I want to help," Connie said, running behind him.

Hewitt ran down the driveway and got into his car, racing away, leaving skid marks behind.

"Wow, why was he in such a hurry?" asked Susan.

Connie kept staring out the door.

"Don't you want to know what I heard?" Susan asked.

"We know. Pastor Dennis died."

"What?" Susan asked. "When?"

"You don't know?" Connie asked, turning around.

"No." Susan went to the living room and sat on the couch. Connie sat beside Susan and let her mind drift to the horrific possibilities.

Hewitt will be taken off the case. Kevin will run around like a madman trying to find Elizabeth and Michael. And now the pastor is dead. What if the pastor was right? What if he was the only one who knew how to find them? Connie shook her head and went back into the kitchen. Pulling a bottle of wine out of the cabinet, she uncorked it.

Susan followed and grabbed her hand. "No. No more of this. Michael and Elizabeth need us. We have to help that agent."

Connie pushed the bottle away, saying, "He's going over to your mom's house."

"Why?"

"I guess to get some answers from the pastor's black book he's been carrying around."

Susan ran to the door.

"Now where are you going?" Connie asked.

"My mother's been sick the last couple of days. Her blood pressure has been bad. I've been spending my time helping her get things done around the house. I should be with her when he's there."

"Wait, what was your news?" she yelled out the door. "Susan?"

CHAPTER 33

FIRST-CENTURY JERUSALEM

MICHAEL SLUNG THE BAG OVER HIS SHOULDER and walked toward a light in the distance. It wouldn't be long before he reached his destination and faced his biggest challenges. He began to consider things he had to remember in order to successfully retrieve Elizabeth. He knew he had to look away when around the Roman soldiers. He must give the impression he would obey their orders. He also had to blend in with the crowd and avoid any confrontation while on the streets. To call attention to himself would invite disaster.

The horizon brightened, making it easier to see Caesarea. It looked massive compared to the other cities he was familiar with in the First Century.

He forged ahead along the shoreline, mapping out his strategy in his mind. He took deep, invigorating breaths. Near the city's edge, there was a small marketplace and staging area where boats were loaded with cargo. It was quiet, allowing his anxiety to ease. He came upon a man shouting instructions to five workers near a very large ship. The men were filling boxes with food and weapons.

"Sir," he said to the big, burly man, "I need to find a friend who is a Roman prisoner. Where might they keep him?"

"Why would you want to find someone like that?" the man asked.

"Captain, how many more boxes should we fill?" a worker said, interrupting their conversation.

"Enough to fill the lower deck," he answered. The captain turned and faced Michael. "The Romans are no friends of people like us. I suggest you leave if you can."

"I cannot. I need to find my friends and daughter. They are somewhere in this city."

The captain fingered his black beard and rubbed his eyes, stretching his back. "We sail soon. I need to organize my men. I wish I could help you. If you wish to seek your friends, you will find them in that building." He pointed to his right. "It is where the Romans hold their prisoners."

Michael put his hands over his eyes, shielding it from the early morning sunrise.

"Can you see it?" the captain asked.

"Yes." He turned back to the captain. "Where are you sailing to?"

"Rome. We have expensive cargo to take there for the empire."

"The Romans trust you to do this?"

"I am the best at this, and I am cheap for them." He smiled. "I do not like them, but they pay with much silver. They help me feed my family so I do it."

"What is valuable about their cargo?"

"They are taking a preacher to Rome for trial."

Michael's eyes widened. "A preacher from Jerusalem named Paul?"

"Yes."

Now what? I guess this is what Jesus meant. I needed to take a journey. Maybe this is where I am supposed to be heading with Paul. But I can't wait for him when Elizabeth ... He heard a commotion and watched four Roman soldiers escort Elizabeth, Leah and Aharon toward the boat. "Oh my God," he muttered.

"We have more cargo," said a Roman soldier, stepping forward.

"I will need more silver."

"You will get your share."

Michael looked at Elizabeth. Her head was drawn down. The Romans walked her onto the boat. "How much do I need to take this trip to Rome?"

The captain frowned. "I thought you were looking for your friend."

"Paul is my friend. Those people are the friends and daughter I am seeking."

"Oh, I would not say that to any man walking around in this city," the captain said, pointing to the boat.

"I cannot walk with fear in my heart knowing my friend may give up his life for so many."

"That is a strange thought. Why is he giving up his life for others?"

"I do not have the time to explain. I have silver." He showed him four coins.

"You will need more. I risk much when I bring aboard other travelers. The Romans are ruthless and will throw any man overboard if they think he is suspicious. I do not interfere with their prisoners. I need my crew to be safe."

Michael looked down at the ground and kicked dirt.

"Do you understand?"

"I do. I still need to get on your ship."

"You will need a handful of silver to do so. You will need to bribe the Romans. They are not as generous as I am."

Michael nodded. "I understand. When do you leave?"

"As soon as the Romans tell us."

Michael turned and looked at the building. The captain walked past him and shouted to a worker to start transporting the carts onto the ship. He rejoined Michael. "My friend, the Romans move when they are ready. You should move soon." He paused. "I hate them all."

Michael left and ran to the building where he was met by a Roman soldier. "What is your business here?"

"I am here to speak to my friend, Paul," he said, out of breath.

The Roman lowered his spear to the ground. "I will see if he is allowed visitors. What is your name?"

"Michael."

The Roman waited.

"Michael from Jerusalem."

The Roman left and Michael gazed skyward at the structure. It stood about twenty feet high and extended many feet to the back and sides. *This has to be where the Roman officials conduct their business. It makes perfect sense. This port provides easy access to the sea, and it would only take a week or so to sail to Rome from here.* Horses pulled carts of fruit and fish so high some of the treats were tumbling to the ground. Beautiful women, clad in shoulder-less long white dresses traveled about in small groups.

"This way," said the Roman soldier. Michael was led through a maze of long hallways lit by tall candles. He was stunned when he saw Paul resting alone.

"We will be sailing soon," the Roman told Paul.

"I will be prepared," he replied.

The Roman left.

"Are you in good health?"

"I am," Paul said. "I am ready for my trip."

"Why must you leave now?"

"It needs to be written."

Michael walked around the big room in a frantic pace.

"You are worried. What troubles you?" Paul asked.

"My daughter and our friends. They are on that boat. The one you are going on."

"Sometimes we need to take the journey to understand our purpose."

Michael knelt down beside him and held his hands. "She is my daughter," he pleaded "She is going on trial. Do you know what they do to citizens like this? I am not a Roman citizen, so I do not have the same rights as you. I know Jesus told me to be here for one of the apostles. I do not remember if there is anything else I must do."

"Think, Michael. Think."

"I am." He shook his head and waved his hands in the air. "I was in shock when I first saw Elizabeth alive. It is possible I did not hear everything."

"Go back to the boat. Let me think," Paul said.

"I need to find more silver. Do you have any?"

A Roman soldier entered the room. "We are ready. We sail soon."

Paul handed Michael a bag. "Use this to free your daughter and friends."

Michael grabbed it and raced to the boat. He was met by two Roman soldiers. "I have silver to free my friends."

"Who?"

"The women and man you brought aboard." Michael emptied the bag and showed them the coins.

"Go," said one Roman to another. "Get two of them."

"No. There are three."

"This is not enough, especially for the murderer of a Roman soldier. We will need one to take the trip with us to face trial for Marcus' death."

Three Roman soldiers escorted Leah and Aharon off the boat.

"No. Please. Where's the other woman?" Michael asked, shouting.

The soldiers pushed him away from the dock. He struggled to fight his way onto the boat. The captain looked at him for a brief moment. "How long before we leave?" he asked the Roman soldiers.

"Soon."

CHAPTER 34

A LONE CROSS HUNG FROM THE TOP OF A WOODEN DOOR, shaking from the breeze that jettisoned off the Long Island Sound. The smell of the ocean tickled Hewitt's nose as he walked around the house. A small playground lay dormant in the backyard, dirt covering a short blue slide.

Disgusting. How do these people live like this? He noticed a shed in the corner of the yard, its door slightly ajar. Hewitt peeked in and opened it wider. He saw a huge plastic cover, pulled it up and saw old baseball bats and a deflated dirty basketball inside. Hewitt wiped the outside of the stroller with a handkerchief, picked up the doll and cleaned its face with slow, soft touches. Walking back and forth a few times, he began to do his own time traveling, thinking of Hailey.

A brisk wind rattled the shed, shaking him out of his trance. He pushed the stroller back into the corner, covered it and closed the shed, making sure the door was secure from the ocean wind. Hewitt cleaned his hands off and knocked on the front door.

A woman looked through a small window at the top. Her eyes pierced through his. "What do you want?"

"I'm Special Agent Hewitt Paul. Are you Cathy Evans?" He showed his badge.

"Yes, I am. What's this in regard to?"

"I want to ask you questions about your ex-husband."

"Go away. I have nothing to say about him."

"Do you care he's been hurt?"

"I know all about the shooting at the church."

Hewitt looked down, forced a deep breath from the salt-filled air. He steadied himself and stared at Cathy. "It's worse than that."

"How much worse?"

"Please let me come in," he said.

Cathy continued to glare and unlocked the door. "This way," she said, leading him into the living room. "Sit down."

"Thank you."

"How bad is he hurt?"

Hewitt fingered the side of the wooden chair. "He's passed on."

Cathy didn't give a reaction. "How?"

"The injury from the shooting."

She faced him. "He was fine only a week ago. I know."

"I'm not sure what triggered the wound to regress," Hewitt said, "but it did."

Cathy was silent and walked into the dining room, stopping at the table and holding onto a chair.

Hewitt stood and noticed a nurse's outfit lying on a dark, wooden table. "Are you okay, Ms. Evans?

"It's Mrs. Evans. And I'm fine."

"I know you must be in shock."

She stared at him. "I don't believe it."

Hewitt took a few steps toward the dining room. "I understand. It's hard to accept death at any time about anyone, especially a loved one."

"He didn't die. Not from that wound. No. I don't believe it."

This is going to be tougher than I expected, Hewitt thought. "I would like to ask you a few questions."

Cathy remained in the dining room, holding the chair. She was staring at pictures inside a credenza. Hewitt joined her. "You have a beautiful family," he said.

She removed one, a portrait of her, Dennis and two boys. "We have great kids," she said, touching them. "They went through a rough time, especially when they were very young. Kids can be so mean to each other."

"How is that?"

"When we divorced, kids teased my boys. It seemed like every day one of my boys came home upset. Dennis didn't help matters."

"I'm sorry. That's just not right."

"Not right? You know what's not right? I'll tell you. One night my husband is the greatest man in the world, my soul mate and all that lovey-dovey nonsense. Then he's a drunk, telling me his world was ending and life was pointless. Out of nowhere this happened."

Hewitt grimaced. "I don't know what to say."

"He drank and drank until I had to tell him to leave. The guy fell off a mental cliff."

"Do you remember the night it started?"

"Of course," she said. "I don't want to." She paused. "Christmas. Christmas night."

She clenched the picture. "He shouldn't have been working. But, people need their food for the holidays. So he was working overtime that night, making sure everybody else was taken care of for Christmas."

"He was a truck driver. Right?"

"Yes. A good one for many years. Always made his deliveries on time. Never a day late for work. Wouldn't call in sick even when he had a one-hundred-three-degree fever. Always made it home to help set the table … until that night."

"He lost his job, didn't he?"

She nodded and handed him the picture. "Our lives collapsed that Christmas night."

"What did he say after this all happened?"

"He wouldn't say. He was like a brick wall. I could never reach him again."

"How old are your boys now?" Hewitt asked.

"Twenty and twenty-four."

"Do they still live at home?"

"Yes. They have jobs. They're doing well despite the last fifteen years or so. I also remarried and had a girl. She's doing well in high school."

"I'm glad to hear that." He paused. "I saw the cross outside. Do you go to church?"

"Why do you need to ask about that?" Cathy asked, taking back the picture.

"I'm just trying to understand how you truly feel about your faith."

"What does an FBI agent care about faith?"

Hewitt didn't answer.

She placed the picture inside the credenza. "So you want me to honestly express myself? Like I'm talking to some therapist sitting on a couch? Okay then, I will. I don't go to that church. Why would I? To see Den talking about love and forgiveness? To see people smiling and shaking his hand, telling him how much they love him? Why must he choose to be a pastor in a church so close to the kids and me? Why?" She looked away. "Sometimes I wonder if he's trying to torture me."

Cathy walked back into the living room and sat down. Hewitt followed. "I don't mean to upset you," he said.

"Well, you did." She looked up at him. "I have so many emotions going through me, even after all these years."

"You mentioned you spoke to him last week. What was your relationship like?"

"Why are you in my house asking me that question?"

"Because I think you might be able to help me find that missing Stewart girl."

She gave him a look of disbelief. "How would I do that?"

"Please answer the question."

"We spoke once a week. More when the kids were younger."

"Why not more now?"

"My boys … they're grown up … they're their own individuals." She sighed. "They'd had enough. They didn't want any part of their father after a while."

"You don't look happy."

"Why would I be? I'm angry at Den, but I want his sons to be part of his life. It's like he's ashamed of us. He's so concerned with that church. It would have been nice for him to spend more time with his sons as they got older."

"Did they want to?"

She shook her head. "No. But I always hoped it would change. Maybe he was ashamed of himself. I've often thought this could be it."

Hewitt sat down. "What I'm about to ask may seem inappropriate. But I need the truth to help me understand what might have happened to the missing girl."

"Elizabeth Stewart?"

"Yes."

"The life insurance policy?"

"Yes."

"It was part of the divorce settlement," Cathy said.

"I know."

"You seem to know an awful lot about us. Isn't that our personal business?"

"Not if it can help me solve this case."

Cathy gave him a frustrated look. "Yes, it's in Elizabeth Stewart's name."

"Why? Why would a great dad bypass his sons? Did he know the Stewarts for a long time?"

"I don't know."

Hewitt paused. Before he could ask his next question, Cathy spoke. "Look, I don't know what you're getting at here. I was hurt when I found out my boys weren't the beneficiaries." She gave a weak laugh and sighed. "Who knows why he did it? Maybe he felt sorry for her."

Cathy stared at him for a few seconds. "It was such an awful story. I remember it like it was yesterday. The entire town was mourning. How terrible it must be to lose your pregnant wife on Christmas night. But I had my own problems, too, that night with Den. Not knowing where he was. I was worried he had been in an accident and they'd find him in his truck in some ditch. I thought I had lost him."

She sighed. "I guess I did. It was a dark day here. It would have been better if they had found him in a ditch."

The words struck Hewitt as harsh. He had already noticed there were no signs of Christmas in the house. No tree. No lights. Not even a wreath.

"You don't feel like celebrating the holidays?" he asked.

"Do you have any more questions to ask?"

"Did Dennis ever talk about Michael Stewart to you?"

"Never."

"Not one mention?"

"No. Why?"

"I would think that if you spoke to him every so often Michael Stewart's name would come up."

"Why?"

"Michael is his best friend."

"Best friends? I thought it was Robert Cantone."

"What?" Hewitt stood.

"Yes. He spoke often about Robert. How he needed him to help himself."

"How would Robert help your ex-husband? Was it financial?"

"You'd have to ask him."

CHAPTER 35

A PICTURE OF PASTOR DENNIS sitting on his motorcycle stood on top of a dark brown casket. The line to pay respects stretched out of the church's front door and down Main Street. The police had asked the media to move their trucks farther down the street so the vehicles wouldn't be a distraction to the somber proceedings.

An organ played soft music as a violinist strummed her instrument. The interim pastor consoled the mourners. Connie and Susan entered the church, bowed their heads and moved forward.

"I can't look at him," Connie whispered, tugging on Susan's arm.

Susan stood on her toes and peered over the line ahead of them. "You won't have to. The casket is closed."

"Really?"

Susan turned and nodded.

"Good."

It was several more minutes before they reached the casket. "Hello. I'm Pastor Timothy. Thank you for showing your love for my brother in Christ."

Susan shook his hand and nodded. Connie did the same and stopped to touch the picture. "My brother loves you. Thank you for loving my brother." She wiped a tear away and joined Susan in a pew.

They watched Hewitt enter the church. "Look who's here now," said Connie. "Surprise. Surprise."

"Wonder what he's around here for?" Susan asked.

"Don't be so tough on him. He's doing his job."

"I can see he's doing his job. But the way he does it is like a bully."

"He has to be tough in his job," Connie said with some edge.

"My, aren't we a bit defensive."

Connie ignored her. "I see he's still wearing his sunglasses."

They watched him make his way up to the pastor. They exchanged a few words and shook hands. He looked left and right for a place to sit and spotted Susan and Connie. He made a beeline right to them. They scrunched over to make room for him, but he sat between them instead.

"So sad, isn't it?" Connie said, taking out a tissue.

"This is awfully soon to have a service," Hewitt said.

Susan shrugged her shoulders.

"I guess," Connie said. "What's the normal time? Two days? Three days?"

"Yes. But certainly not within twenty-four hours, especially when an autopsy is needed. The church refused to give us permission."

"Why would an autopsy be needed?" Connie asked. "The papers said he never recovered from the wound. Are you going to charge Allison with murder?"

"Haven't decided."

"What do you mean?" Susan asked.

"I mean the bureau will make that decision down the road. There's no rush." Hewitt paused. "I don't trust this new pastor. He's hiding something."

"You don't trust anyone," Susan said.

Connie glared at her.

Everyone was seated, and the church became quiet. The pastor invited the flock to come up and share a prayer or a thought near the casket. Connie stood up as her pew advanced toward Pastor Dennis. After whispering some words, she brushed against the casket.

"Oops," she muttered.

It slid off the stanchion. Pastor Timothy caught the end before it hit the ground and pushed it back. "Got it," he said.

"I'm so embarrassed," said Connie, as she returned to the pew.

Hewitt reached over and touched her hand when she returned. "Where's his ex-wife? His family?" Hewitt asked to no one in particular.

"Shh! Are you talking to us?" Connie asked.

He shook his head and whispered. "Where's he being buried?"

"Out east," Connie said quietly.

The pastor said a few prayers and thanked the flock for supporting the church and him during this period of grieving.

Hewitt got up. "That was awfully quick," he said. "I thought a service like this would last a couple of hours."

"Are you leaving?" Susan asked.

"Now I am. I need to check a few theories out. Can I follow you to the gravesite?"

"Sure," Susan said. "I'm the little blue Toyota by Main and Church."

"I'll drive up behind you. Look for me."

"See you then," Susan said and turned to Connie. "You up for this?" she asked, opening the car doors.

"No. But my brother would want me to be here."

"He would," Susan agreed as she sat and closed the door.

Connie looked behind. "There he is, down the block. You can't miss that Cadillac."

"Yeah, what is up with that gas guzzler?" Susan wondered.

"It's all show."

"I guess we've got a little show in all of us."

Connie turned back to face Susan and glared. "What do you mean by that?"

"Nothing."

A horn beeped behind them. Susan adjusted her rearview mirror and pulled away from the curb. They followed a long stretch of cars onto the Long Island Expressway.

"Do you know which exit?" asked Susan.

"Just follow the cars. You won't get lost."

It wasn't more than twenty minutes on the expressway when the cars began to exit onto the service road. "I guess we're here," she said. "That wasn't such a long ride."

Connie opened up her purse and covered her eyes with sunglasses.

"Are you all right?" Susan asked.

"No. I'm worried about Hewitt," said Connie.

"Why?"

"I don't know. I just am."

"Let's talk about this later."

"I don't have many friends since Craig and I got divorced. All of our friends blamed me for the split, so I need a friend. Now."

Susan parked the car as the mourners abandoned their vehicles and walked up a hill.

"Can I count on you?" Connie asked, breaking the silence.

Susan picked up her purse from underneath the seat. She turned to Connie and removed the sunglasses. "Yes, I can be your friend. And you don't need to cover up how you feel or what you look like when you do have that meltdown."

"I hope we won't be doing this for Elizabeth and Michael too."

Susan grabbed some tissues from the glove compartment. "I'm not ready to say we've lost them. I hope you know I've always loved Michael and Elizabeth. They're family to me. They always will be. We can't give up."

CHAPTER 36

HEWITT STAYED MOTIONLESS IN HIS CAR FOR SEVERAL MINUTES, surveying the area. He lifted his sunglasses to get a better view of the activity. Pastor Timothy opened his Bible one more time and appeared to say a few words. After he closed his Bible, the area began to empty. The pastor chatted briefly with four cemetery workers and then left.

The workers began the process of lowering the casket into the ground. Hewitt stared and relaxed his legs as Pastor Timothy drove past him. The workers continued their task and began to backfill the open grave. Hewitt watched every shovelful of dirt pouring into the hole.

He rubbed his eyes a few times as he grew tired. After opening up his windows to catch some cold air, he took a sip of some flat Diet Coke sitting in a cup. *This stuff is vile.* He shook his head and removed his sunglasses.

One by one, shovels patted and swatted the topsoil in an organized fashion. The pound and press routine lasted several minutes until one gravedigger tossed his shovel to the ground. The others did the same.

When the last bit of sunlight scraped the horizon, he closed his windows and got out. He stretched his arms, adjusted his suit jacket and wiped away a lone fuzzy clinging to the lower part of his pants.

He walked to the burial site and kicked at the dirt a few times. He glanced behind him and to his left and right. Grabbing a shovel, he slammed it into the dirt and began digging. He tossed the dirt to the left, he tossed it to his right and when he had a full shovel, he hoisted it over his shoulder.

Hewitt dug and dug, each stab at the dirt deeper than the one before. He rested every few minutes, allowing the strain that swallowed up the energy in his arms to receive some relief. He took a handkerchief from his top shirt pocket and wiped the perspiration off his forehead. Removing his jacket, he looked around for a safe place to leave it. He tossed it aside instead when he noticed a man walking up the hill toward him.

"Hey, mister," a man yelled from a distance, waving his arms. "What are you doing?"

Hewitt continued to thrust the shovel into the ground. He dug to the left. He dug to the right. He dug and dug for several minutes until finally hitting the top of the casket. The metal of the shovel scraped it again on the next pitch down. Hewitt jumped into the hole and fell on top of it. He managed to nudge the casket sideways.

"What are you doing, mister?" asked the man looking down at him. "Did you drop your wallet in there?"

"Nope."

"Well, you better have a good reason for what you did. You just ruined our work."

Hewitt looked up. "I'll put your precious dirt back when I'm done."

"Done with what?" The man snapped a shot of Hewitt with his cell phone.

"FBI." Hewitt flashed his badge. "Step back and don't interfere with an ongoing investigation."

The man walked away, grumbling.

Hewitt gripped the top of the casket and tried to wedge it apart. "Open, you son of a gun," he said, groaning.

He reached up and grabbed the shovel. He battered the top several times, finally prying it open. He tossed the shovel away and wiped his hands.

He strained to lift the top. "Up you go," he shouted, thrusting it open. He stared for a few seconds and reached in, picking up the picture of Pastor Dennis sitting on his motorcycle. He stared at it for a few more seconds before placing it back inside and closing the casket.

"Where are you, Pastor Dennis?" he said as he climbed out of the grave and kicked the shovel away.

CHAPTER 37

HEWITT BANGED ON THE FRONT DOOR OF THE CHURCH. "Hello, anyone in there?" he shouted. He whacked the hard, wooden door a few more times with the back of his gun. "Open up. Now."

He walked around to the side of the church and stood on his toes to look through a stained glass window. The church was empty. The candles near the podium flickered, and the manger scene was illuminated by a light from the high-arching ceiling. Hewitt ran to the backyard and knocked on the lone door.

The door opened. "Yes, how can I help you?" a woman asked.

"I'm Hewitt Paul." He pulled out his FBI badge and showed it to her. "I need to get inside. I may have lost something in the pastor's office."

The woman frowned. "You do know what happened to the pastor?"

"I do. I was in his office a couple of days ago. I thought I might have left an important note behind."

"What kind of note? Was it on a sheet of paper or in a book?"

"It's related to the case I'm working on. I can't share that information."

She opened the door and took another look at the badge he was holding. "I'll be in the basement if you need me."

"Your name?"

"Katie Adams."

"And what are you doing in the church?"

"I'm a secretary."

"Thanks, Katie. I shouldn't be long."

"The door is open. Please close it when you're done."

Hewitt looked to his left and right, moving his hands on both sides of the wall as he walked down the hallway, feeling for any hidden passageways or doors he might have missed on his last inspection. He opened the first door leading down the hallway to Pastor Dennis' office. Inside were several boxes piled one on top of another. He removed the top one and opened it, finding old sandals, dirtied robes and a couple of wooden crosses. He looked inside the next box and found old coins. He dug one out and put the box back. Holding it up, he squinted.

Looks like the image of a soldier, but not from our time.

He heard footsteps coming, and he pushed the boxes back. He jogged a few steps to Pastor Dennis' office and went inside. An old Styrofoam cup stood on his desk, filled with water. Papers were scattered all over the floor. He went behind the desk and picked up the wastepaper basket. Red stained tissues filled the top. Hewitt took a deep breath, took a pair of plastic gloves out of his pocket and put them on his hands. He turned the basket over and dumped it out onto the desk.

He rummaged through several pieces of paper, some starter notes for the pastor's next sermon. He sat down and examined the wrinkled pages. Acts 27-28:10. Hewitt turned around and looked at the bookcase. *There's got to be a Bible here.* He pulled out several black books and tossed them on the ground. "Here it is," he said, holding it up. He paged through it and found the passage. He kept his finger inside the Bible as a bookmark, got up and locked the office door. He sat in the chair opposite the desk and began to read.

When it was decided that we would sail for Italy, they proceeded to deliver Paul and some other prisoners to a centurion of the Augustan cohort named Julius. And embarking in an Adramyttian ship, which was about to sail to the regions along the coast of Asia, we put out to sea accompanied by Aristarchus, a Macedonian of Thessalonica. The next day we put in at Sidon; and Julius treated Paul with consideration and allowed him to go to his friends and receive care. From there we put out to sea and sailed under the shelter of Cyprus because the winds were contrary. When we had sailed through the sea along the coast of Cilicia and Pamphylia, we landed at Myra in Lycia. There the centurion found an Alexandrian ship sailing for Italy, and he put us aboard it. When we had sailed slowly for a good many days, and with difficulty had arrived off Cnidus, since the wind did not permit us to go farther, we sailed under the shelter of Crete, off Salmone; and with difficulty sailing past it we came to a place called Fair Havens, near which was the city of Lasea.

When considerable time had passed and the voyage was now dangerous, since even the fast was already over, Paul began to admonish them and said to them, "Men, I perceive that the voyage will certainly be with damage and great loss, not only of the cargo and the ship, but also of our lives." But the centurion was more persuaded by the pilot and the captain of the ship than by what was being said by Paul. Because the harbor was not suitable for wintering, the majority reached a decision to put out to sea from there, if somehow they could reach Phoenix, a harbor of Crete, facing southwest and northwest, and spend the winter there.

When a moderate south wind came up, supposing that they had attained their purpose, they weighed anchor and began sailing along Crete, close inshore.

But before very long there rushed down from the land a violent wind, called Euraquilo; and when the ship was caught in it and could not face the wind, we gave way to it and let ourselves be driven along. Running under the shelter of a small island called Clauda, we were scarcely able to get the ship's boat under control. After they had hoisted it up, they used supporting cables in undergirding the ship; and fearing that they might run aground on the shallows of Syrtis, they let down the sea anchor and in this way let themselves be driven along. The next day as we were being violently storm-tossed, they began to jettison the cargo; and on the third day they threw the ship's tackle overboard with their own hands. Since neither sun nor stars appeared for many days, and no small storm was assailing us, from then on all hope of our being saved was gradually abandoned.

When they had gone a long time without food, then Paul stood up in their midst and said, "Men, you ought to have followed my advice and not to have set sail from Crete and incurred this damage and loss. Yet now I urge you to keep up your courage, for there will be no loss of life among you, but only of the ship. For this very night an angel of the God to whom I belong and whom I serve stood before me, saying, 'Do not be afraid, Paul; you must stand before Caesar; and behold, God has granted you all those who are sailing with you.' Therefore, keep up your courage, men, for I believe God that it will turn out exactly as I have been told. But we must run aground on a certain island."

But when the fourteenth night came, as we were being driven about in the Adriatic Sea, about midnight the sailors began to surmise that they were approaching some land. They took soundings and found it to be twenty fathoms; and a little farther on they took another sounding and found it to be fifteen fathoms. Fearing that we might run aground somewhere on the rocks, they cast four anchors from the stern and wished for daybreak. But as the sailors were trying to escape from the ship and had let down the ship's boat into the sea, on the pretense of intending to lay out anchors from the bow, Paul said to the centurion and to the soldiers, "Unless these men remain in the ship, you yourselves cannot be saved." Then the soldiers cut away the ropes of the ship's boat and let it fall away.

Until the day was about to dawn, Paul was encouraging them all to take some food, saying, "Today is the fourteenth day that you have been constantly watching and going without eating, having taken nothing. Therefore I encourage you to take some food, for this is for your preservation, for not a hair from the head of any of you will perish." Having said this, he took bread and gave thanks to God in the presence of all, and he broke it and began to eat. All of them were encouraged, and they themselves also took food. All of us in the ship were two hundred and seventy-six persons. When they had eaten enough, they began to lighten the ship by throwing out the wheat into the sea.

When day came, they could not recognize the land; but they did observe a bay with a beach, and they resolved to drive the ship onto it if they could. And casting off the anchors, they left them in the sea while at the same time they were loosening the ropes of the rudders; and hoisting the foresail to the wind, they were heading for *the beach. But striking a reef where two seas met, they ran the vessel aground; and the prow stuck fast and remained immovable, but the stern began to be broken up by the force of the waves. The soldiers' plan was to kill the prisoners so that none of them would swim away and escape; but the centurion, wanting to bring Paul safely through, kept them from their intention and commanded that those who could swim should jump overboard first and get to land, and the rest should follow, some on planks and others on various things from the ship. And so it happened that they all were brought safely to land.*

When they had been brought safely through, then we found out that the island was called Malta. The natives showed us extraordinary kindness; for because of the rain that had set in and because of the cold, they kindled a fire and received us all. But when Paul had gathered a bundle of sticks and laid them on the fire, a viper came out because of the heat and fastened itself on his hand. When the natives saw the creature hanging from his hand, they began saying to one another, "Undoubtedly this man is a murderer, and though he has been saved from the sea, justice has not allowed him to live. However he shook the creature off into the fire and suffered no harm. But they were expecting that he was about to swell up or suddenly fall down dead. But after they had waited a long time and had seen nothing unusual happen to him, they changed their minds and began to say that he was a god.

Now in the neighborhood of that place were lands belonging to the leading man of the island, named Publius, who welcomed us and entertained us courteously three days. And it happened that the father of Publius was lying in bed afflicted with recurrent fever and dysentery; and Paul went in to see him and after he had prayed, he laid his hands on him and healed him. After this had happened, the rest of the people on the island who had diseases were coming to him and getting cured. They also honored us with many marks of respect; and when we were setting sail, they supplied us with all we needed.

Hewitt closed the Bible and stood, retrieving the black book from his pocket. He paged through it a couple of times, stopping near the end. He tucked the Bible back into the bookcase, cleaned up the floor and threw most of the debris from the desk into the wastepaper basket. Hewitt sat and unwrinkled an old newspaper article. He smoothed out the ends and read. *My goodness. What a lot of baggage to carry around.* He folded it back up and tucked it into his side pocket.

It was time to pay Mrs. Farmer a visit.

CHAPTER 38

HEWITT PEERED THROUGH THE WINDOW, noticing an old lady pushing a box into a closet. She returned with a smile and opened the door.

"Mrs. Farmer," he said, holding out his hand. "I'm Special Agent Hewitt Paul." He flashed his identification.

"How can I help you?" she asked.

"May I step inside so we can talk?"

"What would you want to be talking about?"

"Your husband."

"Come in," she said, moving aside. "I've been expecting you anyway."

"Really? Why is that?"

"The local police have been here. The county police have been here. Why not the FBI? Besides, you looked upset at the service for our pastor. You looked like you needed to talk to someone."

"Yes, I am upset. But why would you think I would need to talk to you?"

"You gave me a suspicious look at the service. Like you thought I was hiding something."

"I did a little research on those who attended the church on a regular basis. People who might know the pastor. Or might know Michael Stewart. Should I be suspicious?" Hewitt asked, stepping into the living room.

"Would you like some hot tea?"

"Sure."

"I'll make it just right for you," she said as she turned and walked into the kitchen.

Hewitt walked around the living room and inspected the bookcase.

Several minutes later, Mrs. Farmer returned with a tray. Steam rose from the two cups and two cookies were arranged side by side. Hewitt sat in the bigger of the two chairs in front of an old record player. She handed him a cup and placed a cookie on a napkin in his lap. Sitting down next to him, she took a bite. "One of my best batches."

Hewitt broke off a piece of cookie and chewed it. "Delicious."

She smiled. "You're not here to get my recipe or sample my baking skills. How can I help you?"

He leaned sideways. "First, I want to express my condolences for the loss of your husband."

She nodded and took a sip of her tea.

"I'm trying to find Elizabeth and Michael Stewart. I was wondering if your husband had mentioned them at all."

"He had. He was worried about them."

"Why?"

"George only mentioned him once. I really didn't think much of it because he was always worrying about someone here in town."

"Did he mention anything in particular?"

"He worried about Michael and his daughter, especially when he found out he was a widower."

"Did George talk about Michael having any … crazy as it might sound, ability to travel places?"

She shook her head.

Hewitt sat back in the chair and sighed. "What about Michael? Did you speak to him?"

She broke off a piece of her cookie and nibbled on it. "We spoke. Michael was very generous with his time when I was grieving. He gave me great comfort."

"Did he ever tell you about places he wanted to visit? Anything that bothered him?"

She sipped her tea some more. "He spoke a lot about his daughter. He was worried sick about her. He told me how sad he was and couldn't live without knowing if she was safe. I saw a man with a broken heart."

Hewitt leaned forward. "Breaks my heart too. Were you close to Pastor Dennis?"

"When George was alive, we saw him almost every weekend at the Sunday service. He was a good man. But he's helping George now."

"What?" Hewitt put his tea down.

"George is helping the pastor now."

"Where?"

She pointed to the wall.

"Mrs. Farmer, please forgive my ignorance. We are talking about him, right?"

She nodded.

"Where is George helping Pastor Dennis?"

"There," she said, again pointing at the wall.

Hewitt stood. He went to the wall and stared at the picture. "I see a painting. So what?"

"Is that all it is to you?"

"Yes," he said, turning around to face her. "Did your husband paint this?"

"Yes. He worked on it for many years. What do you think of it?"

Hewitt studied the four-by-two-foot framed picture. There were eight soldiers with spears drawn, towering over women, their arms up, defending their children. "Very disturbing."

"I thought so too."

"Did he talk about why he painted this?"

"Sometimes. He said it kept him mindful of the cruel realities of this world."

"I've read enough biographies about artists," Hewitt said. "Studied it a bit in college too. Tortured souls, some of them were. Most of them had no grasp of reality; that's probably why many drank or committed suicide."

"Oh, that's not true, is it?" Mrs. Farmer asked.

"Well, I may be reaching a little," Hewitt replied.

"Well, my George wasn't like that," she said, taking another piece of cookie off the tray.

Hewitt returned to his seat and took two sips of the simmering tea.

"George said painting helped remind him of his travels."

"Where did he say he traveled to?"

"He would never say. He liked to take long walks. Said it kept him in teenage shape." She laughed and finished the last bit of the cookie. "This is my best batch."

"How did your husband die?"

"Don't you know that?"

He nodded. "I just want to hear what you thought."

"The police would only say he died from a suspicious wound in his chest. They told me they were investigating it as a suicide. George was not that way. He loved life."

Hewitt rubbed his forehead and went back to the picture. He placed his finger around the outline of a soldier. He turned to face her, keeping his left hand on the painting. "What did your husband do before he retired?"

"He was a pastor's assistant. For Pastor Vincent."

"Did you say Pastor Vincent?" asked Hewitt as he walked back to Mrs. Farmer.

"Yes. They were very close, until the incident."

He sat down. "What incident?"

"George came home all bloodied, screaming and yelling. I never saw him so upset. He said he got hurt at the church."

Mrs. Farmer picked up her cup and grabbed his, placing them on the tray. She walked to the kitchen and dropped them in the sink. She rejoined Hewitt and sat down, placing her hand on his. "George was a good man. He cared about Pastor Vincent." She shook her head. "He wouldn't talk about it again." There were some seconds of silence between them. "That's when he started to paint," she said.

"From what I've heard, Michael had a close relationship with Pastor Dennis."

"I believe so. That's what Michael told me."

"Close enough where they would share secrets?"

"I can't tell you one way or another whether they would. But I can tell you it's tragic for everyone here in Northport that the pastor is no longer with us."

"I'm not so sure of that," said Hewitt as he got up from the chair.

"Why would you say that? How awful. You should be praying for him. Pastor Dennis has gone home to the Lord to work with George."

He shook his head. "No. I don't believe he's with the Lord right now."

CHAPTER 39

HEWITT STARED INTO HIS REFRIGERATOR. He saw a half-empty box of pork fried rice, three cans of Bud Light and an unopened bottle of white Chardonnay. He grabbed the bottle of wine and with some difficulty, extracted the cork from the top. Pouring the wine into a tall beer glass, he watched a piece of the cork bob around the top. He put his finger in it and pressed the cork against the side of the glass. He pushed it up and smirked. *Got ya.* It fell back in as he lifted his finger to pull it out.

No. You're not going to get the best of me. Hewitt reached into a drawer near the stove and grabbed a spoon. *Come on. Come to me. Come to Papa.* He twirled the spoon around and the piece dipped on and off of it a couple of times. Frustrated, he started to pour the wine into the sink. *Get out of there. Now.* The wine fell smoothly down the drain while the tiny piece of cork hung on for dear life in the glass. When it was empty, he held it to the ceiling light. *I don't believe it.* He banged the faucet on and let the rushing water flood the glass, finally pushing the stubborn cork into the sink and down the drain. *That'll teach you.*

He stared at the remaining wine in the bottle and then at the glass. *I'm losing it. I've been drinking myself into oblivion, and now I'm fighting a piece of cork. On top of that, I've got a bunch of religious freaks almost convincing me a man time travels to the time of Jesus. Think of that, Hewitt. Think of what these people are trying to sell. This is absolute horse crap. I'm college educated and part of the world's best governmental agency. I am the best at what I do – finding missing children.*

"You're not going to break me," he said as he poured the remainder of the wine into the sink. He opened the three beers and did the same, holding the last can up high to make it more dramatic. "No one is going to make a fool out of me anymore."

Hewitt went upstairs to change and sat on the bed with fresh pajamas in his hands. He listened to the silence of the house for a few moments before going to open Hailey's bedroom door. *She's not coming home. It's time for me to accept this.*

"Daddy, Daddy, help me," Hailey's voice echoed in his mind. He squeezed his head with his hands and dropped to his knees.

"I'm trying, honey. I'm trying."

He sat against the edge of the door for several minutes, keeping his mind blank until his cell phone rang.

"You have something that can help me, Connie?" he asked, answering the phone.

"No. Sorry."

"Why are you calling me then?"

"To warn you. I saw a photo of you at the cemetery. What were you doing?"

"What do you mean?"

"Um, you digging."

"Oh Lord," he said, standing up.

"Yeah. Are you okay? Even the best people lose it."

"I'm fine. I haven't lost anything."

"You can't be fine if you're digging up someone's body after he was just buried. It sure looks like you've lost your mind."

Hewitt put the phone to his side for a brief moment. He took a deep breath and put the phone back to his ear. "Where did you see this photo?"

"I just saw it. It's only a matter of time before every social network is either sharing it or tweeting the link. The captions I saw are funny though. *Crazy FBI guy digging up clues* was my favorite."

"I'm not crazy."

"Sure looks like it."

"Oh, Lord," Hewitt said again. "What am I going to do now?" He paused.

"Do you need a friend?" Connie asked.

Hewitt didn't answer. He went to the kitchen and dropped the phone on the table.

"Hewitt? Are you there?"

He picked it back up and reluctantly placed it on his ear. "I'm here. I can't believe how much I've screwed this up."

"Do you need a friend?" Connie asked again.

Hewitt didn't answer and sighed. A knock on the door shook him out of his momentary trance. He opened it and turned away. "I'm not getting rid of you, am I?"

"Nope," said Connie as she hung up her cell phone. She walked in and looked around. "Well, well, so this is how a big shot FBI special agent lives." She proceeded into the living room. "Not too impressive."

"How did you get my address?"

"You wrote it down on the *business card* you gave me." Connie picked up a pillow off the couch. "What is this?"

Hewitt grabbed it out of her hands. "Don't touch or move anything."

"Okay."

Hewitt went into the kitchen, placing the pillow on the table. "I'd offer you something, but I just dumped whatever wine that was left into the sink."

"Good for you," she said, joining him at the table. "There's been far too much drinking lately anyway. How are you holding up?"

Hewitt gave her a puzzled look. "I'm fine."

"No, you're not. Anyone who has gone through what you have in the last few years has to be hurting."

"I see you've been busy on the Internet."

"The Internet helps."

"I'm fine."

Connie shook her head. "I know what fine looks like. Behind that tough FBI macho-man exterior is a heart that's bleeding. You're human like the rest of us."

"We don't bleed," Hewitt said with a glare. He poured himself a glass of water from the sink. He raised it in a gesture of an offer.

"No, thanks," she said.

"Are we done?"

"You tell me."

"I don't understand where this conversation is going."

"I'm no criminal investigator like you, but when I see an FBI agent digging up a grave, I know there has to be something funny going on. You may as well tell me before you lose your job."

"I won't lose it."

"Come into the Twenty-First Century with me, special agent," Connie said, leaning closer. "Your picture is about to be all over the Internet shoveling out a casket where a beloved preacher was just buried. Do you really believe you're not going to be fired? There will be thousands of people sharing your pretty face all over the world. Or do you not live in the Twenty-First Century?"

Hewitt pushed away his water and stood, rubbing his forehead. He grimaced and looked at a picture of his daughter on the refrigerator door. He stared for several seconds and sighed.

"Are you having a breakdown?" asked Connie.

"No." He took a quick glance at her. "But I'm not all right. I haven't been all right since my daughter disappeared." Hewitt walked into the living room and sat down.

Connie followed and joined him on the couch. "I'm sorry," she said. "I know about loss."

"What would you know?" Hewitt asked. "You were never a parent, never lost a son or daughter like I did, like the parents out there who cry during the day and can't sleep at night thinking about all the terrible situations their kids have gone through." He turned to her. "Tell me, how do you truly know what I have gone through?"

"I may not know how your specific situation feels, but I've miscarried three times. I've had a newly painted room full of baby clothes and toys sit in my house for years because the child I thought I would have was never born. I've had a man who I thought would stay with me during my darkest times abandon me."

Hewitt looked away and moved to the far end of the couch.

Connie continued. "I'm sorry you've gone through it. True, I will never know exactly how you feel. I do know for four glorious months, my ex and I were so happy, watching our baby grow on the ultrasounds, excited when the baby would kick. We were going to be a family."

Hewitt turned to her. "Three times?"

"Yes." She wiped a tear from her cheek. "I guess I wasn't meant to be a mother. I was never the nurturing kind anyway. Look at me. I'm an absolute wreck. I'm chunky now. The hourglass figure is gone. Imagine me trying to carry a baby? I'd be a blimp."

She laughed but Hewitt wasn't sure how real it was. He shook his head. "Why do you do that?"

"Do what?"

"Why do you put yourself down?"

Connie flinched. "I don't know. I thought I would lighten the moment."

"Do you do that a lot?" he asked.

"What are you, a shrink now?"

Hewitt moved closer. "No. But I know a good woman when I see one."

Connie smiled. "You think I am?"

"Didn't I just say so?"

"Why are you answering my question with a question?"

Hewitt sighed. "Why do I have to repeat myself?"

"Because a woman likes to hear she's special over and over again."

Hewitt waved his hands in the air. "Whoa, I didn't say you were special."

"Excuse me, Mr. Special Agent, you did say I was a good woman."

"Yes, good. I didn't say special."

"Why does saying special scare you?"

Hewitt laughed. "Oh, you're good all right. You're good at twisting my words."

"Ha. Men need to be told what they're feeling. And I think you feel something for me."

"Oh, no," said Hewitt. "It's not like that at all."

"Oh, I think it is," Connie said as she moved closer to him.

Hewitt leaned back on the couch and picked up a picture of him and his daughter off the side table. He gazed at it for a few seconds and looked at Connie. "She was special." He took a deep breath. "I couldn't protect her. Me. So big and strong. Mr. Macho. We had all the money in the world, the best security system to keep her safe." He lowered his head and placed the picture back on the side table.

Connie touched his hand. "It's okay to hurt."

"I can't take the time to hurt. Don't you understand? Do you know how many parents and children rely upon me? I can show you cartons of letters from those parents, telling me about their suffering. There isn't any time for me to rest and feel hurt."

Connie squeezed his hand. "Maybe you don't have the time to hurt but you should allow your heart to grieve."

Hewitt shook his head. "I have too much anger inside me to grieve." He tried to pull his hand away.

"I'm not letting go. I'm here for you. I wasn't there for my brother when he lost his wife. I feel terrible about that. I want to help."

"No one can help me. I'm broken." Hewitt watched a drop fall from Connie's eye onto her cheek. "Ever feel lonely?"

"Yes," she said. "Every night."

"Well, that we do have in common." He pulled her close and shivered.

"What's wrong?"

He took a deep breath and sighed. "I'd better explain the picture to my boss."

"Good luck with that," she said.

He clicked his phone to call as he waved Connie away. *I hope Wrightman won't be upset with me.* He ran his hand through his hair a couple of times.

"Why are you calling me at this hour?" Wrightman said when he answered his phone. "I told you I'm on vacation. I don't want to hear from anyone. I'm only picking your call up because of the publicity in this case. Can't you handle this yourself?"

"I've put the FBI into an awkward situation."

"Awkward," yelled Wrightman, his voice shaking Hewitt's ear. "How much more awkward can it get? Do you know how embarrassing it is for the world's top agency to have a middle-aged man elude us when we had the entire perimeter sealed off?"

"I know, sir. I'm working every angle."

"Every angle? If you were working every angle, we'd know where he and his daughter are by now. Right?"

"Sir, he had some help. He had to. I'm working on those who could have helped him escape."

"We're wasting time. Who knows how far he's gotten by now. Isn't it about time we start pulling some agents away from that church?"

"No, sir. Not right now. I believe he made his escape from inside that church, and we have to find the room or area he did it from."

"We've been sitting in that crummy church for several days now. We're looking like the biggest fools since the Keystone Kops."

"I have some breaks in the case."

"Then solve it. Immediately."

"Yes sir."

Hewitt coughed and glared at himself in the mirror. "No one makes a fool of me," he said, forgetting he was still on the phone.

"Excuse me?" said Wrightman.

"Yes sir. I'll solve this case."

"All right, that's my best Knute Rockne speech," Wrightman said. "What's the reason you called?"

Hewitt paced back and forth in his bedroom. "Sir," he said, lying, "I just needed a pep talk."

"You got it," shouted Wrightman. "Now go solve this case and stick it to the media."

The line went dead, and Hewitt dropped the phone on the bed. "I need a strategy," he said. "I can't let my feelings interfere with my work. Not anymore."

Connie snuck into the room. "Are you just using me to help you find my brother so you can put him away?"

"What?" Hewitt said, turning around.

"Using me. Was all that heavy-hearted talk just a bunch of nonsense to get to know me so you can solve the case? I thought you cared. Do you care more about my brother and me or about being a hero?"

"I care about solving the case. I didn't become the best in the business by letting my heart sob for everyone."

"I don't believe that," Connie said, sitting next to him. Her cellphone rang. She held it away from her ear. "Yes, Dad. Is everything okay?"

"You didn't stop by," he said.

"I know. I'm sorry. I am trying to find Michael and Elizabeth. I've been busy with the search parties."

"How's that going?"

Connie stayed silent for a few seconds. "He's not here."

"I guess it's been a waste of time," he said.

"Yes, Dad. A waste of time. I have to go." She hung up and shook her head.

"I know you've got your boss on your butt, Hewitt," she said, "but do you really believe my brother would harm his daughter? Does he fit the profile of such a person?"

Hewitt stood and took a couple of steps to the door. He opened it. "Yes."

CHAPTER 40

THE WORKERS BEGAN LOADING UP THE FINAL CARTS filled with food and supplies. Michael stepped aside as a group of four Roman soldiers surrounded Paul and walked him up the pier and onto the boat. Michael ran to the captain. "I am looking for a girl this tall," he said, holding his hand below his neck.

"The Romans have her below deck."

"I need to get her off this ship. Please help me."

"I cannot disobey orders from the Romans."

Michael shook his head frantically. "I cannot let this ship leave with her on board. She will be killed."

"Is there a problem?" yelled a Roman standing near the edge of the dock.

The captain turned first to the Roman and then back toward Michael. "We are almost ready to sail. There are no problems."

The Roman walked away as Michael took a few more steps toward the ship.

"Michael, you must do something now," said Aharon. He grabbed his arm and pressed it. "Act!"

"My God, Michael, do not just stand there," said Leah.

Aharon reached into a pouch and gave him ten coins. "Bribe them. Save your daughter."

Michael looked at Leah. "Save my daughter," she said.

The captain joined him. "I am trying to do what I can. I am not able to get her off the boat. The Romans have her surrounded. I am trying to bargain with the caretaker to see how much silver will get her released."

"If you cannot get her released, please let me take the journey," Michael said.

"We leave from shore once all the carts are full," said the captain as he made his way to the deck. "Do you have enough silver?"

Michael looked at Aharon and Leah. "I hope so."

The captain picked up a supply cart and handed it to a worker. "This is important," he instructed the man. "This stays below deck at all times. Surround it with the other boxes. Do not let anyone near this."

The captain met up with a Roman on the boat and spent several minutes speaking. Aharon placed a knife in Michael's side pocket. "Do not hesitate in using this. There will come a moment when you will have to kill to save your daughter."

Michael nodded. "I will do what I need to do."

"Good; do not grow weak in the face of death," Aharon said quietly. The whispered words sounded devious to Michael's ear.

The captain came back to them. "The Romans will not release her. There is not enough silver to convince them. You can come with us. I told them you are a friend of the preacher."

"How am I going to get her off the ship?"

"You will have to wait until we get to Rome," the captain said. "I will need to be paid."

Aharon stepped forward. "Four coins should do."

The captain shook his head. "You speak for him?"

Aharon glanced at Michael.

"He does."

"Four coins is all he has," Aharon said. "He will have to use what he has left to bribe the Romans."

The captain turned and took a few steps toward the boat. "Please, sir," Michael said, running to him. "Please, it is my daughter. My only child. She is all I have left in this world."

The captain faced Michael. "I have much cargo to take with the Romans and their prisoners taking up half my boat."

"Sir, I do not have much. What you have on that boat is all I have."

The captain frowned. "Rules are rules. More freight slows my boat down. They want this boat to sail immediately to Rome as we have the wind at our backs."

Aharon stepped forward and handed the captain a round, short cup. "This was handed down to me. I was told it was used by a king many sunsets ago."

"What king?"

Aharon shook his head. "I know it has value. More value than the silver he can give you now."

Michael shook his head. "How are you going to survive? You have given me all your silver."

Leah grabbed Michael's hands. "Elizabeth must be saved. We will find other ways to live."

Michael looked down at Leah's belly. "What about your baby?"

Aharon put his arm around Leah. "We will survive. I hope you can see our child some sunrise."

Michael looked back at the boat and noticed the line of carts was short. "It is almost time for me to go."

He turned to Aharon and Leah. "I hear Rome is a beautiful place to live. Free from tyranny and violence."

"What Rome are you talking about?" Aharon asked.

Michael grimaced. "One from many sunsets, I guess."

"This is our home, our traditions, our land," Leah said. "Free Elizabeth and find your way back to your world."

"I will take her somewhere safe," Michael said.

Leah shook her head. "There is no safe place in this world."

"I worry about you." Michael watched her squeeze Aharon's hand.

"I was born here. I lived here with Yochanan. Now, I have Aharon. I am as safe as God allows."

Michael noticed she tightened her grip on Aharon. He looked down and then away, seeing the captain waving at him. "I have to go," he said.

Leah let go of Aharon's hand and moved closer. "Please protect my dear daughter."

Michael nodded.

"When I lost my daughter many sunsets ago," Leah said, embracing him, "I thought my reasons to live had vanished. Your daughter was a gift from God to remind me during my grieving that I need not bear a child to have another." She pulled back. "You will always be a part of my life whether you stand in front of me or not. You will be right here." She pointed to her heart.

Aharon looked away as Leah hugged Michael again. "I love you." She cried and tightened her hold.

"I know. I know. I have always known." Michael dabbed his eyes with his sleeves. "I have to leave," he said. "Be well."

He stepped back, turned and ran up the pier. The boat pulled away from the dock, and Michael took a quick glance back. He watched Aharon and Leah holding each other.

Goodbye, Leah. He could see her body shaking, her face pressed into his chest. He knew he would never forget the night they had talked while sitting on the rooftop. He had come into her life as an angry man, bitter over what had happened to Vicki. He never thought he would be able to open up his heart to love again. *You did this for me, Leah. No one else could have ever done it.*

Their figures grew smaller and smaller as the boat created distance between him and the shore. He hoped Leah would find a lifetime of happiness with Aharon. He seemed to be a good man. She needed someone like that. His heart's desire was for them to find peace. He hoped they would find a home somewhere to be a family and raise their child. He knew the child would give her great joy like Elizabeth had always given him. *I know there's uncertainty, but your love will prevail.*

Goodbye, my love.

CHAPTER 41

FIFTEEN MEN ON EACH SIDE OF THE WOODEN VESSEL ROWED IN UNISON. The captain bellowed encouragement, demanding the men to pull and push their oars with more speed. Michael watched for a few minutes before descending a short stairwell. He saw Elizabeth leaning against a pile of carts filled with food and supplies.

"Dad!" she shouted.

"Quiet, Elizabeth. Where are the Romans?"

"They're off somewhere drinking. How are we going to get off this boat?"

He shook his head. "I don't know. I have some silver and a weapon."

"A weapon?"

He pulled out a knife. "From Aharon. It's all he had."

"That's the best we can do?" She shook her head. "How long do you think it will be before we get to Rome?" she asked.

"I'm not sure. Whatever you do, do not confront anyone on this boat. Act like a woman would during this time."

"How is that?"

"Do what you are told."

Elizabeth leaned forward, holding her head. "Oh, great."

"What's wrong?" Michael asked, reaching for her. "Are you sick?"

Elizabeth gave him an angry look.

"Tell me what's wrong."

"Behind you."

"What?"

"Look behind you."

Michael turned slowly. "I'm looking. What is it?"

"Look closer," she said, grunting. "Get it."

Michael stood and looked at a stacked group of carts. "Get what. I don't see anything. Do you want something to eat or drink?" He picked up a loaf of bread and showed it to her.

Elizabeth whacked it out of his hands. She staggered to another stack of carts in the corner. Michael heard some footsteps above him on deck. "Sit down, Elizabeth."

He grabbed and pulled her down beside him as a couple of Romans glared. "Be still for the journey. We have our orders to take you back alive. Do not force us to punish you."

"She will listen," Michael said, putting his hand up in front of his face.

"Who are you?"

"He is the friend of the preacher," another Roman said, stepping down off the stairway.

"Then you should go be with the preacher," the Roman said. He picked Michael up. "Go seek him out."

Michael frowned. "Yes."

He took a step away from Elizabeth and turned around, pointing to her cross. He mouthed, "Keep your cross hidden. If a soldier bothers you, call the captain." He pointed upstairs. "I gave him money."

ꝼ

The boat creaked back and forth as the wind inspired the waves to gain some strength. The captain's cries began to lose their vigor as the noise from the elements tumbled across the boat's structure. The fog dissipated and an overcast sky greeted Michael as he took a moment to smell the salty air. The shoreline of Caesarea had vanished as the boat had picked up speed. He was unsure how long it had been since he had said his goodbyes to Aharon and Leah.

The waves bounced against the side of the vessel and sent mists of water into his face. He wiped it with his sleeves and approached the captain. "Sir," he said.

The captain stopped in mid-shout. "Are you being treated well?"

"Yes sir. I am seeking to speak to the prisoner, Paul. Is this possible?"

The captain pointed to the far end of the boat, away from the rowers. "He is there," he said. "You can find him below the topping. Tell Julius I granted permission for you to speak to him."

"Thank you." Michael moved past the men rowing, noticing their arms drenched in seawater. The sky darkened some more, and the wind pinned the sails back. It looked like they were running into a storm. He was glad he was on the boat with Paul. God would not let Paul suffer and die on this journey. He knew Paul had much more to write, much more to share and preach. Surely this couldn't be the end. As he thought about it though, he remembered that most of the apostles died a cruel death. He just couldn't remember what had happened to Paul.

He glanced at the sky one more time before walking down a short stairwell with lanterns on both sides to lighten the dark area. He was confronted by a man holding what looked like a piece of clay. "Are you Julius?" he asked.

"I am."

"I am here to see Paul."

Julius turned around and shouted down the stairs. "Does Paul want to speak to another traveler?"

A Roman soldier appeared at the bottom of the stairway. He raised his spear. "Who needs to see him?"

Julius turned and faced him. "State your name."

"Michael."

"Where are you from?"

"Jerusalem."

"What is your purpose?"

"I am an old friend. I want to wish him my best." He looked past Julius and saw Paul peering up at him.

"Come, my friend. We have much to talk about." He waved him down. Julius stepped aside, and the soldier lowered his spear as he walked past them. Paul was sitting on the floor at a small table with a cup of water and several pieces of bread. His face was full, and he had some color in his cheeks. His outstretched hands held onto the table.

"Sit my friend," he said.

Michael leaned down and balanced himself by holding onto the table with one hand. His stomach rumbled, and he felt some acid jump up into his throat. He took a deep breath as the boat swayed.

"Have you not traveled by sea before?" asked Paul.

"I have. But not in a vessel this small."

"This boat is big."

Michael tugged at his garment and grabbed his stomach. He put his head between his legs for a few seconds.

"My friend, be calm," Paul said.

"I am trying," Michael replied, lifting his head from between his knees.

"Have some bread," Paul said, handing him a piece.

Michael nodded and gulped it.

"You are hungry?"

"This helps my stomach."

Paul pushed another piece of bread toward him. Michael scooped it up and swallowed it whole. "I feel better," he said.

"This pleases me."

Michael eyed the cup of water sitting on the table. "How can I please you?" he asked.

"Tell me what my rabbi said. You told me at the prison you were given a message. We were interrupted before you could tell me."

Michael glanced at Julius standing behind him, speaking to the Roman guard.

"You can talk. They have treated me well."

He leaned closer to Paul. "He told me what is revealed to me traveling by boat with you is of utmost importance."

Paul shrugged his shoulders. "Is there more?"

"No."

"Are you sure?" Paul asked as he rubbed the back of his head.

Michael reflected for several seconds, touching the base of the cup.

"Take some," Paul said.

Michael took a couple of sips, trying to remove the acidic taste in his mouth. "Jesus said you had some words that would carry forth through many sunsets."

Paul took a deep breath and leaned back from the table. He stroked the bottom of his eyes, trying to smooth out the wrinkles beneath them. "My rabbi has a way with words. Sometimes the words he does not say speak with more importance."

"I do not understand," said Michael, now up on his knees and holding onto the table with both hands.

"The words I have yet to speak are the words you need to know."

Michael pulled away and clung to the table as the boat swayed some more. The cup slid off and fell to the floor.

"The wind is talking to us, my friend," said Paul.

"What do you mean?"

"Listen to the wind."

The table shook, and the last piece of bread tumbled onto Michael's lap. He pushed it away and stood, holding his stomach. "Oh no."

"You are sick again? Is the wind speaking words of discomfort?"

"You could say that," said Michael. He bent over and took a few short breaths. The smell of the seawater flooded his senses. He grabbed the cup off the floor and saw it was empty.

"Ugh," he continued. "We can talk later. You can tell me what I need."

Paul stood and grasped his arm. "The words are already being spoken to you. There are no words that need to come from my mouth. Do not close your eyes or ears. It is happening now."

Michael ran to the top of the boat. The waves were overrunning the sides, and water was flooding the deck. He stumbled to the railing and threw up. The next wave ascended the boat and drenched him. He shook his head and stumbled back downstairs. He fell to the floor and felt a hand touch his back.

"Are you all right, Dad?"

"Yeah. Breakfast didn't agree with me."

He stared at her. "Anyway, whatever I did have the last couple of days my stomach just dropped into the sea."

"Sorry. You feel better after throwing up?" she asked.

Michael shook his head. "This boat rocking back and forth like this isn't my ideal way of traveling."

"You wouldn't make a good apostle," she said.

He frowned.

"Sorry. Trying to lighten your agony. Speaking of apostles, what did Paul say? What do we have to do?"

He waved his arms in the air and stood, taking a deep breath. "I'm more confused now after speaking to him."

Elizabeth straightened up. "What was confusing?"

"He told me first the words not spoken are as important as the words Jesus did speak. He also said listen and watch the wind, whatever the heck that means. He said the words being spoken are happening right now. I don't hear anything."

"Maybe he means we have to be on the deck to hear the wind."

"Could be." He leaned away from her and spit. "Sorry. I know it's disgusting."

"Gross is more like it."

"I know." He climbed the few steps and stared at the black sky, ignoring the captain's pleas to stay below. "I am fine. I need some air. It will do me some good."

"The sea is getting worse," the captain said.

He ignored his fears despite the waves crashing against the side of the boat. Michael gripped the railing with both hands as Elizabeth joined him. "Go back down," he yelled. "The Romans won't tolerate it."

"No. The instructions Jesus gave you were meant for both of us. Right?"

"I guess. I'm not sure. He never mentioned you."

"We're in this together," she said, now holding on with both hands. "Four ears and four eyes are better than two of each."

Michael was too nauseous to argue with her. He picked his head up high and closed his eyes. *I am listening. Now, talk to me, Lord. Tell me what I need to know to help Paul. Tell me where I should go to get us home.* The wind howled a tune he couldn't decipher. The waves tumbled over the side with greater height.

"Can you hear anything?" he shouted over the captain's yelling.

"Not one word," she said. He looked at Elizabeth wiping her eyes. She coughed and spit up some water.

"Go back downstairs," he said. "I won't stay up here much longer."

She saw the Romans pointing at her from the far end of the ship. She brushed past Michael and went below.

He watched the waves come aboard one by one. *I'm watching, Lord. What should I be looking for? What message must I give to Paul? Tell me soon.*

Michael turned away and felt the brunt of the wind, pushing him away from the railing. He tumbled to the ground, hitting his head against a cart. The captain lifted him up. "Are you hurt?"

"No."

The captain left him and rushed to the aid of a man who fell overboard. Several men leaned down with their arms. Michael pulled at a stray robe under the cart and brought it to the men. They lowered it and tugged hard as the man held onto it. As they raised him up over the railing, the men cheered.

"Take him down and get him warm," shouted the captain. He gestured to the men to take their positions. "Forward ... back," he said. "Halt." He pointed to Michael and held up an oar.

"Me?" Michael muttered, pointing to his chest.

"You," the captain said. "We are a man short. Look at the sea. We need every man to help now."

The boat slid sideways wave after wave. The black sky pitched a tent surrounding the tiny boat. A man slapped Michael on the back as he sat down and lowered his oar over the side and into the water.

"Forward," screamed the captain. "Back," he said.

The water caromed high off of his side and soaked his lower body.

"Forward, back," the captain pleaded.

As the waves hit the boat with more frequency, the pleas came in shorter bursts. The salt stung his eyes, and his vision became blurry. Some water poured into his mouth, and he coughed each time the captain shouted "Forward."

He spit and tried to wipe the mist from his eyes. The waves of water filled his ears and lungs. Then everything went black.

CHAPTER 42

TIMOTHY PLAYED WITH THE MICROPHONE ON TOP OF THE PODIUM. "Testing, one, two, three." His voice carried from end to end through the empty church. He opened an old, tattered Bible and thumbed through it.

Where is that passage?

He removed his reading glasses and rubbed his eyes. He flipped the pages until he reached the end. *Why can't I find that passage?*

He looked up at the empty pews and scratched his head. "Am I losing it?" he said to no one in particular.

"Katie, I need your help," he called out.

"Yes, Pastor," she said, carrying a stack of papers.

"I know I'm getting old, granted. But I know I'm not crazy. Is this the Bible I read from during the last service?"

Katie put the stack of papers down on the side of the podium. He handed her the Bible. She looked at the inside cover. "Yes. Look at the marking."

Always remember, 12/25. Ask for forgiveness.

"This is the personal Bible of Pastor Dennis," Katie said. "You did want this one, didn't you? You told me you wanted to remember him by using his Bible for the services."

"I did request this. Good. I'm not going crazy. But there are pages missing."

"What pages?" she asked, turning them one by one.

"The Acts of the Apostles. Acts 27-28:10. They're missing."

Katie sat down in the first pew. She looked at each section of the New Testament. He joined her. "I don't see it," she said, looking at him. "You're not going crazy. Let me look through it one more time."

Katie took nearly thirty minutes, carefully examining each page. She shook her head and closed the book. "I don't know what happened," she said. "At the end of your last service, I locked it up in the office." She stood and handed him the book. "I'll get you the spare copy."

"Good. I need to read from one of Paul's works." He held the Bible to his chest. He removed his reading glasses and rubbed his eyebrows.

She returned moments later and gave him another Bible. "This is brand-new," she said. "I'm sorry, Pastor. I didn't notice any torn pages or rip marks. I know I locked it up. This Bible was special to Pastor Dennis. I treated it that way."

"Don't worry yourself about this," he said. "It wasn't your fault."

"Thank you. But how did this happen?" she asked. "It's odd there are no tear or rip marks where the pages are missing. Maybe part of it fell out? Maybe the glue dried holding the pages together?"

"Perhaps," he said, as he began paging through the new Bible.

He kept pushing the pages along. Each time he finished ten or so pages, he looked up toward the church ceiling. "Mary, Mother of God, are my eyes deceiving me?" he asked out loud.

"Is everything okay?" asked Katie.

He put one finger up in the air. "I'm checking."

He finished going through the Bible minutes later and held it up to his face, shaking his head.

"What's wrong, Pastor?" she asked.

"It's not in this one either." He turned to her. "What is going on here?"

He dropped the Bible on the bench and walked to a couple of pews behind them. He grabbed a couple of Bibles used by churchgoers for the services. Sitting down, he instructed Katie, "Take some books. Check again."

Katie went to the other side of the church and took one each from four different rows. She returned and sat down next to him. "Do you think someone came in here and removed the same pages?"

"No. This is too random."

They paged through the books with speed. When they finished, he half ran, half walked to the last pew and took eight more Bibles out of the holders. He gave four to Katie as she joined him in the back near the organ.

"They're all like this," he said, dropping the last one on top of the organ. "Call and check with the company that provided us with the books."

"Yes, Pastor," said Katie. She ran to her office, holding one of the Bibles.

"Why?" he wondered out loud. "How did this happen? This has to be a printing mistake we didn't recognize."

He walked to the front and stopped by the podium. He opened Pastor Dennis' Bible and examined the New Testament again. He glanced upward, catching Katie's blank expression as she stood off to the side.

"What's wrong?" he asked.

"They said it wasn't a printing error."

"What? How could it not be?"

"They said it was the version they were given. They checked their templates."

"Then they got the wrong templates."

She shook her head. "They said all their templates are like that."

Timothy sat on the lip of the service area and grasped the side of the podium. He stared for several seconds at the vacant church. "You can go, Katie."

She didn't move as he turned to her. "You can go."

"But Pastor, what are we going to do about the Bibles?"

"There's nothing we can do here."

CHAPTER 43

MICHAEL FLUNG HIS ARMS, flailing away through a waterfall. He coughed and turned over, tasting sand. He gagged, spitting it out. He felt more water dousing his face.

"Stop," yelled Elizabeth. "Are you okay, Dad?"

"Huh?" He rolled back over as the early morning sunlight hit his face. He squinted and rubbed his eyes with his soggy sleeves. Elizabeth stared at him.

"What happened?" he asked.

"Plenty," said the captain, leaning down. He extended his hand, and Michael grabbed onto it. Lifting him up, the captain slapped his back and gripped his shoulder. "The men thank you."

Michael shook his head as Elizabeth gave him a half hug. "What did I do?"

The captain smiled. "You kept rowing. Do you not remember?"

"I do remember rowing, a little. Then nothing. All was black."

"The storm was unforgiving. Big wave after big wave came crashing overboard. You kept rowing. You have our respect."

Michael looked around at the surroundings and saw the remains of the boat strewn about the shoreline. "Are we in Rome?"

The captain laughed and walked away.

"We're on some island," Elizabeth said.

"Which one?"

"One of the workers told me it's Malta."

"Great. Now what? Did they say when we could get another boat?"

Elizabeth walked a few yards toward the shore. He staggered to catch up to her. "Were there any men lost?"

"The captain said he lost three of his men."

Michael bent over and coughed. "Are you sure?"

"Yes."

Michael rubbed his forehead and stared at her.

"Is there something wrong?"

"I don't recall it happening that way. I wonder if we changed history? What about Paul?"

She looked back at him. "He's safe."

"Thank goodness," he said while gagging on more seawater. "It's so salty. This stuff is awful."

He touched the chain around his neck and felt the cross inside his wet shirt. *Thank God I didn't lose this during the storm.* He joined her at the shoreline's edge and kicked at the waves as they tumbled over his feet. "This complicates things."

"How?" she asked.

"I'm not sure this is where we should be. I thought we were supposed to be in Rome."

"The captain said we will be going to Rome once they get a new boat."

"Yes. But how long will we be stranded on this island?"

"The captain said there is another boat to sail this way on the next sunset."

"Great," he said, backpedaling from a big wave hitting the beach.

She didn't respond.

"What's wrong?" he asked.

Elizabeth walked away and sat down on a big rock near the edge of the forest.

He joined her. "I know it seems bleak," Michael said. "We will eventually get to Rome."

She lowered her head and scooped up a fallen petal from a red flower. A Roman soldier stood nearby, watching.

"Talk to me. What's bothering you?"

"Do you know Paul has someone write for him?"

"What?"

"Paul. The so-called apostle we were told to find and travel with, according to what you were told by Jesus. He has someone write for him."

"I wasn't told which apostle."

Elizabeth sighed.

"I've spoken to him. He's very smart. He's an educated man. I think you have it wrong."

"I'm telling you, he can't write."

"How do you know?"

"He told me."

"Why would he even tell you something like that?"

She smelled the petal. "I heard him talking to a man before about how he needed someone to write his thoughts down."

"What did he say exactly?"

"I can't remember every word. But he told the man he was worried about his work being lost." Elizabeth stood and pocketed the petal. "He asked for you."

"All right. He can't write. Why are you so sad? Many men during this time could not write or even read for that matter. This is not unusual." Michael dug his feet into the ground and pulled them out, watching the sand roll off. "Do you not agree?"

Elizabeth shrugged her shoulders. "What do I know?"

"This doesn't make any sense," he said.

"Is it supposed to?" she asked.

He shook his head. "Where is he?"

She pointed to a dirt path about twenty yards away. "They went toward that big tree over there."

"Come on," he said, tapping her shoulder.

They walked along a narrow road, surrounded on both sides by dense brush and shrubs. They emerged several minutes later into a wide clearing where makeshift sheds were formed in a circle.

In the center, a big fire was pushing flames skyward and several men were warming their hands and feet.

Michael located the captain. He was sitting down, chewing on some charred fish. "Have some," the captain said, greeting him with a smile.

"I will. Thanks."

"I do not know your name."

"Michael."

"Michael, where are you from?"

He thought for a few seconds. "On the other side of Rome."

The captain put his meal down. "That is a long way from where I met you."

Michael nodded. "Way too long."

"My name is Augustus. I can tell you have the heart of a tiger."

"I appreciate your confidence. I seek my friend, Paul. Can you tell me where he is?"

The captain gestured with his free hand. "Over there. He has been requesting you. Be careful of men like him. He tells strange tales. Ask for Julius."

"I will. Please watch my daughter."

"I shall. I owe you."

Michael looked to his left and then his right, making sure no one was following him. He was met by three Roman soldiers. "Where's Julius?" he asked them.

"Wait," one soldier said.

"Do not move," another soldier added.

Michael felt something cold on his leg. He froze and watched the soldier drop his spear. A snake curled its way onto the weapon. The soldier ran to the fire and dropped the spear into it.

"Come," said Julius, startling him. "This way." He waved him inside the shed.

Paul was sitting on a bedroll. "My friend, I am happy to see you. I hear you swallowed much sea water. Are you feeling better?"

"I am glad to see you. I am fine."

Julius left and the remaining Roman soldiers did the same. Michael glanced behind him to see where they were going.

"They are no threat to us now?" he asked.

Paul did not answer and took a sip of water from a cup. "Are you thirsty?"

Michael shook his head.

"I thought so," Paul said with a smile.

"I have many questions for you," Michael said.

"I hope I can answer all of them."

"My daughter ... "

Paul put his cup down. "Yes," he said, interrupting Michael's next thought. "A curious woman."

"She is. She said you have a problem writing."

"Many men do. My eyes fail me sometimes."

Michael dropped his head.

"Are you ill?" Paul asked.

"No. I am not."

"What troubles you?"

"My faith. Just when I think I have all the questions answered, more arise."

Paul smiled. "This is why we call it faith. Is it not?"

"It is," he said in a reluctant tone.

"What part of your faith troubles you now?"

Michael looked up and studied Paul's face for the first time. He shouldn't have been more than thirty-five to forty years old, an average age for a male during this period of time. Yet he looked much older, more like he was in his sixties. He could see his hair was starting to recede. His brown eyes were surrounded with deep wrinkles and had dark circles beneath them.

His cheeks were flushed, and his nose was spotted in red blotches from the ocean's breeze.

"If you cannot write," Michael said in a measured pace.

"Yes, go on," he said, leaning forward.

"How can you help spread the word of your rabbi as I have been told?"

Paul closed his eyes and rubbed them. Taking a deep breath, he opened them just as quickly. "I do not understand your question."

"Your writings are not yours? Am I right?" Michael asked.

"You are right to say I cannot write sometimes. My eyes are not the same as when I was young. I try to do my best."

Paul stared at him. "Why do you have so little faith?"

CHAPTER 44

THE SMOLDERING FIRE signaled it was time for Augustus and his men to sleep. Michael was given a blanket while Elizabeth lay on a bedroll still soaked from the storm. "Here, get up," he said.

She stood as he tossed aside the bedroll and placed the blanket on the ground. "Thanks, Dad." He kissed her on the forehead.

"You haven't said much since you spoke to Paul," she said.

"There's not much to say after we had our discussion. I'm confused. I'm not sure now why we're here with Paul. I'm starting to wonder whether it was Paul we were supposed to help. Maybe it's when we get to Rome that Paul will need our assistance."

He sighed and stretched his arms and legs.

"Maybe we should start worrying about ourselves," Elizabeth replied as she sat up to face him. "Is there a way we can get off this island?"

"I've already looked. I took a walk around while the Romans were fixing the boat. There are guards everywhere. Unless we find another boat, our best chance is when we get to Rome. I've spoken to the captain and have given him enough silver to help us escape when we reach there."

"Are you sure?" Elizabeth asked.

Michael shrugged. "Who can you trust in this time, in this place?" He stayed quiet for several seconds before speaking. "You should sleep. The captain told me it is possible another ship might be here or this one can be repaired by the next sunset."

"How do we really know either way?"

"He said it is a normal stop for another boat."

"What are the odds that will happen?"

"Who knows? I'm just a visitor here like you."

Elizabeth looked away, and Michael let his body relax. He listened to the crackling of the fire outside for several minutes. The birds were boisterous, and the wind brushed the high-standing trees like a paintbrush as he struggled to find a comfortable position.

Elizabeth slipped into a deep sleep.

Michael flinched as he began to dream. He was shaken out of it as an eerie sound alerted him.

He stood, went outside and circled around the shed. *Nothing.* He watched a couple of Roman soldiers drinking wine, laughing and telling stories. One turned around and yelled, pointing at him. "You, go rest. We have traveling to do once the next sunset comes."

"I am going to see my friend first before I do."

"Sleep when you can. It can be a tiresome journey."

Michael nodded and entered Paul's shed without obstruction. Julius and a Roman guard were asleep. Paul opened his eyes as Michael approached.

"What worries you my friend?" Paul asked.

"Much," said Michael as he sat next to him.

"Do you worry about what has already happened or what the next sunrise will bring?"

"Both." Michael faced him. "You have to understand this. I come from another place and time. I've read your works. Your words have lasted thousands of years."

Paul gave him a confused look.

"Many, many sunsets," said Michael.

"What troubles you?"

"You do know the others are in danger."

Paul shrugged his shoulders.

"Peter, Mark, your brothers."

"We know this."

"You need to protect yourself," Michael said, drawing closer. "It's in the words I've read."

Paul raised his hand. "They are still being written."

Michael shook his head. "No. They have been written. Millions of people have read them, not just me. It does not end well for you and the others. The Romans and the haters will kill you."

"Are you troubled staying here with me?"

Michael shook his head. "I do not understand what you mean. I am trying to help you by telling you what will happen in the next several sunsets. Your future."

Paul smiled. "You cannot walk in fear of what is not known."

"I want to help you. I want to find a way to get you to a safe place."

"There is no safe place. I am here for a reason. You are here for a reason. Your daughter is with us for a reason."

"What is the reason?"

"The next sunrise will speak the words you seek. Rest. Sleep. We have much work to do."

Michael returned to the shed and took one more look around. He picked up a couple of stray cups. *I must have heard something else.* He sat and listened to Elizabeth's deep breathing as she slept. *Amazing. Whether it's Jerusalem, Long Island or Malta, she sleeps. Like her mother.* He looked up and nodded. *Yes, like her mother.* He sighed and lay down. *Like you, Vicki.* He closed his eyes and forced himself to remember happier moments. He thought back to when Vicki and he were in love.

"Stop freaking out every time something wonderful happens," he heard Vicki say.

"I'll do my best." He flinched as Vicki faded. "Where are you going? Come back. Don't leave."

Her lips moved, but he couldn't hear her words. "Come back," he struggled to say, holding out his hand.

"Ow," he screamed.

Startled awake, Elizabeth asked, "Dad, what's wrong?"

"I just got bit," he said.

A commotion outside distracted them at first.

"What bit you?"

He looked at his leg, now swollen. "Had to be a snake or something."

They went outside to see Paul battling a serpent near the fire. A crowd had surrounded him. "What is going on?" Michael asked the captain.

"The preacher was bit by that devil." He pointed to the snake in Paul's hand.

Paul stared at it, tightening his grip on the serpent. He whispered some words, looking skyward.

Michael felt dizzy, and his eyes blurred. He tried to stumble around the crowd to get a better look. The vision of Paul manhandling the snake faded. He staggered and fell to his knees.

"Dad," Elizabeth yelled, running to him. She touched his forehead. "My God, you're burning up. Captain! Captain!"

Elizabeth ran around the crowd as Michael thrashed about with his arms and tried to pull himself up. Water rolled out of his eyes and down his cheeks. He could see the blurry outline of the crowd. "Something is wrong," he said in a weak tone.

He crawled toward Paul.

A Roman soldier lifted him up and held onto his shoulder. "What is wrong?" he asked.

"Look," said Julius, joining Elizabeth. "His leg."

"What is it?" Elizabeth asked.

"Another snakebite," Augustus yelled.

The crowd of soldiers and natives now gathered around Michael as the soldier lowered him to the ground.

"Dad, can you hear me?" Elizabeth asked.

He reached out to touch her hand.

Augustus kneeled beside him and gripped his shoulder. "Can you feel your feet?"

"No."

"What does that mean?" Elizabeth asked.

Augustus shook his head, stood and walked away.

"My friend, stay strong, our work has begun," said Paul, who fell to his knees beside him. He gripped his leg.

"I cannot feel anything," Michael moaned.

Paul closed his eyes and whispered some words, keeping his hand on top of the bite.

"What are you doing?" Elizabeth asked. "You are not a doctor. We need a doctor. Is there a doctor on this island? Can someone help him?" She rushed around asking the natives. "Do you know a doctor? Do you? Do you?"

Michael closed his eyes and drifted into a dream, into a place he had never visited, meeting his relatives and friends again. "Mom, I can see you," he said. "Nana. Uncle Ed. Joe. Uncle Jack. Mary. Sweet cousin. I've missed you."

"Wake up," Elizabeth yelled. He felt his cheeks being struck. "Wake up, Dad. You are not leaving me now. Not after what we've been through. I cannot live without you. Stay awake."

He opened his eyes again. Paul's face blocked the sun's light. His brown eyes blinked several times. "My friend, this is not the place for you to leave me. We are now ready."

"What?"

Paul stood and backed away. Michael crawled a few feet and then propped himself up on his elbows. He watched Paul walk through a crowd of people and back to his shed. Elizabeth stared as he struggled to sit up. "Help me," Michael said.

"Did you see that?" Elizabeth asked.

"What? What happened?"

CHAPTER 45

CONNIE'S MIND DANCED AROUND EMOTIONALLY with her favorite memories of Elizabeth. It was a perfect evening to allow herself a break from the struggles of life. The wind off the bay was light, yet the frigid air encouraged her to tighten a bright red scarf over her face. Fluffy snowflakes fluttered from above, touching and melting on her nose. She watched the boats in the dock rock back and forth.

She reflected back to the summers when she'd take a young Elizabeth out for long walks. They would always stop in this particular spot, right at the edge of the pier.

"Someday, Aunt Connie, Daddy is going to get us a boat," Elizabeth would say. "He made a promise to me. We don't break our promises, right?"

"That's true, Elizabeth. We try not to."

Connie bent down, put her arm around her and whispered with a big smile. "We'll spend our Saturday afternoons out there with the others." She would point to the perimeter of the Northport shoreline. "And we'll have peace from this rat race."

Elizabeth would always smile when Connie would say rat race. "Aunt Connie, what is the rat race?" she'd ask.

"It's where people work themselves into an anxiety attack and forget how to live. Never forget that, Elizabeth. Don't ever forget how to live."

Connie stepped away from the pier and stood in front of the town's tall Christmas tree. Its colored lights illuminated the area with holiday cheer, its ornaments tied to the branches, swaying in the breeze. She straightened out one ornament and touched the pines. She breathed deeply, relishing the sweet smell.

Now, this is Christmas. She noticed the bright, white lights in the distance hanging over the gazebo. Connie walked toward it in small steps, letting the glow soothe her anxiety. She stopped near the stairwell as the snow formed a coating on top of the roof. To her right, a mother and daughter were laughing as they went up and down together on a swing in the nearby playground. *This is like a Hallmark Christmas card.*

Connie closed her eyes and listened to the breeze. She wiped a rogue snowflake off her nose and opened her eyes. She watched the mother and daughter walk away, hand in hand, skipping down the concrete path toward Main Street. Connie climbed the five steps of the gazebo and stood in the middle.

She looked around before speaking. "I only ask this for Christmas, God," she said out loud. "I pray for the safety of my brother and niece." She touched what she thought was a flake under her eye.

"Are you out there, God? Can you hear me? If you can hear me, it makes me wonder why would you hear me now and not in another place or time?" She wiped her eyes. "See what you're doing to me, Mike? You've got me all weepy now. I'm a mess. I'm a wreck and sick to my stomach. I'm ready to fall apart."

She lowered her voice and took her scarf off, wiping more tears with it. "Mike, hear me if you can. Come home. Come home, now," she said.

"I miss you," she yelled. "I miss you," she said again as her voice fell. "I miss you," she whispered. Connie sat down on the steps and wept. The wind swirled, and the snow fluttered up and down around her. She closed her eyes once more for a few minutes until she heard someone come up from behind.

"Why are you out here?"

Where did he come from? "Huh? Oh. I can ask you the same thing. What's going on?" She took a tissue out of her pocket and wiped her face. "What are you looking at?"

"Someone falling apart."

"I'm fine."

"Are you sure?" Hewitt asked. "You're crying."

"I just needed a good cry."

He sat beside her. "I can't blame you. I do know you love your brother. And I don't believe you know where he is."

She nodded. "Well, is that supposed to make me feel better?"

"Yes."

She wiped some stray tears off her chin.

"The FBI is doing everything they can," he said. "I spoke to my boss. I'll find them. It's only been a few weeks."

"Is that a short time to find missing people?"

He shrugged his shoulders. "I don't know what to say. I've had every picture I've found circulated to all the field offices. They've looked through phone records and gone through their computers. They're looking everywhere. I think it may be time to go on TV myself and make a plea. What about you? Would you do this?"

"I don't look at the TV anymore," she said. "All they do is show their pictures. It's heartbreaking."

"Would you make a plea for me?" Hewitt asked. "To help me." He shook his head. "No, I said that wrong. To help you. To help your brother and niece."

"What would I say?"

"You would say what's in your heart. How you want anyone who can help find your niece and brother to come forth. We'd post a number for anonymity too."

Connie hesitated.

"I know it hurts to see them on TV, but they have to show their pictures," Hewitt said. "It could lead to someone in this country seeing them somewhere."

She pulled away and shook her head.

"You don't agree?"

"Oh, I agree that what you said is right. They do need to show their pictures. I just don't think he's around where anyone can find him. Showing their pictures is a waste of time."

He placed his hand on hers. "Look, I've checked every angle, interviewed every person, scoured every corner of that church. A man just doesn't disappear like that without help from one or more people. Maybe even from a whole community."

Connie didn't respond.

"Be honest with me," Hewitt said. "Can you?"

"Of course."

"Did he leave the country?"

She threw her hands up in the air. "How do I know? You just said you believed I didn't know. Which is it? Would you feel better if he did leave the country?"

"I'm checking on every angle."

"I don't know. It's all so crazy."

"What's crazy? He either left the country or not."

She shook her head. "It's not like that. I don't know what to believe anymore. Sometimes I think I'm going insane trying to figure out what happened to both of them."

"Where could they have gone then? Did he leave a number behind for you? Something that I can chase right now. I don't have much time left here."

She stood and looked up at the sky, letting the flakes tumble onto her face. "I have no idea how to get in touch with him."

He got up. "Is there something you haven't told me about your brother and Elizabeth? Their relationship? Money issues? Problems they might have had in the past?"

"I've told you what I can."

"What you can? So there is something you haven't told me?"

"If I told you what I thought, you would think I've lost it. I'm not a religious freak. All I've been looking for is a bit of stability in my life. And sanity. Thinking this way hasn't given me any of this."

Hewitt faced her. "I'm here if you need to talk."

She gave him a hug, surprising him. He pulled back at first, noticing her sadness. They looked at each other for a few moments. Connie looked over at the gazebo. "It's such a pretty town," she said. "I remember when my ex and I used to dance over there." She pointed.

Hewitt stayed quiet for a few moments. He watched her walk away, dabbing her eyes with a tissue. "Sometimes we need a break," he called out. He jogged to catch up to her. He put his arm out, gesturing to the gazebo.

"Are you asking me to dance?"

"I'm asking for your friendship," he said.

"Why yes," she said with a smile.

Hewitt walked her up the stairs as the snow came down more heavily. She leaned her head into his shoulder and wrapped her arms around his waist. They swayed back and forth for several minutes until she stopped.

"What's wrong?" he asked.

"What song are we dancing to?"

"Does it matter?"

"It does to me. I need one in my mind."

"What song would you like to dance to?"

"Something hopeful."

"Would you like me to sing it?"

"Hmmm. I'm not so sure how to answer that."

Hewitt smiled. "You just did."

"Oh, I'm sorry. Are your feelings hurt?"

"A little."

"Go ahead. Sing it."

"Oh, oh, oh, oh … It must have been cold there in my shadow … "

Connie stood on her toes and looked at Hewitt. "Your voice is beautiful."

"Tonight's the night where I let go of my worries, it's under this evening sky, where I find my heart can heal, helping me fall where the snow is high…"

"You're making that up," Connie said, laughing. "I've never heard that song."

"Yeah, it's made up. But it's pretty good, don't you think?"

He led her around the gazebo, and she twirled as Hewitt fumbled with some final lyrics.

CHAPTER 46

MICHAEL JOINED ELIZABETH AT THE FIRE. She was munching on charred fish. He nudged her shoulder and grinned. "I never thought I'd see my teenage daughter eating this."

Elizabeth kept chewing, and after the last bit of fish was swallowed, she wiped her hands on her shirt. "You made your adjustments, right?"

"Yes. I had to make several while living in Jerusalem."

"Sorry, Dad."

"Why?"

She dropped her hands to her sides and wiped again. "When you were sick and I saw you struggling to breathe, it hit me how you must have felt when you found out about me."

"It was a gift," Michael said. He paused. "One of the greatest I've ever received."

"To have your heart crushed is a gift? I don't get it."

"Yes, I had that crushing feeling of grief and sadness. I know how it felt, like losing your mom. There's something so unbearable about losing your child. I hope you never have to go through it. But you're here. I will never take another moment we have together for granted. I'll even relish our arguments."

Elizabeth kicked at a stray piece of fish.

He grasped her arm. "We're here. Now. Today. We have this moment. Enjoy it."

A Roman soldier came over and handed Michael a piece of fish and cup of water. "Thank you," he said, giving Elizabeth a surprised look.

Michael took a bite.

"They're not all like Marcus," Elizabeth said.

"I hope not. If you recall your history in school, the Romans weren't choirboys. They were ruthless oppressors, taking what they wanted when they wanted. You do remember that?"

"I do. However, they also built cities, aqueducts, and buildings; some of them were really beautiful places. I didn't think it was possible during this time."

"It was. Jesus didn't live during the Stone Age. Men could communicate in many different ways. The Romans were very efficient in many areas but so was Hitler, and we know what a maniac he was. It doesn't change history."

"Aren't we somehow changing history?" Elizabeth asked.

"I hope not. I'm sure Paul would let me know."

He took a deep breath and sipped his water. "History. What is it about this time that we are needed here?"

"I guess we'll find out," said Elizabeth, pressing down the piece of fish. She squished it into the dirt. "For the ants."

Michael ate the fish and offered his water to Elizabeth.

She declined. "Paul was asking for you."

He swallowed and took the last sip of water. "When? You should have told me."

"You were still sick. The captain told me not to bother you. He wanted you to sleep, recover. There were guards around you. The captain said he needed healthy men for the next journey."

"Oh, great." He stood and watched Julius walk past him. "What is that Julius has in his hands?" he asked, looking down at Elizabeth.

She got up and stared. "I have no idea."

"Stay here," he said, taking a few steps in the direction of a shed across from the fire. He followed Julius and knocked on the outside of his shelter.

Julius faced him. "Paul is in the shed at the far end of the camp. He has requested your presence when you have recovered. Do you feel up to it?"

"I do," Michael said.

"Good. He will be pleased," said Julius, turning away and placing an object on a pile. They all looked similar in structure.

"What are those?" asked Michael.

"These?" asked Julius, pointing to the pile.

"Yes. I have never seen them."

"You are not from a place that has these?" Julius pulled a short, metal rod out. One end featured a slight bend in it. "This piece goes with this item," said Julius, picking up another object. "I am recording our journey for the Roman Empire."

Michael approached him. "Is this what men used during these times?"

"Times?"

"I am sorry. Do you mind?" Michael put out his hands.

Julius nodded and handed him the metal tool and tablet.

"Is this wax?" he asked as he touched it.

"It is. I am surprised," Julius said.

"Why?"

"I sensed you were a man of this world. A man who could read. A man who could write. Yet you have no knowledge of the tools used to do so."

"Where I come from, we are still learning."

Julius took the objects. "It gives me joy you have discovered them with me."

Michael watched him pack the items away. He approached him as he placed the last one in the wooden cart. "Would you have one for me to use?"

Julius frowned. "My friend, these tools cost silver, a handful of silver."

"I do not have much." Michael dug into his pockets, still moist from the sea travel, and pulled out two silver coins. "I lost much of it during the storm."

"I cannot let such important materials for my recording go for a petty price."

"It is all I have."

Julius moved his hand through his gray hair. He looked at Michael and shook his head.

"Wait. Let me find some silver," Michael said. He left the shed and rushed to Paul.

"My friend, come in. I hope you are healed," Paul said when he saw him.

Michael got on his knees. "I owe you my life."

Paul smiled. "I did what my rabbi asked. I am with great joy that you are feeling better."

"All to you," Michael said.

"All to my rabbi," Paul responded. "How can I help you?"

"Do you have any more silver? It can help us."

"I do not travel with much, so I do not have enough to give away. I gave you what I had back in Caesarea."

"Of course," Michael said and walked back to the shed.

Elizabeth was asleep on the blanket. He stood at the opening, thinking, watching birds sprint around in the sky at a frantic pace. The skies darkened, and the clouds covered the little light left. Workers and soldiers eating and resting near the fire scattered quickly to their sheds for shelter. The rain began to drop from the sky, easing the humidity. The water tumbled off the small roof and onto his head. He wiped the moisture from his hair and leaned against a stack of carts filled with supplies.

His mind drifted to thoughts of Northport. Strangely, the struggles he faced there seemed to be wonderful memories now. The times he dug for change to buy a slice of pizza – anguishing as it was back then – the memory forced a smile on his face. The moment when Elizabeth told him she had walked home instead of waiting for a bus that was late gave him a sense of pride in how independent she was. He turned around and watched her sleep, relishing the calmness in her breathing. Life seemed normal.

He took a happy, deep breath. "Beautiful. Peaceful. Why can't it be like this all the time?" He smiled and took one more peek at her. *Sleep. We have a long trip ahead. We'll make it back. I promise that.*

Michael faced the opening again and jumped back. A shadow covered the opening. "My God," he said. "Where did you come from? How did you get here? Did you travel through the church too?"

"I did. I am needed here now."

"Here now? It's a long way from Northport, Dennis."

"I know. My work there is done."

"Done? Are you not going back?"

"I am not."

Dennis approached him and put several pieces of silver in his hand. "You will need this. You have your instructions. Do it well."

"What about you? Why are you not able to come back with us?"

"I have my instructions too."

"You knew all along about the church?"

"Only when I read the black book you gave me. There was a reason why I was driving the truck that night. There was a reason why I became a pastor there. There was a reason why you found the book and gave it to me, Michael."

"I guess this is why I have been asked to take these journeys."

Dennis stepped back. "The answer is before you. Travel with an open heart. Protect your daughter. There is another ship to come by this island. Not all will have friendly faces."

Dennis walked out of the shed and toward the shoreline.

"Where are you going now?" Michael called after him.

"I am taking my next journey."

"Please don't go. I have no friends back home."

Dennis stopped, turned around and extended his hand. "I have not left you."

Michael shook his hand. "Will I ever see you again?"

"There will be a time when we do see each other."

"When?"

"When it is needed."

He released his grip and headed to the water.

"Where are you going? There are no boats out there. What the – ?"

Dennis walked into a wave and disappeared.

Michael sprinted into the sea, tumbling into the water. He swam several yards and submerged. He flailed and kicked a few feet and stopped. Gasping for air, he surfaced. "Where did you go, Dennis?"

He looked behind him and saw the smoke from the fire rising. He felt a hand on his shoulder. He jumped and glanced around, but he was all alone in the waves.

CHAPTER 47

HEWITT RETURNED HOME ALONE and stared at the tall pine tree in his living room. Its branches were bare except for a lone ornament attached to the highest one, made by his daughter when she was in kindergarten. He kicked at the box holding the strands of lights, wondering if it was worth the effort to decorate the tree. He turned his attention to the TV, flipping through several channels, preferring to watch without sound. The vibration of his cell phone prompted him to drop the remote.

"Yes sir," he answered. "Merry Christmas."

"Merry Christmas to you," said Wrightman. "This isn't a social call. Normally I would have you in my office for such an issue, but since there is urgency in this Stewart case, I needed to get in touch with you as soon as possible."

"Has anyone called in with a lead?" asked Hewitt, straightening up in his chair.

"No, it's not that. I have to make a change."

"Change?"

"Special Agent Paul, are you aware of a picture of you digging up a grave?"

"I am. I had no choice."

"First, I'm embarrassed I had to find out from Holligan. Why didn't you tell me about this during our last phone call?"

Hewitt hesitated. "Sir, I'm ashamed."

"You should be!" Wrightman yelled. "What on earth prompted you to do that?"

"I was given a tip that there wasn't a body in that casket."

"Who gave you that tip?"

Hewitt hesitated and stood up, taking a turn around his living room. "I saw something."

"You're your own tip?"

"Yes sir."

"Why didn't you inform the office of this before you made a fool of yourself?"

"I didn't want you to be involved with this in case it didn't work out."

"That's admirable, Special Agent. I appreciate you trying to protect me. But it didn't work out. In fact, you embarrassed the entire FBI bureau. Do you know how it looks when one of our top agents is digging up a dead body without having filled out the official paperwork? Do you know how insensitive it looks to the average guy on the street? The soccer moms are flooding our offices with emails and phone calls now."

"Have there been a lot of calls?"

"Why don't you stop by the office and ask the clerks who have been fielding them the past couple of days? Your timing couldn't be worse."

"I know but I didn't have time to wait."

"No time to wait? Was the pastor going to jump out of the ground like a zombie and start eating the people of Northport?"

Hewitt took a deep breath and growled.

"Special Agent, is that your response?"

"No sir. I saw something. I acted. Perhaps I could have waited, but I wasn't wrong."

"You weren't wrong?"

"No. There was no body. I have no idea where the pastor's body has gone. I didn't tell you because I wanted to be sure. Once I had proof, I was going to show you."

"Well, I've got news for you. You were wrong. We already checked out what was going on over there after your picture showed up on the Internet. The area you were so happily digging up is a memorial place for the church community to visit in remembrance of their beloved pastor. The pastor's body was sent to his family for a private burial."

"What? That is highly unusual, sir."

"It may be unusual, but we're not in the business of judging morality here. You were assigned to this case to find Michael and Elizabeth Stewart, not to dig up bodies."

"I'm sorry, sir."

"Sorry isn't going to help us. My boss is up my ass because of what you did."

There was a pause in the conversation. Hewitt held out hope that his boss would say goodnight. He didn't.

"Where do we stand with this case?"

Hewitt rubbed his forehead. "I've checked every lead, every part of that church, interviewed every person connected to the Stewarts."

"And?"

"And I don't know. I don't know how he escaped the perimeter. I know we had every door and window accounted for when he disappeared."

"I need you to turn over all your notes and contacts to Special Agent Holligan."

Hewitt stood. "Why, sir?"

"Holligan's in charge of the case now. Perhaps we need some new blood here. You don't have anything to go on. Maybe Holligan will find something you haven't."

"Sir, please. I'm the best you have."

"Yes, you are. But you're exhibiting signs of stress with this case. Between the therapy you've been going through and your wife leaving you, I'd say it's time for you to take a break from this. So, I formally have removed you from the case."

"Am I suspended?"

"No. But you're on leave."

"What's the difference?"

"You're still getting paid."

Hewitt tossed the phone on the couch and walked upstairs to his bedroom. He sat and folded his hands over his face.

What have I done? I've destroyed everything – my marriage, my family, my job. There's nothing left for me. Nothing.

He went to the dresser and opened the top drawer. A plaque honoring his service to the FBI lay atop several citations. He grabbed a long, brown envelope and opened it, letting the contents flutter to the bed. One by one, he read the letters and e-mails from parents professing their gratitude to him for bringing their children home safely.

Dear Special Agent Paul,

Today was Isabelle's fifth birthday. She wanted the biggest choco-late cake she'd ever seen, so we made one with seven layers. It towered over her head while she was sitting down! Her smile lit up the world when we had her blow out the candles and we sang happy birthday. We've enclosed a picture.

Hewitt held the photo in his right hand as he continued to read.

You gave us this smile back, Mr. Paul. You gave us another mem-ory we will have for a lifetime. You gave us our greatest gift, our most beautiful love. You are an angel that came into our lives. Thank you, sir. God bless you.

He dropped the letter. "Bless me?" he said while standing. "How has God blessed me?" His tone was washed with rage.

"Who blessed me when my Hailey was taken from me? Who is blessing me now that I'm sitting in this empty house?"

He fell to his knees and battered the pile of letters. "Some bless-ings." He gripped a letter and mangled it. He stood and glared at the mirror above the dresser. "I hate you," he yelled.

Hewitt grabbed another letter and ripped it open. His anger raged more as he read line after line from grateful parents. "Where is my reward for doing this?" he asked, waving the letter. "I don't hear you, God. A dead daughter. A wife who left me. A job I might not have much longer. What kind of a reward is this? Talk to me!"

He tore the letter apart and sprinkled the pieces everywhere. He swatted a picture of him and Veronica against the wall. The glass frame shattered, and the tiny splinters littered the floor. He stared at the picture, torn in the middle. "What have I done?"

CHAPTER 48

MICHAEL BANGED ON THE SIDE OF THE SHED. The wooden structure shook. He saw Julius sitting by the far wall, his feet up against one of the makeshift carts. He opened his eyes and frowned.

"You have my attention, traveler. How can I help you? Did you not speak to Paul?"

"I did. I have good news."

"I can always hear good news. What is it?"

"I have more silver."

Julius got up and examined the money in his hands. He stepped back. "I am curious. For a man who has never seen these tools, what is your interest in them now?"

"I am a writer. Like you."

"You are? What have you written?"

"Much of what I have written is stored at my home."

Julius walked back to him. "You said you have never seen these objects before, yet you say you have written. How?"

Michael glanced at the tablet. "On stones, scratching with a sharpened piece of metal."

"Like a man who lives in a cave?"

"I guess you can say that."

"Do you live in a cave?"

"I did."

Julius shook his head. "You are wise for a man who comes from a cave. I have never met someone like you. I do not know whether I can believe you."

"You can. I did live in a cave. I do read. I can write." He dropped four more pieces of silver in Julius' hands. "Is this enough?"

Julius paused and nodded. He removed a tablet from the pile and gave one to Michael.

"The other tool?"

"You need this? Do you not carry one of your own? You did say you had one back home."

"It is not like the one I have there, and I do not have it with me. I need one now."

Julius held out his hands.

"Will two pieces be enough?"

"It shall."

They made the exchange, and Michael rushed to Paul. "I have this," he said.

"Sit down," said Paul.

"Is this why I am needed here to travel with you?"

"I do not think so," said Paul. "It is me who is needed here to be with you."

Michael shook his head. "No. Your rabbi told me I had to travel with you."

"Indeed. I am here for you."

Michael placed the tablet down. "Me?"

"Yes. You."

He looked at the bent part of the short rod. He let it slide through his fingers a couple of times. *Just like a pen or pencil.* "Let me try this," he said. *Paul – Malta.* "I can make this work," Michael said in a surprised tone.

Paul smiled. "Why would you think you could not? Are you not a writer?"

"I am. How did you know I was?"

"You had your instructions. I have mine."

"I am ready. What do you need me to write?"

"You do not need me to tell you what to write. What have you seen while on our journey?"

"Much."

"What do you feel? What is in your heart?"

"Plenty. I have so many emotions."

"Write."

Michael moved the tool across the tablet, writing about the boat trip, the encounters he saw, the people who survived and the miracles he witnessed. He transcribed the emotions of the journey. He looked up as he was almost done and saw Paul was staring. "Is there anything wrong?"

"No. Much is right about our moments together. I am praying for us."

"Why us? Will not God protect us?"

"Our Father is not here to protect us. He is here to guide us."

"You seem worried," Michael said.

"My sunsets ahead are few."

"Are you in danger now?"

"In a world full of hate and anger, those who believe with their hearts that peace and love is the way and dare to proclaim it in front of many, risk far more than those who stay silent."

Michael leaned forward. "Are they going to kill you when you get to Rome?"

"You do not know?" Paul asked. "I thought you already read the words."

Michael didn't answer.

"They cannot kill what is in my heart. Write, Michael. Write."

So he did. He transcribed how first Paul survived a snake bite and how he amazed the natives with his strength. He told the story of how Paul united the island to accept the workers and soldiers so they had more time to plan an escape. When he had no more room to write another word, Michael dropped the rod and held up the tablet.

"A work of love," Paul said.

"Might be my best writing," Michael answered.

"Your most important writing cannot be questioned now."

He nodded and handed Paul the tablet.

"No," said Paul, giving it back to him. "You must carry this to Luke."

"Now?"

"Yes. He will know what to do with it. Keep your eyes open and listen. Write."

"How will I find him?"

"He will find you." Paul grabbed his arm as he stood up. "Do not let anyone know you have this."

"I will see you on the boat."

"Pray that you do."

CHAPTER 49

Hewitt tucked a parent's letter into his top pocket before unplugging his laptop. He slid it into a black leather case and placed it on top of a small table in the hallway. He straightened his tie while looking in the mirror above the closet door. *I may be off this case, but I have an obligation to that girl. To Hailey too. Holligan isn't going to have a clue what to do with this case. If I can't find her, nobody will.* He touched the keys on his cell phone. "Hello, Susan. I know it's Christmas Eve. I just need a few minutes of your time."

"I'm here with my mom. Please don't frighten her. She's old and has a hard time remembering anything."

"All I want to do is find your friend and his daughter."

"We're here," she said.

Hewitt pulled out the black book. He fingered through it again and tucked it back in with the computer. He walked to the door and stopped. "No. I need it." He retrieved the black book. *Should I be taking potential evidence? Can this really be evidence?*

The doorbell rang and Hewitt froze. He gripped the book tighter as he heard a knocking too. *What would Holligan think of this book? Would it help him in the case? Or would it steer him off course? Jeez. I need this.*

The doorbell rang again. "Coming," he shouted. Hewitt placed the book on top of the case and opened the door. "Holligan."

"Hewitt. Nice picture on the net. Where's your computer?"

"It's in the hallway," Hewitt said.

Holligan picked up the black book and read the first page. He glared at Hewitt. "This is some of the evidence you found? Are you kidding me? Is this what you've been working from?"

Holligan tossed the book back. "Does your laptop have all the contacts and notes?"

Hewitt handed him a sheet of paper. "Here are all the file numbers and descriptions of the content."

"Impressive," Holligan said as he read the sheet.

"If you have any questions, you have my cell number," Hewitt said.

"I think it's best a new pair of eyes moves on with this investigation, Special Agent. I don't believe I'll need to talk to you anymore. It's time to try other methods of finding my niece. It's obvious the way you have handled this case you weren't close to finding her at all."

"And him."

"What?" he asked as he closed the case.

"Michael Stewart. We are trying to find him too. Right?"

"This case may have baffled you, Paul. But, knowing my brother-in-law as I do and his history, it's a pretty safe bet he has my niece. And he's not sitting around here in Northport."

"What history is that? I didn't find anything alarming after digging into his past. I interviewed every person close to him."

Holligan tucked the case under his arm and poked Hewitt in the shoulder with his hand. "A guy who couldn't keep a job his whole life. Does that not ring a bell?"

"Maybe he was unlucky?"

"Six times losing his job? That says something more than unlucky."

"Probably got laid off due to the economy. It hasn't been good in a while."

Holligan brushed past him and turned around. "So, this is what happens to someone who loses their perspective? Goes all soft?"

He shook his head and walked away. "Good luck with your next assignment," Holligan said. "I hope you enjoy pushing papers across a desk." He slammed the door shut.

Hewitt stared at the lone Christmas card swaying back and forth, stuck to the back of the door. *Maybe he's right.* He sat down on the stairs and wiped a speck off his black shoe. *Have I gone soft? Is this the reason why I can't think clearly with this case? Has it affected my ability to deduce in a rational way and notice the evidence? Am I not being tough enough during the interviews?*

He left the house and sat for a few minutes in his car. He gazed into the rearview mirror. "I guess we're going to find out how tough I am." He inserted a bullet into his gun.

ᛏ

Susan's mom's house was decorated in green and red Christmas ribbons. A wide, live pine tree reached high, the top of the angel's head touching the ceiling. Colored lights blinked in rhythm while soft holiday music played. The smell of baking filled the living room air, apparently from a big plate of chocolate cookies shaped like Christmas trees sitting in the middle of the coffee table. She placed a bag of crackers on it too, with a bowl of candy.

Susan handed Hewitt a cup of coffee, its steam dancing up to his nose.

"Where is your mom? I'd like to speak to her too."

"She's unavailable."

"Where is she?"

"Sleeping. She needs her rest. Whatever you need I can help you with it."

"She isn't ill, is she?" Hewitt asked.

"She has her good days. She has her bad days. I guess that's all you can ask for. Right?"

Hewitt nodded and took a sip. "I'm sorry to bother you this evening. I know it's been a difficult time for you, and it should be spent with your family."

Susan glared. "Then why aren't you spending it with yours?"

Hewitt put his cup down and wiped his mouth with a napkin. "I apologize. I feel I'm at the end of the investigation and I have nowhere else to turn."

Susan leaned forward. "At the end? Are you giving up?"

"Should I?" he asked, picking up a cracker.

"How would I know? You're the FBI guy."

"Look, Susan. There's a lot at stake here. Two lives could be in danger. I know you were close with Michael."

Susan sipped her tea, staring at him.

"If Michael Stewart was going to confide in anyone, it would be you. I know about your relationship with him."

Susan dropped her cup onto the table. Some of it spilled down the side and onto the floor. "Did you hack my emails? I'll call a lawyer before you can step out of this house."

Hewitt shook his head. "I spoke to your buddy."

"My buddy?"

"Connie."

"Oh, please. She may be his sister, but she has no idea what kind of a person Michael is."

"And you do. It's why I'm here now. Help me. Please." He leaned forward. "Help me."

Susan finished a chocolate bar in three bites. "I've seen some extraordinary things happen since I've been back," she said. "What should make sense doesn't. What shouldn't make sense does. Does that make sense?"

Hewitt stood up and reached into his back pocket, pulling out the black book. He held it up as he sat back down. "Do you know about this?"

"I've read it."

"You have?"

"Yes. So what?"

"Is this for real or are you like me, wondering how much whiskey the people drank before writing such stories? Are these the type of people that see Jesus in their toast or oatmeal in the morning?"

Susan began nibbling on another cookie. "I've read the book, yes. But I've never seen any of the events described in it. For all I know, Michael is in Aruba with his daughter."

Hewitt placed the book beside the plate of cookies. "It's either real or it's not. Do you believe it's possible? What did Michael say to you? Did the pastor speak to you about this book? I've had the handwriting analyzed for the last few pages, and it was written by Pastor Dennis."

Susan put her half-eaten cookie down and wiped her mouth with a napkin.

"Tell me, what is going on in that church?"

She picked up her cup, walked into the kitchen, and poured herself another cup of tea.

"Would you like some more coffee?" she asked.

"I'm fine."

Susan returned and took a small sip. She flinched and put it down. "This is what I can tell you."

"I'm listening," Hewitt said.

Susan told him about the accident and Michael's cloth.

"Where is the cloth?" he asked.

"I don't know. I last saw Michael with it."

"What kind of a cloth was it? What could it mean?"

"It looked like any cloth you would use to clean a car or dust a lamp," Susan said. "I don't know what it could mean. I've thought about it many times. I've tried to rationalize it in every way and I can't. I can't really tell you with an honest heart what it means. Was it a miracle? I don't know. But have you ever thought about the miracles that happen around us every day?"

Hewitt leaned back against the hard wooden chair. It creaked so he reached down to hold the sides. "What miracles are you talking about?"

"They happen every minute, every day in this world. For instance, birth – a baby being born. Think about the enormity of it. Just because it happens every day doesn't mean it isn't a miracle."

"I'm not following your train of thought," Hewitt said.

She sighed. "There are many miracles mentioned in that book. Do we agree?"

He nodded.

"People finding their way to God or Jesus or whatever name you prefer. Maybe it's an everyday miracle like birth. Maybe this happens but we just don't see it."

"Come on, you don't believe that, do you?"

"To be honest, after experiencing the last few weeks here, I don't know what to believe." Susan got up. "Wait here. I want to show you something."

She returned minutes later with a big, brown box. "I'm not the most spiritual woman in this world, so I've refrained from sharing this with most people."

Susan moved the plate of cookies and her cup of tea. She opened the box and began dropping the contents on the table. Hewitt rummaged through them. "Look at the coins," she said.

He picked one up. "So?"

"They're from the First Century. Right?"

"Could be. There are many like this around, especially in Europe. Not a big deal."

He continued to go through the articles. "What is this?" he asked. "Something to sew with?" Hewitt leaned to his side and looked at it under the lamp.

"Looks like a bent rod. Can't use this for knitting," Susan said.

Hewitt felt the object. "This isn't your ordinary, everyday rod used for knitting." He got up and looked around the living room. "Do you have a computer, a laptop?"

"Over there," said Susan, pointing. "Why?"

"Show me."

She led him into a small room. A big, wide plastic box filled the old wooden desk.

"You've got to be kidding," he said.

Susan shrugged. "My mom never upgraded."

Hewitt sat down, and the chair wobbled. "Terrific."

"It's not meant to hold a heavy person."

"Do you know how to use this?" he asked as he moved the mouse around.

She leaned over his shoulder and grabbed it, clicking away. The buzzing sound of a dial-up modem erupted.

"Wow. I thought this way of connecting went out the same time as the dinosaurs."

"It works for her," she said, letting go of the mouse.

They waited for several moments for a connection. Hewitt typed in a URL and pleaded. "Come on, this is torture."

"You would know," Susan said.

Hewitt glared at her as she shrugged her shoulders. "Did I say something wrong? Here it comes," Susan said as she leaned over him again.

"Come on, work with me," Hewitt said.

A picture of a metal rod began to emerge on the screen. Only the top portion was visible. "I need to see more. Give me more," he said. The picture continued to download slowly. "More, more, come on." As he removed the cell phone from his front shirt pocket, the last part of the picture downloaded.

"Wow," said Susan.

"Just what I thought," Hewitt said, holding up the rod to the screen. He turned around and grasped her hand. "Can I keep this?"

CHAPTER 50

WORKERS WERE PACKING CARTS AND LOADING MATERIALS while Roman soldiers were putting on their armor. Michael spent some time near the shore, looking for Dennis. He gazed into the distance wondering if his best friend would return. *He did say he would be there if he was needed. I know he said this. This means he will come back. But when? Where are you, Dennis? Where did you go? I do need your help. I need you now. Can you hear me?*

He juggled the remaining silver Dennis gave him and returned to the camp. He dried himself off and bought two more tablets from Julius. He spent the final moments on Malta watching, listening and transcribing the experiences Paul was living.

He only rested when his hand would tire, taking periodic breaks to drink water and eat bread. Elizabeth joined them later in the day and helped write some thoughts of his time on the island.

"You are like the brave women that follow us," Paul said to her. "Smart," he said, pointing to his head. "Loving," he continued, touching his heart. "Loyal."

Elizabeth smiled and kept writing. When she tired, Michael would resume.

"There will be men who will try to destroy the work," Paul said as Michael wrote on the last empty space. "There will be men who will try to poison these words. You must be careful of whom you give this to."

"We shall."

Paul gave him a big piece of cloth. "Place the works inside this. Carry it with you until you are approached."

"Until I see Luke?"

"Yes. Only him."

"What does he look like?"

"Much like me. More hair." Paul pointed to the top of his head.

Michael nodded and wrapped the cloth around the tablets.

"You would be wise to eat before we take our next journey," Paul said.

"Elizabeth, go get something. I'm fine."

She left and Michael sat back down across from Paul. "I have so many questions for you."

"It is I who have questions for you," Paul said.

"Really?"

He nodded.

"I guess you want to know about our progress, the technology that has made our world so wonderful."

"Is it? Are there no more wars? No more hate?"

Michael hesitated and shook his head.

Paul looked down for a brief moment and rubbed his forehead. "This is confusing. During our last talk, you told me so much about your world, where you come from. All this progress man has made. I want to know how such progress can still lead to hate. If man communicates better in your time, why is there still anger? Still wars?"

Michael sat back. "I never thought of it that way."

"I sense men from your time look at us as old relics and believe they are more wise than we are. More aware. Yet the men of your time still kill, still destroy, still do not respect life."

Paul shook his head. "We live in an unforgiving time where new ideas become reasons to silence the faithful. I do not see much difference between our time and the time you have told me about."

"I think we are a more tolerant society."

"Are you?" Paul leaned forward, his eyes as wide as Michael had seen them. "Your time is only possible because of what my rabbi has done and taught. Perhaps someday the men of your time will be grateful and shun the tables of silver your men place before you."

"There are many good men and women who give from their hearts," Michael said.

"There are. Seek them out. They will not be present in tall buildings or tables that are full of glitter." He raised his hand high. "They will not ask you for your silver in my rabbi's name. The people you need to seek will live in poverty, limp with ills, and love more with little."

"Paul, we are almost prepared to travel," said Julius, peeking his head into the small tent. "Are you ready to leave?"

He nodded and looked at Michael. "Are you prepared to travel?"

"I am," he said.

Paul left while Michael noticed several men with buckets dousing the remaining flames of the campfires. A long line of workers stretched from the tents to the shoreline as they hauled boxes of supplies. "How long is the trip to Rome?" Michael asked Augustus.

"How the wind blows is my best guess."

"Is it wise to leave now while there is no light?"

"There is danger behind us. Another ship. Warring soldiers we are told."

"Who said this?" Michael asked.

"A soldier from the other ship that has just arrived. He said there is a soldier named Titus seeking some vengeance. I gain more silver when I bring my prisoners in alive than dead. I have lived enough to know that I should stay out of such a man's way."

"We must leave now," Michael said, with urgency.

"Remain calm. We are almost ready."

"Do you know where my daughter is?"

"She is in your shed."

Michael rushed back and found her talking to Paul. "We need to be ready to leave as soon as possible."

"You look pale as a ghost. What's wrong?" asked Elizabeth.

"Your father understands this journey now," Paul said. "Rome is not the only city where your journey should go." He walked past them and out of the shed. Three Roman soldiers followed, their spears drawn around him.

Elizabeth joined Michael outside. "He is coming. Am I right?"

He nodded and gripped the cloth with the tablets, tucking them under his right arm. "Whatever happens on the ship, protect this. Do not worry what happens to me. If need be, it will be you who carries it to Rome."

"You aren't going to stay behind, are you?" she asked.

"It's not my intention to do so. But if need be, I will."

"No. We have taken the journey this far together. We either leave together or we stay together."

He held the tablets with both hands. "This is why we were asked to take the journey."

Elizabeth nodded. "I know now. I know why you're here. I just don't know why I am."

The last boxes were removed from the sheds and taken to the shoreline. The captain thanked the natives and left behind some supplies and food for the community. Michael and Elizabeth followed Julius along the narrow dirt road to the beach. A bigger boat awaited them. The last bit of light on the horizon faded as they found a corner below deck to rest. Paul was huddled in the far corner across from them, his eyes open. The soldiers sat on wooden boxes facing him, their helmets off and spears on the floor. A lone light shone between the four on a cart.

"There's something wrong," Michael said.

"What? I do not see anything different. He is not being threatened."

"No, he's not but look at his eyes. I do not know him well, but I have looked into his eyes many times. Before I saw hope. Now I see sadness."

Elizabeth pushed herself forward with her hands. She leaned back. "Maybe he's worried about the ship."

"No. He knows something. I am going to have to see what is wrong when the soldiers fall asleep."

"What if they don't?"

Michael moved a few yards behind her on his knees. He opened a cart and removed a tall jug. He stuck his nose inside the container and held it up. "My weapon."

"What is it?"

"Wine. The heavy stuff."

"Heavy stuff?"

"Yes. No water added."

Elizabeth grimaced. "Oh, God. Not again." She put her head between her knees.

"Are you getting seasick?" he asked as the ship bounced a little. She shook her head.

"What's wrong?" Michael said, touching her shoulder.

"I'm seeing people again."

"What?"

Michael tried to lift Elizabeth's head. She pushed him away.

"What is the problem?" shouted a Roman soldier standing near Paul.

"Nothing. My daughter is feeling a little sick."

"Keep her silent," the Roman said.

Elizabeth rocked back and forth, moaning.

"You have to keep quiet," Michael said, rubbing her back. "I know about sea sickness. You may just need to go to the deck and get it out of your system."

Elizabeth turned and glared. "I'm not seasick." She started to cry.

"I'm sorry, honey. I don't mean to upset you. You've been through a lot. Rest."

"We can't rest. We're in danger."

"I know that."

Elizabeth shuddered and leaned into Michael's shoulder. "No. We're in danger now."

CHAPTER 51

CONNIE STROLLED ALONG THE PIER ALONE. There was a period of peace as she had the dock to herself. She thought about Elizabeth and Michael, wondering if they were somewhere safe so they could celebrate Christmas. She also questioned if Hewitt was right – that her brother had skipped town and was in another country with her niece.

As she neared the end of the pier, his voice startled her. "Hewitt, what are you doing out here? I thought you were going back home."

"I did," he said.

"Why are you back here?"

"I got more bad news," he said, facing her.

Connie's heart sunk into her stomach. "My God, you found them?"

Hewitt pulled away from her. "No. I haven't."

"Well, what's the news? Oh dear Lord, please tell me they're alive."

Hewitt took a few steps to the edge of the pier.

"What are you doing?"

"I have nothing left in my life. My boss just took me off a case for the first time in my career. I live alone at home. I stare at the walls after I finish my job. Now, I may not even have a job."

Hewitt sat down on a bench as the wind pushed the docked boats around Northport Bay. Connie sat next to him. "Divorce happens, and we all fail at our jobs every so often."

"I can't afford to fail at my job. When I fail, it means little boys and girls are coming home in body bags. Can't you understand that?" He stood and went to the edge again.

"Why don't you come back here and sit and talk?" Connie asked, patting the old wooden bench.

"I've done enough sitting and talking." He took off his coat and dropped it to the ground.

"Whoa," Connie said, standing. "Come back here."

"For what? To tell you how I can't figure out where your brother and niece have gone? To give you advice on how to handle a divorce? To tell you how I screwed up the only worthwhile aspect of my life? To cry about how I couldn't protect my daughter despite having all the money in the world?"

Hewitt slumped. "I used to think playing basketball was my identity. Then it changed when Hailey was born. She became my world. I was a father. I thought that would be my identity. When Hailey was taken from us, I had nothing. So, I made sure her disappearance wouldn't be in vain. I gave up everything – the money, the glory, the crowds. I knew if I were to make anything worthwhile out of my life, I had to do something big for Hailey. So I did. I became the best at what I did. Now, I have nothing. I am nothing."

Connie ran and put her arms around him.

"What are you doing?" Hewitt asked.

"I'm not letting you go."

"Then I'll take you with me," he said.

"Fine. We'll both sink to the bottom of the bay. But I'm going to try and convince you it will get better."

"Better," he said, trying to pull her hand off of him. "It doesn't get better."

She stuck her hand inside his belt, latching onto it.

"Let go," he said.

"I know you're bigger and stronger," she replied, gripping it tighter, "but you've helped so many people. And you still have to help me find my brother and niece. You can't give up."

Hewitt pulled her hand out from under his belt. "I suggest you leave. I wanted to find you and at least apologize. I had my doubts at first whether you truly cared about your brother. I do know now that I was wrong."

"I'm not leaving until we leave together."

"We're old and divorced and broken, Connie."

"We may be broken, but we're not dead," she pleaded. "There's no reason why we can't still think young, right?" She held onto his shirt pocket and put her hand on his cheek.

He grasped her hand and pushed her away.

"Don't," she screamed. "You're such a selfish bastard."

Hewitt shook his head and turned to her. "What? Selfish? Do you understand how many parents I've made happy the rest of their lives by finding their children? Do you realize how much commitment and emotional strength it takes to do such a job? Do you know how I felt when the only news I could give to parents was when their kids' bones were found? Do you? How dare you call me ungrateful! All that work I've done. I gave up my life."

Connie started to cry.

"That won't work," he said. "It worked before but not anymore."

She continued to weep, never letting her eyes move away from his.

"Go ahead, keep crying. It's typical of a woman to use tears to manipulate a man. I deal with women like you strictly with my brain and not my heart."

Hewitt continued to batter Connie with his classroom knowledge of how to cope in stressful situations. "This is the problem women have," he said, digging into his pocket. He pulled out a tissue. "It's why there are no females in our department. You need to remove the emotional attachment you might feel in these cases."

Connie glared and rushed him. Hewitt backed up slightly, holding onto a pole. She slapped him. "Your work isn't done. So put your jacket on and get back to finding my brother and niece."

Then she kissed him hard. "And I mean it." Her phone rang. She pulled it out of her purse and looked at it. "I've got to go and help a friend."

She stared at him for a brief moment. "Do you still want to take a swim?" She pushed him into the bay.

"Why'd you do that?" fumed Hewitt, flailing around. He grabbed onto the wooden pole and started to climb out of the water.

"I don't have any time for sulkers," she said, walking away. "Find my brother and niece!"

CHAPTER 52

THE SEA WAS QUIET. Only the bellowing sound of Augustus' voice stirred the evening calm. Michael watched Paul close his eyes. The three Romans scattered across the floor, armor removed. Two lay asleep on their sides, while the third sat on a box facing Paul. Michael could see his back slump and head lower.

"Go to sleep," he whispered to Elizabeth.

"How can I sleep? I'm a nervous wreck."

"You shouldn't be. There is no storm tonight."

"It's not the weather I'm worried about."

Michael put a finger up to his mouth. "Quiet." He reached into a cart behind him and retrieved a jug of wine. Michael grabbed two cups and got up. He steadied himself, holding onto a beam. *Relax. The sea is not so bad. Not like the last trip.* He bent over and took a short breath, running some saliva around his mouth to get rid of the nauseous taste.

"Are you sick again?" Elizabeth asked, holding onto his arm. "Sit down."

He put his hand out and took another breath. "I'm fine." He wobbled a few steps toward Paul, grabbing a beam every few feet.

Paul opened his eyes as Michael approached. His eyes widened as he pointed to the soldiers.

Michael held up the jug and winked. The Romans snored and shook, one kicking his spear away.

The soldier facing Paul tumbled off the cart. "What?" He turned and clenched Michael's arm. "Where are you going?"

"To share this," he said, handing him a cup. The Roman held onto his arm and glared. "You take risks, traveler. Not a wise one."

"I am sorry. I had this and it was fulfilling. Can I pour you some?"

The soldier released his grasp and nodded. Michael filled the cup to the top and sat down beside him. "Why not enjoy the journey?" he asked. "Michael is my name." He raised his cup.

"Alexander. Are you a Roman?"

"No."

"What is your business traveling this way?"

"I am with my friend, Paul," he said, lying.

"For how long?"

"A few sunsets."

Alexander stretched his arms and yawned.

"You look tired, my friend," Michael said.

"I am. This is my first journey. They sleep. I do not."

"I understand your superior does not give you much respect."

He nodded.

Michael poured wine into his cup. "Relax. The prisoner has nowhere to go. He cannot swim."

Alexander looked puzzled. "A man of the world like him cannot swim?"

"He is old, feeble."

"I am," Paul agreed.

Alexander gulped the wine and yawned again. "I need sleep. It will be a long journey to Rome."

"Rest then," Michael said.

"I will lose my pay if I do."

"I will watch him and wake you if he tries to move."

Alexander shook his head. "I cannot risk my pay. He is not to be touched. His safety fetches us all more silver."

"Well then, let us celebrate your first journey," said Michael, taking a sip and raising his glass again. "So good. I feel wonderful. Do you?"

"Let me have more of that," said Alexander. He took the jug away from Michael and emptied the last drops into his cup. He leaned on the cart and stretched his body after swallowing the remainder of the wine. As he rubbed his eyes and tried to straighten up, he held onto the wooden box. "Keep an eye on the prisoner," Alexander said. "I will share my silver with you."

He closed his eyes and lay on his side. His pouch fell to the floor, and two silver coins rolled toward Michael. He clamped his foot on them and placed the coins in his pocket. "Never know when I might need this," he said, looking at Paul.

Michael watched Alexander slip into a deep sleep, his snoring reaching a high pitch within minutes. He inched his way to Paul and looked behind him, noticing his hands were shackled.

"What happened?" Michael asked.

"Their kindness is no more," Paul said.

"I do not understand. What did Julius say?"

"He is frightened of me. He heard of your snakebite and how you were healed."

"I thought he knew."

"He only saw you getting up."

Michael rubbed his forehead. "That makes sense, but how did he find out?"

"A worker told him about your writing. He wanted to know why you needed the tablets."

"What are they going to do with you now?" Michael asked.

"I am preparing."

"For what?"

"The worst."

Michael stood. "We have to do something. We need to escape." Paul bent over and showed him the chains.

"I know. It is another problem to deal with." Michael held up the silver coins. "This money speaks here and anywhere I have been."

"It may not be enough."

Michael held onto a beam and looked around. He noticed another soldier sound asleep whose pouch lay near his face.

Paul shivered. "No," he said. "There is much risk for you and your daughter. Remember the tablets."

He grimaced. "I will not stand by and do nothing. I can tell Julius you did not heal me. I can say it was a spider bite, not a snakebite. He will believe me."

Paul shook his head. "The truth is the truth. Why change it? Is the truth not worth defending with one's life?"

"Do you not fear what the Romans will do to you?"

"No. I fear what you will do."

Michael sat beside him. "I see sadness in your eyes."

Paul did not answer. Michael noticed Elizabeth's eyes wavered, shutting and then opening several times.

Alexander rolled over on his stomach, his pouch wide open and showing more silver. Michael stared at it for several seconds and sighed. He crawled over to him and put back the two silver pieces. He rejoined Paul, took a deep breath and leaned against a beam.

"You are a good man, Michael."

Augustus' shouting had quieted on deck, and the rowing sounds of the oars striking the water were silent. The boat swayed back and forth. Julius came down the stairs in a frantic rush.

"We must leave. Now," he said, leaning down to unlock the shackles on Paul.

Michael got up. "Why? Are we there already?"

"No."

"Wake up," said Julius, nudging Alexander.

"What is wrong? Did the prisoner escape?"

"No, you fool," Julius said. "You fell asleep. We must swim the last part of the journey."

"Swim? How far?" Michael asked.

"I do not know. It is still dark. I cannot see the shoreline."

"We must go now," said Julius. "Alexander, get the others up. The prisoner and you will go. I will stay."

"Why must we do this now?" Michael asked.

"There is a rogue ship approaching us. They seek the prisoner. I have my orders to get him to Rome safely."

"I will go with him."

"Can you swim?"

"Does it matter?" He rushed to Elizabeth and shook her shoulder. "We need to go now."

"We're there?" asked Elizabeth, stretching her arms.

"No."

"Where are we?" she asked as she stood.

"I don't know." Michael emptied two carts. "Here," he said, handing her one. "Use this as a float."

He tucked the cloth with the tablets under his arm.

Julius stared at him.

CHAPTER 53

CONNIE SAT ON A COLD METAL BENCH IN FRONT OF JAX'S BAR. She pulled the cell phone out of her purse and touched the screen. She watched Hewitt running to his car across the street. "I owe you," he shouted while shivering. "Big time."

She glanced at him as he stopped his car in front of her. She waved with a smile and spoke. "Hey, Virginia. I got your call. Are you okay?"

"I am."

"How do you feel?"

"Nervous."

"Do you still need my help?"

"Yes, I'm scared. I know it's a strange question to ask, but you are my new best stranger."

"What do you need?"

"I know I have terrible timing. Of all nights I'm bothering you."

"You're not, Virginia. I'm here for you."

"I'm at Northport General."

"Now?"

"Yes," Virginia said.

Connie reached into her purse for a tissue. "What a night to have your baby. How many centimeters are you dilated?" she asked while wiping a tear away.

"They tell me eight."

"Are you being given any painkillers?"

"Yes."

"Okay, sweetie. I'm on my way."

"Thanks."

Connie put the phone back in her pocket and watched Hewitt get out of the car. "Well, my night is about to become more exciting."

"More exciting?"

"I'm sorry for pushing you in, but you deserved it. Mocking a woman in distress isn't a very smart move."

"You were trying to manipulate me."

"No. I was expressing how I felt. I need to go."

"Where?"

"A friend is about to have a baby."

Hewitt didn't respond.

"Can you give me a ride?"

Hewitt's eyes widened. "Wow, you have some gall."

"You owe me," Connie said.

"Owe you?" Hewitt turned around for a second and then faced her.

"Yeah, you do," said Connie as she stood. "I stopped you from becoming a whining hot mess."

"You pushed me into the bay."

"Yeah, I did. I'm glad I did. I bet it shook some sense into you."

Hewitt sighed. "Where is your car?"

"I walked."

"I'll give you the ride."

She nodded. "Thanks. She's three weeks early."

"Is that important?" he asked.

"I don't know. But I want to support her. And I hope everything turns out all right."

"Have the ultrasounds been good?"

"I believe so," she said, following him to his car.

"Then what's the problem?" he asked.

She stopped on the passenger side of the Cadillac, waiting for him to open the door. "She doesn't feel she can handle having a child in her life at this time."

"I'm sorry."

"I need to help her."

"How?" he asked, opening the door.

"Any way I can, even if I have to adopt the child."

"Wow," he said, sitting down and turning on the ignition. "That's a huge responsibility."

"I'm ready for it."

"Does she know you're willing to do this?"

Connie nodded. "Oh, yeah. Take me to Northport General."

"Sure. Do you have it in writing? You know there are no guarantees."

"I have her word."

"Having her word doesn't mean it would stand up in any courtroom."

Connie faced him. "I'm not interested in going into any court-room over a child."

Hewitt drove up Main Street. "We're about twenty minutes from the hospital. Are you sure about doing this? I've seen it turn out bad in situations like this."

"I'm not going to listen to your sad stories anymore," Connie said. "She needs my support. She has no one."

"She might feel differently after she has the baby."

Connie looked away. "I know. I don't need to be reminded of what might not happen. I just want to be there for her."

"Sure."

Connie stared outside as they passed the stores along Main Street. She noticed the toy store, beautifully decorated with a big green ribbon in the front window. "I want to be a mother, Hewitt," she said. "I want it so bad I can feel the baby in my arms. But I'd give it up if it meant having Elizabeth back home safely."

"I know you would."

She gave a faint smile and was surprised when he placed his hand on hers. "Stop."

"Why?"

"I want to go in the toy store and pick up something."

"Now?"

"It'll only take a couple of minutes."

Hewitt turned the car around and parked. "It might not be open now. It's starting to get late."

"I'll be right back," she said, shouting.

"I'll wait here."

"I won't be long."

Minutes later, Connie returned with a small bag.

"My Christmas present?" Hewitt asked.

"Ha. Next year, maybe," she said with a smile.

Hewitt turned off Main Street and gave her a quick glance. "You would make a good mom."

They sat in silence until they pulled into the hospital parking lot. Connie stayed motionless in her seat for a few moments while Hewitt rubbed his eyes. "You don't have to go in," he said.

She shook her head and took a tissue out of her purse. "That wouldn't be fair to Virginia. She has no one. It's about time I'm there for someone else."

. "Do you want to do this because you really want to or because of some guilt you need to erase?"

She wiped her eyes. "Probably both. No matter what happens I want to support her."

Hewitt touched her hand again. "Do you want me to come in?"

"That would be nice."

Hewitt smiled and Connie laughed. "What's funny?" he asked.

"You look like a dork," she replied.

"I thought dorks were cool today."

"Tonight they are."

They stopped at the main desk and received their visitor passes. Hewitt didn't flash his FBI badge. Instead, he went to the bathroom.

"Going to dry off?" asked Connie.

Hewitt raised his eyebrows. "Give me a few minutes."

Connie could hear the dryer blowing in the bathroom. She giggled a bit and stopped when Hewitt appeared. She smiled when Hewitt's shoes squished as they walked down the hallway. "I told you I was a great date," she said.

Hewitt grinned.

A nurse greeted them with gowns. "You are cleared to be in the room with Virginia. Sir, are you a friend?"

"He is," Connie said.

"Can I get some clothes?" Hewitt asked. "I had a little accident." Connie smirked.

The nurse nodded and returned minutes later with a robe.

"Please wear these," the nurse said. "Please listen to any instructions by the doctors and nurses in the room. Any questions?"

"No," said Connie.

The nurse guided them through two hallways and into a room at the far end. The area was quiet except for three nurses chatting outside a small desk.

"How eerie is this?" Connie said.

"What's wrong?" asked Hewitt.

"This is the same place I saw Elizabeth when she was born." She pointed to a big glass window. They stopped and looked. Row after row of babies lay in incubators.

"This way," said the nurse.

"Are you sure about this being the place?" asked Hewitt.

"Yeah. Very sure. You don't forget a place or a night like that."

He touched her shoulder. "I can go in there alone if you want."

"I'm fine."

"This way," the nurse said again, opening the door.

Virginia lay on a short bed with an IV protruding from her hand. A nurse in the corner wrote on a chart.

"Hey ya, sweetie. How are you doing?" Connie asked.

Virginia winced and struggled to say a few words. "I could use some more pain medicine."

"Nurse," Connie said.

The nurse continued to write on the chart.

"Nurse?"

"Here, hold this," said Connie, offering her hand to Virginia who squeezed it hard. "Wow, that's some grip you've got there, girl."

The smell of clean sheets and pillows softened Connie. "Excuse me. Can you help Virginia? She looks like she's in a lot of pain."

The nurse looked up and put the chart into a plastic holder attached to the back of the bed. "I'll be right there."

"Well, can it be right now?" asked Connie.

"Okay, Connie. Let's let the nurse do her job," said Hewitt.

"You're right," Connie said. "I apologize." She turned, looked at him and grinned. "See, the new me."

The nurse adjusted the pump. "How does that feel now?"

"Better," Virginia said.

"Hold my hand, sweetie," Connie said. "Squeeze it as hard as you want."

Virginia let out several small moans. "How many centimeters dilated is she now?" asked Connie, turning to the nurse.

"Nine. Almost ten."

"Okay. You're almost there, Virginia."

"Dr. McKenna will be in soon," the nurse said while dropping ice chips into a plastic cup. She placed it on a tray and swung it in front of Virginia. "Dr. McKenna's our best. He's been doing this for over twenty years."

"Do you hear that Virginia?" Connie said. "You're going to be fine."

"If I am going to be fine, why do I feel so awful?" She released a loud moan. Hewitt grimaced.

The nurse patted Virginia's forehead with a towel and placed it on the tray. "If you need anything else, press the red button." She handed her a device. "It won't be more than a few minutes before Dr. McKenna arrives."

Hewitt sat and Connie stroked Virginia's hair. She held the cup of ice chips to her lips. "Do you need anything else?"

Virginia shook her head. "Just stay." She moaned again, gripping Connie's hand.

"Crap," Connie said.

"You all right?" asked Hewitt.

She turned and mouthed the words, "That hurt."

Hewitt smiled.

"It's not funny," Connie said out loud.

"What's not funny?" screamed Virginia.

"Nothing, honey."

"Huh? Is that your husband?"

Connie looked behind her at Hewitt. He stood and joined them. "He's a good friend."

"You're a lucky woman to have him. Not many men would want to be around a screaming woman."

"I am."

"What's your name? I need to know if I'm about to moan some more. Do you scare easy?"

"Hewitt's my name."

"What an odd name. Oooooooh, God. That was a long one."

"What a way to meet, right?" he asked.

She half laughed and half moaned.

"Where is that doctor?" Connie asked.

"I'll go look for him," Hewitt said.

"Hang in there, Virginia," Connie said. "The doctor will be here soon."

She moaned and struggled to sit up.

The beeping sound of the heart monitor started to bother Connie. She took a deep breath as she watched Virginia grimace. "Are you feeling the drugs?"

"A little."

"Well that's not enough. Where's Hewitt? Where's that doctor?" Connie asked.

"The doctor is in," said a man entering the room. "Dr. McKenna at your service." He held out his hand to Connie.

"About time," she said.

"No. Perfect time," he said, examining Virginia. "She's ten centimeters dilated now."

"How do you know?" Connie asked.

"Well, when I did the internal exam, I could feel the head in the birth canal. This baby is ready to be born."

He stood and moved the tray out of the way.

"What are you doing?" asked Connie.

"It's showtime. Are you ready to push?"

Virginia screamed. "Yes."

"Oh, that's a good attitude. I'm glad because we need your full cooperation."

Dr. McKenna moved to the back end of the bed. "Nurse, please. Here," he said. A tiny table with several metal instruments was wheeled in and placed on the other side of the bed.

"Hold my hand, sweetie," Connie said. "Break it if you have to."

"Okay, Virginia, hold your breath and push," said Dr. McKenna. "Good girl, I think the head will be through with the next push. This contraction is over, so try to relax and rest for a few seconds until the next one starts."

"Oh my God," said Connie. "You're almost there."

"Oh no, here comes another one," groaned Virginia.

"All right, let's have another good push," Dr. McKenna implored. "Keep going, keep going."

"I can't. I can't," Virginia shouted.

"Yes you can," urged Connie, pressing her hand.

"No. No. He's staying in here until I have more money saved."

"Too late for that," Connie said. "He's coming and he's wanting his Christmas presents."

Hewitt joined Connie.

"I have no presents under the tree for him," Virginia said.

"There'll be plenty of gifts for him," Connie replied. She turned around and motioned to the shopping bag in the corner. "Get it."

Hewitt handed her a neatly wrapped small box with a red ribbon stuck on top in the middle.

"Do you see this?" Connie asked, showing it to Virginia.

"Yeah. So what?"

"The first present under your tree for your boy."

"My boy?"

"Yes. Your boy."

"But … "

"Quit the chitchat, ladies," pleaded Dr. McKenna. "Here's his head." He pushed the head in slightly and adjusted the child so one shoulder would come out first. "Give me another good push," he pleaded. "Come on Virginia, push."

"Push, honey, push," Connie said.

"Nice job!" Dr. McKenna said.

"Am I done?" Virginia asked, panting.

"Almost. One more push," he said. "There he is, a handsome little fellow."

"Wow," Hewitt said.

"Is he beautiful?" Virginia asked, gasping. "What color is his hair? His eyes? Connie, tell me."

"What?"

"Tell me what he looks like."

Connie let go of her hand and went behind Dr. McKenna.

"Tell me. What color is his hair?"

"Hold on a second, sweetie." Connie watched the nurses care for the baby, assessing his condition. They took a couple of minutes cleaning the blood and amniotic fluid off of his reddened skin, finally drying him with three white towels.

"His hair is brown, Virginia," Connie said.

"His eyes?"

"They look blue."

"Is he beautiful?"

"Yes. Like you."

Virginia cried.

Connie glanced at the baby one more time and then stared at Hewitt.

CHAPTER 54

SOLDIERS RAN IN DIFFERENT DIRECTIONS, as Augustus demanded his workers find hiding places for cover. An emerging fog obstructed Michael's and Elizabeth's vision as they rushed to the deck. The workers dropped a small boat overboard and threw two oars down.

"Help the prisoner to the boat," Julius said. "Hurry." He approached Michael. "The boat is not big enough for two more people," he said.

Michael pushed Elizabeth toward him. "She will go."

She shoved back. "I will not. I am not leaving you here with those butchers coming."

Julius waved his arms in the air. "Decide. One will need to go. Rome demands it. Go to the boat now." He walked away.

"Elizabeth – "

"Hold on, Dad. Can you hear that?" she asked, looking over the railing.

"What?"

"The noise. Come here."

"We do not have time to sightsee, Elizabeth." He grabbed her arm, but she wrestled his grip away.

"Listen, Dad."

A small buzzing sound hovered several yards away. He leaned over the railing. "Quiet," he said.

Out of the fog, about fifty yards away, emerged a big ship with several Roman soldiers lined up in military fashion, amassed on the deck. A man shouted from a top tier of a bridge. As they drew closer, the man's shouting became more audible. "You have a prisoner of mine," he yelled.

"Get the plank," Julius demanded. Two workers grabbed a long, wide wooden board and extended it out into the ocean. It was big enough to march soldiers two by two across. "Hold," he told the workers. He climbed up and took several steps out.

Michael grabbed Elizabeth's arm and dragged her to the other side of the boat. "Get down," he ordered.

They watched Julius take two more steps as the approaching ship stopped. "We have our instructions to take the preacher of Jerusalem to Rome, Titus. My orders are clear."

"It is not the preacher I seek," Titus said. "I am looking for a man named Michael who kept company with my sister-in-law."

"What are you talking about?"

"This man Michael of Jerusalem has committed many crimes against the Roman Empire."

"What crimes are they?"

"Obstructing a trial. Freeing a Jew and her peasant daughter. The women are wanted for the murder of Marcus, a decorated Roman soldier. The man is also wanted for assaulting a Roman soldier."

"I know about your brother. My condolences." Julius put up his hand.

"Let me examine the ship," Titus demanded. "I have a right as a Roman soldier."

"No need," Julius said. "I will seek this man out. Perhaps he has hidden somewhere."

"You must go now, Elizabeth," Michael whispered. "One of us should be with Paul. Take these." He handed her the tablets in the cloth.

"I won't be safe going to Rome," Elizabeth said.

"You're not going to be safer on this boat. We have to take a chance with you going to Rome."

"Where will we meet?" she asked.

"Just keep your eyes and ears open."

"That's not an answer," she said as she was helped by one of the workers into the small boat.

"It's the best one I have." Michael glanced at Alexander, who stood frozen, glaring.

"Go," Augustus pleaded to them. "Now!"

Michael crawled to the opening of the stairway and tumbled down the steps. He opened a cart and grabbed his writing tool. *I guess this will have to do. What a way to defend myself. It better be mightier than a sword.*

"What are you doing down here?" asked Julius as he entered the lower deck.

"Just getting some rest," Michael said, lying.

"Where is your daughter?"

"I told her to go. My friend will need her."

"Good. Titus will not let this ship move until they have someone. I do not want him boarding this boat because I have cargo that would be of interest to him."

"I will surrender," Michael said.

Julius nodded and looked around. "What you did to save your daughter is noble," he said. "I must now save my cargo."

Michael walked past him and up the stairs. Julius instructed Augustus to push the board closer to the other ship while Titus stepped onto the wide board. "We will take the prisoner now," Titus said. He met Michael in the middle, aided by one Roman soldier wielding a spear. They pushed Michael ahead a few steps. "You are hereby arrested for aiding two women accused of murdering a decorated Roman soldier. You will be tried before a court at the Antonia Fortress in Jerusalem."

Titus pulled Michael's hands behind his back and tied them with a thick rope. "Walk slowly," he said.

"I am, you jerk." He swung his hands back, hitting Titus.

"Janikus," Titus said. "If he jumps, bleed him with your spear."

"Yes sir," he replied, keeping his weapon pressed into Michael's back.

The buzzing sound escalated to a low hum as Michael inched his way along. *What is that?* He looked up and saw a bit of clearing in the fog. The hum rose louder, and he moved a few more steps to get a better view.

"Slow down," said Titus.

Michael could see the deck of the other ship and stopped. Soldiers were moving up and down, swinging their spears. *Looks like locusts. Or is it? Something is certainly wrong.*

"Keep moving," said Titus.

"I am not taking another step."

Janikus poked his back. "You heard him. Move."

"I do not think it is wise to move this way anymore."

"Shut up and walk," Titus shouted.

The hum closed in and surrounded them. Michael froze and pushed the spear away. He stared as the cries from soldiers rang out. *They are jumping into the water.*

"Sir," Janikus said. "Our ship. What is happening?"

Titus and Janikus edged past Michael. "What is going on?" Titus yelled to the soldiers in the water.

Michael moved a few steps backward. "See you on the other side, boys."

"Janikus, do not let him escape. Kill him if you have to."

The Roman lunged at Michael as he backed away from the spear's edge.

"Whoa," Janikus said, stumbling. He steadied himself on the plank. The board wobbled and Titus fell, holding on with one hand.

"Sir," Janikus said, reaching down. "Are you all right?"

"I cannot swim. My leg is wounded. Help me."

The board bumped up and down when Janikus fell to his knees, letting his spear fall into the water. Michael slipped and tumbled into the sea.

"Help me," Titus screamed.

Michael submerged several feet. He kicked and flailed away. Titus grabbed his leg as he struggled. *Get off of me.* He kicked him several times, pushing him away. *Oh, Lord. I don't want to die.* He kicked harder, struggling with the knot. *I am not letting my daughter grow up alone. I am going to hold my grandkids.* He twisted his hands and wrists, managing to loosen the knot. He swam to the surface about thirty yards from the ships.

Michael coughed up some water and gazed at what was in front of him – white birds hummed and floated around Titus and his soldiers. Their ship's deck was empty. *My God.*

"Sir, I cannot hold onto you any longer; you will need to swim," Janikus yelled to Titus, releasing his grip. He stood and shouted at some soldiers floating in the water several yards away. "Help him," he said.

Two soldiers started to swim toward Titus. Michael looked back and watched as he reached Augustus' ship. The swarm of birds drew closer, skimming off the water. "They're doves," Augustus said as one flew past him.

"There have to be hundreds of them," Michael said, looking up in amazement.

"Grab my hand, my friend," he said.

Michael grasped it and was pulled back onto the deck by two other workers.

"Row," Augustus shouted to the men. Their oars struck the water, and the ship began to move. The plank fell. "Faster. Faster. Move your arms. Faster."

The ship created some distance between the two vessels. The doves continued to hum and swarm as the soldiers waved their hands in frantic gestures, trying to keep them away.

Michael and Augustus stood side by side, staring. Michael tried to communicate his thoughts, yet he couldn't muster any words. The doves swirled around the soldiers much like a tornado. Michael walked to the far end of the ship to get a better look. Some soldiers covered up their faces and others kept submerging, avoiding the swarm.

"I have never seen anything like that before," Augustus called out. "Have you?"

Michael shook his head. "Never."

When there was enough distance between the two ships, Michael shook himself out of his daze. He rushed down the stairs. "Julius, I escaped."

"I was a witness. It is time we get you to Rome."

"My daughter?"

"She left a while ago with the prisoner."

Michael dropped to his knees. "Thank goodness."

Julius bent over. "You must leave this ship once we reach land. They will hunt you down. I hope you made some friends on this boat."

Michael nodded.

Julius walked away and climbed the stairs.

Michael looked across and saw Alexander glaring at him.

CHAPTER 55

THE CHILD WAS WASHED AND CLEANED on a table a few yards away from Virginia. The nurses wrapped him in a long, white baby blanket as Connie filled a plastic cup with ice and water. She gave it to Virginia and wiped her forehead with a towel. A nurse offered her tea or juice and placed some crackers in front of her.

"You did great," Connie said, holding her hand.

"We haven't known each other long, but I feel there's a reason why you're in my life now," Virginia said.

Connie smiled. "I was thinking the same thing."

"Where did your friend go?" Virginia asked, sitting up.

Connie looked behind her and noticed Hewitt had taken his coat. "Maybe he needs some air. Men aren't as strong as we are."

Virginia laughed. A nurse pushed her forward and removed a pillow, replacing it with a fresh one. Connie helped her adjust. "How are you doing now? I was worried. You sounded worried about everything."

"I'm all right now," Virginia whispered. "Thank you. It's okay because of you. You're like the big sister I never had."

"Sister?"

"Yes."

Connie let go of Virginia's hand and moved away from the bed. "I guess I can live with that."

The nurse handed Virginia the baby. She smiled. "My God, he does have blue eyes. I wonder if he will keep them."

"Like the father?"

"Yes. He does have the most beautiful eyes." She paused and looked up at Connie. "When I met you, I was so freaked out about becoming a mother."

"You were scared," said Connie, moving back to the bed. She put her hands on the metal railing. "I could see you had the deer-in-the-headlights look. I've seen it a few times when I've looked in the mirror."

"Really," said Virginia as she touched the baby's hands, placing her finger inside.

"Yeah, on my wedding day." Connie laughed.

"You know the night we went out to talk at the diner? First, thank you for answering my call so late at night." She paused and stroked the baby's light brown hair. "I wasn't in a good place."

"I didn't think so. I heard the desperation in your voice." Connie watched her whisper a few words to the baby, then kiss his rosy pink cheeks. "I'm always here for you. Always. Okay?"

Virginia put a blue cap on the baby's head. "Can we continue to talk? About anything?" she asked her.

"Anything?" Connie hesitated. "Sure. I can handle whatever you need from me."

"It was an emotional time for me. I've been under a lot of stress."

"I know," Connie said, turning away for a second. *Where is Hewitt?*

"I guess it's true what they say about a mother and her baby," she said.

"What's that?"

Virginia sighed and rubbed the baby's back. He cooed a little. "Once you hold your baby, you can't let them go."

Connie nodded and rushed to get her purse. She dropped it back to the seat and put on her coat.

"Do you want to hold him before you go?"

She took a few steps toward the door and turned around, noticing Virginia was holding the baby up.

"Please, Connie, I want you to be his godmother."

She nodded. "That would be nice," she said, wiping away a tear.

Virginia handed the baby to her, and Connie rocked him back and forth in her arms. "You are so beautiful," she said. "You have the best looking eyes."

"He does," Virginia agreed.

"I'm going to sing you a song. I sang this many years ago for my niece. Are you ready, young man?" She glanced at Virginia and saw her eyes were moist. "To market, to market to buy a fat pig, home again, home again, jig a jig, jiggety-jig." Connie steadied her emotions and began the next verse. " … home again, home again, away from that cranky nurse."

Virginia laughed and wiped her eyes with a tissue.

Connie handed her the baby. "Talk soon," she said, picking up her purse. She rushed out of the room, down the hallway, and out into the nearly empty parking lot. She sat on the curb and lowered her head.

"I'm sorry," said Hewitt. He placed his hand on her head and sat beside her. "Come here." He gave her a hug.

She looked up at him. "Did you know she wouldn't go through with it?"

"I peeked in and saw her reaction when she held the baby. I've seen it a few times. It's much like when I've reunited kids with their parents. That first touch is much like the first touch when reunited." He handed her a couple of tissues.

"You're so prepared about life," said Connie.

He gave her a faint smile. "No. I'm lost."

"I should have realized this would happen," she said.

"How would you know? You opened up your life and offered a wonderful solution to a broken-hearted mother. There's no greater gift you could give to a mother in need."

She wiped her eyes. "Since when have you become so wise about relationships?"

"I can grow as a person too."

"We both have grown, haven't we?"

He touched the top of her head. "Yeah, we have. Once you stop your whining and feeling sorry for yourself, you can actually see how wonderful your life really is. Even someone like you can be tolerable."

She smacked him on his shoulder. "Tolerable?"

He laughed.

She put her wet tissues into her purse.

"You know you can still adopt," Hewitt said.

"Takes time. Takes a lot of money."

"Yes, I know. I've been doing some research. But it's worth it."

"When have you been researching this?" asked Connie.

"The past couple of days. I know you would be a great mother. Haven't I said this already?"

She nodded. "Can we take a walk down Main Street?"

"Sure. Let's enjoy this Christmas."

"There's a novel concept," Connie said. "Enjoying Christmas." She took a deep breath and gazed at the evening sky. As they walked through the parking lot, she felt her worry return for just a brief moment.

CHAPTER 56

WOODEN BOXES SLID A FEW FEET SIDE TO SIDE as a strong wind whistled below deck, catching Michael off guard. He clung to a beam and landed on a pile of carts. He watched Alexander lurking at the far end.

"Look away," he said to Michael. "You are no friend of mine."

"What you may have heard is not true," Michael said. "My daughter did not murder the Roman soldier. Our friend did not murder Marcus. They defended themselves, just like you would if another man threatened you."

Alexander stood and gave him a menacing stare. "Why would I believe a man who speaks strange words and cannot tell me where he comes from?" He took a couple of steps toward him, spear in hand.

Michael staggered to his feet as the cart beneath him slid a few feet away. "Whoa, I have got to find a better way to get around."

"There," Alexander said, holding his spear forward. "You talk not like any man I know." He pointed it at his face. "Where are you from?"

"Jerusalem, outside the city wall."

Alexander shook his head. "You do not speak like any man from Jerusalem I know."

"I live way beyond the city wall."

"How far?"

"Beyond the aqueduct."

"Are you like the prisoner? A preacher?"

"No," Michael said, putting his hands up. "I am just a man who lives with his daughter on a farm."

"Where is your wife?"

Michael lowered his head. "She died many sunsets ago."

Alexander took a couple of steps back and lowered his spear. Michael looked up and saw him sitting on a box. The rocking motion of the boat slowed. Michael peered up through the opening by the small stairway and noticed Julius was talking to Augustus. *I wonder what is going on. No one is rowing.*

"Do you know why the ship has stopped?" Michael asked Alexander.

"I do not know. I do know I get paid whether we sail or not."

Michael raced up the steps and to the deck. He waited for the two to finish their conversation. Julius turned toward him and frowned. "We must change our journey."

"Augustus, what is going on?" Michael asked.

"We have a problem with this ship. There is that, too." He motioned to the horizon.

"I cannot see anything," Michael said.

"Feel the wind," Augustus said. "Listen."

"I am. The wind is brisk. So?"

"What?"

"It is strong."

"Turn," Augustus instructed his rowers.

"This is a bigger ship than the last one. This one should be able to get through a storm."

"No, my friend. This ship leaks, and I am wasting men removing the water when they can be pushing it forward."

"We are going back to Malta?"

"No. Back to Caesarea."

"Why there?"

"Because it is the safest place for us."

"No, Augustus! Please. My daughter! She is on the other boat, going to Rome. You must keep going to Rome. Please!"

Augustus shook his head and walked away. "Julius is the man with the silver," he said. "What he says goes." His voice became faint.

Michael raced to Julius and grabbed his arm, struggling with him. "Stop! Release me," Julius said.

"No. I am not letting go until you head back to Rome."

They jostled for several moments before the altercation alerted a couple of Romans at the far end of the boat. "Sir, is there a problem?" one shouted to them.

Julius glared at Michael. "Is there, traveler?"

Michael gripped his arm tighter and twisted it. "Guards!" Julius shouted.

Michael released his hold and pushed him away. Julius pointed at him. "You take many risks for a man whose head can fetch silver." Michael stayed on deck, still glaring at Julius walking away.

"I need to calm down," he said to no one in particular. He saw the horizon was shining its last light. *I am going to have to find a way to turn this ship back. I'll have to steal a weapon or two. There's no way this ship can go to Caesarea.*

He pounded the top part of the wooden deck. *I never should have let her go. She would have been better staying here with me.* He sighed. *No, she wouldn't be safer here. She was protected with Paul.* He shouted at the top of his lungs, looking skyward. "I've helped Paul. I've written what needed to be written." He took a short, deep breath. "I made the right decision, didn't I? I've risked a lot. Where is my reward?"

Michael spent the next few minutes trying to convince himself that his only choice was allowing Elizabeth to be free of this boat and Titus' pursuit.

Michael staggered back down the stairs and fumbled with a cart. He managed to open it and pulled out a loaf of bread. He tore off a piece and dropped the loaf. He fell back onto a cart.

"Alexander, do you know when the next ship leaves Caesarea for Rome again?"

"Why do you ask?"

"I need to get to my daughter. She has gone with the prisoner."

Alexander walked over to him and put his spear through the loaf of bread lying on the floor. He lifted it up to his mouth and bit into it. He swallowed and shook the remaining bread off his spear.

"There is much silver at stake for the return of your daughter and friend," he said, bending over to whisper in his ear. "You would fetch a nice reward."

"I understand," Michael said.

"You do?"

"Yes."

"Good. Silver is the only language I understand."

Michael nodded as Alexander lifted his head.

"May you have much silver to give me when we arrive back in Caesarea."

"I will get you what you need."

"I will help you if you do," said Alexander.

"I will give you silver only if my daughter is found," Michael replied.

Alexander gave a devious smile. "Your daughter has been found."

"What?" said Michael, jumping to his feet. "Where?"

"She is safe. When Titus said she was wanted for the murder of a decorated Roman soldier, she was taken off the boat. She is worth more to us here on this ship than in Rome."

"Tell me where she is," Michael said, grabbing the spear. He lifted it up and pinned it against Alexander's chest. "Tell me or I will cut your heart out and feed the sharks."

Alexander gripped his hand, twisting it. "Traveler, you are not making many friends on this journey. You hurt me, your daughter will not leave this ship. Put the spear down."

Michael lowered it.

"You need not worry about her safety if the silver fills my hands when we reach land."

"I will not give you any silver until you show me she is safe."

Alexander shook his head. He grabbed away the spear and swatted Michael with the metal rod. He gripped Michael's neck with his hand. "Your choices are clear. You can give me the silver I want and your daughter will be freed. Or you can be a problem for the rest of the journey and end up overboard swimming for your life."

Alexander shoved him into a stack of carts. Michael groaned as he reached to hold onto one, but he fell back again as the cart toppled off a pile.

"I will be watching you," Alexander said. "The murderer of a Roman soldier would fetch any man a big bag full of silver. I hope you have done well." He turned around and glared. "I hope it is good enough to save your daughter."

Michael got up, taking a couple of steps up to the deck. "I would not seek help from Julius or Augustus," Alexander said. "If they know your daughter is aboard, they will seek the same silver I do." He walked to Michael, clutching his arm. "I will not lose my chance. If it is taken from me, I will take it from you."

Alexander released his grasp and turned away. Michael glared. "I do not believe in killing another man. But if you harm or hurt my daughter in any way, I will give up my life to take yours."

Alexander faced Michael.

"Do you understand me?" Michael asked him.

"We can agree there is much at stake," Alexander replied.

"You're damn right," said Michael as he took a step up to the deck.

"Be careful with your words, my friend," Alexander shouted. "The wrong word spoken could mean death to your daughter."

Michael rushed back down the stairs and tackled Alexander. His spear bounced away. They wrestled and rolled into a pile of carts, the top one falling off and onto their heads. Michael swung and struck Alexander's nose. A cart opened and two jugs rolled out, striking Michael in the back as the water rushed out.

"Stop," yelled Augustus. He removed Michael's grip and picked him up as Julius stepped in front of Alexander.

"What is your dispute about?" asked Augustus.

"There is no problem here," said Alexander as he wiped blood from his nose. "Just a couple of men having fun, discussing a bet."

"A bet?" Augustus asked. "What kind of a bet leads men to try and kill each other?"

"A bet over a woman?" Julius asked.

"Men, I will say this only one time," Augustus said. "There is no woman in this world worth killing each other over. No woman."

Michael stared at Julius. *Should I tell him? Would it put Elizabeth in danger? Can I trust him? Can I trust Augustus?*

"We will reach land in the next few sunsets, maybe sooner. The men are working hard. Rest. Relax. We have plenty of food and drink." Augustus pointed to the carts. "Put these back in order."

"I will rest," said Alexander. "Let the farmer from Jerusalem work." He retreated to the far end of the room and retrieved his spear. "I am bound by the rules of the Roman Empire."

"I know," said Augustus, turning to face him. "On this ship, you are now bound by my rules or you can swim with the rest of your friends. We have lost enough men on this journey. Let us make the rest of this trip a safe one."

Alexander raised his spear in the air. "I agree. What about you, Michael?"

CHAPTER 57

MODERN-DAY LONG ISLAND

HEWITT DECLINED AN INVITATION FROM CONNIE to spend the rest of Christmas Eve with her. Their walk was brief as he flooded his mind with new theories. "I'm still working this case," he said.

"What if you get caught by Kevin or your boss?" she asked.

"Then I do," he said. "It's only a matter of hours before they decide to bury this case in the public's mind. If they sense there's a cold trail, they'll try to divert attention to another case."

"I don't believe it," Connie said.

"It doesn't matter if you do or not. I know the next twenty-four to forty-eight hours are critical in finding something my boss can sink his teeth into."

They shared a brief hug, and he left after dropping Connie off at Michael's house.

He arrived back on Main Street minutes later. The last stores opened were finally closing up. He stared at a few couples holding hands, leaving the Variety Store. He found a spot for his Cadillac a block away from the church. The steps were jammed with churchgoers leaving the last service of the evening.

Beautiful. Perfect timing. Maybe I'll get lucky. I could use a little help. He gripped the black book and raced inside the church. The pew area was empty except for a lone woman at the front bending down. *I'll wait until she leaves.*

He sat in the last row and pulled out his cell phone. He ignored a woman removing books from a pew. He clicked his cell phone. "Sir, I'm sorry to bother you, but I have a lead now in the Stewart case."

"Did you forget our conversation we had earlier?" asked Wrightman. "You're off the case. Did you give your notes and laptop to Special Agent Holligan?"

"I did. But – "

"There are no buts. I don't want to hear from you again about this case. Good night."

Hewitt sighed and put his phone away. He watched the pastor instruct Katie to gather up the rest of the Bibles.

"How many more books are left to package up?" said Pastor Timothy, his voice carrying to the back of the church.

"I'd say about ten or fifteen," she said.

Hewitt jogged to the front. "I'm sorry to bother you, Pastor. I need to talk to you."

Pastor Timothy adjusted his glasses. "One moment." He pulled a book out of the carton and paged through it. "Hold on," he said. "This one is fine."

Katie shook her head. "I'm afraid not. I checked every one of them earlier today."

"You must have made a mistake," Pastor Timothy said as he continued to page through the book. He handed it to her. "Take a look."

She stared at the page. "Am I losing my mind?" She showed him. "Look. I marked it to be sent back."

"Is there a problem?" Hewitt asked.

"No, no," Pastor Timothy said, waving at him. "We're just sending back a bunch of defective Bibles with missing pages."

"Printing problem?" Hewitt asked.

"Looks like it. Katie, let's go through this carton again. I want to be sure. We'll look stupid if we're sending back good books."

"Pastor, I need to talk to you," Hewitt said. "Now."

Pastor Timothy bent down and grabbed five books. He turned and handed them to Hewitt. "I could use some help too. Help me and I'll help you."

"What am I looking for?" Hewitt asked.

"Look for anything from the Acts of the Apostles, specifically Acts 27-28:10. Those are the sections I need. In the defective books, this writing was missing. If it's missing, throw the book in the carton."

Pastor Timothy emptied the box and sat beside Hewitt. They leafed through the books, page by page. A pile of good Bibles grew between them. Katie did the same in the pew in front of them.

"I only see books with it," Hewitt said, putting the last one down.

"The material about Paul being on the island of Malta, right?" asked Pastor Timothy. "Acts 27-28:10."

"Yes."

Pastor Timothy stood and leaned over the pew in front of him. "Katie dear, are you sure we have the right books?"

"If they're marked, we have the right ones."

Pastor Timothy stepped back. "They are marked, but they're not the books we looked at before."

"I know," Katie said, throwing her hands up in the air.

"Where are the books with the missing pages? Did you throw them out by mistake? It's okay. I won't be mad."

"I didn't throw any books out," she protested, turning around.

Hewitt glanced at Pastor Timothy and shrugged his shoulders.

"Now I know I've lost my mind," Katie said.

Pastor Timothy sat back down on the bench.

Hewitt handed him a book. "Got nothing here," he said.

"Strange," Pastor Timothy said. He got up again. "Go home, Katie. We'll figure this out tomorrow after the morning service."

"Yes, Pastor. I'm so sorry. I don't know what I did. I was sure I had the right collection of books."

"Wish your family a Merry Christmas from me."

"I will. Merry Christmas to you."

They watched Katie gather up her purse and a big bag of presents.

Pastor Timothy walked her out the door. He pushed the latch across and turned off the back lights. "Need to conserve electricity. Our church isn't doing well now after what happened here."

He sat next to Hewitt. "Very odd," he said. "She's been reliable."

"Um. Okay, Pastor," Hewitt said, moving the pile of books to the side. "She's like most people during this time of the year – stressed."

"You are right, sir. Forgiveness is the ultimate gift to give at this time of the year."

"I could certainly use some of that," Hewitt said.

Pastor Timothy nodded. "A church member came by my office today all upset and in a frenzy. She showed me a picture of you she had downloaded from the Internet. You were digging up Pastor Dennis' grave! Are you here seeking my forgiveness for this?"

Hewitt grimaced. "I'm sorry."

"What were you thinking?"

"I thought I had a clue that would help me find Michael and Elizabeth Stewart."

"Down there in Dennis' grave?"

Hewitt shook his head.

"How, son? How?"

"I'm not sure how. But I need you to tell me about this." He held the black book up.

"What is this?" asked Pastor Timothy.

"A book that describes some events that have happened in this church."

The pastor took the book and began reading. He pushed back his graying hair and read several more pages. "Some of it is rather miraculous."

"Some?" Hewitt said as he took the book back. "I'd say all of it."

"What do you need from me?"

"I need honest answers. I need to know if you knew about this book. Have you heard about it in any way? Is this some hokey way for religious nuts in this community to conjure up publicity for the church? I know the church has been struggling to meet its bills. Pastor Dennis told this to me as well. Or are these just tales, like the tales you read in the Bible?"

"What tales are you talking about?"

"The healing nonsense. The religious wacko stuff you read about on the Internet."

Pastor Timothy smiled.

"Did I say something funny?"

"You referenced the Internet as your source. My, we have come a long way in how we preach God's word."

"I didn't write the tales."

"What makes you say they are just tales?"

"I work with physical evidence, Pastor." Hewitt took out the short, metal rod. "Like this." He gave it to the Pastor.

"Interesting," he said while examining it first with his hands and then inspecting it in the lone church light. "I hate to break this news to you because I know you're looking for a good tale." Pastor Timothy paused. "This," he said, holding it up, "is nothing more than a device pastors used a couple of hundred years ago to press down pages in their journals. Many preachers carried it with them as they wrote. They used it often as a bookmark. Look at the bend. It fits perfectly to keep track of a page."

"Are you sure?"

"Would I lie?" asked Pastor Timothy.

Hewitt looked away.

Pastor Timothy slapped him on the back. Hewitt took a deep breath, gathered some energy and stood. He brushed by him.

"Can I help you with anything else?" he asked Hewitt.

"No. I'm done."

"Merry Christmas."

Hewitt waved his hand in the air as he touched each pew on the way to the back door. He turned around and began his thought. "Pastor, my ... where did he go?" He stood there for a few more seconds and gave up. He pushed the old latch back and pushed the door open. A cold breeze kissed his face. The street was empty and the lamp above shone the only light, illuminating a small tree with an angel sitting atop.

I've got nowhere to go. How about that? The man who helped so many families find their children. The man who has a drawer full of plaques and citations. The man who has all the money in the world. The man who can travel to any city he wishes. The man who has a closet full of Italian-made suits and shiny shoes. The man who has everything.

He opened the door wide. "I have nothing," he said, letting the wind pummel his body. "There is nothing out there for me tonight. Nothing."

Hewitt stepped back inside, closed the door and locked it. He turned and walked to the front and knelt down in the first pew.

CHAPTER 58

SUSAN HELD A VINYL RECORD IN HER HANDS. On the front, Bruce Springsteen wore a plaid shirt. She turned it over and touched the pictures on the back, one a bride dressed in her wedding dress, standing with a groom. She sighed. *I wonder if this will ever be me.*

She held the album to her heart and rocked back and forth on her knees. She reached to grab scissors off the living room table and cut the wrapping paper neatly, measuring the length and width of the album. After folding the bright red and white paper with Snoopy dancing in a Christmas hat, she taped up the back. She held it up for a brief moment. *Perfect. I hope he likes it. If I ever get a chance to give it to him.*

She placed it under the tree and kneeled before it for a few seconds. The colored lights blinked in no particular order while the angel that topped the highest branch leaned over. She stood and straightened it.

"Are you going to bed soon?" her mom asked as she walked down the stairs.

"What are you doing up?"

"I couldn't sleep knowing you're upset." She held onto the railing and took her steps down at a slow pace. Susan sat by the tree, picking up her gift to Michael.

"You aren't going to make me sit down there with you?"

"No, Mom." Susan got up and helped her mother to the couch. "Can I get you some coffee or tea?"

"No, no. I'll be up all night in the bathroom. One trip is the limit at my age."

"You're not that old."

"It's okay to tell me the truth, Susan. I know I'm old. I don't have many good years left. I have no friends anymore."

Susan frowned. "Do we have to talk about this tonight?" She lowered her head and sat beside her. "I have enough on my mind."

"Why are you upset on Christmas Eve? It's not that boy again, is it?"

"Mom," Susan said. "He's a man. I'm a woman. When are you going to treat me like a grown woman? I'm forty-four now. Not fifteen."

Her mother's fingers trembled as she struggled with her glasses. "I'm not perfect, Susan," she said. "I'm sorry you don't feel I treat you like a woman, whatever that means. Is this a feminist thing I should be up on?"

"No, Mom. It has nothing to do with that."

"You will always be a little girl to me, the one making sandcastles at the beach during the summer or building a snowman in the winter."

Susan sighed. "I remember those times. But those days are gone. I'm not that person anymore."

"Oh, forget about that boy. I mean man. He was never going to stay around for you. And you have changed. You didn't have to. Why did you stop being a little girl? Age shouldn't determine what you enjoy."

"Mom," Susan said with an aggravated look. "Really? Sandcastles and snowmen?"

Her mom sat back and leaned her head against the back of the couch. "Were you happy the days you made those sandcastles and snowmen?"

"Of course. But life marches on. We become adults."

"Yes we do. Time does move forward for everyone. I know that. I can tell you all about the aches and ills that go with it too."

"We're not going to talk about doctors and prescriptions, are we?" Susan asked.

"No."

"Good. I know it's no fun getting old."

"True. But you don't have to be miserable. You have many more wonderful years ahead of you. You wonder why I'm hard on whoever you are interested in at the time?"

"Let's face it, Mom. No one is ever going to be good enough for your little girl."

Her mom leaned over and grabbed her hand. "And I should feel that way. Your happiness is what matters to me most."

"Sometimes I wonder," Susan said. "You always give Michael a hard time. Always. I love him, Mom. Just like you loved Dad." She took a deep breath and hugged the record. "Now it doesn't matter."

"You're right. I am hard on him. I guess I never had a good feeling about him when he came over."

Susan gave her an astonished look. "When did you ever have a good feeling about any guy I was interested in?"

Her mother didn't answer.

"It doesn't matter," Susan said, getting up and placing the present back underneath the tree. "He's not here, and he may never come back. People in this town have judged him. I doubt he would return to live here. Everyone thinks he has something to do with Elizabeth's disappearance."

"Does he?"

Susan returned to the couch and glared.

"I'm sorry. I needed to ask. I may have been hard on him, but I do understand that anyone who cares about my daughter must have a good heart."

"He has a beautiful heart, one of the most beautiful hearts I've ever known. He has his faults. We all do." Susan lifted her eyebrows.

"I get the message."

"I saw the hurt in his eyes when he spoke about his daughter," said Susan. "I felt his sorrow when we held each other. I felt the sadness in his kiss."

"Kiss? Oh no."

"Yes, Mom," said Susan, waving her arms in the air. "Your daughter has kissed a man. And to make your worst nightmare come true, I enjoyed it."

Her mom twitched and looked away. "Did you also … ?"

Susan hesitated. "No."

"Oh, thank God."

"But I wanted to."

There were a few seconds of silence between them. "You know what, Mom, you and Michael have something in common."

"Michael and me? Oh, please."

"Yes, you do. The look you had the night you told me Daddy had died was the same type of look Michael had when he told me his daughter was missing."

She wrapped her arms around Susan, startling her. "I know it hurts. I know the feeling of seeing the hurt in someone's eyes you love. I've seen it in your eyes too."

Susan pulled back. "When?"

"Just now."

They hugged each other tight. "Boy, we haven't done this very often," Susan said.

"We need to do it more. We are all we have tonight."

"Mom, tonight it's enough." They held each other for a few more seconds. "You're going to love what I got for you too."

"Susan, you being here is the best gift I could have gotten. But I would like one more gift."

"And what would that be?"

"Let's take a trip to the beach and build a sandcastle."

Susan stood and put her hands on her hips. "Whoa, I'm not building a sandcastle in this freezing cold weather. Why do we need to do this now?"

Her mom hesitated. "I think it's time we both make a moment. For too many years, I watched them pass me by. I was always too busy chatting with my friends to create a moment with you. I'd like to do that now. It would be nice if you joined me. No pressure."

"But plenty of guilt," said Susan.

"Okay, some guilt."

Susan nodded and extended her hand. "Let's go. Let's make this a memorable Christmas."

CHAPTER 59

AUGUSTUS WATCHED HIS CREW ROW WITH WEARY ARMS while another set of men pitched buckets of water back into the sea. "Land is nearby," Augustus told Michael. "I can smell the fires burning in the distance."

Michael wasn't sure whether he believed him. *He could be saying this to keep me calm. But he is a man who has taken many journeys. He is a better judge of time and distance on the sea than I will ever be.*

He paced back and forth, end to end along the top deck several times, looking for any clues where Elizabeth might be. *What if Alexander is lying and will take whatever money I can find? What happens if I cannot come up with enough silver to free her if he really has her? Do I give whatever I can without any proof that she is safe?* He shook his head, growled and kicked at some long carts at the far end of the boat, away from Augustus and the rowing men.

Thump. *What was that?* He kicked at a pile of long carts with his feet again and then pushed the top one. He shook the second and swatted the bottom one again, this time three times with each foot. He heard a muffled noise. Thump. Thump. Thump. He dropped to his knees and took a quick glance behind him. "Is anyone in there?"

Thump. He heard muffled noises again. He placed his ear to the cart. "If this is Elizabeth, knock twice."

Thump. Thump.

"Dear Jesus." He stood and tried to budge the top two carts off the bottom one. He pushed at the sides and noticed holes about two inches in diameter on the carts. He fell to his knees again and whispered in the hole. "Are you okay? Can you breathe?"

Thump.

He peeked in the hole and saw her mouth, tied with a cloth. He stood again and shoved the top cart with his shoulder.

"Sir, what are you doing?" asked one of the workers.

"Oh, I am just putting these carts back. They must have slid off each other during the journey."

"Let me help you," he said, as he pushed the top one. The worker stopped and wiped his hands. "They are wet." He turned to Michael. "Help me."

"Oh, right, sorry," Michael said.

They both shoved the box back on top. "There, we did it," he said with a smile.

"Yes, we did," Michael replied. He waved to the worker. Once gone, he slammed the top cart with his fist. He dropped to his knees, bent over and spoke into the hole. "Stay calm, Elizabeth. At least I know where you are. I need some time to think of a way to get you out of there without anybody noticing."

He left the carts and approached Augustus. "How long before we reach Caesarea?"

"Not much longer. Look," Augustus said. He pointed to the horizon where some light had emerged at the lower portion of the sky.

"Your eyes are better than mine," Michael said. "I am having a hard time seeing that far."

"You must be old," he said, laughing.

Michael paused a moment. "Blurry eyes. Another name for it." He leaned closer to Augustus as they stood by the railing. "I have a problem and I – "

"What might the problem be?" asked Alexander.

Michael turned and saw him emerge from the stairway, holding his spear.

"How can we help you?" Alexander asked, taking a few more steps forward.

"I was getting ready to ask Augustus how long before we reach land."

Augustus gave him a confused look. "Soon. I said this."

"You have your answer, my friend," Alexander said. "You should get some rest below. You have a long journey home."

"He is not going home. He is going back to Rome to find his daughter," Augustus said. "Did you not know his daughter went with the prisoner on the safety boat?"

"No. I did not know that," Alexander said, lying. "How fortunate it was for her to be on that boat. Or was it with that storm approaching?"

Augustus glared. "You need not remind a father about the hazards of our journey. You should do your best to help him."

"You are right," said Alexander. "I will do my best."

Augustus smiled and looked at Michael. "Let him help you."

Michael pushed Alexander away, who lifted his spear to his chest. "Whatever help I get will be met with a grateful heart."

Alexander laughed. "Let us hope there is more than that." He withdrew and headed to the far end of the ship where the long carts lay. Michael faced the sea and watched from the corner of his eye as Alexander inspected the area. He looked away and began chatting with Augustus, very aware that Alexander was staring at him.

"What a journey, Augustus. Was this the worst one you have been on?"

Augustus' face lit up. "Why no. Let me tell you about my first trip to Rome. You thought the last storm was terrible? The first one I was on makes this last one look like a small rainstorm."

Michael saw his mouth move yet never heard the words. He was too busy watching Alexander move the carts around with two other Roman soldiers. "Augustus, what is in those long boxes?"

"Huh? Oh. At the end of the deck?"

"Yes, where Alexander is right now."

Augustus lowered his head. "The bodies of three of my workers. They died from illness two sunsets ago."

"Oh," Michael said. "I am sorry."

"They were good men."

"What do they do with the boxes?"

"The Romans will take them and give the bodies to the leaders of the cities where they lived."

"What cities are they being taken to?"

"Jerusalem. The three men were skilled fishermen. They had children."

Augustus lifted his head and left the railing. Michael turned around and saw Alexander sitting on a small cart next to the coffins.

"Julius," Michael said as he saw him pass.

"Yes," he said, stopping. "Do you have enough food and drink? It will not be long before we reach land."

"I have enough. I do not know how to tell you this," Michael said with a concerned look. "Can we talk away from the guards?"

Julius guided him down the stairs to the lower deck. "What is wrong?"

Michael hesitated and took him a few more feet away from a soldier who was sleeping. "What I am about to say could risk my daughter and her safety."

"We are fine here. The soldier cannot hear us. Tell me, why is your daughter in trouble? She left some time ago. You will be able to go back once we reach land. It may take a while."

"No. Alexander has imprisoned my daughter."

"How is that possible?"

"She is in one of those carts or boxes or coffins up on deck. Check them. Now!"

"What carts or boxes are you talking about?"

"At the far end of the boat upstairs. You have to believe me."

"The coffins?"

Michael glared. "Yes."

"Augustus said he lost three men," Julius said. "There are three carts. You must be mistaken."

Julius took a few steps toward the stairway and shook his head. "I saw your daughter get on the boat with the prisoner."

"She did," Michael said, grabbing his arm, "but while Titus was here trying to take me, Alexander had her returned."

Julius removed Michael's hand from his arm. "This is a hard story to believe."

"Go and look inside those carts."

"Coffins ... "

"Okay, coffins. Look in them!" Michael grew agitated.

Julius climbed a few more steps and looked back. "I cannot. Those coffins are resting places for men. Men with families and children."

"Please," Michael pleaded.

"The Roman soldiers are responsible for this journey and the dead. We would be violating Roman law. I am powerless over the rules."

Michael moved forward. "Do you have a daughter?"

"I do," said Julius, stopping on the stairs.

"What would you do if you knew your daughter was imprisoned?"

Julius kept his back to him. He waited several seconds before speaking. "I will try and look when we reach shore, if we are alone," he said. "I cannot promise any more than this."

"She is in one of those coffins. I saw her."

"Let us hope you are right," Julius said as he climbed back to the deck. "If not, we could both lose our lives."

CHAPTER 60

JIM STEWART SETTLED BACK IN HIS NEW CUSHIONED ROCKING CHAIR, TV remote in one hand, his evening juice in the other. He stared at the blinking screen as he zipped through several channels.

Figures. Nothing on tonight. No one around. I hate Christmas. A travesty – the gifts, the phoniness of everyone being nice to each other.

He leaned forward and pushed hard on the remote. *Great. Is the battery going? What a stupid device.* Jim took a deep breath and winced. *What is that awful smell?* He looked to his right and noticed the dried up tree in the corner. An unused metal stand lay nearby while a pile of boxes were stacked against a corner chair.

I should dump that piece of garbage. Connie knows I won't put it up or decorate it. Where has she been anyway? I'd better toss this tree outside before the whole house has that stench.

He placed his drink on the end table and stood for a brief moment. His head spun around, and his vision blurred. He fell back into his rocker.

He tried again, gripped the arm of the chair and got up. He walked forward to the TV and held on, taking a few short breaths. He rubbed his eyes to clear them and walked toward the tree before stumbling. He tripped and the tree landed on him as he fell to the floor.

Jim pushed the tree off and examined his hands. He pulled a few pine needles out of his arm and swore under his breath.

Blood trickled down his hand as he rolled the tree over. He grabbed onto the edge of the couch to lift himself up. He wiped the debris off his sweatshirt and pants, tucked in his shirt and took a deep breath.

He wiggled his toes and reached into his pocket, pulling out a small bottle. "Who says flying doesn't have its benefits?" he said, waving the bottle in the air. He opened it, took a sip and rested for a minute. After he emptied it with another gulp, he reached down and grabbed the top of the tree, dragging it. He squeezed it past the screen door and tossed it down the front steps, watching it tumble onto the snow-coated sidewalk.

He slapped his hands together and steadied himself on the wooden railing as he turned around, taking his time on the slippery ground.

He managed to reclaim his chair and proceeded to settle on watching the movie, *It's a Wonderful Life*. He poured another glass of whiskey and sipped it while waiting for the commercials to end. Growing impatient, he pressed the button on the answering machine next to him. "There are no new messages," said the robotic voice.

He poured more whiskey into his glass, drinking and remembering his dead wife. *Christmas is not the same anymore, Becca. How many years has it been since God took you away from me? I've forgotten. Seems like yesterday. I'm sitting here alone on Christmas Eve. How about that? Did you ever think we'd raise such ungrateful kids after everything we gave them?*

"Everything," he said out loud, taking a big gulp of whiskey. The alcohol dripped down his chin before he slurped it up with his tongue. He wiped his face with his sleeve.

Michael is the most ungrateful one of them all. Walking away from his home and church after his daughter disappears. What kind of a father runs away when his family needs him most? A coward. He must be guilty. A guilty man runs. I know if that happened to Connie, Becca, I'd be busting down every door in town and kicking every sleazeball until I found her.

He nibbled on crackers and clicked the television off. "Yeah, what a son I've got. Not like me. Nope. Not like me at all." Jim laughed and poured the remaining portion of the bottle into a taller glass.

He rocked back and forth, sipping and staring at the blank TV screen, examining his reflection.

"The hell with him," he said, flipping up the footrest. He grabbed the phone from its holder, dialed and waited for his daughter to pick up. Her answering machine clicked on.

"Connie, where are you? It's Dad. You remember me, don't you?" He paused and then decided to wait for the instructions to delete the message and start over.

"How's my wonderful daughter doing on Christmas Day, um, Christmas Eve? Where in God's name are you? I haven't heard from you in over two weeks. Are you busy at work? Is there a new man in your life? Your dad is sitting here once again." He paused. "Alone." Jim sighed. "Again."

He hung up and lowered his head, fidgeting with his wedding ring. "You're the only one for me, Becca. I'm faithful. Always."

He rocked back and forth. *I thought we would grow old together. Why did you have to leave me? You knew I couldn't handle the kids alone. Why did you have to die so young? We had many more good years to live.* "Why?" he asked out loud again. He shook his head. "Why? Can someone out there tell me why?"

Jim leaned his head to the right, numb from too much whiskey. He squinted and blinked several times to clear his vision. He noticed a box-shaped object lying near the tree stand. Wondering what it was, he staggered over to the box and picked it up. He returned to his chair and took another quick sip from his glass. Putting it down, he reached inside the box and chose an ornament. The face of the ornament contained the picture of a bride and groom holding hands. *Rebecca and Jim's First Christmas.*

His hands trembled as he held it. He grimaced and squeezed the round ornament in his hands. It broke into several pieces falling on his lap. He swatted the remains to the floor and stared. A tear dropped from his right eye, sliding down his cheek and onto his top lip. "No. What have I done?" he said, falling to the floor.

Jim pushed the pieces into a pile and carefully placed them on a napkin. After removing a plastic bottle from the cabinet drawer, he sat on the floor and attempted to mend the old ornament. He only managed to connect four pieces before it broke again. He stood and rolled the napkin into a ball and threw it against the wall.

"Oh no. What have I done again?" he shouted. He fell to his knees and crawled to the napkin. He smelled it and leaned his head against the wall. "Why did she have to die that way?"

He emptied the napkin, dropped the pieces to the floor and wiped his face. He closed his eyes and lay against the wall for several minutes. His mind wandered to another place and time, but he was unsure where he was. Ring. Ring. *Connie? Could that be her? I knew she'd call. She's the grateful child.* Jim rushed to the phone and grabbed it from the holder. He looked at the screen. *Who is this?* He waited until the answering machine came on. No one left a message. He slammed the phone into the holder. "Ungrateful children," he shouted.

Jim fell back into his chair, picked up his glass and resumed his drinking. When he had finished the remains of the whiskey, he wondered, *Now what?* He looked inside the box again and noticed an ornament shaped like a baseball. The inscription read, "Our first baseball game. Mets-Cubs, August 1969."

"What happened?" he said, throwing his hands up in the air. "I gave you everything, Michael. Everything."

Jim put the ornament back into the box. He picked up the telephone again and pressed several buttons. "I didn't think you would pick up, Michael, but that isn't going to stop me from calling you. This is your father speaking. Where have you been? Do you know there are a lot of people wondering where you've gone? I've had the police and FBI over here asking about you. Do you know how embarrassing this is to me? The neighbors are talking."

He struggled for the next words. "It's time for some tough love, Michael. You get your butt back here and start looking for your daughter or I'll find you and ring your neck. Don't make me come after you. You remember the night you called me to announce your engagement? Do you remember what I said to you that night? I said you needed to straighten yourself out."

Jim fingered his empty glass and placed it on the side table. "Well, I'm saying it again. Get yourself straightened out. Enough of your pity party. It's time you act like a man. I don't care if you hate me. It's what parents say to their kids." He paused for a second. "Call me. I love you."

Jim put the phone back in the holder and went to the cabinet in the kitchen. He leaned down and opened the little door. "There you are," he said, pushing bottles around. He held one up to the light and smiled. "I hate to open you up now, my friend," he said, "but what are friends for?"

CHAPTER 61

THE BOOMING VOICE OF AUGUSTUS YELLING OUT INSTRUCTIONS kept the adrenaline pumping through Michael's body. His eyes stung from the spray of saltwater crashing aboard.

"My friend, you should go below," Augustus said. "You have another long journey ahead of you."

"I cannot sleep."

"I understand. I have a daughter myself. She always asks me before each journey why I have to leave. I try to stay strong when I tell her I need to make a living. I miss her."

Michael stood and rubbed his eyes. He squinted and looked to the far end of the boat. Alexander was gone, but three other soldiers milled around the coffins. He got lost in thought, staring at the area.

He had no plan. He knew he needed to get help from someone who knew how to talk to the Roman soldiers. However, he had no idea whom to trust. There was something about Julius that made him cautious. He seemed like a nice person, but on the other hand he was just like the soldiers. His only concern was silver and how to get more.

Michael heard Augustus say something, but the words were muffled as he trended deeper into thought. He considered talking to Augustus, wondering if he might be his only hope. He seemed like a noble man, a family man – someone who would understand what was at stake. Maybe he could convince the soldiers there was a better bargain to be had. Then again, they all understood silver.

Perhaps Augustus would give him a loan. He could work it off on the next journey.

He turned to say something to Augustus. "I have to tell you." He stopped. Augustus was gone. Michael glanced around and was surprised to see that no men were rowing.

Michael went below and saw the area was vacant. "Hello? Is anyone down here? Julius?" He walked from one wall to the next, pushing away boxes, carts and armor. *Strange. I guess I should take advantage of everyone being gone. I can stockpile some food before we hit shore. I may not get this chance again.*

He tugged and pulled at the top of a cart. It wouldn't budge. He picked up a stray spear. *Odd. A Roman soldier would never leave behind such a weapon.* He thrust the sharp part of the weapon into the top of the box. It splintered open about a foot wide and long.

Michael dropped the spear to the floor, stuck his hand inside and wiggled his fingers around. "What is this?" It felt like an old, grubby cloth, much like a Brillo pad back home. He pulled it out and in the dim light, he could see it was light brown and folded over several times.

He unfolded it and stared. Michael snatched a lantern sitting on the floor nearby and held it over the cloth. "Looks like someone's face."

He lowered his head, holding the lamp over the cloth. He stared again, feeling the texture of the picture. *Does not feel like any ink from this time. No wax on it. Cannot be a tablet like the one I wrote on before for Paul.* Michael moved the lantern closer to the picture and stood up. "Whoa," he said. "Is this ... "

No. Can't be. Maybe? It could be the relic Julius was talking about. Why would he be transporting it on this boat? Did it belong to Paul? Maybe this was evidence for Paul? Could this keep Paul alive longer? Save him from a brutal death?

Michael folded it back up and placed it back inside. He picked up the spear and carved a cross on top of the cart before climbing back upstairs. He looked for Julius and noticed the deck was nearly empty except for the soldiers milling around near the coffins. They were without their helmets and armor but still carried their weapons. He approached them with caution. "Can you tell me where all the men are?"

They didn't answer. "Sirs, sirs," he yelled at the Romans, "where is Augustus? Where is Julius? I need to talk to them." None of the soldiers responded.

"Where is Alexander?" The Romans continued to ignore him. "I have silver for him."

"Silver? Go below," said the soldier. "He is with the others."

"This way?" Michael asked, pointing to another stairway.

"Yes."

Michael rushed down and stepped into several inches of water filling the area. "Terrific," he said.

"There you are," shouted Augustus. "Grab a bucket. We can use all the help we can get now."

"Where?"

"Over there," Augustus said, waving his arms to where some debris was floating. Michael waded over to the far end and retrieved a bucket. He joined Augustus and his men, throwing water out over the side. They dipped and tossed the water at a frantic pace.

"It is not doing any good," said a worker to Augustus.

"Are we going down?" asked Julius, peering into the stairwell.

"We are," said Augustus. "We are only saving a few moments. The ship is taking in more water than we can get out."

"How far are we from land?" asked Julius.

"Not far. A good swim. A short boat trip."

"My cargo? Can we save it?" asked Julius.

"I am afraid not. Save yourself," Augustus said. He gave him a look of doom.

"Oh no," Michael said, tossing away his bucket.

"Where are you going?" asked Augustus.

"To save my daughter."

"What? Your daughter is not here. Save yourself."

"She is here," Michael said. "In a coffin up on deck!"

Augustus stopped passing a bucket up the stairs. "You are seasick. She is not here." He shouted to his workers. "It is time to leave. Save yourselves, men. Take the rescue boats. There are not many. The older men first. The younger men can swim."

Michael looked back at the workers coming up the stairs as he reached the deck. He stormed the area where Elizabeth was being held. "Move out of the way," he told the Romans.

"We do not move until Alexander tells us," one soldier said.

"Do you see Alexander? Look around," Michael yelled. "He is not here."

"You speak lies," a soldier said as he stepped forward, drawing his spear to Michael's chest.

Michael ran to the side where the small rescue boats lay. He leaned over the side and looked into the sea. "There," he said, turning around to face the soldiers. "Come here."

One soldier walked over to him. "Look, that is him," Michael screamed. "Rowing away, probably with all the silver. There is your fearless leader."

"He has left us," shouted the soldier, rushing to his comrades. The three Romans raced to a rescue boat, dropped it in the water and climbed down into it as the ship began to submerge.

"Help me," Michael yelled to them.

"Save yourself," shouted a soldier as they rowed away.

Michael rushed to the coffins and pushed at the top box with his shoulder. He stopped, glanced around the deck and saw no help was coming. He picked up a spear left behind.

"Watch out, Elizabeth!"

He rammed the spear into the far end of the coffin, cracking a chunk of wood off. Her feet were visible. He slammed the spear into it again and saw her stomach. He thrust the spear inside the coffin one more time and broke off several more pieces.

"Come, my friend, we have to go now," pleaded Augustus.

"I cannot go," Michael said. "My daughter is in here."

"The water, look," Augustus said.

The deck was submerged, but Michael continued, ramming the spear near her head. He reached inside, ripped out the cloth stuck inside her mouth and quickly untied the rope around her wrists. "Use your hands, Elizabeth. You've got to help!"

Michael stood and jerked back on the wood, sending one piece floating away. "Do not open your mouth," he yelled. He pulled and tore more pieces away and dropped them into the water. "Close your eyes." He heard her gag. "Close your mouth too." Michael gripped the opening and with every bit of strength he had, he ripped it apart. He grabbed Elizabeth and pulled her out, lifting her above the water. "Spit it out," he said.

Elizabeth coughed and gagged. She vomited a couple of times and tried to catch her breath.

"Spit it all out," Michael demanded.

She held up her hands and waved him away, gasping for air. When she settled down moments later, Elizabeth hugged him. He wiped a gash from his hand on his garment, letting the salt water sting it.

He pushed her away. "Help me," he said. "Push this coffin with me."

"What?"

The water rose to their knees. "Push," he ordered. They shoved the top coffin off and into the water. "Use this as a floatation device," he said. The water rose to his stomach as he pulled the second cart away. He leaned on top of it. "Swim," he said. "Kick."

"Where?"

"Follow the boat," he said, pointing to where Augustus was.

"Where are they going?"

"Back to Caesarea."

"We are not supposed to be going there," Elizabeth said.

"We need to get to shore first."

Michael glanced behind him and watched the ship sink. Carts and boxes floated up to the top all around them. He swam past a couple, examining their lids.

"What are you doing?" Elizabeth asked. "We should be swimming toward that boat."

"I'm checking the boxes."

"Why? Does it matter if we have food now?"

"No, but there is something very important in one of them."

"There are so many of them," Elizabeth said.

"I found it!" Michael said as he pulled the cart toward his body. He pulled out the cloth and examined it, saying, "Not too bad. A little water on it. Thank goodness I folded it." He swam over to Elizabeth. "Just keep kicking. I have no idea how far we have to go."

They swam and swam, taking a few moments to float and rest. Every time they did, the distance between them and Augustus increased. The sea was calm for the next couple of hours as an early morning fog made the once distinct shoreline hard to see.

"Are we close?" asked Elizabeth.

"I can't see."

"Where is the boat?"

Michael shook his head and spit out some seawater. He wiped his eyes. "Everything is blurry to me. I can't see Augustus anymore."

He laid his body on top of the coffin for a few moments, taking deep breaths.

"What are you doing?" asked Elizabeth, looking back at him.

"Give me a moment. I'm resting."

"We're almost there, right?"

Michael didn't answer her but closed his eyes, holding on to the coffin with one hand and the box with the other.

"What's wrong?" Elizabeth asked.

He let go of the cart and put his hand up in the air, letting his body fall into the water as if he were diving off a board. When his head failed to submerge, he opened his eyes and smiled. "My feet just hit the ground."

Elizabeth did the same and said, "Well, enough of this kicking and swimming stuff. I'm walking to shore now." She pushed the long box away.

"Whoa, grab that," Michael said.

"Why? We do not need these anymore."

"We don't. But somebody out there does."

"What?"

"There's a body in there."

"Are you kidding me?"

"No. There's a body in there. A dead one. We need to push these to shore."

"I've been swimming with a dead person?"

"Yes."

"Yuck."

"That dead person just saved us."

Elizabeth frowned and pushed the coffin to shore. They left them at the edge and sat down. "I need a few moments to rest," he said.

"Now what?" she asked.

He turned around and saw some men pulling a small boat ashore. "Hold this," Michael said, handing her the small box with the cloth in it. "Do not give this to anyone."

"Where are you going?"

"To speak with them," he said, pointing to two men chatting. He jogged over to Augustus and Julius. "My friend, you made it," Augustus said with a smile.

"We did."

"We?"

"Yes. My daughter is with me."

"She is alive?" Julius asked.

"Yes."

Julius gave Michael an angry look.

"What is wrong with him?" Michael asked Augustus.

"He has lost much. His cargo is floating in the sea. He was hoping for much silver with his cargo. Everything is gone. His relics too."

"I am sorry. I need your help."

"What is it you need?"

"A way back to Rome. I have something to give to my friend, Paul."

"Your friend was taken. I do not think it is wise to make that trip anymore."

"I thought it was supposed to be a friendly trip."

Augustus shook his head. "No. The Romans have wanted Paul for many sunsets. He does not have many more sunsets to live."

"That cannot be. I thought the first time he was to go there he was to be set free."

"You confuse me. Your friend Paul was taken to Rome some sunsets ago and returned here. This is the second trip for him."

"Are you sure?"

"I do not forget a face."

Michael lowered his head.

"I am sorry, my friend."

"I need to go. I need to help him."

"You are a noble man. The next ship does not leave for several sunsets."

"I thought you were leaving soon to go back," Michael said.

"No. I am done with traveling for now. We were fortunate to have survived this journey. Who knows what happens on the next one? I will not take another for a while."

"Why though? You are a man of the sea," Michael said.

"I am, but I am a man of my family as well. I need to see my family more. My daughter. My son. My wife."

Michael lifted his head and extended his hand. Augustus gripped his shoulder and smiled. "You are a strange man, my friend, but a good man."

"As are you, Augustus."

"May you travel in safety, Michael," he said.

He watched Augustus sling a small bag over his shoulder and leave.

"Dad," Elizabeth yelled. He turned around and saw Julius struggling with her. "Oh no." He raced to her and pushed Julius away. "What is your problem?"

"I have lost all my silver because of the journey," he said in anger. "There is a reward for your daughter and her friend."

"You will not take her." He swung at Julius, hitting the side of his head. He fell to the ground. Julius tripped him. Michael tumbled over him, pulling Julius to the ground. He clamped both hands around his neck. "Leave us alone," Michael yelled. He squeezed harder, pressing his thumbs into his skin until Julius gagged.

"Dad," Elizabeth shouted. "Stop. Stop now. Please."

Michael released his grip and watched Julius struggle to find a comfortable breath. He held his hands up to his face, seeing them tremble. He got up and looked at Elizabeth. "I hate this place. Let's go."

He grabbed her arm.

"Where are we going?" she asked.

"Home."

CHAPTER 62

MICHAEL AND ELIZABETH RESTED IN THE MIDDLE OF A MARKETPLACE near the edge of Caesarea. Hundreds of people were beginning their shopping. "This reminds me of Jerusalem," Elizabeth said.

He didn't respond at first, still trying to steady his hands.

"Are you all right?" she asked.

He ignored the last question. "You're right. This city was built by the Romans for the richest of rich people. It is considered one of their greatest accomplishments. We will stand out. We cannot rest too long here."

He bent down near a wall, behind a fruit stand. He opened the small wooden box and grabbed a pouch. Opening it, he pulled out several pieces of silver.

"What are you going to do with that?" Elizabeth asked.

"We are two days away from getting to Jerusalem, according to Augustus. We need a more efficient way of transportation."

"But this is not our money."

Michael gave her a frustrated look. "What other way do you suggest? We cannot walk through the desert in our condition."

She shrugged her shoulders.

"I thought so." He handed the box back to her and began counting the silver. "Hey wait just a second." he said. "What happened to the tablets?"

"I dropped them in the boat."

"Did Paul see you do that?"

"Yes."

Michael sighed and looked up at her.

"Is he going to be okay?" she asked.

Michael shook his head.

"What will they do to him?"

"They'll kill him. They hanged Peter. Most of the apostles met a terrible death. If we aren't careful, we'll meet the same fate."

He stood and peered around the wall. Drawing back, he pulled out a small knife and took the box from her. "Is that Aharon's?" she asked.

"No. I took it off the dead body."

"Why? Where's Aharon's knife?"

"I needed it back on the ship to defend myself against a guard."

He glanced at Elizabeth before placing the box on the ground. He removed the cloth and unfolded it. He cut a portion of it away, leaving only about a foot of fabric surrounding the face.

"Is that a painting?" she asked.

"You could say that."

He folded up the portion of the cloth he had cut away and put it back inside the box. He then folded the main portion of the cloth, placing it in his pocket for safekeeping. He handed the box to her.

"Why are you doing that?" Elizabeth asked.

"Just in case we need to lead people astray," he said, getting up. "We need to move now."

He took another peek around the wall. "Stay right behind me. The marketplace is getting crowded. Let's not lose each other."

Michael and Elizabeth moved along a line of storefronts, stopping for a few moments at each stand, examining the merchandise. They finally came upon a man selling carriages with horses. "Let us hope we have enough silver to buy a decent one," he said, turning around to face her.

He took a few more steps before putting his hand up. "Stay here. Wait for my signal. Do not approach until I say it's okay."

"Why?"

"Blend in, Elizabeth," he said. "Don't forget to act like a woman of this century. Behave like one."

"Wow," she said. "I never heard you refer to me as a woman."

"Here you are," he said, handing her a cloth. "Cover your face with this."

She frowned.

"Do it now. This isn't Northport in the Twenty-First Century."

She wrapped the bottom part of her face, only her eyes showing. "Okay? Won't this make them more suspicious?"

"Maybe. But we have to make sure no one recognizes you." He left her to approach the man. "I have this many," he said, showing the man.

"No. Not enough. I need much more than that to give up one of my animals."

Michael returned to Elizabeth. "Well, that did not work out so well."

"Now what?"

"Bend over," he said. "Roll the cloth you have into a ball. Stuff it inside your garment."

She did and straightened up.

"No. That will not convince him at all." He glanced at a fruit stand. "Wait here."

Michael returned moments later with a nice-sized watermelon.

"Are we eating?"

"No. But you have to pretend you are eating for two."

"What are you talking about?"

"Wrap the cloth around this," he said, handing her the watermelon.

"Done."

"Put it under your shirt and hold it."

"Are you kidding me?"

"I kid you not. Do it."

Elizabeth did as he asked. "This is kind of heavy," she said.

"Stay hunched over," Michael said, as he walked away. "Do not move from there. I want him to see you."

"Whatever."

Michael left and approached the man again. He walked around, inspecting several carriages and horses. He opened his hand again, showing him the silver. "No. That is not enough. I told you," the man said.

Michael pointed to Elizabeth. "My brother's wife. My brother is away on a trip to Rome. I am here to take care of her. She is expecting before the next sunset."

The man turned around and looked at her.

"Look. She is sick. Please. I would be grateful. We need to get to Jerusalem."

The man continued to stare at Elizabeth. She bent over and grabbed her stomach, letting out a few groans that Michael was able to hear.

"Please, sir," he said, grabbing the man's shoulder.

"Go. Take the small chariot and the last horse." He led him to the animal.

Michael dropped the silver in his hands. "You have my gratitude."

"I gave you a bargain," the man said.

"I know." He retrieved the horse and after tying it to the small chariot, he climbed in, sat down and maneuvered the horse toward Elizabeth. He stopped beside her saying, "What do you think?"

"I think you're nuts," she said. "It's so tiny."

"Excuse me. I'm sorry it's not a Porsche. Get in."

"Where? There's no room."

He squeezed over. "Now there is. We need to go."

"Do you know how to drive one of these?" she asked. Elizabeth went to pick up the box and dropped the watermelon. It rolled over toward the man.

"Get in," Michael pleaded.

"Okay," said Elizabeth as she quickly climbed in, holding the box.

"Stop, stop," yelled the man as he picked up the watermelon and ran after them.

Michael urged the horse to move faster.

"Wow, my dad knows how to drive a chariot here," said Elizabeth.

"I learned while working in the fields," he said.

"Surprise, surprise. Look who is handy around the house now."

"Sit down, smart aleck."

"I am," she said, holding her hands up. "I'm afraid to put my hands in because I may not be able to get them out."

"Hold on. This can get up to high speeds."

"Yeah, you're like a NASCAR driver."

"You're so skeptical. Hi, yo," Michael shouted, jostling the ropes attached to the horse. The animal picked up speed, and the chariot bounced up and down a few times.

"Just like a roller coaster," Elizabeth said, waving her hands in the air. The chariot squeaked and squealed on the narrow dirt path. "Ouch," she said. "My butt."

Michael stood up and pulled back on the ropes to find a more manageable pace.

"How long do you think it will take to get to Jerusalem?"

"Your guess is as good as mine," he said over the noise of the wheels.

"How about a guess?" Elizabeth asked.

"After sunset."

"Then what?"

"Then we bury this box with the cloth in a cave or somewhere in the side of a mountain."

"Why?"

"So someone can find it."

"Why not bring it back?"

"We can't. It's an old relic. How would it look if two people from Long Island in the Twenty-First Century possessed such a relic?"

"Oh," Elizabeth said. "No one would believe us anyway, right?"

"Yes. They would think we stole it. Someone in the next few centuries needs to find it. No one would ever believe we found it. We would be arrested if we had possession of this."

After they had traveled some distance, he slowed down. He opened the box and dumped out the cloth he had cut from around the face. "We don't need this anymore. We should be there in a few hours." Michael removed the cloth with the picture from his pocket and placed it inside the box. He closed it up and gave it back to her.

"When we find a cave we'll get some stones and metal and seal it shut."

"How will they find it?"

"Sometime in the future they will dig it out and discover it."

"We can do that?"

"Sure can," he said as he jostled the ropes more to encourage the horse to pick up the pace.

"Can this horse make it the whole way?" she asked.

"We're about to find out."

Several miles later, the sun began its descent. Michael and Elizabeth stopped by a well not too far from Jerusalem. They gave the horse some water. "There you go," she said, letting the animal slurp the water from her cupped hands. "Drink it all."

It was only a short while before they came upon a small neighborhood of identical stone homes. The dwellers were herding their animals to a holding area nearby. "This must be a really poor town," Michael said. "It can't be too far from Leah."

"Should we stop and see if she's safe?"

"I doubt she has gone back home."

"We should check, should we not?" Elizabeth asked.

"We should not. It's time to move on."

"Are you sure?"

"I have never been more sure in my life. In two centuries." He gave her a wink.

They glanced at each other for a moment. She gave him an astonished look. "Did I say something stunning?" he asked.

"Yes. I never thought I would hear you say you must move on with anything."

Michael nodded. "It's about time I do. I've trapped myself in many sad and wonderful memories. What is the point of making a memory when you can't go forward and make a better one?"

Elizabeth folded her arms behind her head. "I hope we can make some better ones in Northport," she said.

"We will. I know this."

"How do you know?"

"Trust me."

"Look," said Elizabeth, standing up. "There is the aqueduct. We're near Leah."

"We've passed her town," Michael said. "Are you ready to go home?"

"No."

"Why?" he asked in surprise. "Are you going to miss this place?"

"No, but I will miss Leah."

"I will too. But there is so much more for us back home on Long Island. Our friends. Our family. Your classmates. Even Matthew."

He looked at her and she nodded. "I wish we could have taken Leah back home with us."

"This is where Leah lives. What about her husband? Her friends? Her family?" He slowed the horse down as they came upon a small mountain. "Here," Michael said, getting out of the chariot. "This should be the place."

"Why here?"

"It's where the Sermon on the Mount happened. I'm sure of it. I remember the terrain, the trees and bushes." He took the box from her, saying, "Tie the horse to that tree."

She did and raced up the hill to join him. As they ascended several more feet, he could hear voices. "Where is that coming from?" he asked, looking behind him.

They stopped to listen for a moment as darkness settled. They resumed walking, and the sound of the horse jostling alerted them. Michael put his hand on Elizabeth's mouth. "Quiet." He pulled her behind some brush and listened again. Peering around it, he squinted. "My eyes are too blurry."

"Let me look," Elizabeth said, taking a couple of steps out.

"Can you see anything?" Michael asked.

"The horse is gone, and I can't see anyone."

"Oh, great."

"Do we need to get to the tunnel after this?" Elizabeth asked.

"Yes, it's the only way back I know."

"Hey Dad, here's a strange question."

"Yes?"

"Are there lightning bugs during this time?"

"What do you mean by lightning bugs?"

"The bugs that fly around and light up."

"I know what they are, but why ask about them now?"

"I thought I saw some down the hill."

"What?" Michael froze and turned his head. He saw several bright lights in formation walking up the hill. "Those aren't bugs. Those are people carrying torches."

He grabbed her arm and picked up the pace, climbing as fast as he could. The voices of men drew closer as they moved past some dense brush. The noise of wolves howling filled the mountainside.

"This is creepy," Elizabeth whispered.

They came upon a dark cave around a sharp bend. There was a faint echo inside it. "Get inside," he said. "The lights are getting closer."

They backed into the cave. Michael leaned down, putting his hands on some boulders. He stumbled and grabbed onto Elizabeth's arm. "Stay with me. Get down."

"I see nothing up here, Alexander," a man called out.

"They are here," Julius said. "He took that chariot, and the tracks lead to this mountain. They are somewhere around here. Keep looking. I will continue walking up. You stay and look around here."

Michael took a deep breath as the man staggered inside. He put his fingers up to his mouth and looked at Elizabeth. The man took several steps past them. Michael gripped a rock and flung it at him, striking the man in the head. The man tumbled to the ground. Michael ripped the torch from his hand. "You will be fine. Sleep." He pushed his eyes closed.

"Is he dead?" Elizabeth asked, alarmed.

"No. He will sleep for a while. Hopefully he has some pleasant dreams." He motioned to her. "Stay behind me. We need to get deeper into the cave."

They walked for several minutes, coming upon a steep embankment while the sound of running water filled the area. Michael looked out the opening, his foot striking a rock. It fell, plunging into the water seconds later. He turned around. "That is one long drop."

Michael fell to his knees and grabbed a large rock. He grinded it against the wall, sharpening the edges. He plunged it into the soil and began digging. "Do the same," he told Elizabeth.

"I don't see any more rocks like the one you have," she said.

"There are more along the sides a few feet back from where we came."

She left and Michael splattered dirt and pieces of rock all around him. "Elizabeth, hurry," he shouted. When he turned, several men holding torches stood in front of him.

"Well, how is my friend from our journey doing?" asked Alexander, as he stepped in front of a group of soldiers holding Elizabeth. He pressed his spear against her neck.

She kicked his feet, and he slid the weapon across the side of her face, creating a small gash.

Michael stood and two Romans drew their spears to his chest. He kicked away the cloth behind a rock. "What do you have there?" asked Alexander.

"It is not yours."

"It is now," Alexander said, pushing Elizabeth into a group of soldiers.

"No!"

The two soldiers pushed Michael to the ground as Alexander picked up the cloth. "Ah, this is what Julius was hiding. He will not be able to enjoy the riches from this." He turned to the soldiers. "Kill Julius."

He turned back to Michael. "This should fetch me a mountain full of silver."

Michael reached up and grabbed the cloth, running to the edge. He held the cloth out as the water's mist moistened it. "You are a fool," said Alexander.

"Let my daughter go or I will drop this."

"Throw her over the cliff," Alexander said, walking away. "I can wait for you to hand it over."

"No!" Michael's cry echoed through the cave as a soldier pushed Elizabeth toward the cliff. He dropped the cloth and tackled the Roman. He struck him in the face. "Leave my daughter alone!"

Michael smashed him again, bloodying his nose. He gripped the soldier's neck and pressed hard. "I will take every breath you have."

"Stop, Dad!" yelled Elizabeth.

He watched the Roman's eyes turn back into his head. Another soldier grabbed Michael, trying to pull him away.

"Kill him," shouted Alexander.

Michael wrestled free of the solider and picked up a large rock. He held it high over his head. "I will take your life like you have taken so many others." He felt a shiver inside and trembled. A man grabbed his hand and took the rock from him. Michael looked back.

"Leave your anger here," Jesus said. "You have done well, my son. Your journey is over."

Michael got up off the soldier, still shaking with rage.

"Leave your hatred behind," Jesus said. "Their empire will end. My Father's Kingdom will live."

He walked around the cave, staring at the Romans as they drew their spears. "When you leave here to go home, remember these words. Do not be deceived by the treason of those who speak my name to gain personal riches."

The spears inflamed, and the soldiers screamed, dropping their weapons. "Those who use swords and spears to defend what cannot be taken from one's heart only contribute to the evil of the world."

Jesus picked up the cloth. "There will be those who say holy words in my name yet will never walk in my shoes."

The cave shook. Rocks from above and around them fell and rolled, splitting and splintering into many pieces, sending the soldiers running from the cave.

"When the ground trembles from doubt, take the step of faith to find your way home." Jesus stepped aside and motioned toward the waterfall. "Be baptized on this day. The water given to you from my Father is pure and good. Beware of those who stain it and use it for their personal gain."

Alexander rushed Jesus and gripped the cloth. "You are a madman, preacher," he said.

His hands crumbled, and fire filled his feet. Flames engulfed him, and Alexander screamed in pain as he fell to the ground. He crawled toward Elizabeth. "Murderer," he said, groaning.

Michael clamped his foot on Alexander's arm. "You are going nowhere, Roman." Jesus took Michael by the arm and guided him to Elizabeth.

"Where there is man, there are fools," Jesus said, standing over Alexander. "Where there is man, there is greed. Where there is man, there will be war. Do not be like man, Michael and Elizabeth. Look at the fool beneath you, guided by power and weapons."

They watched as Alexander crawled and then slithered like a snake out of the cave. "Where there is oppression, let the angels sing from your heart with tolerance. Where there is poverty, may you spare a meal. Where there is pain, may you share your comfort." He took a few steps back from the waterfall. Jesus motioned to it. "Let your faith take you home."

Jesus smiled and moved his hands forward. A soft, warm wind brushed up against them. "Your world is beautiful. Make it more so."

A bright light shone down upon Jesus. His body glowed.

"Are you ready, Elizabeth?" Michael asked, taking her hand.

She nodded and closed her eyes. A hot gust of air blew against them, pushing them into the waterfall.

CHAPTER 63

MODERN-DAY LONG ISLAND

HEWITT SAT IN THE FIRST PEW and stared at the beautifully decorated manger. He lowered his head and let his mind take him back to the last Christmas Eve that he and his wife had spent with Hailey. Hewitt had put together her first bike, a pink tricycle with training wheels. A shiny silver horn was attached to one handle while red ribbons hung from the other.

He could still hear her laughter and see the unobstructed joy on her face when she came downstairs. "Wow, wow, yippee," she squealed. "Can I ride it, Daddy? Can I?"

Hewitt grinned. "Just don't run me over."

"I won't, Daddy."

She hopped onto the bike and beeped the horn twice. "Watch out. Here I come. Miss Hailey is coming through. This is her street now. All aboard."

"All aboard, what are you riding? A train?" he asked.

"No, Daaaaaaddy," she squealed. Hailey rolled forward a few feet and put her hands up in the air. "Just like a roller coaster."

Hewitt grasped Veronica's hand and gave her a kiss.

"Yucky. Mom and Daddy kissing in a tree, kissing, first comes tub, then comes marriage then comes a puppy in a baby carriage."

"A puppy?" Hewitt asked.

"Yes. A puppy," said Hailey. Her voice started to fade as she rode the bike around the living room.

"Son? Hewitt? Are you feeling okay?" A voice jarred him back to the present.

Hewitt lifted his head. "Sorry, Pastor. I was lost in thought."

"Good ones, I hope?"

He nodded and sighed.

"Are you sure you're okay?"

"I'm fine, Pastor. I was just reflecting."

"Anything I can help you with?"

Hewitt took a deep breath. "Yes."

Pastor Timothy sat next to him. "I'm here to listen."

"Why did God take my daughter from me?"

Pastor Timothy moved closer. "I wish I had the answer to that difficult question. I ask many questions similar to yours every day."

"I didn't think you had an answer."

"I'm not sure God wants us to have the answers. He may be asking us to find the answers instead of him sending them to us. What would we learn from life if the answers were always available? I don't think we would learn much."

"That may be true, but all I know is tonight I'm sad. I'm sad for my ex-wife. For what I've done to our lives. How I've failed in our marriage. I can't seem to shake my anger. Our joy was taken far too early." He glanced at him. "She was only five years old."

Pastor Timothy turned to face Hewitt. "There's no rational reason why someone so young and innocent with much to live for is taken from us in such a way."

They sat in silence for several minutes until the pastor stood. "I must go pay a visit to a special friend of ours. Do you need to talk more?"

Hewitt stared straight ahead, mesmerized by the manger scene set up by the podium. *That's where Michael disappeared. It has to be right around the manger. Yeah, we looked at it before and couldn't find anything.*

"Hewitt?"

"Huh?" He looked at Pastor Timothy. "I'm fine."

Pastor Timothy held out his hand. "Merry Christmas, Hewitt."

They shook hands. "You have a great day of celebration." He remained seated in the front pew and pondered whether he had been attentive enough to the security around his house. *I was in the public eye. People knew I was rich, and they knew about my daughter. We should have kept her picture out of the newspapers and off the Internet. We invited every wacko out there to come take her.*

He put his hands over his face briefly as the weight of his thoughts overwhelmed him. Suddenly, the church shook, interrupting his contemplation. *What was that? The wind?*

He stood and noticed he was the only one left. He approached the manger and admired how the light shone on the face of the baby Jesus, like a laser from God's hand. Hewitt dropped to his knees. "Why, Lord? Why won't you help me find that girl? Haven't I suffered enough losing my own daughter? Why should another girl suffer? Don't we have enough pain in this world? Enough grief? How many times must I call some parent about finding their kid dead? How many more times must I do this? Tell me. Please, in the name of Hailey, help me."

The strain of his voice echoed through the old church. The wind, once full of intensity, was silent now. He looked at the baby Jesus and saw some moisture on the face of the child. He took out a tissue and wiped his eyes, embarrassed that his tears had fallen on the infant. As he dried off the baby's face, he began pleading, "I've got no more energy to fight the good fight. I have no clues as to what happened to them."

He shook his head. "No. No." He decided he had to fight back. The fear of having to call Connie about finding Elizabeth dead somewhere unnerved him. "I need to do this for Hailey," he said to the baby.

He took out another tissue and wiped the baby's eyes again. He stared and wondered. *What is that?* He dried another tear coming from the right eye and watched as yet another tear dripped down the cheek. Hewitt stood up and backpedaled a few steps.

"Pastor, are you still here?" he said loudly.

He spun around, inspecting the entire church. "Special Agent Ramirez? Are you still in the back?"

There was no response. Hewitt went to the pastor's office and knocked. "Anyone in there?"

He tapped the door again. "Hello. Pastor. Anyone?" Hewitt stepped back and rubbed his forehead. "What the ... " He placed his hand on the metal casing that held Pastor Timothy's name. It read "Pastor Vincent."

Hewitt pulled out the black book and flipped through the pages until he came to Pastor Dennis' scribbling. He read through his notes on Michael Stewart's journey. He turned back a few pages and stopped. "GF believes he traveled to the time of Christ. Here are his thoughts." – Pastor Vincent.

Am I dreaming? Have I finally lost it? Hewitt tapped several more times on the door. "Pastor, are you in there?"

A thumping noise in the church area alerted him to return. "This is Special Agent Paul of the FBI. Show yourself." Hewitt pulled out his gun and held it shoulder high. "I have my weapon out." He grabbed his flashlight and held it out in front of him as he searched pew by pew.

He retreated to the manger, noticing a tear again trickling out of the baby's eye. *This has got to be one of those automated dolls that cry.* Hewitt picked it up and turned the baby over, looking for a small screw with an attachment. There was none. He held the baby on its back and stared. A tear dropped again from the right eye and dribbled down the cheek. "Whoa," he said, holding the baby away from himself.

Another tear fell. "Is this some joke, Ramirez?" he asked, shouting in the church. "I know I'm off this case, but this isn't funny. Did Holligan put you up to this?"

Hewitt touched the tear with his finger. "Ouch," he said, feeling a burning sensation run up his hand, arm and shoulder. The heat rippled through his body, sending him to his knees. A young voice called out. "Daddy, Daddy, help me, help me!"

Hewitt placed the baby back in the manger. "Who's that? Where are you?"

"I'm here, I'm here," the voice called out.

"Who are you?"

"Hailey."

"Hailey? Dear. Honey. Where are you? Tell me! Daddy will come and get you."

Hailey touched his hand. "Here, Daddy."

Hewitt stared and took a couple of steps back. He fell to his knees and pulled her to his chest. "My Lord, you're alive. How is it you're here? Why are you here? Where have you been hiding?"

"Here."

He looked up at her. "Here? In the church? I've looked everywhere for you. I looked in every pew, every closet, every office, every door, every stairwell and I didn't find anyone."

"Here," she said, pointing to his heart. "I'm there every day."

Hewitt closed his eyes and absorbed the feeling of holding his daughter. "I wish I could bottle this and feel this forever," he said.

He opened his eyes and saw he was surrounded by older children. They were smiling and holding hands. He stood and turned around, looking at each child. "Do I know you? Were these your classmates, Hailey?"

"No, Daddy."

"Who are they?"

"You don't know them?"

"I can't be sure. Were they at your parties?"

"No."

He turned to each one. "Tell me."

The older children moved around counterclockwise, singing.

"Why are they singing, Hailey?"

"They're happy."

"Why?"

"You don't know?"

"No. Tell me, honey." He bent down on his knee and touched her face. "Tell, Daddy."

She smiled.

He shook his head. "Are you really here?"

"Do you not see me?"

"I do. I want to believe you're here."

"Well, then I am. You saved them, Daddy. You saved them from the bad people."

He stood and looked at each of the older children. Hailey held his hand. He squeezed it harder.

"You are a great daddy."

Hewitt kept staring at the older children singing. He wiped a tear away and saw Hailey was gone.

"No, Hailey, come back," he yelled. "Don't leave."

Chapter 64

A BIG PILE OF SALT STOOD IN THE MIDDLE OF THE PARKING LOT. Susan maneuvered her car around it as kids were tumbling down the side. Once parked, she grabbed a bucket from the back seat, helped her mother out of the car and up the concrete steps. A piece of wood stood straight up in front of them, left over from the last super storm. They walked around it and were greeted by a brisk wind off the water.

Susan held her mother's arm as they walked down the next set of stairs and onto the sand. They stepped through an opening of a plastic fence, leaning at a sharp angle. "Are you sure you want to do this?" she asked. "We can come back when it's warmer. Maybe summertime?"

"Look at me, dear," her mother said.

"Yes, so?" she said, stopping.

"I don't have many more days to make memories with you."

"Mom, stop talking like that. You could live to a hundred and twenty."

"Not likely."

"I'm not listening," Susan said, covering her ears.

"Well, you're going to listen to this. I've spent my whole life watching others make memories, others make moments." She walked a couple of steps toward the shore and lifted her head toward the sky.

"What are you doing?" asked Susan.

"My grandfather would tell me around Christmas to look up in the sky and you would see ... "

"Santa Claus. Yes. I know the story, Mom."

"Oh, Susan, no. He said if you looked up in the sky, you could see him traveling."

"What?"

"My grandfather said he could travel to the end of time."

"Well, you said he spent time in a psychiatric ward too."

They took a few more steps toward the ocean. "He did. Yes. But was he really crazy?"

"Sounds like it. I thought you believed he was crazy."

"I used to think so."

They stopped at the edge of the water. "Now, what do you think?" Susan asked.

"I'm not sure."

Susan got to her knees and placed the plastic bucket down. She extended her hand to her mother. "Do you need help getting down?"

"I'm old, not feeble."

"Glad you've got some spunk left," Susan said.

"That I've always had."

They pushed the wet sand into the bucket, packed it tightly with their hands and turned it over. "Time it, Susan," her mother said.

"How long?"

"Ninety seconds should do it. Long enough to dry."

"Okay, you're the expert."

Susan set the timer on her cell phone. The waves rolled softly up to her feet. She took her shoes off and let the cold water caress her toes. Her mother sat, hands folded over her knees, her hair pushing back from the breeze. Susan noticed her smile. *I wonder why I didn't see more of it.*

The wrinkles, once seen as a stark reminder life was leaving less time for them to be together, instead gave Susan a sense of hope that they were embarking on a new relationship. The buzzer rang, and she tapped her mom's shoulder. "Are you ready?"

Her mom didn't respond. She closed her eyes.

"Are you feeling all right?" Susan asked.

"I am. This is the best I've felt in a long time."

"I'm glad," Susan said as she dug her toes into the wet sand.

Her mom put her hands on the bucket. "On the count of three," she said. "One, two, three." They pulled the bucket up and began to build. Three buckets later, a sand castle was born.

"Beautiful," Susan said.

"It would have been beautiful even if it crumbled," she replied.

"Spoken like a true mom," Susan said with a laugh.

"I've been fortunate to be a mom," she said.

"Ouch. Sorry, I haven't been able to give you any grandkids."

Her mom grabbed Susan's hand. "I didn't mean it that way. I meant how lucky I am to have a daughter, someone to share and make memories. Like tonight."

Susan nodded and stared at the waves coming ashore. The sounds of seagulls flying around were like white noise for her as if a fan were blowing on a hot August day. She closed her eyes and dreamt of a better tomorrow.

"Do you think you will get married to him?"

"Married to who?" Susan asked, opening her eyes.

"You know, him."

"Him as in Michael?"

"Come on, honey. You told me you love him."

"As a friend."

"I don't believe that."

"I know. You don't believe men can be friends with women. I've heard the talk before."

"No. I believe they can. I just don't believe you and Michael are just friends."

Susan kicked at the sand. "We have an understanding we are friends."

"Is he your best friend?"

"I think so."

"Best friends do get married."

Susan wiped away some sand from in between her toes. "Gee, no pressure there, Mom."

"I only want what's best for you."

"Michael is hard to read. I get mixed signals."

"He's a man, Susan. Men don't know how to express their true feelings. He's also had so much to deal with in his life. Sometimes, you need to give them a little push."

Susan stood and wiped more sand off her legs. "There's no point in discussing this. I have no idea where he is. Or whether he's alive. Or whether he's coming back."

She watched the sky clear as the horizon sparkled with the evening's stars. "Maybe you're right, Mom," she said, looking down at her.

Her mom stared straight ahead.

"Hello? Mom?" She waved her hand in front of her eyes. "What's wrong?"

Her mom pointed to the sky.

"What is it?" asked Susan, turning around.

The sky lit up with a bright white light, and two dark blue streaks flashed across the sky and then downward. Susan waited for an explosion. "Was that a plane?" she asked, glancing down at her mom.

The light dimmed moments later, and the sky darkened again as the stars returned. "That was no plane," her mom said.

"It wasn't Santa, either," Susan added. She noticed a flickering light in the distance as she looked to her left. "Is that a fire?"

Her mom got up. "I can't see that far."

"My God!" Susan said, standing. "It looks like it's on top of the church." She grabbed her cell phone and called 911. "Hello! I'm at Crab Meadow Beach, but I can see a fire not too far away."

"Where is the location?" the operator asked.

"It looks to be the church on Main Street."

"Town?"

"Northport."

"Thank you."

"We have to get to the church," Susan said, putting her phone away.

"The firemen will take care of it," her mom said, holding onto Susan's arm. "I need to go home. I'm cold."

CHAPTER 65

MICHAEL FELT A RUSH OF WARMTH SURGE THROUGH HIS BODY. He glanced at Elizabeth, noticing a glow illuminating her face. Her expression was one of contentment, and her eyes shone a bright blue. As the air blew against him, images of his life in Jerusalem surrounded him and then faded away. His body felt weightless for a moment and then heavy. He flailed away, but his arms were rubbery. He panicked for several seconds until his feet hit the ground.

He looked behind him. Elizabeth stood frozen, her body drenched with moisture, water falling off her face and onto the ground. He took the cross and chain off his neck and hugged her. "We're home. Take this off," he said, touching her chain.

She did and squeezed him tight. "Where are we?"

Michael watched her eyes widen. "What's wrong?"

"Are we back home?" she asked. "What's happening? Are we really here? Am I dreaming again?" She held her head and groaned. "I'm hearing a lot of voices, Dad. I can't make it stop." She squeezed her hands over her ears.

He turned around and saw several children encircling a man near the makeshift manger. Michael approached the children.

"My name is Samantha," one tall child said, touching the man's shoulder. "You rescued me five years ago. Do you remember? I was ten years old and scared. The man hit me many nights when I cried. You stopped that man from hitting me. We're so happy now. Our family. My mother and father saw me graduate from middle school. Do you know what they said when they gave me flowers?"

"Are you all right, Elizabeth?" Michael asked. He put his arm around her as she stayed hunched over, holding her head.

"We're home," he said, raising his voice. "We're finally home." He rubbed her back, and she lifted her head. She gave him a forlorn look.

"What's wrong?" he asked. "We're home. We're alive. We're here."

She nodded and leaned her head into his chest.

"Wow," Michael said, putting his arm around Elizabeth's shoulders.

"What? What is it, Dad? What's going on?"

"That's the FBI agent. The one who thought I was responsible for your disappearance. What's he doing here, and who are those children?"

They moved closer to the group and listened to a girl speaking. "They told me how they cherish each day," the girl said. "How they never take for granted having time with me. How their lives have meaning now."

Hewitt nodded and lifted his head.

Another girl stepped forward. "My name is Lynn Ann Wallace." She brushed her light red hair out of her eyes and bent down, looking directly at Hewitt. "Mr. Paul, I was taken by a man as I was coming off a school bus. He told the bus driver he was my uncle. He knew everything about my family, so I went with him. He hurt and touched me. I found out later that my baby brother had fallen and gotten hurt. That was why my mom was late getting to the bus stop.

"I spent six months being abused by this man. I had no hope. I cried night after night, wondering if my mom would ever hold me again." The girl wiped some tears away. "Then you saved me." She gave Hewitt a kiss on the cheek.

One by one, girls and boys stepped forward, each one telling a story. The oldest appeared to be about seventeen years old. She spoke in a clear, defiant tone. "I will never forget the day when I was abducted by this man and woman. I was walking to the grocery store to get milk for my mother. They tied me up and put me in this van. They blindfolded me so I couldn't see where they were taking me. I lived in this dirty basement for a couple of years. They only gave me bread and water. I wanted to kill them for what they were doing to me. They laughed and mocked me when I told them I had to go to the bathroom.

"My mom told me after I went missing, she spent the time finding ways to hate herself. She thought about killing herself too. Each day that went by, she cried herself to sleep at night. But because of you, my mother doesn't have to cry anymore. If she does cry, they are happy tears. She's forgiven herself, and we have a new life together, all because you saved me. In a couple of months, I will be graduating high school and going to college. I am going to be the president of the United States someday and make sure all children are protected in this country."

The girl smiled and kissed his forehead. "You should see my mother smile when I come home from school. It's a smile that could light up every lighthouse here on Long Island. You made it possible. Your dedication. Your love."

The children faded away, and Michael watched Hewitt hold out his arms.

"What's he doing, Dad?" Elizabeth asked.

"I don't know."

"Don't leave, honey," Hewitt said.

"Don't you see now, Daddy," a voice called out. "Don't you see the families you saved?"

"I do. I do," he said.

The little girl smiled. "It's because of me." She hugged him. Then she was gone.

Hewitt stayed on his knees, wiping his face with his sleeve.

"Oh my Lord, it can't be," Michael said. He ran past Hewitt to the door behind the manger.

"Dennis," he said, running to him. "Dennis, I thought I'd never see you again."

"I had one more task to complete, Michael."

"You're not staying?"

He shook his head. "There's more work to be done."

"Where are you going?"

"Wherever time needs me," he said with a smile.

Michael turned and motioned to Elizabeth. "Come here," he said.

She joined him. "What's wrong?"

"Look who's here," he said, turning back. "Where did he go?"

"Who?"

"Dennis."

"The pastor?"

"Michael Stewart? Where did you come from?" Hewitt asked, jumping to his feet.

He joined them behind the manger. "Elizabeth Stewart? Is that you?" He pulled a small photo out and looked at her. "Are you all right? Are you hurt in any way?"

She looked at Hewitt. "I'm fine. Dad, are you all right?" she asked.

"He was here. Now he's not," Michael said.

"You're both here," Hewitt said. "You're both here and safe." He hugged Michael and then Elizabeth. "Incredible! This is incredible!" He paused and looked around the church. "No one is going to believe me."

There was a noise in the back of the church. Michael squinted to see who was in the rear opening the door. "Who's that?"

"Pastor Dennis?" Hewitt said. "Pastor Dennis! He's alive!" He and Michael ran to the back. Hewitt opened the door as Michael stayed a few feet behind him. TV lights lit up the area and reporters shouted questions.

"Special Agent, is there a problem in the church?"

"Did any of you see someone walk out this door in the last few seconds?" Hewitt asked the mob.

"No," shouted back several reporters.

"Special Agent, what about the situation in the church?"

"What are you talking about?"

"The cross on top of the church. It lit up. Looked like the church was on fire."

"I don't know anything about that. Everything is fine in here." He shut the door and locked the latch. He stared at Michael. "Where in God's name did you go?"

"You wouldn't believe me."

Hewitt dialed his cell phone. "Sir, we have a big break in the Stewart case."

Michael could hear the screaming from the other end of the phone as Hewitt moved it away from his ear. "You're off the case. Why are you bothering me again? Do you know what time of night it is? I told you not to call me anymore regarding this case. Do you want to keep your job?"

"Sir, calm down." He placed the phone back against his ear. "I have Michael and Elizabeth Stewart here in the church. Safe. Unharmed." Hewitt shook his head. "No, I'm not drinking."

He shook his head again. "Sir, I'm fine and sober. I have the Stewarts." Hewitt glanced at Michael and waited a moment before talking again. "No. I can take care of this myself. He's not threatening to escape. Yes sir. Yes. Yes. I won't answer any questions from the media."

He put the phone away in his pocket. "Were you here all the time?" Hewitt asked.

"No, but you won't believe my explanation."

"You'd better think long and hard about what you're going to say," Hewitt said, "for your sake and your future."

Michael turned away from him and looked at Elizabeth. "I wouldn't know what to say."

CHAPTER 66

HEWITT GUIDED THEM TO THE BACK OF THE CHURCH. He opened the door and was met again with glowing TV lights and reporters shouting questions. He shut it quickly saying, "Wrong move. We have to find another way. There's too much of a crowd out there."

"I can help you," said Michael. "Let me show you. Follow me."

Hewitt pulled back the latches to lock the door. "Is this how you escaped, Michael, though another hidden door? Did Dennis know about this? Where is he? Are you going to show me?"

"What? Escaped? I wasn't running from anyone. I was running to save my daughter."

Michael slid behind a curtain and opened a door. A narrow, dark stairway stood before them. Hewitt nudged Michael aside. "I know this. It leads to the other places on Main Street, right?"

"Yes."

"You escaped through here?"

"No, as I said before, I didn't escape. You wouldn't believe me, so I won't try to explain it."

"The FBI is going to want to know how you did it."

Michael didn't respond. He took a couple of steps down the stairs.

"Is there a car in one of these lots we can get to?" Hewitt asked.

"No. Let me use your phone. I'll call my sister."

"Okay," he said, handing him his phone.

He touched the screen and held the device up to his ear. "Guess who?"

"Michael?"

"Yes."

"Where are you?"

"In church."

"In Northport?"

"Yes. I need your help. Do you have a car?"

"Is Elizabeth with you?"

"Yes. She's here."

Connie screamed into the phone. "Thank God! Thank you, Lord. Thank you."

He could hear her cry. He looked at Elizabeth and lowered his head. "I love you."

"I love you, too," she said while weeping. "Let me talk to Elizabeth."

He handed her the phone. "Aunt Connie. Yes. I'm fine. I missed you too. I love you. I know you do. I know. I know. I know. I'm putting Dad back on the phone."

"Connie, I need you to calm down," Michael said. "I need your help."

"Now you ask me for your help? What took you so long?"

"Look, I'm with the FBI agent."

"My Hewitt?"

"What? Your Hewitt?"

He waited for Connie to respond.

"Hello, Connie?"

"What do you need?" she asked.

"Where are you?"

"At your house."

"Good. Get over to the temple on Main Street. In the back. The parking lot. We'll be there. Hurry. There's a mob in front of the church. Come up Norwood to avoid the mess over there."

"Coming."

He gave the phone back to Hewitt. "Let's go," Michael said. They walked down the steps and onto a concrete walkway. Hewitt held up a small flashlight.

"Here," Michael said, stopping. He turned to his right and walked up a couple of steps. He turned a knob, and a door opened. "We're lucky the rabbi is so trusting."

They entered the temple, made their way to the back and out into the parking lot. From there, Michael could see the glow of the TV lights a few blocks away shining on the top of the church's cross. Connie pulled in moments later. Before she put the car in park, she turned off the ignition, jumped out and ran into Elizabeth's arms. "My God, I thought I would never see you again. I love you. I love you so much. I know I haven't said it enough so I'm going to keep saying it. I love you. I love you. Do you know how much I love you?"

Elizabeth nodded.

Michael smiled and watched tears fall from Elizabeth's eyes.

"We have to go," Hewitt said, tapping his shoulder.

"You heard the special agent," Michael said.

Connie released her embrace and hugged him. "I love you too."

Michael slowly wrapped his arms around her. "We've waited way too long to say this to each other." He pulled back. "I love you."

The three sat in the back while Hewitt drove. Connie turned around to face Michael. "We have a problem."

"What problem is this?" asked Hewitt. "I have to get them to the New York City office."

"It's Dad, Michael."

"What's wrong?"

"He's drunk."

"Well, nothing's changed since I left."

"This time is different. He told me there's nothing left for him to live for."

"When did he say this?"

"Right after you called."

Michael looked at Hewitt. "It's on the way to New York City. In Queens. Please."

Hewitt grimaced and looked at his phone. "Fine. It can only be a few minutes though."

"Thank you."

They all sat in silence for the forty-minute drive. Michael shivered at the sight of the old white house. The porch light was out, and a piece of a torn screen on the side fluttered in the wind.

"I'll wait here," Hewitt said. "I have some calls to make. This is not under my jurisdiction either. However, if you need me, come and get me."

"Stay here, Elizabeth," Michael said as he got out of the car.

Elizabeth pushed back. "But ... "

"No buts. I have to handle this myself."

She looked away.

"She'll be fine with me," Hewitt said.

They walked up the brown wooden stairs. The porch door squeaked and shook as Michael opened and closed it. "I don't have the key to the front door," he said.

Connie took a keychain out of her purse and unlocked the door. Inside, the hallway was dark. The living room had a lone light on, and Jim lay on the floor near his chair. "Dad! Dad!" Connie yelled. "Are you all right?"

She lifted his head, and he opened his eyes. "You came. Oh Connie, you came," Jim said, trying to sit up. He put his hands to her face as she tried to lift him. "Michael? Is that you? Oh God, I'm dead. Am I dead?"

"You're not dead," he said. "What were you doing on the floor?"

"I must have fallen asleep. No one answered my calls tonight. Where were you two?"

"Dad, I was out looking for Michael."

"What about you, Michael? Where were you? Where did you go?"

"I wasn't home."

"I know you weren't home. Do you know the FBI and police were over here almost every day asking about you?"

"No, I didn't."

"Well now you do."

Michael pulled him up and into his chair. Jim started to rock back and forth. Then he stopped and began to cry.

"What's wrong Dad? We're here for you," Connie said.

"I don't want to live anymore. I'm so alone."

"You're not alone."

Jim shook his head. "I didn't do enough to help your mom."

"What are you talking about?" Connie asked.

"I tried," Jim said. "I tried to get her the best doctors, the best hospitals, the best medicine. That horrible breast cancer. I hate it. I wish I could kill it."

"We've spoken about this before," Michael said. "You did the best you could."

Jim shook his head. "No. I didn't make enough. I couldn't afford the best care for her. We weren't rich, you know."

"I know," Michael said. He knelt down in front of him. "Dad, you did the best you could. That's all anyone can ask."

Jim wiped the tears from his eyes and held Michael's hand, shaking it. "She was so young. So young."

"I know. I know," Michael said, "but it's about time we both stop blaming ourselves."

Connie knelt beside Michael. "No one is blaming you, Dad. No one ever has."

Jim sighed and straightened up. He stared at Michael. "I don't know what happened to us. I don't know why we ended up not talking to each other. I wanted to be better than my father."

"I'm sure Grandpa was proud of you," Michael said.

Jim waved his hands in the air. "He was disappointed in me," he said. "I could tell by the way he treated me, spoke to me."

"How do you know?" Michael asked.

"I remember when I came home from the war I was so proud and couldn't wait to see him," Jim said. He smiled. "I thought I had done something noble and brave. My father would surely respect me for what I did for our country."

Jim took a deep breath that lasted a few seconds. He looked away from Michael. "I walked up the steps and said, 'I'm home, Dad.'"

"What did he say?" Michael asked.

Jim looked up at him. "He laughed at me and said, 'So what. Go out and get a job if you want to live here.' I thought he was going to throw me down the steps."

Michael lowered his head. "I'm sorry. I didn't know. I wish you had told me this before."

"Why?" Jim asked. "Why would I tell you this? I wanted you to love my father. I wanted you to love me. It's why I gave you the only love I knew – tough. Just like my dad. I wanted to be like him."

They sat in silence for a minute or so until Elizabeth walked inside. "Dad, is everything all right?" she asked, entering the living room.

Connie and Michael turned around.

"Elizabeth," said Jim, standing.

"Grandpa."

Connie and Michael stood and moved away as Elizabeth hugged him. "Grandpa, are you all right?"

"I am now," he said. "Where in God's name did you go?"

"You wouldn't believe it."

"Well, you're going to tell me. Aren't you?"

"Someday, Grandpa. Someday."

Michael saw Hewitt standing at the door.

"Can I help?" he asked.

"Thanks," Connie said. "We're fine now. We're like any family. We have our issues. Nothing a little intensive therapy and a good cry can't help."

Hewitt nodded and looked at his phone. "Wow," he said.

"What?" Michael asked. "Something wrong?"

"Not at all. It's Christmas." He looked away and walked back toward the door. "Merry Christmas."

Michael looked at the old clock on the wall. "Merry Christmas to you." He went outside and looked up into the dark. "Happy birthday, Jesus."

CHAPTER 67

MICHAEL STARED OUT THE WINDOW, watching the snowflakes coat the front lawn. He sipped hot chocolate and marveled at the feistiness of a bird, sitting alone atop the big, green pine tree that partially covered his big window.

He tapped the glass with his knuckles. "Hey, I thought you guys are supposed to fly south for the winter?"

Michael took another sip, relishing the sweet taste of a melted marshmallow. He breathed in deep, letting the aroma fill his lungs. The bird wiggled its head sideways and around and flew off.

"Well, well, look who is up early on Christmas Day," Elizabeth said as she came down the stairs. "Did you open my gift yet?"

Michael turned around. "Absolutely not."

"Did you peek?"

"Perhaps."

Elizabeth let out a short laugh. "No, you didn't."

"Maybe I did."

She hugged him. "Merry Christmas."

"Merry Christmas to you."

She pulled away and smiled. "Are we keeping the tradition alive this year?"

Michael put up his hand. "Look at the weather. It's awful out there. The wind is really coming off the Sound." He went to the window and cleared away some condensation with the sleeve of his robe. "Look, Elizabeth. It's terrible out there."

"Dad, come on. You know we only have a little time together before I go back to school."

Michael nodded. "Dress warm."

"Should I wake her up or will you?" Elizabeth asked.

"I'm not sure she will be up to making the trip. She's been feeling sick a lot."

"I know. I heard her last night in the bathroom. I wish I could do something to help."

"I'll see how she feels."

"It would be fun to have her along. Maybe the cold air will help." Elizabeth ran up the stairs.

Michael placed his cup in the sink and took a quick glance at the tree. "Wonderful," he said. "Everyone understands." There were only three presents underneath the understated, decorated tree. *Perfect.*

He went upstairs and lay down on the bed, lifting the covers up. "Peek a boo, guess who?" Michael laughed. "Hey, beautiful, how are you feeling today?"

"I'm fine, better than last night," Susan said.

She sat up and Michael placed his head on her belly. "I can hear the heart beat," he said.

"He's been kicking up a storm over the last couple of nights."

"Are you up for our little tradition?"

Susan took a deep breath and touched her stomach. "Sounds like this one will be a drummer."

"You don't have to go," Michael said. "Elizabeth will understand."

"Yes. I'll go. I'm fine. Give me a few minutes to get myself together."

"I was thinking about names," he said.

"Oh. What are your suggestions?" she asked.

"Paul. I love the name Paul. It says courage to me. What do you think?"

"I like it. Let's discuss it more later. Let me get changed."

Michael gave his wife a kiss. "Let me know if you need any help." He dressed and took a gold wedding ring out of the drawer. "Fits perfectly," he said, looking at it in the mirror.

"All right, Elizabeth, where are you?" he asked, walking down the stairs.

"Right here," she replied, popping out in front of him in the hallway.

"Wow. This is a change," he said. "Usually it's me waiting for you women to get ready."

"Don't say that in front of Susan," Elizabeth said.

Michael laughed. "Oh, yeah. This I know."

Susan joined them moments later, and they made their way into the car. As they approached Main Street, Michael glanced into his rearview mirror.

"Are you okay?" Susan asked, placing her hand on his.

"It's the weather. I hate it. So cold and windy. Are you sure you want to do this?"

"Yes," squealed Elizabeth, sitting in the back.

Michael stopped his old Toyota by the park. He helped Susan out of the front passenger side and watched the boats shake from the dock as the wind zipped from the bay and into their faces. "Yikes," Michael said. He jumped up and down.

"It's not that bad," Susan said.

"You must be hot-blooded," Michael said.

"Is Aunt Con coming?" Elizabeth asked as she did a pirouette in the snow.

"I left her a message," he said. "Is that boy coming?"

"You mean Matthew?"

"Yes. Who else would it be?"

"Yes, he's coming. You did say you liked him."

Susan held Elizabeth. "You did," she said. "You told me several times."

"Ah, I see why Elizabeth wanted us to be together, Susan. She needed an ally."

"Women stick together," Elizabeth said with a grin.

"You betcha," Susan added.

A horn beeped, and Connie got out of a van. She was holding a little girl's hand.

"I never thought my sister would ever want to be a mother," Michael said.

Susan walked over to him and placed her head on his shoulder. "It's wonderful they were able to adopt. All children deserve to be loved."

He nodded. "I need to make another stop later."

"The fish."

"Yes. Mrs. Farmer looks forward to my visit."

Susan smiled. "So do you."

"I do."

He watched Elizabeth run to Connie. She dropped to her knees and embraced the girl. "Hi, Sophia. You look so pretty today."

"Thank you, cousin Elizabeth."

Elizabeth jumped to her feet. "Oh, I love the sound of that."

Hewitt and Michael shook hands.

"So, this is a tradition," he said to him.

"Yes. We needed one to remember why this is such a great day."

"Yeah, the presents and drinks and parties and relatives," Hewitt said.

"No. Just being able to have the gift of breathing this air right now at this time," Michael replied.

Hewitt nodded and Michael looked up, watching a stray flurry hit the ground. He felt Connie give him a playful shove. "Hey, bro, are you going to take a ride with me like we did as kids?"

"With you? I should know better."

"Yup. Let's go."

Michael raced ahead of her to the slide. He stumbled as he began to climb up the metal ladder. Michael heard a pinging sound as something dropped out of his pocket, hitting a rung as it fell.

"What's wrong, old man?" Connie asked, pushing him in the back. "A few steps up and you're winded?"

Michael got to the top, still looking at the snow-coated ground. As he struggled to dig into his pockets, he felt his feet slip out from under him. Connie pushed him down the slide, and he could hear Elizabeth and Sophia laugh as they watched.

Thump. He landed face-first into the snow. He sat up as Connie barreled into him.

"Nice," Connie said. "A real soft landing courtesy of my bro."

"Yeah, now I can't get up," said Michael, wincing. He rubbed the lower part of his back.

"Are you hurt?" asked Susan as she came over.

"Oh, my back. I can't get up," Michael faked.

Susan bent over. "Here, let me help you."

He pulled her down and kissed her lips. "Thank you for coming."

"Of course. What are best friends for? Why would I miss this?"

"Because we're crazy," said Elizabeth.

"Who says we're crazy?" Michael asked.

"Oh, only everyone here in Northport," Elizabeth replied.

"What does crazy mean?" asked Sophia.

"It means we're cool," Connie said. "Yeah, cool."

Michael lay in the snow, and Susan did the same. He began to move his arms up and down, forming a snow angel. "This is for you, Vicki. This is for you, Dad. This is for you, Dennis."

"This is for you, Mom," Susan said.

"What are they doing?" Sophia asked.

"Why, they're sending messages to all the people they love who are now in heaven," Elizabeth said.

Sophia grabbed her hand and said, "Help me, cousin." They lay down in the snow and held hands, moving them up and down.

"For you, Leah."

CHAPTER 68

SPRING HAD BRUSHED IN SOME WARM TEMPERATURES on a late March afternoon in Northport. It was a perfect opportunity for Marc Smith to take his children out and give his wife a break from the parenting responsibilities. Many in the town had the same idea to seek outdoor activities.

"Let's go down the slide," screamed a little girl with ponytails.

"Don't go too far, Jessica," said Marc, looking at his cell phone.

"Yes, Daddy."

He looked up and put his cell phone away. "Where's your brother?"

Jessica inched her way down the slide and pointed. "Over there, reading on the bench."

"Bobby, over here, I can't watch you and your sister in different places."

He closed up his book and joined his father at the bench, facing the bay.

"What are you reading, son?"

"A really cool story about this man and daughter living here," he said, holding up the book.

"Interesting. I believe this was in the papers a couple of years ago. Fiction."

"Fiction?"

"Yes. There are all kinds like that out there."

"The author says it happened."

"Can he prove it?"

"How would he prove he was able to time travel back to First-Century Jerusalem?" Bobby asked.

Marc waved his hands in the air. "Evidence. Some sort of physical evidence."

Bobby joined Jessica at the slide and took a few turns. As he went to climb up for another try, he glanced down and saw something shiny.

"What do you see there?" his father asked.

"Looks like money."

"Finders, keepers." Marc stood and watched Bobby dig into the ground with his hands.

"What is this?" he asked, holding it up.

Marc pulled a tissue out of his pocket and cleaned the object off. "Never saw anything like this," he said.

He walked back to the bench while Bobby took another turn down the slide. Pulling out his cell phone, he searched the Internet for a description of the shape.

"Hey, Bobby, come here," he said.

"What's up, Dad? Did you find out what it is?"

"I'm not sure. But I remember reading a bit of the book you have. I need you to refresh me on the ending. What happens?"

"The family ends up in the park, one like this. They have this unusual family tradition."

"Thanks. Go ahead and play. I need some time alone to think."

"Are you going to write about them in the paper?" Bobby asked.

"Perhaps," he said, pressing the screen with his fingers.

He stood and went back to the spot where Bobby found the metal rod. Kicking around some dirt, he bent over and smoothed it out. He looked up and saw Jessica climbing.

"Are you watching me, Daddy?"

"I am. I am."

He heard her squeals as he got off his knees. Wiping some dirt off his jeans, he grabbed Jessica's hand. "Time to go."

"Why? We just got here."

"Daddy needs to do one thing, and then we can come back. Bobby. Come with us."

He made sure his kids were buckled up and stopped in front of the Lady by the Bay Church. "I'll be back in one minute," he told Jessica and Bobby. He locked the doors and went inside the church.

"Hello," he said, walking up the aisle. "I'm looking for the pastor of this church."

"That's me. I'm Pastor Timothy. How can I help you?"

"I'm Marc. I'm trying to get in touch with a Michael Stewart."

"Why is that?"

"I work for the local newspaper, and I wanted to do an interview."

Pastor Timothy turned and whispered something to a woman. He turned back to Marc. "He's a private person. I'm not sure he would do any interviews now. I don't think he's done any since, well, you know that Christmas day."

"Why won't he do any interviews?"

"There are many reasons. The first one is he wants to get back to living a normal life."

"How can one live a normal life if what he says is true happened?" Marc asked.

"Many do not believe what he said," Pastor Timothy replied.

"Do you?"

Pastor Timothy shook his head. "It's not up to me to believe or not to believe. Every man has his own way of dealing with his faith. If it helps him draw closer to God, then it is a good way as long as no one is being hurt."

Marc pulled out the metal rod and held it in the air. "Look at this," he said. "I've Googled it. I've looked at several pictures online. There is only one conclusion. This is a genuine writing tool from the days of the Roman Empire."

Pastor Timothy examined it. He gave it back to him. "Give me one minute," he said. Pastor Timothy returned moments later with a metal rod in his hand. He held it up and compared it to the one Marc was holding.

"They match," Pastor Timothy said. "They match."

He sat down in the front pew and rubbed the metal rod with two fingers. "So it was so."

Marc sat down next to him. "You believe this is a writing tool?"

"Yes."

"Where did you get yours?"

"Does it matter?"

"Perhaps." Marc stood and put the writing tool back in his pocket. "Michael Stewart has to know if people read about this they will believe him. I'll write an article about it. Please help me find him."

Pastor Timothy left the pew and took a few steps to the pulpit. "He lives near the beach. It's an old house up on a hill, off of Bayside Avenue. You can't miss it."

"Thanks, Pastor."

Marc dashed down the steps and into the car.

"Are we going back to the park, Daddy?" Jessica asked.

"No. In a few minutes. I need to run one more errand. Bobby, let me see that book you're reading."

Marc paged through the book. "Yes. Yes. This is making sense." He handed it back to Bobby and pulled away.

It took about ten minutes to get to Michael's house. An Easter egg flag hung from a stanchion near a big bay window. It flapped in the breeze as the wind off the Sound whistled in his ears. "Come with me, kids," Marc said while removing their seatbelts.

He rang the doorbell and waited. A man peered through the blinds and closed them.

"Maybe no one is home," Jessica said. "Let's go back to the park."

"Just a few more minutes, honey," Marc said.

"Is this where the author lives?" asked Bobby.

"Yes." He rang the bell again.

The door opened. "Yes. Hello. I'm not interested in buying any magazines or touching anyone or healing the sick. I'd suggest a doctor. I don't have the ability to create miracles either. Of course, I can buy a magazine if I wish, but I'm not any more special than you are. Okay?"

"Mr. Stewart?" Marc asked. "I just need to show you something."

"Show me what?"

"This," said Marc, holding up the writing tool.

Michael's eyes widened, and he took it from Marc. "My goodness. You found it. I've been looking all over for it."

"So, it's true."

"What's true?" Michael asked.

"Your trip. Meeting Paul. Helping him write some of his journeys."

"Where did you find this?"

"In the park," Marc said.

Michael smiled. "Right. I lost it on Christmas day. May I have this back?"

"Of course."

"Thank you." Michael began to close the door.

"I can help you," Marc said. "I'm a reporter for the local newspaper. I can prove what you said is true. People won't think you're crazy anymore."

Michael pushed the door open and smiled. "It's not important what others think. I'm happy now with my wife and children. I've spent too many years worrying about what others were thinking about me. I don't need a newspaper reporter to defend me. I do appreciate the thought, but I know what I saw and experienced."

"You're more courageous than me," Marc said.

"Courageous?" Michael shook his head. "No, Paul was courageous. To write and preach what he did during that time. To do it with the threat of death in his face every time he spoke to the crowds. That's courageous."

"What about proof? We can show you were there. Isn't it better to have someone on your side? I think the article would convince others."

Michael stepped out and sat down on the stoop. "You have beautiful children. Treat them well, but give them room to grow. It's something I had an awfully difficult time doing when my Elizabeth was younger."

Marc nodded. "What about showing the proof?"

"Proof? I don't need to show it to anyone. It's all in here." He pointed to his heart and then his head. The trees nearby shook hard, and the rustle of the branches distracted Marc for a brief moment.

Marc persisted. "If you can just give me a little bit of your time," he said to Michael. "I think the article will quell the doubters and the people that mock you. Don't you want that for yourself? For your family?"

Michael stood up and went back inside. "I'm fine. My family is fine. And this day is far too beautiful for us to spend time worrying about who mocks and who doubts me. Besides, I don't have much time these days."

"Why is that, if you don't mind me asking? Are you spending a lot of time speaking about your experience?"

"No. I'm not a big speaker. I prefer to let my actions do my speaking. Besides, I like to do some traveling at this time of the year." He winked.

Marc pulled his kids close to him as Michael closed the door.

Dear Readers,

I hope you have enjoyed my time travel trilogy. The first book, *Necessary Heartbreak,* started out as an idea two decades ago when I found myself homeless, riding a New York City subway train at night. The wonderful outcome from this time of struggling to find shelter is it helped transform me into the person I am today. I believe I'm a more compassionate, loving person after seeing so many of my brothers and sisters living on the trains at night during that time.

I first thought of publishing it as a memoir. Life moved forward and I put the idea aside as I worked hard and fulfilled my responsibilities as a parent. I revisited the idea in 2006 and thought I needed another element to the story to make it work. I installed the aspect of time travel and what it would be like to witness some of Christianity's most important moments. *Necessary Heartbreak* was born.

After an initial self-publishing period, Simon & Schuster purchased the publishing rights. I revised the story, added more depth to the plot, and it was published in 2010. I thank Anthony Ziccardi for believing in my story.

The second book of the series, *Everybody's Daughter,* draws less on my personal experiences and more on my spiritual philosophy. I thank Lou Aronica of Fiction Studio Books and The Story Plant for publishing it in 2012.

Lou's company, The Story Plant, also published *The Greatest Gift.* Originally, I had a much different ending to the trilogy. But as I went along in the writing process and had my own personal battles in life and in my relationships, the theme of the book changed.

I've had to endure my own challenges and struggles over the past few years due to many factors. The economy has hurt my family as it has millions of Americans and many more millions worldwide. I've suffered the loss of loved ones and scuffled with doubts in some relationships. Due to these conflicts, I've made sure to be honest with the current emotions while writing the last story.

What I've learned is that good can come even through tragedy and hardships. I wanted each of the main characters to come to this conclusion. I wanted to show how they come about in understanding this important message.

It's also vital to remember there will be instances in which some relationships can't be saved as they once were but can be rediscovered in other ways.

The ending I presented is one that time marches on and waits for no one. We have today – this moment – to make it special.

I've decided to allow you, the reader, to view both endings. The one that follows this letter was written a few years ago. I still love it, but I feel the one I've recently written presents a wonderful message for us all – live for today and appreciate the beauty that is around us now.

A trip into the past can only benefit us if it helps us to be grateful for the present.

Thank you so much for supporting me on my healing journey. I hope it has helped you in some way too.

Michael John Sullivan

MICHAEL, ELIZABETH, AND HEWITT STOOD BEFORE THEM as the wind's fury settled down to a peaceful breeze. They watched the proud parents attend to the baby.

"You got your answers. Right?" asked Hewitt.

"I don't have the answers I want," Michael said. "We need to find a way back."

"Back? There's nothing back where I have been except anger and more anger."

"I don't think we are here to demand answers from anyone."

"We aren't," said Elizabeth. "We should give them what we have found."

"Do you think it's any coincidence that we've ended up here?" Michael asked Hewitt. "I have to give them this."

They approached the family. They saw Joseph stop packing his belongings. "I will take care of them," he said to Mary.

"We need to travel now," Mary replied.

"Please do not leave," Michael begged.

"My daughter," Hewitt said. "My daughter. I need to know if she is at peace."

The baby let out a short cry as Mary wrapped a blanket around Jesus. She gave him a kiss and reassured him.

"My friends, it is cold and not a night for anyone to be out," said Joseph. "I must find a safe and warm place for my family. Can you understand this?"

Michael stepped closer to him. His eyes were dark brown. He could see him shivering from the brisk wind. "We have come a long way. We need to give you these."

He took out the cloth and handed it to Joseph. He looked at it and put it to his face, closing his eyes. He breathed deeply, letting the smell fill his body. His eyes opened, and he handed it to Mary. She touched it and held it up to her right cheek, rejoicing in how it felt. She removed the blanket and placed the cloth around Jesus before tidying him up again with the blanket.

"Can you help us?" Michael asked.

"What do you need?" Mary said.

"My daughter, Hailey," said Hewitt. "Is she safe?"

"She is."

"Why was she taken from me? What good has come out of this?" Hewitt approached Mary as Joseph gave him a nervous look. "What happened to my daughter has caused my ex-wife and me so much pain. I hate this world for what it has done to us."

Mary held the baby close to her chest, rocking him back and forth.

"You should leave," Joseph said.

"There is no need," reassured her husband. "They will not harm us."

Hewitt started to cry. Michael put his hand on his back. "We should go."

"No, I need answers. I want to know what God who controls this world would allow such a terrible act to occur. I thought God protected his children. He never protected mine."

"Look in your heart for the answers," Mary said.

"My heart? I do not have any joy left in my heart."

Mary handed Jesus to Hewitt. His little legs were kicking up a storm as the blanket unraveled from around his arms. "Do you not see what has happened because of your daughter?"

Hewitt frowned. "Pain. Doubt. Anger. Bitterness."

"Look deeper beyond these emotions. Look into your heart. How have you changed? What do you feel?"

Michael listened yet stared at the baby swinging his arms and legs. He let Jesus grab his thumb as the baby smiled.

"I want to protect every child like he or she is mine," Hewitt said. "I want to stop the madness of this world. I want every family to be able to hug their children at night, free from danger."

Mary smiled. "You want what our Father wants. You are doing the work of our Father. You are helping protect the children of this world like our Father wishes."

Hewitt sighed as Michael gripped his shoulder. "Your son is so beautiful," Hewitt said.

Michael smiled, remembering the day Elizabeth was born. Strangely, he previously only recalled it with much pain as Vicki passed away that night. Now, he was only remembering the joy of his daughter's smile. He hugged her with one arm.

Mary put her hand on Hewitt's face. "You decided to live your life in love for others so many mothers and fathers would sleep in peace."

Mary turned and handed the baby to Michael. "Let your heart beat with new life."

He felt his knees weaken, and he dropped to the floor, holding Jesus tightly. Mary's face faded, and he could see Elizabeth reaching for him. In a moment, she disappeared from his sight. The church shook, and the walls vibrated around him. The concrete ceiling cracked, and a gust of hot air whipped an inferno toward him. "No!" Michael held onto Jesus, gasping for air. "Elizabeth! Go!"

Her voice was faint. "Dad, Dad, where are you?"

"Don't wait for me. Get outside," he shouted.

The lights went out, and a mist surrounded him. Michael pulled his body up and took a deep breath. He looked in his hands. *Where did he go?* He surveyed the area and saw only darkness, except for a little crack of light. He started to crawl on his knees toward the opening. The mist became heavy, so he got to his feet. "Elizabeth, are you up there?" he cried out.

There was no answer. "Elizabeth!"

He squinted and lowered his head, gasping for any clean air. "Elizabeth," he mumbled.

Michael took several more steps, stumbling side to side. "Ugh," he said, struggling to breathe. "Elizabeth," he whispered.

The mist clogged his lungs, and Michael fell to the floor. He crawled a few more yards before lying down. "Elizabeth," the words barely left his lips.

"I love you."

The mist dissipated a few minutes later. Michael lay motionless, his body numb and his mouth soaked with moisture. Unable to move his arms or legs, he picked his head up. A wider light shone off a small opening.

There. There it is. The opening out of the church.

He crawled like a snake for several yards, pushing toward his freedom. "Are you there, Elizabeth?" he asked with a little more force.

Michael made his way out and pulled himself up, finding a small flight of wooden stairs. Each step creaked as he walked. It was a familiar sound, one he had heard often many years ago. He gathered some strength. He felt the texture of the wallpaper. "What?" he said.

A lone picture hung on the wall near a door. He wiped away some dust and staggered backward, his face etched in bewilderment. *This can't be.* "Hello, is anyone in there?" he asked through the door. "Elizabeth!" he shouted. He knocked four times and listened for a response. There was none.

Michael looked down the hall and saw three more doors. He took a few steps toward the far end and retreated. *No. This can't be.*

He went back to the picture and wiped it again with his sleeve. "Hello," he yelled. "Is this some sick joke?"

He pushed on the door. A creaking noise snaked its way up his spine. He jumped and his heart skipped. Michael leaned hard on the door, opening it wider. A dresser stood in front of him. The top of it was empty, except for a lone, gold ring, sitting near the far edge. His footsteps squeaked as he walked toward the dresser. He reached across and picked up the ring. He quickly read the inscription and dropped it just as fast.

My God. "Is anyone home? Elizabeth, are you here?" he shouted. Michael ran back to the hallway. He checked the next room and raced out. He entered the far room and exited quickly.

Michael peered up the stairs and then ascended the flight two steps at a time. Out of breath, he slammed open the third-floor door. Pictures hung on the wall, covered in dust. He wiped the white coating away and stumbled back against an old wooden dresser.

"Mom!" He jumped three steps at a time and searched the rooms on the second floor.

Empty.

What's going on? Am I dreaming? Maybe I died? Maybe this is part of going to heaven? Oh God, I hope so. Or maybe I've gone to the other place?

Michael took a few steps down the stairs leading to the first floor. Family pictures graced the walls. He stopped at the first one and placed his hand on it. He began to cry. "Mom," he said. "Dad." He touched each person in the picture. "Sammie." He wept harder. "Connie." He kissed the picture, noticing the reflection showing the redness in his eyes and sadness in his face. Michael took a couple more steps and looked at another family portrait. "The day Connie got us all together for Mom and Dad's big anniversary," he said. Michael smiled, recalling how they went up to Jamaica Avenue to sit for a picture. "Mom and Dad were so happy that day."

He wiped his eyes and realized his hair had no more gray. "Bizarre," he said to the picture, obviously not expecting a response.

Michael found the next picture hanging a few more steps down. He didn't notice who was in it but just looked at his own reflection again. He pushed back his hair, now thick and dark brown. His eyes were clear, and the wrinkles below them had faded. He stared for several minutes. *I'm dreaming or else I've died. I don't know where Elizabeth is either. Is she alive? Did she get back safely? Is she with me?*

Michael's head began to throb. The slicing pain stretched from the bottom of his neck through his eyes. The room spun around several times, so he closed them. He clung to the banister and tried to compose himself. He lay on the stairs for several minutes, taking deep breaths.

Some time later, still groggy, he sat up and pushed away a robe lying near his legs. *Whose is this?* It was light pink, thin and small, certainly not a robe for any man. *Where am I now?* He placed his feet on the ground, trying to determine the texture as brown floaters filled his eyes, darting back and forth like pinballs off walls. His left hand hit a pillow, big and fluffy in size. *This isn't mine.*

He rubbed his eyes, trying to steer his vision in a steady fashion. *Why is the bed facing the dresser?* He saw the top of a small jewelry box, slightly closed, with a gold chain dangling from the opening. Michael shook his head, trying to remove the black spot-like figures from spinning side to side in his eyes. As he took a couple of steps toward the door, his feet stumbled upon a pair of slippers, dark pink in color. He wobbled and sat down on the bed.

He gazed at the slippers, puzzled as to who owned them. He stood back up and opened the closet, filled with women's shirts, blouses and sweaters. Several pairs of shoes lined the floor. *Am I in the right house? What happened to my father's house? This looks like Northport.*

He walked deeper into the closet and came out with a bright red sweater. Michael put his face in it, absorbing the smell. His eyes widened.

"Elizabeth! Elizabeth, are you home? Please Lord, please." He raced down the hallway and barreled through her bedroom door. "What?" He didn't move. The room was a light green and pink, with painted balloons on the walls. A bassinet was cradled in one corner while a half-made crib lay in the middle of the room, parts hanging out from a big, cardboard box.

Michael didn't move a muscle, still gazing at the interior of the room. A small, stuffed Pikachu doll was sitting inside the bassinet. Chills swept through his body as he returned to the hallway. He walked slowly down the stairs, noticing the spotlessly kept floors and sparkling carpet. His heart started to race, yet his headache was dissipating. The sink was clean, the counter wonderfully organized, and a stack of mail was arranged in fine order. He picked up the envelopes and strummed through several of them. "Medical bills," he said softly. Michael opened one up. "A doctor's bill?"

He pulled open a drawer and saw the utensils placed carefully in the proper slots. The small cabinet was devoid of liquor, featuring plates and cups. His heart pounded, and adrenaline surged through his body. He looked on the far wall and walked closer to see the calendar. *December 25.*

He raced back into the kitchen once more to make sure he had read the date right. Michael scurried back up the stairs, checking first his room, falling to the floor, peeking under the bed. He dashed again to Elizabeth's bedroom. "The crib, the crib I never finished."

Michael slammed the bathroom door open, breaking a piece of the bottom off, catching a glimpse of his face. He stared. His hands felt his skin. He noticed his reflection was much younger now. He pinched his cheeks.

He raced down the stairs, taking two steps at a time, tumbling the final few but unfazed. The newspaper lay on the floor near an unfinished Diet Coke.

Michael stood in the middle of the first floor, hyperventilating, the adrenaline pouring inside his chest and squeezing his breathing. He settled himself down and bent over.

Beep!

A car horn from outside shook him. His body shivered. He ran to the front door and opened it. Sitting inside his old Toyota was a woman on the passenger side.

"My God," he said softly, half happy, half crying. He raced down the steps and pulled open the door, falling to his knees, grabbing at her hands.

"Are you proposing again?"

"Vicki!"

"What were you doing inside? Did you finally fix the crib like I've asked for the past few weeks?"

He stood up and pulled her out of the car. "I love you! I love you!"

Michael squeezed her, absorbing her warmth and body against his, touching her hair and pulling her head to his nose to smell.

"Take it easy or you'll push the baby out now," she said with a laugh.

He pulled away. "Elizabeth."

"Well, we haven't finalized the name yet. Right?"

Michael kissed her on the lips, her cheeks and neck.

"Okay, okay, you don't have to put together the crib yet. But the baby is due soon. Can you get it done this week?"

He pulled away from her. "Elizabeth!" He dropped to his knees again and leaned his head against her belly. He smiled. "She's kicking." Michael looked up at Vicki. "She's kicking!"

"I know. Kicking like crazy today, more so than any other time. It's like she's upset about something. Strange. Put your head against my belly again."

She placed her hand on the back of his head and he listened. "Wow, is she really ready to come join us in this world?"

Vicki helped him up.

"I love you. I love you so much," he said.

"What did I do to deserve this today?"

"You can't imagine." He continued to caress her cheeks with butterfly kisses, touching her hair, and placing his hand back on her belly. "Keep kicking, Elizabeth."

She smiled. "What happened inside? Only a few minutes ago you were griping about putting together the crib. You were being cranky about seeing the relatives again."

"I'm sorry. I'm really sorry." He kissed her again and again.

"All right, we should get going to Sammie's house."

He froze in fear. "Not today."

"But it's Christmas. Are you crazy?"

"No. I'll fix the crib."

"You can fix it when we get back."

"No. It should be fixed today." Michael hugged her again, touching her cheeks and moving a strand of hair from her eyes. "You're so beautiful."

"What will Sammie say if we don't come over?"

"We can go tomorrow."

"Why not today?"

He closed the car door and held her hand. "Because I want to live today like it's the last day of our lives."